D0265361
WATERFORD CITY AND COUNTY
WITHDRAWN
LIBRARIES

THE LEOPARDS OF NORMANDY:

DUKE

David Churchill is the pseudonym of an award-winning journalist, who has conducted several hundred in-depth interviews with senior politicians, billionaire entrepreneurs, Olympic athletes, movie stars, supermodels and rock legends. He has investigated financial scandals on Wall Street, studio intrigues in Hollywood and corrupt sports stars in Britain, and lived in Moscow, Washington DC and Havana. He has edited four magazines, published seventeen books and been translated into some twenty languages. *The Leopards of Normandy* reflects his lifelong passion for history and his fascination for the extraordinary men and women of the past who shaped the world we live in today.

www.david-churchill.co.uk

The Leopards of Normandy

Devil

As David Thomas

Girl
Blood Relative
Ostland

As Tom Cain

The Accident Man
The Survivor
Assassin
Dictator
Carver
Revenger

THE LEOPARDS OF NORMANDY:

DUKE

DAVID
CHURCHILL

headline

First published in Great Britain in 2016 by
HEADLINE
An imprint of HEADLINE PUBLISHING GROUP

1

Cataloguing in Publication Data is available from the British Library

ISBN 978 1 4722 1922 0 (Hardback)
ISBN 978 1 4722 1923 7 (Trade paperback)

Typeset in Garamond MT by Avon DataSet Ltd, Bidford-on-Avon, Warwickshire

Printed and bound in Great Britain by Clays Ltd, St Ives plc

Headline's policy is to use papers that are natural, renewable and recyclable products and made from wood grown in well-managed forests and other controlled sources. The logging and manufacturing processes are expected to conform to the environmental regulations of the country of origin.

HEADLINE PUBLISHING GROUP
An Hachette UK Company
Carmelite House
50 Victoria Embankment
London EC4Y 0DZ

www.headline.co.uk
www.hachette.co.uk

THE LEOPARDS OF NORMANDY: DUKE

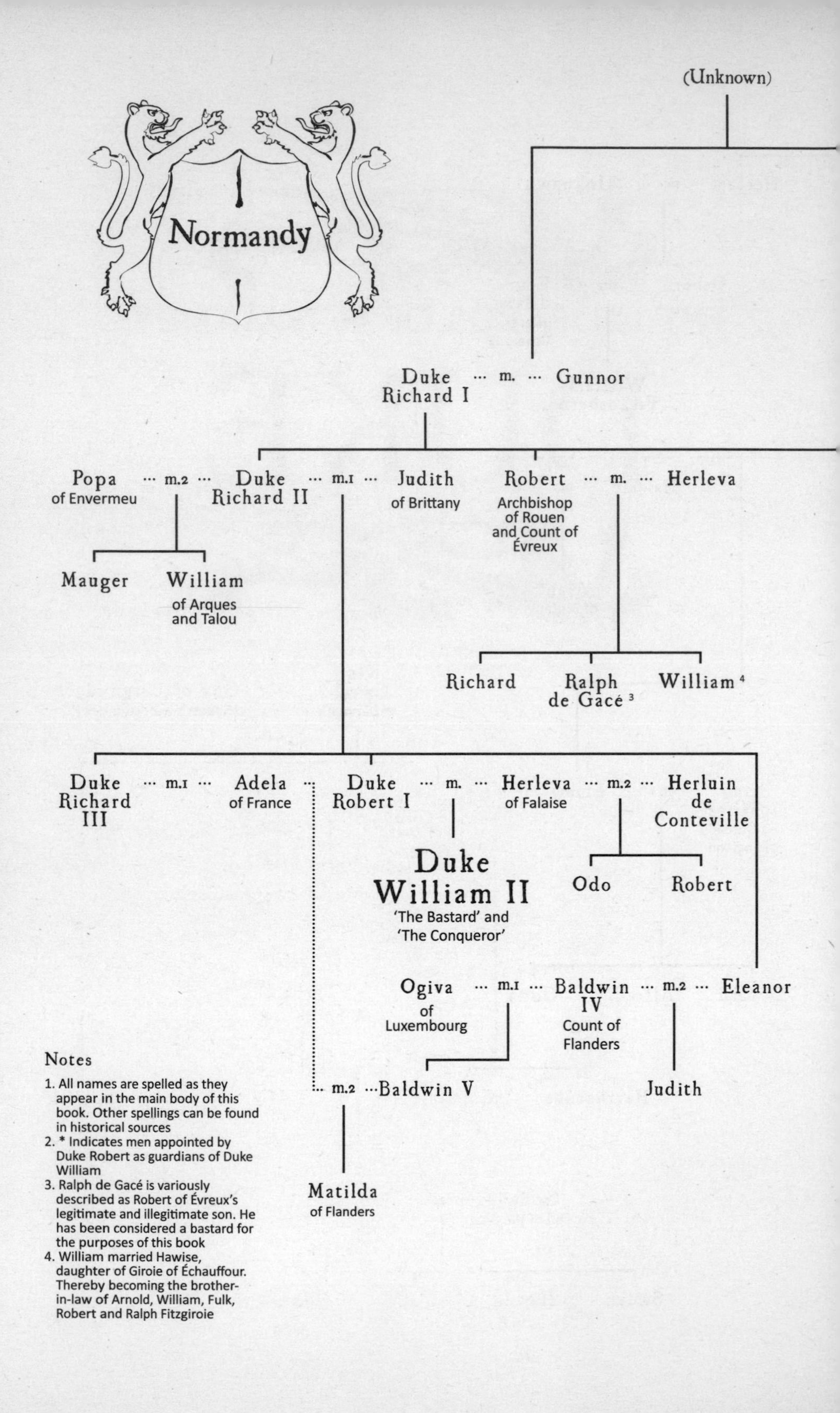
Normandy
(Unknown)
Duke Richard I ... m. ... Gunnor
Popa of Envermeu ... m.2 ... Duke Richard II ... m.1 ... Judith of Brittany
Robert Archbishop of Rouen and Count of Évreux ... m. ... Herleva
Mauger
William of Arques and Talou
Richard
Ralph de Gacé 3
William 4
Duke Richard III ... m.1 ... Adela of France
Duke Robert I ... m. ... Herleva of Falaise ... m.2 ... Herluin de Conteville
Duke William II 'The Bastard' and 'The Conqueror'
Odo
Robert
Ogiva of Luxembourg ... m.1 ... Baldwin IV Count of Flanders ... m.2 ... Eleanor
m.2 ... Baldwin V
Judith
Matilda of Flanders
Notes
1. All names are spelled as they appear in the main body of this book. Other spellings can be found in historical sources
2. * Indicates men appointed by Duke Robert as guardians of Duke William
3. Ralph de Gacé is variously described as Robert of Évreux's legitimate and illegitimate son. He has been considered a bastard for the purposes of this book
4. William married Hawise, daughter of Giroie of Échauffour. Thereby becoming the brother-in-law of Arnold, William, Fulk, Robert and Ralph Fitzgiroie

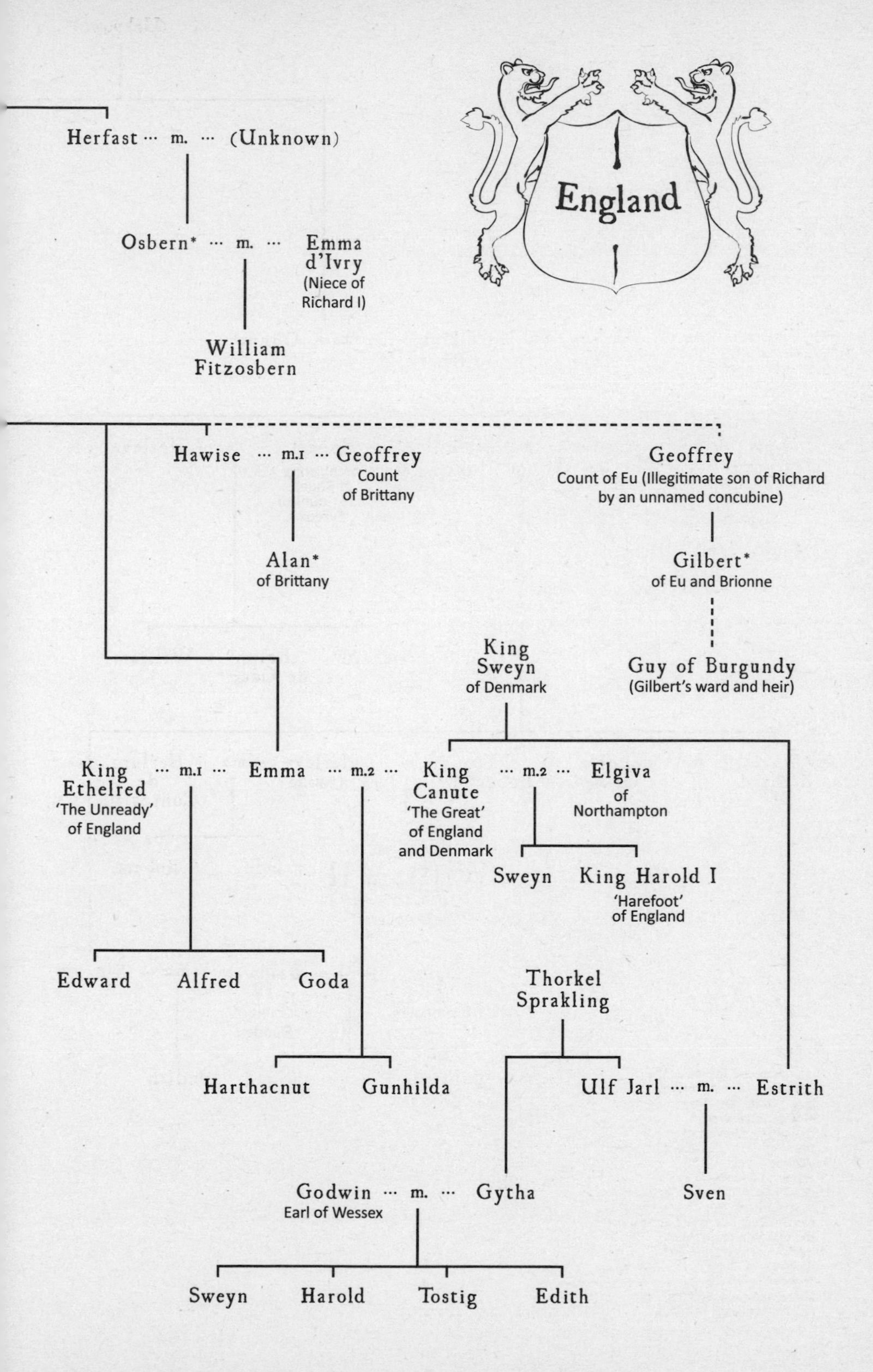
England
Herfast ··· m. ··· (Unknown)
Osbern* ··· m. ··· Emma d'Ivry
(Niece of Richard I)
William Fitzosbern
Hawise ··· m.1 ··· Geoffrey
Count of Brittany
Alan*
of Brittany
Geoffrey
Count of Eu (Illegitimate son of Richard by an unnamed concubine)
Gilbert*
of Eu and Brionne
Guy of Burgundy
(Gilbert's ward and heir)
King Sweyn
of Denmark
King Ethelred
'The Unready'
of England
··· m.1 ···
Emma
··· m.2 ···
King Canute
'The Great'
of England and Denmark
··· m.2 ···
Elgiva
of Northampton
Sweyn
King Harold I
'Harefoot'
of England
Edward
Alfred
Goda
Thorkel Sprakling
Harthacnut
Gunhilda
Ulf Jarl ··· m. ··· Estrith
Godwin ··· m. ··· Gytha
Earl of Wessex
Sven
Sweyn
Harold
Tostig
Edith

List of Characters

Historical Characters

The First Dukes of Normandy

Rollo 'the Strider' (846–931)

William I 'Longsword' (900–942)

Duke Richard I 'the Fearless' (933–996)

Duke Richard II 'the Good' (978–1026)

Duke Richard III (1026–1027):	first husband of Adela of France (below)
Duke Robert I (1027–1035) known as both 'the Devil' and 'the Magnificent':	William's father

The House of Normandy

William II (1035–):	'the Bastard' later to be better known as 'the Conqueror'
Emma of Normandy, Queen of England:	widow of two Kings of England, Ethelred 'the Unready' and Canute 'the Great'
Eleanor, sister of Richard and Robert:	married to Count Baldwin IV of Flanders

Robert, Count of Evreux and Archbishop of Rouen:	died immediately before this story begins
Richard and William:	the archbishop's legitimate sons and heirs
Ralph 'Donkey-Head' de Gacé:	Archbishop Robert's illegitimate[1] son and William's cousin
Mauger, later Archbishop of Rouen; and William, Count of Arques and Talou (referred to as 'Talou' in this story):	sons of Richard II by his second wife Papia, and William's uncles
Gilbert of Brionne, grandson of Richard I:	William's cousin and guardian
Guy of Burgundy, grandson of Richard II:	Gilbert's ward and heir
Osbern Herfastsson:	William's distant cousin and guardian
William Fitzosbern ('Fitz'):	son of Osbern, later William's friend and steward
Barnon of Glos:	Osbern's estate manager
Thorold:	William's tutor and guardian
Robert Champart:	abbot of Jumièges
Odo the Fat:	a killer in the employ of Ralph de Gacé
Goles:	a court jester

1 Sources differ as to Ralph's legitimacy, or otherwise. For the purposes of this fictional account he has been assumed to be a bastard, in every respect.

The Houses of Fulbert and Conteville

Fulbert the tanner:	William's grandfather
Doda:	his wife
Herleva:	his daughter, William's mother
Osbern and Walter:	Fulbert's sons, William's uncles and guardians
Herluin of Conteville:	husband of Herleva
Odo and Robert of Conteville:	sons of Herluin and Herleva

The Kingdom of France

King Henry I (1031–):	William's liege-lord
Princess Adela of France:	his sister

The House of Flanders

Baldwin V (1035–):	Count of Flanders and second husband of Adela of France
Matilda:	their daughter
Judith:	Baldwin's half-sister, his father's daughter with his second wife, Eleanor of Normandy

The House of Brittany

Count Alan III (1008–):	first cousin of Richard and Robert of Normandy and guardian of William

The House of Bellême

William 'Talvas':	Count of Bellême
Hildeburg:	Talvas's first wife
Arnulf and Mabel:	their son and daughter
Rohais:	Talvas's second wife
Ivo Bishop of Sées:	Talvas's brother

Norman Barons (in order of appearance)

Giroie of Échauffour:	a Breton-born soldier, bent on creating a dynasty
Gisela:	his wife
Arnold, William, Fulk, Robert, Ralph (known as 'the Ill-Tonsured' or 'the Clerk') and Hawise:	their children
Roger de Tosny:	another old soldier, recently returned to Normandy from Spain
Helbert and Heliband:	his sons
Wakelin of Pont-Enchanfroi:	a friend of Gilbert of Brionne
Roger de Beaumont and Hugh de Grandesmil:	enemies of Roger de Tosny
Roger of Montgomery:	a rebellious baron
Hugh, Roger, Robert, William and Gilbert:	his sons
Thurstan Goz 'the Dane':	a baron, trying his luck

Nigel 'Falconhead':	Viscount of the Cotentin; Grimauld de Plessis; Ralph 'the Badger'
Taisson, Lord of Thury; Rannulf, Count of the Bessin and 'Longtooth' Haimo de Crèvecoeur, Lord of Torigni, Évrecy and Cruelly:	conspirators against William
Hubert de Ryes:	a minor baron with land between Caen and the Channel coast
Hardret:	a Norman knight who wants to make a name for himself

The Kingdoms of England and Denmark

Edward, son of King Ethelred of England and his second wife Emma of Normandy:	living in exile in Normandy
Alfred, his brother:	murdered shortly before the start of the story
Goda, sister of Edward and Alfred:	married to Count Eustace of Boulogne
Harthacnut and Gunhilda:	Emma of Normandy's children by King Canute
Elgiva of Northampton:	Canute's first wife/concubine
King Harold I of England, known as 'Harefoot' (1035–):	Canute and Elgiva's son

Leofric: Earl of Mercia (c.1017–)	
Lady Godiva:	his wife
Aelfwine:	Bishop of Winchester
Brihtric Mau:	a Saxon landowner and ambassador to the court of Count Baldwin
Sven Estridsson:	son of Ulf Jarl (brother of Gytha Thorkelsdóttir) and Estrith (sister of Canute): close ally of Harthacnut
King Magnus I of Norway (1035–)	
Kalv Arneson and Einar 'Strongbow' Eindridesson:	two Norwegian barons loyal to Magnus
Thrond:	an executioner employed by Harthacnut
Tofi the Proud:	King Canute's former standard-bearer
Gytha:	his bride
Osgood Clapa:	Gytha's father, an East Anglian landowner

The House of Wessex

Godwin, Earl of Wessex (1020–)	
Gytha Thorkelsdóttir:	his wife
Sweyn, Harold, Tostig, Gyrth, Leofwin, Wulnoth:	Godwin and Gytha's sons
Edith:	their daughter

Named Fictional Characters

Judith:	Herleva's best friend and William's nanny
Jarl the Viper:	a professional poisoner, also known as Jamila
Agatha:	a young Flemish girl in need of charity
Mahomet:	Jarl's servant, but Jamila's husband
Eudo:	a poacher's son
Father Osmond:	a monk seeking justice
Rörik Ingesson:	captain of Harthacnut's flagship
Conan:	a soldier, turned monk
Turkill:	William's trainer in the art of swordsmanship
Tallifer:	a maker of fine pies
John of Saltwich:	one of Earl Godwin's men
Brutus the Great:	a strongman in a travelling show
Martin:	one of three useful poachers
John:	a blacksmith's boy
Solomon ben Yehuda:	a Jewish scholar in Narbonne
Mildred:	a servant at the royal palace of Winchester
Father Louis and Father Rodulf:	two rural priests
Bishop Bertrand:	chaplain to the King of France
Peter of Tewkesbury:	an English boy in Flanders

Prologue: The Carrion Field

The countryside south of Caen, Normandy, early 1047

The spring rains had been heavy and the River Orne was running fast and full. By rights the mills at Borbeillon should have been turning at a good, steady rate, the air filled with the sounds of the grinding of the wheat between the rotating millstones, the splashing of the water against the paddles of the waterwheels and the groaning of wood and rope.

But the millstones were still, the wheels were not turning and the only noise that came from them was the repetitive banging of wood against metal. Again and again the same staccato clatter as jammed paddles beat back and forth against the objects that were obstructing them: the helmets, shields and chain-mail coats of dead men, hundreds of them, whose bodies had been carried downstream by the river in which they had drowned.

The day was drawing to a close, but in the oyster-grey expanse of the sunless sky a multitude of birds – crows, rooks, ravens, buzzards, even seagulls drawn inshore by the promise of a feast – wheeled and screeched and cawed as they surveyed the devastation beneath them. Across a great swathe of flat, featureless countryside the corpses of mighty aristocrats, their attendant barons, vavasours and men-at-arms lay alongside their slaughtered mounts, contorted and disjointed as if picked up and thrown back down against the ground by the hand of

God himself. Here they had fought, retreated and then fled pell-mell towards the banks of the river, which had claimed the lives of any who survived long enough to be driven into its chilly waters.

The battle that had taken place that day would not inspire troubadours to compose songs praising the bravery and chivalry of its combatants. No playwright would take it as the subject of his work, writing speeches filled with virtue and courage to place in his characters' mouths. It was, in many respects, just another bleak day in an age of violence and disorder, a battle between two cousins, both barely out of their teens. Like their fathers and forefathers before them, the pair were typical examples of Norman nobility: ambitious, greedy, impatient men, whose blood was as much Viking as French, ready to seize by force whatever was not theirs by right. Each one of them knew that his allies one day might be his enemies in the morning, and vice versa too, for loyalties only lasted as long as there was profit in them. There was not a man present who had not fought in other, very similar engagements, and many of those who survived would one day fight and even die in others just like it. And birds would flock to pick at their bodies, too.

Yet for all that it appeared unexceptional, this was a conflict that changed the course of history. Two cousins met on a featureless plain, and when their battle was done, one of them slipped into a millennium of obscurity, unknown to any but the most devoted scholars.

And the other?

Well that is another story entirely . . .

Book One:
The Prelate's Legacy

Spring 1037–Autumn 1039

1

Rouen, Normandy

The Duke of Normandy's nanny placed a hand on his shoulder, shook it a little and said, 'Time to get up, Your Grace.'

William the Bastard gave a dismissive shrug, rolled over in bed so that his back was towards her and muttered, 'Don't want to.'

William was nine years old, and Judith had known him since he was just a seed in his mother Herleva's womb, tended to him from the day he was born and stayed with him when cruel political calculations had forced Herleva out of the ducal household, leaving William behind. The two women had grown up together in a cluster of cottages on the outskirts of Falaise: one the daughter of a skinner who stripped the hides off dead animals, the other of the tanner who turned those hides into leather. Their homes and their fathers' workplaces had been set aside from the rest of the town because the gruesomeness, filth and stench of their chosen trades was so repellent to decent folk. Now Herleva was the wife of a viscount, the mistress of a great estate and the mother of a duke, while Judith was still just a servant, when all was said and done. Yet she felt no sense of injustice, for though she had once been able to make the town lads come running, she was never going to win a great lord's heart. It was thanks to Herleva that Judith had spent nigh on a dozen years living and working in the ducal household, where she was far better off than she would ever have been in Falaise. So she had no cause to complain, except, of course, for those moments when William decided to defy her requests.

The boy was as stubborn as he was strong-willed. He was tall and strongly built for his age, with a bright thatch of ginger hair to match his fiery temper, and once he'd said no to something, wild horses couldn't drag him to a yes. Still, Judith had to try.

'Forgive me, Your Grace,' she implored him, 'but you must get up. It's His Grace the archbishop's funeral today, and before that the reading of his will.'

Judith allowed herself occasionally to treat her charge just like any other child, for his sake as much as hers. So her next effort was more informal. 'Come on, William, you really do have to be at the funeral. The people need to see their duke on such an important occasion, and the archbishop was your great-uncle, after all.'

'Don't care. Won't go.'

Judith reached down and took hold of his arm. 'Up we get,' she said, giving a gentle tug.

In an instant, William wrenched his arm from her grasp, rolled his body out of her reach, cast off his bedcover and sprang to his feet. 'How dare you touch me?' he shouted. 'I am the Duke of Normandy! I don't have to go anywhere if I don't want to! Not unless the King of France himself tells me to.'

Judith knew she was beaten, for now at any rate. She needed reinforcements, and she had just the man in mind.

William watched Judith walk disapprovingly out of the room. Then he fell back down on to his bed and wriggled under the covers. He had decided he was going to stay in bed all day. He didn't know what the reading of a will even was, and he certainly wasn't going to the funeral. His great-uncle's body was lying in Our Lady of Rouen Cathedral for everyone to see, but that was the very last thing in the whole world that William wanted to do. He'd never seen a dead body, not close up, anyway, and certainly not someone he knew. He didn't want to start with his own great-uncle. And there was something else too, something he couldn't tell anyone that meant he absolutely could not bring himself to set eyes upon the archbishop's corpse.

William hated even thinking about it. He rolled on to his side and pulled a pillow over his head, as if it could block his thoughts as effectively as it cut out the light and sound of the outside world. Within a couple of minutes, he was dozing again.

'Your Grace . . . Your Grace?'

William opened his eyes at the sound of a familiar, male voice. Osbern Herfastsson was much, much older than William, so old that his hair was almost entirely grey. He was William's steward, the most important man in the ducal household, having been his father's steward before that. And he was a member of the House of Normandy, descended on his mother's side from Duke Rollo, the founder of their dynasty. So even though he was William's vassal, Osbern was a man who had to be treated with respect.

'Yes?' said William cautiously.

'May I ask you a question?'

'What question?'

'Well . . .' Osbern let the word hang teasingly in the air, 'would you like to see a man who has a face like a donkey?'

William hadn't been expecting that. His surprise made him do something very unusual: he giggled. 'What, an actual, real donkey?'

'Yes, an actual donkey,' said Osbern. 'In fact, he looks so much like a donkey that he's known as Ralph Donkey-Head.'

William frowned. 'Are you sure, Osbern? I mean, have you seen him?'

'No, not yet. Ralph was raised in the country, away from

everyone else. For all I know, he spends his days in a field and sleeps in a stable overnight.'

William burst out laughing. 'No one lives in a stable!'

'A man with a donkey's head might. Anyway, he arrived here last night, and he'll be at the reading of the will. So if you want to see him, you have to be there too. Archbishop Robert's widow doesn't want him to come to the actual funeral.'

'Why not?' William asked.

Osbern did not know how to reply. Ralph was illegitimate, the son of a long-forgotten concubine. But William was a bastard son too, and it would hardly do to tell a duke, even one so young, that there was something dishonourable about his status.

William, however, saved Osbern's blushes. 'Doesn't she want a donkey in the church?' he sniggered, before collapsing in hysterics at his own joke.

'Something like that, I should think. Come on now, get dressed and we'll go and see if this Ralph fellow really does look like an ass.'

This time William leapt to his feet and was dressed and breakfasted in no time. He and Osbern, accompanied by a troop of mounted guards, rode from the ducal palace in Rouen, across the city to the abbey of Saint-Ouen, where the abbot was waiting to greet him.

He led William and Osbern to the chamber where he would soon be reading the archbishop's will. The document's principal beneficiaries were already there, waiting for the event to begin. Among them were the archbishop's three sons – he had never seen any reason to practise chastity, reasoning that as well as being Normandy's most senior prelate, he was also the Count of Évreux, and as such had a duty to produce an heir. Not everyone in Normandy, or the Vatican, come to that, agreed with his self-serving justification for ignoring the priestly vows of celibacy, and there were those who suggested that God Himself might be of the same view, for He had not blessed the archbishop with the offspring that a man of his strength, good looks, animal vigour and brilliant mind might have expected.

His oldest son, and the heir to the title of Count of Évreux, was named Richard, after the archbishop's father, Duke Richard I, whom the people knew as 'Richard Fearless'. Sadly, his younger namesake was not so much fearless as desperately mediocre. There was nothing particularly wrong with him. He was healthy, decent and lacking in any apparent vices. He gave generously to a number of religious foundations, just as any proper Christian with money to spare was supposed to do. But compared to his father, he was a docile carthorse next to a rearing, snorting charger.

The archbishop's second son, William, had been a sickly boy, and the very fact that he had survived at all seemed the most that could be said for him.

Then came the third, apparently even less well-favoured child, who was now nearly twenty years old. This was Ralph de Gacé, and the moment Duke William clapped eyes on him, he called out in his piping treble voice, 'You're right, Cousin Osbern, he does look like a donkey!'

Ralph de Gacé winced like a man being whipped on an open wound. Though he had grown in the years since he first acquired his nickname from the taunting bullies in the village that butted up against the small, run-down castle in which he had been raised, he remained a deeply unattractive specimen. His eyes, half covered by an unkempt mass of dull brown hair, were watery and bulged from their sockets. His nose and face were long and framed on either side by a pair of oversized ears, while his lips were barely able to stretch over protruding upper and lower teeth, beneath which was a weak receding chin. There really was no denying that he did look very much like a donkey.

His eyes narrowed for a moment as he shot a look of undiluted noxious hatred at William. The young duke did not see the venom in Ralph's eyes, being too busy saying hello to his uncles Mauger and Talou. Though their father was Duke Richard II, William's grandfather, they were barely a decade older than the boy duke. They were also legitimate, which William was not, and thus, as they both well knew, had reason to insist that their claim to the dukedom was at least as great as his.

As he lay on his deathbed, the archbishop had summoned William and warned him that these two uncles of his were reaching an age when they would become ambitious for power. 'Beware them both, my boy!' he'd said in a weak, trembling voice that had upset William because it was so unlike the all-powerful great-uncle he had known. Now he looked at the pair of them, his face furrowed in concentration as he wondered how he was supposed to spot the signs of his uncles' ambition. Mauger didn't look like someone who could do him any harm. He was thin and nervy, forever glancing around and giving little twitches of his mouth and head. Talou, on the other hand, reminded him of Osbern's descriptions of his dead Uncle Richard, the one that people said his papa had killed. Richard had been big, strong, and warlike, but his weakness, said Osbern, was a lack of intelligence. 'He had no kindness, either,' the steward had added. 'In time, perhaps, he might have earned his people's fear and even their respect. But he would never have had the love that a truly great ruler receives.'

Talou didn't look like someone who was interested in being clever or kind. He was big, with a face covered in white-tipped red spots, and he walked with his shoulders hunched forward as if he was constantly searching for someone to punch.

'What are you looking at, Cousin?' Talou asked, catching William's eye and taking a single, menacing step towards him.

'Don't you dare speak to your duke in that fashion, boy,' Osbern Herfastsson growled, placing himself between the two of them.

'And don't you dare speak to the son of a duke in that one,' Talou retorted. He stood there smugly, obviously pleased with his reply.

Osbern leaned forward so that his face was up close to Talou's. 'You haven't been to war, have you, boy?'

William was fascinated. He'd always known Osbern as a friendly, even loving figure. He'd never seen this side of his character before.

Talou shook his head dumbly.

'Well I have. When you weren't even a glimmer in your father's eyes, I stood side by side with him in the blood and the shit, fighting the English, the Bretons, the French and anyone else who thought they could take what belonged to Normandy. I was proud to call Richard the Good my commander and my duke, and he was gracious enough to call me cousin and friend. When I see you fight – I mean, really fight, when your life could be lost at any moment God chooses – then I'll decide whether to show you the respect you seem to think you deserve. But until then, I will address you as the boy that you are.'

The abbot observed the whole scene with a growing sense of foreboding. He'd caught the way Ralph had looked at William. He'd seen how Mauger glanced around like a jackdaw, ever in search of something shiny to take for himself; and there had been no mistaking the resentment in Talou's eye. Once again the abbot asked himself whether the archbishop had done the right thing in choosing to gather together the boy duke and the young men with the greatest reason to oppose him. 'That is the whole point!' the archbishop had insisted, as he prepared to dictate his wishes to a monk from the abbey, in the presence of the abbot and one of his chaplains. 'My only hope is to craft a will that ties them all closely to William, that gives them the maximum reason to follow him and offers as little incentive as possible to rise up in rebellion.'

The two men had been colleagues in the Church and friends for more years than either could count. So the abbot had felt able to be frank. 'Honestly, Robert, do you really think this will make the slightest bit of difference? I fear that dissension and even open revolt are inevitable. When there is a weak hand on the tiller, stronger hands will seek to steer the boat.'

'I expect you're right,' the archbishop replied with a sigh. 'But if I can just distract them and keep them from making their challenges until William has grown strong enough to repel them, then I will have done as much to save my family as it could possibly expect.'

'Or deserve,' the abbot had added wryly.

Now the archbishop was dead, and it was time to reveal the contents of his will. The abbot picked up the parchment that lay rolled and sealed on the table in front of him. 'Your Grace, my lords, this is the final will and testament of His Grace Robert, Archbishop of Rouen,' he began.

'I can attest that what I am about to read to you represents His Grace's true intentions, vouchsafed when he was sound in mind and body and sworn to in the sight of God. His Grace wrote as follows . . .'

2

Five knights mounted on mighty chargers forced their way through the crowds in Rouen's Cathedral Square like dogs through a herd of milling, empty-headed sheep. Their wooden saddles were as high as the heads of the common folk who scurried to get out of their way, and they were followed by a troop of foot soldiers and a large uncovered horse-drawn wagon in which sat a middle-aged matriarch and her four daughters.

At the head of the column rode a man who wore no armour, yet whose entire demeanour somehow suggested that his body alone was as impenetrably hard as the iron from which his horse's shoes had been forged. His name was Giroie, Lord of Échauffour. He had come from a modest background in Brittany, but though he lacked the education and finesse of those with more noble blood, he possessed one very valuable, tradeable skill: he knew how to fight. He was equally competent with a sword, a lance, an axe or just his bare hands, and to this skill he added unmatched courage and fortitude, combined with raw cunning and boundless ambition.

More than twenty years had passed since Giroie first made his name. An army from the county of Maine had crossed the border into south-east Normandy. The local Norman forces, led by the Count of Bellême, fled rather than fight the invaders, but Giroie and his small band of men stood their ground against overwhelming odds and then went on the offensive themselves, chasing the enemy right out of the duchy. A grateful Duke Richard II had given him two fine estates and the lordships that came with them. Now Giroie was part of the aristocracy, but he knew as well as anyone that he was just a parvenu, a self-made man. The favours that had been bestowed on him could be removed just as swiftly. So he had abandoned his military campaigning and devoted his energies to the creation of a dynasty.

Giroie had been blessed in this enterprise with a wonderfully fertile wife, Gisela, who had given him seven sons and four daughters. The oldest of his boys, Arnold, was his heir and had been set aside to run the family estates. The others were being farmed off one by one to serve other, more eminent families. His daughters, meanwhile, had been groomed for the marriage market. By these means Giroie wanted to create a warrior clan linked by ties of service, marriage and eventually kinship with as many of the great houses of Normandy as possible, so that in time, they too could count themselves among the highest in the land.

Now Giroie rode through the middle of Rouen with four of his sons, who all bore the newly minted family name of Fitzgiroie. No passer-by would need a name, however, to know that they were related. It was obvious at a glance, not just from the heavy jaws and prominent, glowering brows they shared with their father, but also from a general belligerence. No son of Giroie's had ever turned his back on a fight, and it showed.

All around them, however, the atmosphere was anything but combative. As sad and even shocking as the archbishop's death might have been, his passing was rapidly turning into an impromptu feast day. Food stalls had been set up around the square, and traders were taking advantage of the mass of hungry and thirsty townsfolk to tout their wares. Minstrels and clowns competed with gipsy fortune-tellers for the attention and pennies of the crowd, and small children raced between the grown-ups playing games of tag, fighting, giggling or simply burning off their boundless energy and high spirits.

Giroie led his column through the teeming multitudes. Those who recognised him and knew his reputation hurried to get out of his way. Anyone who, through ignorance or unwise defiance, failed to move voluntarily found that Giroie and his sons were happy to use their horses as battering rams and simply barge their way through, lashing out at those who strayed within kicking range and shouting curses and threats at any man who dared approach the wagon in which their womenfolk were riding.

Up ahead, Giroie could see the cathedral. Much of its facade was hidden behind a web of flimsy wooden scaffolding, for the archbishop had commissioned a tremendous programme of expansion and improvement. Masons had come to the city from all over north-west France and the provinces of the Low Countries. One tower to the left of the main entrance, which stood as tall and massive as any castle keep, had already been completed and dedicated to St Romain. Another was under way. Giroie had not visited Rouen since the first tower's completion, but he barely gave it a second glance. He had no interest in architecture. He wanted to build a dynasty, and his materials were not bricks and mortar but flesh and blood.

The family and their retainers made their way to a large inn that stood in a muddy street to one side of the Cathedral Square, along which ran an open, stinking drain overflowing with filthy water and thick with excrement. Their wagon, horses and men were stabled and barracked, the Giroies themselves were shown to the two rooms in which they would be staying, and large quantities of food and ale were ordered to fortify them for the funeral. The innkeeper and his servants were left in no doubt that their guests needed to be catered to at once, and as soon as the meal arrived, Giroie was ordering his wife and children to wolf it down. 'Hurry up, we haven't got all day! It won't be long till the service starts, and we've got business to conduct before then. Wife, let me take a look at our daughters!'

The men were left to carry on eating while Gisela lined up the four girls in ascending order of age. Giroie inspected them as if they were troops, which in a sense they were, though they would do their duty in the marital bedchamber rather than on the battlefield.

'This isn't good enough,' he told his wife, having finished his examination. 'Hawisa's clearly the one who's going to catch a man's eye and get his cock swelling, but we can't have her spawning brats while her three big sisters are still sitting around waiting for a proposal.'

'Don't say that,' Gisela replied, though she knew perfectly well that her baby girl, as she still thought of her, was the pick of the crop. 'They're all lovely in their own way and I'm sure that any man, no matter how highly born, would be happy to have any of them as his bride.'

Giroie gave a sceptical grunt, then turned away from his womenfolk and picked up a wooden tankard of ale. He drained it in one, and after a single mighty belch gave the order to move out.

3

The abbot began to read the archbishop's will. William thought he had a voice like a cross old woman: high-pitched, fussy and disapproving – as though all the men in the room were just boys, and he was about to tell them off. He sounded like a preacher giving a sermon, or William's teacher, Brother Thorold, becoming impatient when William or one of his classmates couldn't translate a passage of Latin.

'"I declare this to be my will in the name of the Father, the Son and the Holy Ghost, thanking the Good Lord for the many blessings He has bestowed upon me and vowing to serve Him in the hereafter as I have done in this life on earth",' the abbot declaimed.

'"To the Cathedral of Our Lady of Rouen, my spiritual home and sanctuary, I leave the decorated psalter known as the Benedictional of Athelgar that I received as a gift from my beloved sister Emma. I ask that prayers from it be said on the anniversary of my death, in commemoration of my soul.

'"To my first cousin and most loyal friend Osbern Herfastsson I leave a gift of gold coins to the value of one thousand pounds as a token of my appreciation of all he has done to assist me and support the cause of the House of Normandy."'

William was pleased about that. He loved Osbern and was happy to think that he would have lots of gold. But Talou and Mauger looked furious. Why are they so angry to see Osbern doing well? William wondered.

'"To my beloved eldest son Richard, who becomes by right the Count of Évreux, I leave all the estates and properties that by custom belong to that title, along with the castle of Évreux and all its furniture, tapestries, goblets and serving vessels of wood, pewter and assorted precious metals, and all the bed linen, fur rugs and clothing contained in its wardrobes. I commend him to continue the many excellent charitable deeds and benefactions for which his life to this date has been noted.

'"To my younger son William I leave my estates at Lieuvin and Baiocasino and all their rents, vassals and contents likewise, in the hope that he will live well and conduct himself properly as a loyal vassal of the Duke of Normandy, whomsoever may be the holder of that title."'

The abbot paused. He was frowning as he looked at the paper in his hand. Maybe he can't read the writing, William thought. Or maybe he can, but he doesn't like what it says. The moment the abbot started speaking again, William knew by the sound of his voice and the words themselves that the second possibility was the right one.

'"To my natural son Ralph I bestow the castle of Gacé at which he has been raised, along with the further estates of Bavent, Noyon-sur-Andelle, Gravençon and Écouché. I myself was born illegitimate. My parents Richard and Gunnor married when I was a young man, so that I might be ordained as archbishop, a post that can only be held by one of legitimate birth. Likewise, many of those who have ruled Normandy as her duke were the offspring of concubines rather than wives. It cannot therefore be said that there is anything inferior or unworthy about the status of bastard, and it is in this light that I beseech those who now assist our duke in his God-given duty as ruler of Normandy to take my son Ralph under their wing and train him well, so that he may one day serve his ducal masters as I have served mine. Of all my sons I believe he is the one most blessed by God with the particular qualities that have allowed me to advise and guide those whom I have served."'

William looked around at half a dozen incredulous faces and one brazen, triumphant one. 'Now who's the donkey?' cried Ralph, pumping his fist in celebration.

William was frowning, deep in thought. He was sure that the archbishop had included Ralph on the list of people to beware of. The old man had said Ralph was bitter, and had blamed himself for not being a more attentive father. I think he's trying to make up for that, William concluded. If he makes Ralph feel better then he won't be nasty to me. So should I still worry about him?

He considered the matter for a moment, as an angry conversation broke out between Ralph and Talou.

'Do we really need another bastard at court?' Talou asked, and William felt himself blushing with hot, burning shame as a sudden silence descended on the room and everyone looked at him, their eyes like daggers piercing his skin. He said nothing, but he was raging inside as he gazed steadily at Talou, who blinked and turned away, unable to look him in the eye. William felt a measure of victory at out-staring his uncle, who was twice his age and far bigger and stronger than him, but at the back of his mind, something was nagging at him, a question he'd not yet managed to answer. He tried to remember what he'd been thinking: something about Ralph . . .

Before he could retrieve the lost memory, the abbot cleared his throat very loudly, so that everyone turned their attention back to him. 'If I may continue,' he said. 'His Grace goes on to say, "It is not, of course, in my power to name my successor as archbishop. It is, however, in the gift of the duke and his advisers to do so. I therefore beseech Duke William and his guardians to consider the claim of my nephew Mauger. Just as it is right that the line of ducal succession has passed through the sons and grandson of my brother Duke Richard II's first marriage, so the archbishopric should be bestowed upon a son of the second. Mauger is still very young, but so was I when I received my consecration. I trust that he will be blessed with as long a time in which to serve God and Normandy as I have been."'

Unlike Ralph, Mauger managed to contain his enthusiasm, which manifested itself solely as a broad smile and a series of quick little pecks of the head.

Do I really have to make him the next archbishop? William asked himself, examining his eighteen-year-old uncle. He doesn't look old enough to be an ordinary priest. And why was Great-Uncle Robert so kind to Mauger as well as Ralph? He's meant to be dangerous to me, but if I'm the Duke of Normandy and he's the Archbishop of Rouen, I'll see him all the time and . . . oh!

Something had just occurred to William. If Mauger and Ralph are close to me, then I'll be able to see what they're doing. Or my guardians will see it, anyway. So they won't be able to do anything bad in secret.

The abbot looked as cross about Mauger as he had been about Ralph. But it wasn't his place to complain. He began reading once again.

'"I beseech His Grace Duke William to show favour to his uncle the Count of Talou and grant him the right to build a castle of his own on the hill at Arques, which lies within his lands, close to the fishing village of Dieppe. The hill commands a wide area of countryside, and there is a fine hunting forest between it and the sea to provide both game and sport. A good stout castle there will help secure the north-east corner of our duchy against incursions by forces from Boulogne, Flanders or France.

'"I feel sure that you, Talou, will have no hesitation in

thanking your duke for his generosity and favour by devoting all your energies to his service and being a loyal and true support to him in the arduous task, bestowed on him by God, of ruling Normandy and his peoples. And be in no doubt at any time that any acts of dissension, rebellion or treachery on your part will fully entitle your duke to strip you of your property, seize your castle and, if it pleases him, even go so far as to destroy it.

'"Finally, I commend all those assembled to hear this will, and all the people of Normandy, across the duchy, to be loyal and faithful servants of my great-nephew Duke William. He holds his title by the grace of God, and any rebellion against that title is, likewise, a most sinful and unpardonable assault upon the sanctity of our Holy Father and will therefore constitute a sin whose punishment will surely be an eternity in the fires of Hell."

'So concludes the reading of His Grace's will,' said the abbot, rolling the parchment back up again. 'I trust that no one has any objections to any of its stipulations.' He looked around and met with no obvious dissent, though William had the strong impression that a lot of the grown-ups around him were much crosser than they were letting on.

'Very well,' the abbot concluded. 'Our business is finished. Let us hasten to the cathedral for the funeral.'

As everyone stood, exchanging brief words of conversation, and prepared to be on their way, William stood alone, chewing his bottom lip. Now that the will had been read, other thoughts were crowding back into his head: the same thoughts that had made him so unwilling to get out of bed.

The abbot must have noticed something, because he walked across and looked down at him kindly. 'Is anything troubling you, Your Grace?' he asked.

William uttered a muffled 'No,' and gave a single, decisive shake of the head.

He glanced up at the abbot. He doesn't believe me, he thought. What will I say if he asks me any more questions?

But the abbot didn't pursue the matter. 'Well, if you do think of anything, you can always come and talk to me. Nothing you say will be passed on to anyone else, except, of course, He who hears and knows everything. And He is very forgiving, you know, to one who is truly penitent.'

William started. He knows that I've committed a terrible sin! And God knows too! His eyes widened in alarm, and then he gathered his composure, remembering that a duke of Normandy could never show anyone if he was worried or frightened or didn't know what to do. He had to stay in control at all times.

'Thank you, Brother Abbot,' he said. 'That is very kind.'

'You're welcome . . . God bless you, my son.'

William nodded his thanks, and then, wanting to get as far away from the abbot as possible, ran off in search of Osbern.

4

All night and day the mourners had stood in line to pay their respects to the dead archbishop as he lay in his open coffin before the altar of Rouen cathedral, his features set in an expression of wry amusement that suggested he regarded his passing as just one more event to be confronted, managed and bent to his own ends. An entire generation had been born, lived their lives and died in the forty-eight years that Robert, Archbishop of Rouen and Count of Évreux, had spent on his episcopal throne. Four dukes of Normandy had ruled and departed in that time: his father, brother and two nephews. Only Duke William, his great-nephew, had outlived him. The archbishop's permanence as both the spiritual leader of the duchy and the worldly adviser to its dukes had led the Normans to believe that he was all but immortal. Even now, as they bent their knees to kiss the heavy, bejewelled gold ring on the fourth finger of his right hand, there were those who could not quite believe that their protector had departed this world for the next.

The woman who had assassinated the archbishop just a few days earlier was now close enough to study the results of her handiwork. She looked down on him through the fabric of a veil woven in Damascus from thread finer than any the haughtiest noblewoman in Normandy could even imagine, let alone afford. When she was born, on a longboat journeying down the Dnieper river in the lands of the Viking Rus, her parents had christened her Finna Bjornsdottir. More recently, however, she had gone by the name of Jarl the Viper. It was a matter of commercial necessity in a profession that had brought her great wealth. Customers hiring a killer expected him to be a man, even if Jarl's chosen method – poisoning, using potions concocted from ingredients she had in many cases grown herself – was, to her mind, a very feminine means of administering death.

In the archbishop's case, she had gone to his bedchamber and given him a warm, soothing drink scented with honey, berries and spice. Her victim was a very sick man, whose end was imminent no matter what. But she'd feared that before he died he might want to give a final confession, including the admission that he had ordered the death of his nephew, Duke Richard III. Jarl had carried out that particular assignment and wished to avoid the slightest possibility that she might be caught and punished. She had thus added to her sweet brew a fatal dose of an opiate tincture derived from a particular form of poppy, grown from seeds that had come with her from the ancient city of Damascus, where she had first been taught her deadly art.

She was pleased to see that the archbishop looked at peace, and that something close to a smile was frozen on his grave-cold lips. She bore him no ill will and had chosen the poppy as her weapon because it induced a contented, even blissful state before the body finally succumbed. It was therefore almost certain that she had provided him with a gentler journey to St Peter's gates than his ailments would have done if left to their own devices. She felt no guilt whatever as she took her turn beside the coffin, bent her head, lifted her veil a fraction, lightly kissed the blood-red ruby that was mounted on the golden ring and murmured, 'Farewell, Your Grace, rest in peace.'

As she rose gracefully to her feet, the calm of the cathedral was shattered by a blare of trumpets that cut through the incense-laden air like an axe through an unprotected skull. She turned her head to see a boy and four men striding directly towards her through the nave of the cathedral. She recognised them all, for it had long been her business to know such things, if only to make sure that should any of them become her target, she would get the right man.

To the right of the group was Count Alan of Brittany, the archbishop's nephew. He was a short but powerfully built man whose swept-back mane was beginning to show the first traces of grey, just as his swarthy face was softening somewhat around the jowls. His eyes, however, were still jet black. Even at a distance Jarl could detect their mischievous glint of confidence, bordering on arrogance, and for all her cool detachment, she was still woman enough to be intrigued, if only for an instant.

The man beside Alan was taller, older and far more weather-beaten. This was Osbern Herfastsson. Jarl wondered how many of the people here today, who were all familiar with Osbern's steadfast, unflinching loyalty to the archbishop and to the two dukes he had served as steward, understood how astutely he had used his proximity to power to further his own ambitions. There were few men in Normandy who could rival the extent of Osbern's estates.

Apart from him, perhaps, thought Jarl, looking at the third member of the group, Gilbert, count of both Eu and Brionne. Like Alan, Gilbert had known the archbishop as 'Uncle'. His father, Godfrey, had been the illegitimate son of Duke Richard I, born to one of the duke's many concubines but raised as if his blood were true.

These three men were the effective rulers of Normandy now that the archbishop, who had long been the greatest power in the land, was gone. They were dressed in gowns of the finest Flanders cloth and their scabbards and sword hilts were chased with silver and gold. The final member of the quartet, however, was entirely unarmed and wore nothing more than the rough woollen habit of a monk. Brother Thorold served as tutor in the ducal palace. He, like the others, had been named as a guardian of William the Bastard, seventh Duke of Normandy, who walked ahead of them past the congregation packed into the pews on either side of him.

Jarl took a good long look at the lad on whose young shoulders the future of his dynasty and duchy alike now rested. He had a sturdy body and a proud, combative bearing that belied his age. There was a determined set to his jaw and a fierce expression in his eyes, as if he were daring the men around him to take him on and see how far it would get them. Some children might scuff their feet as they slouched into a church. Others would break into a playful run. But this one strode like a man, with his back straight, his shoulders squared and his head up. Jarl smiled at the sight of this stripling warrior, even as soldiers from the Norman militia, whose shields bore the two golden leopards that were the duchy's symbol, began to herd her and the other mourners away from the coffin and away down one of the aisles that ran either side of the nave.

There were shouts of protest from those who had been standing in line for hours but had yet to see the archbishop's body. The soldiers paid them no attention and formed a line abreast, creating a human barrier that pushed its way between the coffin and the waiting mourners. As she was caught in the press of people being herded to one side, Jarl darted one final appraising glance at the duke and thought of the last times she had seen him: first in the archbishop's chamber, and then, very soon afterwards, playing with his friends in the garden outside.

William had been hit by one of the other boys' wooden toy swords and had fallen to the ground, rolling around groaning and making his friends shriek with laughter as he pretended to die. Jarl had been deeply affected by the contrast between this child's-play imitation of death and the reality she knew only too intimately.

Now, as she watched William walk through the cathedral, she felt certain that all too many of the men thronging its pews believed that they, not he, should be master of Normandy, no matter what it took. She knew she would probably be called upon to poison William one day, but she realised, to her profound surprise – for she had never before been squeamish – that she could not bring herself to kill so young and undeserving a victim. An instant later she understood that the only way she could avoid being asked to do the job was to retire from her calling, immediately and absolutely. Someone else might end this boy's life, but she would not be the one to do it.

Now that he was here in the cathedral, where his great-uncle's body was lying, the bad thoughts that had been bothering William since he'd first woken up were more overwhelming than ever. He was desperately afraid that he'd done something very wicked, but as he walked up the centre of the nave, feeling all the eyes following his every step, he had no idea what to do about it. If the people around him found out, they'd kill him, he was sure of it.

They were calling out to him from all sides, most exclaiming, 'Your Grace!' though a few ill-wishers hissed, 'Bastard!' But then he heard a woman's voice, much gentler than the rest, saying, 'Willie, my darling . . . over here!' He turned his head and saw his mother, Herleva. Months had passed since he'd last been with her, but there she was, waving at him. His half-brothers Odo and Robert were standing next to her, and beyond them was his stepfather, Herluin of Conteville, giving him a broad, friendly smile. William longed to run over to them and wrap his arms around Mama's waist and feel her pull him tight against her dress. He could tell her his secret and she wouldn't be cross, he knew that for sure. Herluin would be very calm about the whole thing and say something sensible. Then the boys would beg him to play with them and everything would be all right.

But William could not run to his mother like any other boy. He had to think about his duty to his duchy and his people. So he just gave Herleva and the rest of her family a little nod of the head, keeping his mouth tightly pursed without any hint of a smile, and walked on as grimly as a condemned prisoner marching to the gallows.

A moment later, he found himself by the open coffin. Forcing himself to look down, he was struck by Great-Uncle Robert's extraordinary stillness. When he and his friends played soldiers, they often fell to the ground pretending to be dead, but even when they tried their very best not to move or breathe, they couldn't help being pink and warm and bursting with life. But his great-uncle's body looked so like a statue, so completely sucked dry of life, that William could hardly believe this was the very same man he'd seen just a few days earlier, lying in bed and giving him lessons on all the people he could and could not trust. That man had been ill, but he breathed and spoke and smiled when William asked a good question. And . . . and . . .

William burst into tears.

Now it was Osbern's turn to comfort him. He crouched down on his haunches, laid one hand on William's shoulder and lifted the boy's chin with the other. 'There, there,' he said. 'It's all right. There's nothing wrong with being sad when someone you loved and who loved you very much dies.'

William gulped and screwed up his eyes, trying to staunch the tears. 'I know . . .' he sniffed. 'But . . . but . . .'

'Don't worry, William. Your great-uncle's in heaven now. He's surrounded by saints and angels and archangels. He's standing by the throne of God Himself.'

'But . . .' William sniffed again and wiped his eyes. For a

second he seemed to be recovering, but then he gave another convulsive sob and blurted out, 'I think I killed him!'

Now Osbern placed both hands on William's upper arms, holding him tight. 'Don't say that, Your Grace,' he said, deliberately using a more formal mode of address. 'His Grace the archbishop died because his time had come and Our Lord took him to stand by His side.'

'But I was the last person to see him, apart from the servant woman who came in to give him his medicine and she doesn't count. Great-Uncle Robert died after I'd been with him. Maybe I said something that made him cross, or there was a demon in me that leapt on to the bed and killed him.'

Osbern's heart bled to think of the burden of guilt the poor boy had been carrying. 'No, no . . . I promise you that didn't happen,' he reassured him. 'Great-Uncle Robert was a very old man. Death came to him as it comes to us all. There's no need to despair. We should be thankful he led such a long life and did so much good before he died.'

He paused. A thought had struck him, the memory of another death ten years earlier and a conversation he'd had with Tancred, the chamberlain of the ducal palace, now dead himself these past four years. 'You should have seen the slut the duke had with him that night,' Tancred had said with a lascivious lick of the lips, although women were never his pleasure. 'I'm not surprised his heart gave out. Even I might have been tempted.'

The duke in question was Richard III, William's uncle, and although it seemed certain he'd died of natural causes, no one could stop the gossips whispering of murder. Maybe there was some substance to their tittle-tattle after all. An empty flagon of wine and a pair of goblets had been found in the chamber, but no one had paid them any attention. It would have been far more unusual if Duke Richard had entertained a whore without the benefit of strong, sweet wine to heighten his ardour. Now, though, as William reported seeing a woman taking medicine to the archbishop shortly before he died, Osbern wondered whether both men might conceivably have been poisoned, and by the same killer.

He heard a cough from behind him and twisted his head to see Alan of Brittany looking down at him with a quizzical look on his face. Alan gave a quick jerk of his head as if to say, 'Get up.'

Osbern held up a hand. 'One moment.' He turned back to William. 'Your Grace, do you remember the woman you saw in your great-uncle's bedchamber? Was she very beautiful?'

William twisted his mouth from side to side and shrugged. 'S'pose so.'

'Don't be shy, just try to imagine her. Did she have a pretty face?'

William nodded.

'And would you recognise her if you saw her again?'

Another nod.

'Very well then, let's not say another word about this to anyone. You did not kill anyone. You've done nothing wrong. Do you understand?'

'Yes.'

'Good lad. Now, wipe your eyes and your nose and stand up straight. Your barons want to pay their respects to you. Better look like you deserve them, eh?'

5

Giroie was leading his family through the west door of the cathedral when he heard his name being called by a voice that, even as it greeted him with apparent good humour, seemed somehow to be sneering. He looked to his right and saw a familiar figure leaning against one of the huge stone pillars that supported the cathedral roof. He turned back to his oldest son, Arnold. 'Get your brothers and the women somewhere to sit. I'll find you.' Then he walked across to the man who had attracted his attention.

'Good day, Talvas,' he said.

Talvas of Bellême, master of the castle of Alençon and a great swathe of land in southern Normandy, gave a smile that, as was his custom, did not extend to his eyes. 'And to you, Giroie. Brought your family with you, I see.' He chuckled to himself. 'You're like a farmer bringing his prize pigs to market. They're all for sale if you get the right price.'

Giroie looked at Talvas. Even at his age, he'd have no trouble dismembering the arrogant little shit if they ever went at it, one sword against another. And yet, though Talvas was a poorly built specimen, with legs as skinny as a heron's, there was an air of danger about him.

'How's my lad doing, then?' Giroie asked.

'William?' Talvas replied. 'He's doing very well. He's been busy expanding my territory into Maine – that's why he's not here, actually.'

'Doing your fighting for you, eh? Just like I did for your father.'

Talvas gave a polite laugh, but the chill in his eyes became even frostier. 'Oh yes, he's a great fighter, your lad. Of course, my brother Robert would still be alive if it hadn't been for him. There is that to consider.'

Even by the standards of the never-ending swirl of mayhem and criminality that surrounded the Norman aristocracy, the House of Bellême was more than usually delinquent. Three of Talvas's older brothers had died violently, which explained why he, the survivor, was currently in possession of the family stronghold at Alençon. The previous occupant, Robert, had gone to war with the Count of Maine, whose lands shared a border with Bellême. It was not a wise move. Robert was defeated, captured and thrown into a dungeon beneath the castle of Ballon. As a loyal soldier of the House of Bellême, William Fitzgiroie had set out to even the score with Maine and defeated the count. In the course of that action, a company of Bellême soldiers had captured one of the count's followers, Walter Sors, and two of his five sons, whom they promptly hanged, against William Fitzgiroie's orders. Unfortunately for Robert of Bellême, the three remaining Sors boys were at the castle where he was imprisoned when they heard that their father and brothers had been killed. They immediately picked up their battleaxes, went down to the dungeon and smashed Robert's skull to pieces.

'I know what really happened, as does every man in this cathedral. And it wasn't William's fault,' Giroie said, stepping closer to Talvas to make his point and presence felt. 'Don't even pretend you give a damn about your brother. If he was still walking the earth, you wouldn't be sitting in Alençon Castle lording it over Bellême.'

Talvas shrugged. 'That's true, very true . . . There's not much to be said for older brothers from a younger one's point of view. The fewer the better, eh?'

Giroie said nothing. Talvas looked around at the congregation, in which virtually every noble house of Normandy was well represented. 'So, speaking of brothers . . . I've got your son William. Am I right in thinking that one of his brothers wears the colours of Brionne?'

'Fulk.'

'Ah yes, of course. Got any takers in mind for the rest? You should have a look at young Ralph de Gacé.'

'Donkey-Head?' exclaimed Giroie. He looked at Talvas. 'Are you mocking me, boy?'

Talvas was entirely unperturbed by the very obviously threatening tone of Giroie's remark. 'Not at all, not at all. Ralph arrived a few minutes ago and promptly started telling everyone that the archbishop's will more or less ordered our beloved duke's guardians to add him to their ranks. He may be the ugliest, most ridiculous-looking man in all Normandy, but dear old Donkey-Head's going up in the world.'

'You're serious?'

'Never been more serious, Giroie. Besides, I'd never make a joke in your presence.' He turned away and murmured under his breath, 'You wouldn't understand it.'

Giroie was certain he'd heard Talvas right, but he couldn't be starting a fight in a cathedral if he wanted his family to become respectable, and certainly not on a day like this. Instead, he bade a curt farewell and strode up the centre of the nave, wishing he'd had the chance to grab Talvas in both hands and smash his arrogant, conniving head against the nearest pillar until it burst open like a ripe peach against a stone wall.

Just then, he saw a commotion up ahead. A tall, scrawny knight with a hairless scalp burned as dark as his leather boots by the sun was trying to make his way past a small group of much younger men who were blocking his path towards the altar and the young duke. Giroie could hear him calling out, 'Let me pass! By all that's holy, let . . . me . . . pass!' He shook his head in wonder. The last time he'd heard that voice had been on a beach more than twenty years ago, shouting obscene insults at fleeing English soldiers as they desperately waded out to the ships that had brought them to Normandy and were about to take them straight back home again. In those days that head still had some hair on it, but the gangly physique and high, grating speech, more like a querulous preacher than a grizzled soldier, were unmistakably the same.

As Giroie drew closer, he could not so much smell as feel the stench of stale wine rising from the knight, overpowering the lingering scent of incense that hung in the cathedral air. He stepped in front of the youngsters. 'You can go now,' he said to them. 'I'll take care of this.'

One of the group opened his mouth to speak, then caught Giroie's eye and knew that he was outmatched. 'Very well, sir. But you must not let him pass.'

Giroie looked at him for a second, giving not the slightest hint that he had heard, let alone acknowledged that ill-judged command, then turned back to the old soldier.

'By God, Tosny, you stink like a dockside tavern. What are you doing here, anyway? Shouldn't you be off in Aragon, killing Moors?'

'I was. Then I heard my wife had died. Fever. So I came back.'

'Sorry to hear that.'

'I left her to run the estate, thought she'd be safe . . .' Tosny gave a long, drink-drenched sigh. 'Now she's dead, and look at me. All these years at war and I'm still fit as a fiddle.'

Tosny looked like a man on the point of drunkard's tears. Giroie had no intention of indulging him. 'Right,' he said, briskly, 'what are you doing trying to barge your way through a cathedral?'

'Want to see this boy who calls himself the duke. Come on, Giroie.' Tosny leaned forward conspiratorially, almost asphyxiating Giroie with the booze on his breath. 'You're a man who speaks his mind . . . always used to be, anyway. What do you make of the brat?'

Giroie shrugged. 'What is there to make? People call him the Bastard because he's illegitimate. I say, so what? So were most of the dukes before him. But there are plenty who don't think he's got any right to the title.'

'So why hasn't someone killed him already? Tell me that.' Tosny suddenly sounded much more sober.

'They'd have to get past Brittany, Brionne and Herfastsson first. Also, Duke Robert did one clever thing before he left on that pilgrimage to Jerusalem. He took William off to Paris to see King Henry and had him sworn in as the king's vassal, and if that's the case . . .'

'The king has a duty to protect him.' Tosny nodded thoughtfully as he finished Giroie's sentence. 'You're right, that was a shrewd move. But if a man could get those guardians out of the way and control William himself, he'd as good as rule Normandy anyway, wouldn't he? Still, what do I care? I refuse to pledge allegiance to the brat either way. I came here to tell him that face to face.'

Now Giroie understood why people had been trying to stop him. 'For God's sake, Tosny, don't be so stupid. You can't just go up to a duke and spit in his face, no matter how old he is.'

'I've earned the right. I've fought for Normandy and I've fought for Christ Almighty, and now I'm going to say my piece. Let me pass.'

* * *

Roger de Tosny had spent his entire life sobering up in a hurry. There had been countless times when he'd been called straight from the bottle to the battlefield. Now he squared his shoulders, held his head high and marched towards the knot of fellow knights and nobles clustered around Duke William. He endured their blatantly insincere protestations of loyalty and devotion to the boy for as long as he could bear, then barged his way through them all until he stood opposite the child who was supposed to be his lord and master. To his surprise, Tosny liked the look of the lad. He did not flinch at the sight of a large armed man forcing his way into his presence, but stood tall, stayed calm and looked him right in the eye.

'I do not know you, sir,' William said, in a strong, clear voice, without a tremor of alarm. 'But I would be glad to hear your name.'

'Roger de Tosny, that's my name. I've been away these past twelve years, keeping the heathen at bay in the lands of Aragon and Castille.'

'Then you have been doing good work, Sir Roger. Can I count on you as my vassal?'

Tosny said nothing. A silence fell around him, and with it came a feeling of discomfort and unease.

Osbern Herfastsson was the first to speak. 'Your duke asked you a question, Tosny. You would do well to answer it.'

'I'll give him an answer, Herfastsson. But it's not the one that you or he wants to hear. I won't lie to him like these flatterers and arse-lickers, all professing to serve him now when you and I both know they'd betray him tomorrow if they thought they'd profit by it.'

'What does he mean?' William asked Osbern.

'Nothing. He means nothing. Don't listen to him, Your Grace.'

'What I mean,' Tosny said, 'is that I will do you the favour of honesty. As long as I live, I will never lift a sword against you. You can count on that. But I won't serve you either. You look like you've got good strong blood in you, but you're just a boy and you don't stand a chance. If, by God's grace, you live long enough to become a man, then maybe I'll give my pledge to you. But until then, I'll keep my counsel. Good day to you, Duke . . . and to you, Herfastsson.'

And with that, Roger of Tosny turned on his heel and stalked away towards the cathedral door.

'Pay him no heed,' Osbern said to William as Tosny made his way back down the aisle. 'He's just an old soldier who's spent so long in the Spanish sun that his head's been fried.'

'What did he mean about flatterers and arse-lickers?' William asked.

'Nothing. Just more stuff and nonsense.'

William said nothing, but as he watched the burly old soldier make his way out of the church, he wanted very much to chase after him and fire one question after another at him. He knew that Osbern had been infuriated by Tosny's insolence, but he himself had taken the man's words very differently.

I'm sure Tosny meant it when he said he'd be honest with me, he thought. He told me he wouldn't serve me. No one else did that, though I bet they were thinking it. And if he's telling the truth about that, then he's probably telling the truth about never rebelling against me too.

He thought about another one of the archbishop's deathbed warnings: 'Your enemies will often pretend to be your best friends.'

Men like Tosny won't hurt me. It's the ones who are smiling at me now but plotting against me when they think I'm not looking that I have to worry about.

William was struck by how strange his life was. I bet other

boys don't have to think about things like this. They don't look at their cousins and their uncles and wonder if one of them is secretly their enemy. Why should I have to do that? It's not fair!

He was about to put this point to Osbern, but just then the cathedral was filled with the sound of voices praising God to the heavens. The choir had started singing. The funeral service had begun.

6

Bruges, capital of the county of Flanders

Emma of Normandy, the twice-crowned and twice-widowed queen of England, once wife to Ethelred the Ill-Advised and to Canute the Great, and mother to three princes, rose from her pew in St Donaa's Cathedral, stepped out into the aisle and crossed herself as she genuflected before the altar. A day had passed since she had heard that her brother Robert was dead. She had realised at once that there was no time to get to Rouen in time for his funeral: certainly not in the painfully slow and uncomfortable carriage, little more than a covered cart, in which she would, on the grounds of womanhood, age and propriety, be obliged to travel.

How times had changed. As a young girl, she had ridden a horse with just as much speed and daring as any of her brothers, and far more courage – or was it simply foolhardiness? – than Robert. He had always, from his earliest boyhood, been one to weigh up the odds and act accordingly, while she threw herself at the highest, riskiest jumps she could find, just to prove that she could. In later life, however, as she experienced both the strengths and the very glaring weaknesses of a royal consort's position, she had come to value Robert's shrewd, unsentimental counsel with every passing year. His letters had been a constant source of support throughout her time in England and her more recent exile in Bruges. For years he had been her only source of news about Edward and Alfred, her two sons by Ethelred, whom Canute had insisted on banishing to Normandy. Robert was never afraid to say things he knew she would not want to hear, but only because he believed that she needed to know the truth, as he saw it, when so many others around her would only give her flattery or deceit. She would miss that, and the pleasure of the sly wit with which he commented on people and events.

And so, since she could not say goodbye to her brother in person, she had requested a mass to be sung in his memory, in return for which she was expected to make a suitable donation to the cathedral. She was not surprised by the requirement for money. She had rarely met an abbot or bishop who did not hide the mind of a Levantine moneylender behind his mask of simpering piety. Even so, Robert had been an archbishop, a prince of the Church. Surely they should not have required payment to pray for one of their own.

As she rose to her feet, Emma looked up, past the altar and the strong, squat arches supporting the eight-sided church, past the second row of much taller arches, each one subdivided by two rows of Roman columns, past the stonework covered in richly patterned marble and into the roof. Figures of saints and apostles, picked out in mosaic, gazed up towards the figure of Jesus, who looked down from the apex of the dazzling golden dome. Here the glory and majesty of the Saviour was made manifest in glass and stone, in a physical embodiment of the exultation of the priests and worshippers below.

Emma had always joined wholeheartedly in that worship. Her love of God and trust in His blessings had carried her through crises and tribulations that would have broken a lesser woman. But over the past few years her faith had been tested to its absolute limit. The sudden, entirely unexpected death of Canute had wounded her deeply, for though their union had been agreed as a matter of political expediency, it had become a true, loving marriage. But that pain turned out to be nothing compared to the agony she had suffered when Alfred was mutilated and murdered. That atrocity had ripped out her heart and shredded her soul. Night after night he came to her in hellish dreams, gazing at her with a sightless stare from empty, bloody sockets, his eyes cut out by Harold Harefoot's knife as the English king took revenge for her son's attempt to claim his throne. Every morning when she awoke, her exhaustion was a fraction greater and her nerves stretched a little closer to their breaking point. Her grief was a crushing weight bearing down upon her heart, and she went through her waking hours desperately trying to suppress the cries of agony and despair that beat against her chest like prisoners hammering on the door of their cell.

She looked back up at the face of Jesus and her mind screamed: *How could you do that to my boy? You suffered up there on the cross – why did you look down from heaven and let another man suffer even more?*

An unsayable, blasphemous thought came unbidden to her mind. What if the Saviour was not looking down, and there was no heaven, or hell – just the good and ill mankind did here on earth, in the brief flicker of life between a baby's first tears and that final breath?

She was walking now, hardly knowing how she had made her way from the aisle to the ambulatory – the sixteen-sided walkway that ran around the cathedral. There were people waiting for her, as always. Some had heard of her generosity to the poor and ailing and came seeking her charity; others were simply curious to set eyes on an actual flesh-and-blood queen. Emma did not disappoint. She was tall for a woman, taller than most men. But there was nothing remotely manly in the slenderness of her figure, the grace with which she carried herself or the fine-boned elegance of her face. Age and suffering had made her less pretty than she had been as a girl, but that loss was more than made up for by the way in which the fine lines etched so faintly around her features seemed to convey both grandeur and suffering, so that she was somehow regal and yet vulnerable at one and the same time.

Supplicants cried out for her attention, but Emma's sympathy was caught by a young woman standing in the shadow of an archway with a baby in her arms. She was little more than a baby herself, Emma saw, as she walked closer: twelve or thirteen at most.

'Come here, my child,' she said.

The girl looked up at her with frightened eyes that darted between Emma, her baby and the other alms-seekers. Emma could feel the envy and hostility in their stares, and so she turned and swept her eyes over the tightening circle of hungry, desperate faces, saying nothing, forcing them to retreat by the sheer force of her personality, as a man might use the flame from a burning torch to keep a pack of wolves at bay.

Now she looked back at the mother and child. 'Come here,' she repeated. 'Don't be afraid.'

The girl took a couple of nervous steps and then stopped. Emma smiled at her and took two paces of her own across the flagstone floor to bridge the gap between them. 'What's your name?' she asked.

The girl just about managed to say, 'Agatha,' but then paused, not sure how to end the sentence. 'Your . . . um . . .'

'Majesty,' said Emma, gently. 'But please, don't trouble yourself with that.' She looked down at the tiny figure of the infant.

'Is it a boy or a girl?' she asked.

'Boy.'

'Does he have a name?'

Agatha shook her head.

'Well, he's very new, isn't he? Plenty of time to think of a name. When was he born?'

'Five days ago.'

'I see . . . and do you have any family to help you look after him?'

Agatha's face crumpled. She shook her head. Emma pulled out a linen handkerchief, decorated with finely worked lace, and gave it to the girl, who wiped it across her face and then stretched out her hand to give it back.

'Keep it,' Emma said, sensing the intake of breath from the onlookers, who were gradually edging closer again. That handkerchief alone was more valuable than any possession any of them was ever likely to own, and yet to Emma it was nothing.

The girl had gathered herself enough to speak. 'Got a mother and a father, but they don't want nothing to do with me. They say I'm a disgrace, let the whole family down. But I didn't want to do it. Haakon made me.'

Haakon . . . that was a Norse name, Emma thought. Well, that was no surprise. Bruges had been a Viking settlement, just as Normandy had been a Viking duchy, and God only knew how many poor, unwilling girls the men in her family had impregnated over the generations. 'Come with me,' she said firmly, placing a hand on the filthy rags in which Agatha was clothed and guiding her through the growing crowd.

'Where are we going?' the girl asked as they emerged from the cathedral on to the square outside.

The cathedral occupied one whole side of the square and the Count of Flanders' castle another, so that the centre of the city was perfectly balanced between the power of man and that of God.

Emma had stayed for a while at the castle after she had fled England. Now, though, she resided at a house of her own, not far away, provided by Count Baldwin. It was there that she led Agatha and her baby. As they got closer, she said, 'When we arrive, I want you to go to the kitchen. It's across the yard at the back of the house. Tell my housekeeper Berenice that I sent you to her and that she's to find you some proper clothes and give you a hearty meal. You need food in your belly if you're to have milk for your baby. Once you're fed and dressed, we'll decide what to do about your parents and . . .'

Emma fell silent and stood still. Up ahead, four men were dismounting in front of her house. Three of them were men-at-arms in chain-mail coats, while the fourth, who seemed to be of noble blood to judge by the deferential way in which the soldiers stood aside for him, was dressed in a woollen riding cloak and tunic.

'What's the matter?' asked Agatha, sounding frightened.

'I have a visitor,' said Emma. 'Don't worry, it's nothing to do with you. Run along now and find Berenice. I'll talk to you later.'

The girl scuttled away, clutching her baby even more tightly to her as she passed the armed men. Emma ignored them and made her way towards the nobleman, who was standing by her front door. He was modestly built, half a head shorter than Emma, with a weak, soft physique, unhardened by labour, hunting or war. His hair and beard were both white blonde and his skin was eerily pale, with just a splash of pink in either cheek to indicate that he had been out riding on a cold winter morning. Now that she was close to him, Emma could see that he appeared to have fallen on hard times, for though his clothes were made of finely woven material, they were well worn and bore the marks of the darns and stitches that had been used to mend them. The embroidered decoration around the hem of the cloak was faded and patchy.

Emma felt oddly troubled. She did not believe that she had ever met this man, and yet there was something familiar about him, something in the way he looked that reminded her . . . And then he smiled – a cold, smug expression that suggested pleasure with himself rather than anything or anyone else – and she suddenly realised who he was as he said, 'Hello, Mother, don't you recognise your own son?'

King Edward of England, as he liked to be titled, though he had long lived in Rouen, watched his mother struggle to retain her composure. He had wondered whether he would recognise her – it had been more than twenty years since they'd last clapped eyes on one another, after all, and he'd only been a boy of twelve then. He'd changed a lot, whereas she had merely grown older, greyer and more careworn. Poor Mother – events really hadn't worked out as she'd planned. She'd married a fit, virile young king, several years her junior. She'd have expected a few more years out of him than he'd given her.

'Edward, you came,' she said, and smiled at him, the hypocritical bitch. 'I'd almost given up hope, but—'

'You seem to have settled very comfortably here,' he said, ignoring her as he looked around the substantial hall that rose to the full height of the building. He made what might have been a compliment sound like a criticism, as if she were being somehow indolent and self-indulgent by living so well while in exile; as if it were somehow all at his expense.

'Count Baldwin has been very generous,' she said. 'And I managed to salvage a few belongings when I left England. Harold tried to rob me of everything, but he didn't quite succeed.'

'From what I gather, you were as rich as Croesus, Mother. I'm sure that even a small part of your fortune will be more than sufficient to keep you in suitably queenly style.'

His words had wounded her, Edward saw. Good. He wanted her to hurt. She had caused him enough pain; it was time she knew how it felt.

'Please, Edward,' she said, and suddenly there was something almost pathetic in her yearning voice and the desperation in her eyes. 'Have a heart. I've lost my husband, my son and my brother too. Now here you are, after all these years, and I just want to be your mother again.'

'No you don't, you just want to get one of your boys on to the throne of England – the throne that is rightfully mine – and since Harthacnut is more interested in ruling Denmark, you had no . . .' Edward paused in mid-diatribe, suddenly struck by something his mother had just said. 'What do you mean, you've lost your brother?'

'Hadn't you heard? Your uncle Robert is dead. I thought that was why you'd come. I thought you might . . . well, you might think I'd be upset and need,' she sighed, 'I don't know . . . comforting, maybe.'

Edward was fascinated. Everything he had ever thought about his mother had been based on the notion that she was tough, calculating, ruthless – very much like his uncle Robert, in fact. And yet the woman before him now was nothing like that at all. Unless, of course, she was deceiving him. That was very possible. One only had to study the Bible to know how females from Eve to Jezebel to Delilah had used their powers to trap and weaken men. But she would not fool him.

'I knew that His Grace the archbishop was ill,' he said, aiming for an air of kingly detachment. 'But I have spent this past week in Boulogne with my sister Goda – your daughter, madam, though you have not seen fit to honour her with your presence, either.'

'You know as well as I do that it's not a matter of what I see fit. I long to see Goda. But I'm a woman and, what's more, a guest of Count Baldwin, dependent on his favour. I can't just go riding off the way you can, unless he consents to permit it.'

Edward was entirely unimpressed by his mother's protestations. 'Be that as it may,' he went on, 'the news had not reached Boulogne when I left to come here. You have entreated me to visit you for a while now and, being so close, it seemed like an apt opportunity. But now you say my uncle is dead, eh? Well I'm sure he had his reasons . . . That man did nothing unless he planned to benefit from it.'

For some reason Edward could not fathom, his words seemed to jolt his mother out of her feebleness. She visibly grew in stature before his eyes as she drew herself up straight, and actually looked down on him as she snapped, 'For pity's sake, Edward, do you not have a single kind or compassionate bone in your body? He was your uncle, your own flesh and blood. Is it really too much to ask you to mourn him just a little?'

'How dare you!' Edward was disturbed to find his voice rising much higher than he had expected, so that he sounded more like a whining boy than a full-grown man. 'How dare you accuse me of lacking kindness or compassion? How dare you think that I should be giving you comfort! You talk about flesh and blood; well, I'm *your* flesh and blood, but how much kindness, or comfort, or compassion did you show me? You abandoned me so that you could go and fuck that Dane, Canute. A man who had waged war on your true husband, my father . . . And talk about mourning. Father was hardly cold in his grave before you were spreading your legs for Canute and—'

He barely even saw his mother's hand before it slapped him across the side of his face, wrenching his head half off his neck and almost knocking him off his feet. The pain of it was unlike anything Edward had ever known, and it was all he could do not to cry.

'You can't do that,' he mumbled, bent almost double with his hands cradling his wounded face. 'You can't strike the King of England.'

'But you aren't the King of England, Edward. Harold Harefoot is. He murdered your brother, and if you were any kind of a man, you wouldn't be visiting your sister, or your mother. You'd be burning with vengeance, raising an army, putting together a fleet, finding allies to join your cause, doing absolutely anything you could to find a way back to England to kill the man who slaughtered your brother and to take back your throne.'

Edward thought back to his one, not even half-hearted attempt at invading England. He'd sailed up the Solent, seen the English forces massing on the shore ahead, watched in horror as his commander, Rabel, insisted on landing and engaging the enemy, heaved a huge sigh of relief when the battle ended in victory and then ordered his men straight back on to their boats to sail back to Normandy.

He knew that some men had branded him a coward for his refusal to press home the advantage and march into England. But look what had happened to Alfred. When he came ashore, he hadn't turned back. And a fat lot of good it had done him.

'I've not forgotten Alfred,' he said, doing his best to stand upright again. 'Sneer all you like. Hit me, despise me; you've never loved me, why should you start now? But just remember this, Mother. Your beloved Alfred may have been your favourite – don't even pretend to deny it – but he's dead and I'm not. I'm alive, and I intend to stay that way until the time is right. The people of England know that Harold Harefoot is no true king. I've heard tell he's not even Canute's boy at all. They say his mother Elgiva, who sounds like a proper slut even by Canute's standards, couldn't have a baby, so she bought one off a cobbler's wife and passed it off as her own.'

'I've heard that too,' Emma said.

'Well then, the man's as common as muck, and the people know it. They'll want a proper king soon, one who can prove he has royal blood in his veins. Not some Dane, but an Englishman who—'

'Can you even speak English any more?'

'I'm sure I'll pick it up again soon enough,' said Edward, who had never even considered this before. 'It doesn't matter, no one will know. The point is, the people will call for me. I know they will. Then, and only then, I will answer their call.'

'If you really had the guts it takes to rule a country, you would not wait to be called, any more than a real man waits for a woman to beg him to take her. You're not married, are you?'

Edward found himself quailing before the power of his mother's gaze. 'No,' he replied, unable to suppress the involuntary shudder that seized him whenever he found himself forced to contemplate union with a woman.

'Well perhaps you might see to that while you're waiting to be called to your throne,' Emma said. 'The people like to see a queen standing beside their king. And sons . . . they expect those too.'

Edward felt himself floundering. This had not gone at all the way he had expected. He knew, because she had written to him often enough, that his mother wanted him to join her in some madcap expedition against England. His intention had been to see her, dismiss her foolish plans out of hand, put her properly in her place and then ride away having satisfied some of the sense of vengeance that he felt far, far more strongly towards her than he ever had against Harold Harefoot. For a moment, the whole scheme had been working even better than he had imagined, but somehow he had lost control of proceedings. Now he did not just feel abandoned and betrayed by his mother, but humiliated and unmanned by her too. Well, enough of that.

'I don't have time to waste on women's talk of marriages and babies,' he said, decisively. 'I will be on my way. I'm sure Count Baldwin will be happy to put me up at the castle. Good day.'

With that he walked straight out of the hall and back on to the street. All these years he'd waited to see her, and now he knew for sure how much she despised him. Well damn her! Damn them all! He'd have nothing to do with the conniving bitches. Ever.

Emma watched her oldest son make his spiteful way out of her house and sighed. She'd always found Edward hard to love, he was right about that. There had just been too much of Ethelred about him; that mean spirit came straight from his father. Alfred, on the other hand, had been a little charmer from the day he was born, always ready with a smile, able to wind his wet nurse and nanny and anyone else he ever met around his little finger. He was open-hearted, brave and true, and yet – again Edward was right – what good had it done him?

She sighed for all the love that was lost and the love that never had been, and then told herself to stop feeling so glum. There was a little girl in her kitchen in need of help, and it would make her feel better to give it to her.

She found Agatha, wearing a woollen dress far too big for her meagre form, sitting in front of a trencher of bread that was empty save for a few traces of gravy.

'Two bowls of my best chicken stew that one's gobbled down,' said Berenice cheerfully. 'I'm worried there won't be any left for Your Majesty.'

'Give her a third if she needs it,' said Emma.

'Did you hear that, girl?' Berenice said. 'Queen Emma is giving up her food so that you can have your fill. What do you say to that, eh?'

The girl looked up at Emma. 'Thank you . . . Y'Majesty.'

'That's all right. If I know Berenice, there will be plenty more food in the larder. Your baby looks peaceful.'

'I fed him,' the girl said proudly. 'My own milk.'

'Good for you. And now, I wonder, will you do something for me in return?'

Agatha fell silent, frowning, trying to understand how she could possibly do anything for someone as unimaginably grand as Queen Emma.

'Course she will, won't you, girl?' said Berenice.

Agatha nodded.

'Thank you,' said Emma. 'I want you to have your little boy christened properly. I will have one of the priests at the cathedral do it for you. And I want you to call him Alfred.'

7

Rouen

There was no point Ralph de Gacé standing around waiting for the ducal guardians to take him under their wing, as his father's will had put it. He had to take matters into his own hands, and the sooner the better, while the old man's wishes were still fresh in the mind of Osbern Herfastsson, the only guardian to have been present at the reading. The archbishop's grieving widow had kept him out of the church, presumably as punishment for being the spawn of the old man's philandering. But he was damned if he was missing the feast, not when there was so much he could accomplish there. So before the roistering got under way, while all the guests were milling round the great hall of the archbishop's palace, he sidled up to Osbern and asked, 'When does my training begin?'

The older man must surely have known what he was talking about, but he affected an air of bafflement. 'Sorry, what training?'

'The training my late father, our beloved archbishop, stated that you and your fellow guardians should provide for me, so that I can best serve the duchy of Normandy.'

'That's what you have in mind, is it, a life of faithful service?'

'Absolutely, my lord. I plan to dedicate myself to a life of selflessness such as you have shown over the years. You are the master and here I am, waiting to be your pupil.'

Osbern looked at de Gacé through narrowed eyes. He had a strong feeling that he was being mocked, and that what this strange young man most wanted to emulate was his wealth and influence. But now he realised that Donkey-Head's appearance gave him certain advantages. Since he looked so grotesque to begin with, it was more difficult to read his precise expressions than with someone more normal. Finally Osbern nodded. 'Very well then, wait here a moment while I talk to the others. I'll come and get you when the time is right.'

De Gacé watched as Osbern walked across the hall towards the nearest of his fellow guardians, Gilbert of Brionne. The two men started talking. Gilbert flashed a look in his direction and de Gacé imagined with relish the annoyance that his father's will would be causing. The three nobles must have found it unwelcome enough to have a mere monk included in their number. But that had been Duke Robert's decision, made before he left on his fatal pilgrimage to Jerusalem and justified by Brother Thorold's day-to-day experience of teaching William. The monk knew the boy's character and appreciated his strengths and weaknesses in a way that his fellow guardians did not, and was thus well placed to advise on what was best for him. It was also no bad thing to have a representative of the Church amongst them, and so, however grudgingly, Thorold had been accepted. Now de Gacé too was supposed to be granted if not equal status, then certainly a position that stood somewhere between apprentice and anointed successor, on no other basis than a dead man's command.

Osbern had not yet returned to him when the archbishop's funeral feast began, so de Gacé took his seat by his half-brothers and the three of them toasted their father's memory and the good fortune he had bestowed on them all. The meal began with a splendid array of seafood. Crabs, lobster, shrimp and mussels were piled high alongside jellied eels. Whole pikes were served with their heads still on and their underslung jaws jutting out indignantly at the diners about to eat them. Having sampled all those treats, de Gacé helped himself to thick slabs of meat from the mighty joints of beef and pork that had been laid out upon the table, then devoured the pastries and sweetmeats that followed. He made sure that his wine glass was never empty for long, too, for he was greedy and thirsty, and not just for the things that a man could eat and drink.

William was seated at the place of honour in the centre of the high table. It was his duty to say a few words of welcome to his guests and to propose the toast giving thanks for the life of the man in whose honour the entire event was being staged. Thanks to the training that had begun while his father had still been alive, he managed that duty as well as most adults would have done. He enjoyed the entertainment provided by the musicians, acrobats, clowns and a bawdy poet who had been invited to perform at the archbishop's particular request, even if some of the latter's verses, which had the adults around him in stitches, sailed right over his head. That aside, the entire occasion was torture. William had to sit still in his place, pretending to be interested in what the grown-ups were saying, while all the time he could see his friends dashing back and forth across the great hall as they played. They could behave however they liked while he, who was meant to be the ruler of Normandy, was forced to behave himself. It just didn't seem fair at all.

Finally, when he was practically dying of boredom, Osbern got up from his place, stepped across to his chair and whispered, 'You can get down now, if you like.'

William leapt to his feet, waited for a moment as everyone in the hall stood in his honour, and then stepped away from the table, jumped down off the dais and left the hall. The moment he was out of sight of the guests, he broke into a run, dashing up the winding stone stairs that led to the solar – the room where the women and children of the household spent their days. His mother Herleva was waiting for him there. William dashed across the room and threw himself into her arms, almost knocking her over with the force of his impact.

Herleva stumbled backwards, regained her balance and laughed. 'Oof! You need to be a bit more gentle with women, William. You don't know your own strength!'

Still holding her son in her arms, she ran a hand through his thick mop of ginger hair. William frowned. It worried Herleva that he looked so serious so often. He was much too young to be weighed down by the cares of the world. 'What is it?' she asked.

William stepped back a little and looked up at her. 'Did Papa look like Great-Uncle Robert when he died?' he asked.

'Oh my darling boy . . .' Herleva sighed, pulling him close again. 'I don't know what Papa looked like. He was in Asia Minor, on the other side of the world. But I do know one thing for certain. He is in heaven now.'

William wrestled himself free of her grasp so that he could look her right in the eye. It was all Herleva could do not to turn away from his gaze. It was so determined, so unflinching.

'But people said he was the devil, that he killed his own brother,' he argued, as if he were accusing his mother of deceiving him. 'What if he's in hell and being tormented and burned in the fire and—'

'No, William, your father is not in hell,' Herleva insisted. 'I know he's not.'

'How? How can you know?'

'Because he went on a pilgrimage to Jerusalem and prayed at the Church of the Holy Sepulchre, which is built on the very place where Christ Our Lord was crucified. That act alone meant that he was absolved of all his mortal sins, so that he died in a state of grace and went to heaven.'

'Even if he killed his brother?'

'William! How can you ask such a thing? What on earth makes you think your father did that?'

'Because people keep saying he did. I've heard them.'

'What kind of people?'

'I don't know . . . servants, some of the men-at-arms, grown-ups. They think I don't hear them, but I do. And my friends have heard people say it too. Guy of Burgundy teased me about it.'

'But that's awful! What a mean thing to do!'

'Oh, don't worry, Mama,' William said, matter-of-factly. 'I hit him and made him cry, and then he stopped.'

'Hmm . . .' Herleva knew she should scold William for hitting another boy, but privately she was delighted that he was so well able to stand up for himself. She decided to get back to the point. 'Listen to me. Your father did not kill his brother Richard.'

William gave her an even more piercing glare than usual. 'How do you know?'

'Because he gave me his solemn vow that he hadn't, and I know that he never lied to me. He loved me too much to do that. I can prove it too. There was a time when your father could have killed Richard in battle and no one would have thought the worse of him. But he refused to hurt him even when he had the chance. So why would he kill him later?'

William's attitude changed in an instant from fierce scepticism to eager interest. 'When did Papa and Richard fight? What happened?'

'Well, when I first met your father, I was just a girl—' Herleva began.

'Yes, I know, a tanner's daughter,' William interrupted, wanting her to get to the good bit.

'That's right, and I lived in a little cottage by my father's tannery in Falaise, with my parents and my brothers. Now, your father lived at the castle. But his brother, Duke Richard, said that he didn't have the right to live there. So Richard brought a big army to Falaise and laid siege to the castle. The siege went on for months and months—'

'Were you in the castle with Papa?'

'No, I was hiding in the woods, because I had you in my tummy and Papa didn't want you or me to be hurt.'

Herleva laughed at the look of horror on her son's face as he gasped, 'In your tummy? Ugh!'

She went on. 'After your uncle Richard attacked the castle, your father went looking for him and they had a fight.'

'Who won?' asked William, getting straight to the only thing that really mattered so far as fights were concerned.

'I was just about to tell you, if you'd stop being so impatient! Your father won.'

'Yes!' shouted William triumphantly. Then he stopped and thought for a moment before asking, 'But he didn't kill Richard, even though he'd won?'

'No,' Herleva replied. 'He had Richard at his mercy. Richard's sword was broken and his shoulder was wounded so that he couldn't fight. But Papa couldn't bring himself to kill him.'

'Why not? I'd kill him, I'd go like this!' William lunged forward, swinging an imaginary blade. 'And this! And I'd stick my sword right through his guts and—'

'That's enough! Do you want to hear the rest of the story or not?'

William's shoulders slumped crossly. 'All right.'

'Good. Well, the reason Papa didn't kill Richard is simple: he loved him. Even though they argued and fought and even went to war, they were still brothers, and brothers should love one another.'

'That's true,' William agreed. 'I wouldn't kill Odo or Robert.'

'I should think not.'

'Not unless I was really, really angry . . .'

Herleva sighed. No matter how hard she tried to soften the edges of William's personality, he couldn't help but be abrasive. But perhaps that was a good thing. What chance would a boy with a more gentle, contemplative nature have of surviving the life that William now faced? From the day she first set eyes on Robert of Normandy, her life had changed in ways she had never anticipated, and her children would have lives she could not even have imagined. She had undergone a magical transformation worthy of a troubadour's tale. Yet her dreams of a life spent as Robert's wife had been snatched from her, and when she thought of the future that awaited William as Duke of Normandy, she sometimes wished that she had married the baker or farrier or peasant farmer who would otherwise have been her destiny, and that their son had been nothing more than an ordinary village lad.

De Gacé was watching the duke leave the feast when he felt a tap on his shoulder and heard Osbern's voice in his ear quietly telling him, 'Don't make a fuss. Just get up and follow me.'

De Gacé did as he was told. Osbern led him up a twisting stone staircase and along a gallery that looked down upon the great hall. They entered a small chamber hung with tapestries showing scenes from the life of Jesus depicted in vivid colours, so that the blood flowed in bright scarlet torrents from the Saviour's nailed hands, and the halo around His head gleamed with golden thread.

'This was your father's private study,' Osbern said. He introduced de Gacé to the other three guardians. Alan of Brittany and Gilbert of Brionne were polite but curt in their greetings. Thorold was more friendly but correspondingly less sincere.

‘We are agreed that you are to be given the right to attend and observe our meetings, though we may need to ask you to leave if particularly sensitive matters are going to be discussed,’ Osbern informed him.

De Gacé was about to protest that those were the very matters he most badly needed to observe, but caught himself in time. It would do him no good to be uppity now; far better to play the dutiful young man wishing to learn from his elders and betters. ‘I understand,’ he said.

‘It goes without saying that everything we discuss is confidential and you are never to repeat it to anyone without our express permission.’

‘Of course not. I can assure you all, my lords, Brother Thorold, that you can count on my discretion.’

‘We hope so, de Gacé. For if you were ever to say anything that could help an enemy of the duchy, or of the duke himself, that would constitute an act of treason . . . with the usual penalty.’

Osbern is threatening me with death, thought de Gacé. They really don’t want me here, do they? And then it struck him that these four men now had effective day-to-day control of Normandy, and yet they did not dare defy the old man, even in death. That was power. That was something to aim for.

‘As I say,’ he assured them, ‘I will absolutely respect the confidentiality of our meetings. Or rather, your meetings. Please, forgive my presumption, it was not intended.’

Osbern gave him a long, searching look. Then he turned to the others. ‘While we’re all together, there’s something I wanted to mention. I’m sure you all saw William become upset at the cathedral. When I asked what troubled him, he said that he was worried he had killed His Grace the archbishop, because he was the last person to talk to the old man before he died. Then he added, “Apart from the serving woman who came in to give him his medicine." And that puzzled me, for I was not aware that the archbishop had called for medicine before he died. William, however, remembered this woman very clearly. He was particularly struck by her extreme beauty. And it made me think of someone.'

'Moriella,' Brother Thorold interjected. 'The tart who serviced Duke Richard's needs on the night he died. There was a lot of talk in the abbey refectory about her, I can tell you.'

'And what did you and your fellow monks conclude, Brother Thorold?' asked Alan of Brittany, suppressing a smile at the thought of a dining hall filled with gossipy, sex-starved monks.

'That she had been the weapon used by the duke's killer to gain access to his chamber. I dare say she let the killer in when no one was looking. Or maybe she gave the duke poison without even knowing she was doing so.'

'Or maybe she was the killer herself,' Alan of Brittany interrupted, in a bantering tone that drew laughs from the men around him.

'Don't be ridiculous,' said Brionne, though even he had a smile on his face. 'If someone killed the archbishop – and I'd bet every dog and falcon I possess that they didn't – then that someone was a man. Women exist to make life, not take it. It's not in their nature to kill in cold blood.'

De Gacé took Brionne's point: it was ridiculous to go looking for a woman who went around killing people. But when he had the opportunity and the means, he'd start trying to track down the man who might be doing so with such quiet efficiency. And then he'd bide his time until he had need of his services. In the meantime, there were two other men, both much easier to find, whose friendship he needed to acquire.

Returning to the feast, de Gacé made his way through the crowds of raucous guests, who had cheerfully abandoned any pretence at funereal piety now that the serious eating and drinking had begun. He stepped over discarded bones, puddles of spilled wine, fresh vomit and even the occasional semi-conscious body of a reveller who had already succumbed to overindulgence, all the while keeping his eye out for Mauger and Talou. Finally he found them and wormed his way into their conversation.

When he finally had their attention, de Gacé did his unconvincing best to produce a charming smile. 'May I offer my congratulations to you, Cousin Mauger, on your forth-coming appointment as Archbishop of Rouen? It is surely no less than you deserve. And you, Cousin Talou . . .' He beamed affably. 'I can't wait to see the castle you build at Arques. I'm sure that its strength and magnificence will bring you a position of tremendous stature and respect within the duchy.' He chuckled. 'I hope you won't mind if I steal your mason's best ideas for the place I'll be building at Gacé.'

'Not at all,' said Talou, who had never in his life drunk so much and was suddenly filled with a tremendous surge of affection for his poor, ugly bastard of a cousin. 'Not . . . at . . . all.'

'Thank you so much, your lordship. You have no idea how much that means to me, coming from the legitimate son of a duke of Normandy. I wonder if I might ask you both a question? I don't need an answer right away; it's just a thought, really, for you both to ponder. And it is this: as great as the title of archbishop may be, and as splendid as the castle of Arques certainly will be, do you really think . . . oh, I don't know . . . are they actually quite enough? You both have a duke's blood in your veins. I don't know about you, but I think you're entitled to a great deal more. To everything, in fact . . .'

8

Rouen, August 1039

Two years had passed since the archbishop's funeral. It was a rainy Sunday morning and the long, empty hours between mass and the midday meal were stretching out into what seemed to William like an eternity of boredom and inactivity. Desperately looking for something to do or someone to talk to, he was wandering around the palace when he saw his English cousin Edward up ahead. He was just bidding goodbye to a priest – in William's experience, Edward was rarely far from a member of the clergy – and as always, he looked like the family's poor relation, which indeed he was.

'Hello, Cousin Edward,' William said.

'Good morning, William,' Edward replied.

A deep, deathly silence fell. There was not a sound to be heard anywhere. It was as if they were the only two people in the entire building. And neither of them could think of a thing to say.

William racked his brain for a topic of conversation, and just as Edward was about to move on, he came up with one.

'You know how you're the King of England?' he asked.

'Yes.' Edward stood just a little bit taller and pushed his shoulders back.

William frowned, thoughtfully. 'There's something I don't get. I mean, if you're King of England, why aren't you in England, instead of living here?'

'Because my kingdom was stolen from me by my mother,

and a very bad man called Canute,' said Edward, with feeling.

William was shocked. 'Your mother?'

'Yes,' said Edward, and now a distinct edge of bitterness entered his voice. 'My own mother. Can you imagine that, William, to have your rightful inheritance taken from you by the woman who brought you into the world, whose most sacred duty is to attend to your well-being?'

'No,' said William slowly, shaking his head, shocked at the very idea. 'My mother would never do that. She loves me. But . . .' He twisted his mouth to one side as he tried to phrase his next question. 'How can you steal a whole kingdom?'

'By violence, treachery and deceit.'

'I don't understand . . .'

Edward sighed. 'It's a very long and complicated story. The only important thing is that my father was King Ethelred of England, the rightful king. And I am his rightful heir, just like you are your father's heir. Your father was Duke of Normandy, so now you are Duke of Normandy. My father was King of England and so—'

'*You* are King of England!' answered William, for if there was one thing he understood, since it had been drilled into him from birth, it was the significance of inheritance.

'Exactly.'

There was, however, a catch, and William spotted it. 'I'm a duke, and I have a palace, and soldiers and things. And you're a king . . . but you don't have a crown, or any land or treasure or anything. That's why you have to live here with us.'

Edward gave a sharp little intake of breath, as if he had just been pricked by a needle. 'I don't have a crown or property here in Normandy, that's true,' he conceded. 'But I shall have all England when I am king. In any case,' he added, recovering his dignity, 'I am more interested in the spiritual treasures waiting in the kingdom of heaven than the material ones here on earth.'

'I want both,' said William, decisively.

'How very Norman of you.'

William was rather pleased that he'd hit upon the subject of kingship. This conversation was turning out to be much more interesting than he'd expected, and he wanted to pursue it further.

'So when will you be the actual King of England . . . in England, I mean?' he asked.

'I don't know, William. But I have faith that my cause is just and that God will deliver me from exile. Just as he delivered Moses and his people from bondage in Egypt and took them to the Promised Land, so He will take me to my promised land too.'

A picture came to William's mind and he couldn't help but share it.

'It would be funny if you could part the waters and walk across to England, like Moses parted the Red Sea!' he said, and laughed. He hoped that Edward would laugh too, but no such luck.

'You should not make jokes about the stories in the Holy Bible, William,' the self-styled king rebuked him. 'They are the word of God and not to be taken lightly.'

'Oh . . .' said William, feeling squashed. But it wasn't in his nature to let himself be beaten, so he had another go. 'You have *sailed* to England, though, haven't you? I remember you went there just before your brother Alfred died. I liked Alfred, he used to play games with me. He was nice. So when you sailed to England, was that because you thought you would be able to become King of England properly, with a crown and a throne and everything?'

'I am the proper King of England already,' snapped Edward. He looked quizzically at William as if trying to work out whether the boy was deliberately mocking him. His abortive expedition to England was one of the sorest of his sore spots. 'It is that bastard spawn of the usurper Canute, Harold Harefoot, who is the impostor . . .' he added, then changed tack in mid-sentence. 'What's the matter, boy? Why are you looking at me like that?'

'You said "bastard",' William told him, with the cold, hard anger that was his immediate response to any mockery – real or imagined – of his illegitimacy. 'I don't like that word.'

'No, no . . .' Edward was taken aback by the unmistakable air of menace that this mere child could project. 'I don't suppose you do.'

Another silence fell. Once again it was William, his temper now subsiding, who broke it.

'You didn't say if you went to England to become king . . .'

'Not exactly. I went . . .' Edward gave a barely perceptible squirm of discomfort. 'Well, I suppose you could say I was on a sort of reconnaissance mission. You know, when soldiers go in advance of an army to see what's up ahead.'

'Was that why you came back so quickly? You were only gone a few days.'

'When I got to England, there was a large force of Saxons on the shore.'

'Why didn't you fight them? I would have.'

I'm sure you would, you beastly little boy, thought Edward. He did his best to sound magisterial. 'We did engage the enemy, as it happens. There were, ah . . . skirmishes on the beach and these were actually quite successful. The enemy withdrew, but I made the judgement that they were merely regrouping and would return in much larger numbers, and so it was best to make an orderly retreat while we still could.'

Even William, young as he was, could tell that Edward was talking nonsense. It sounded to him very much as though there was a simpler explanation.

'Did you run away?'

'No I most certainly did not! There is all the difference in the world between a defeated army running away in a blind panic, like an absolute rabble, and a calm, considered withdrawal. You will learn this in time William, when you are leading your own army. There are times when it is foolhardy to stand and fight. I withdrew and am here, alive, in front of you. My brother Alfred insisted on marching on into England . . . and look what happened to him.'

'Harold Harefoot killed him,' said William with eager relish. 'He took out his eyes with a hunting knife . . . well, that's what Cousin Ralph told me.'

'Cousin Ralph should mind what he says to impressionable boys.'

'If anyone did that to one of my brothers, I'd kill him. And whatever he did to my brother, I'd do it right back to him, only worse.'

'And what do you suppose God would make of that?' said Edward, seizing the moral high ground. 'It is not for us to take revenge on our fellow men, William. Our Lord will judge us all soon enough, and those who deserve to be punished will be sent to suffer in hell for all eternity.'

If he was hoping to win the theological argument, Edward was to be disappointed.

'God said, "An eye for an eye and a tooth for a tooth",' William riposted. 'I know because Brother Thorold told us so in Divinity. Harold took out both Alfred's eyes, so you should take out both of his.'

Edward had heard enough. 'Really, this is too much! I'm going to have a word with the abbot of Saint-Ouen. Clearly his monk has been filling your head with a great deal of dangerous nonsense.'

Now he had struck a wounding blow. Getting someone else

into trouble went against any self-respecting small boy's deepest code of honour.

'Oh please don't do that, King Edward . . . Your Majesty . . .' William pleaded. 'It's my fault, not Thorold's. I shouldn't have said bad things about the Bible.'

'Hmm . . .' Edward tried to adopt a suitably regal, forgiving air. 'Do you promise to tell the priest about your sin the next time you go to confession?'

'Yes, Your Majesty.'

'And to obey whatever penance he gives you?'

'Yes, I promise.'

'Very well then . . . Our Lord and Saviour taught us the value of repentance, and I'm delighted to see that you are suitably penitent. So I wish you good day, William. I will see you later, no doubt.'

With that, Edward walked off. As William slumped, relieved but exhausted, against a wall, another figure appeared in the corridor: Ralph de Gacé. *Don't call him Donkey-Head!* William reminded himself. These days, Ralph was quite a power in the duchy.

'Oh dear, have you upset the king-without-a-kingdom?' Ralph asked. 'I was watching you both. He seemed to be giving you quite a dressing-down.'

'He was cross because I said that if Alfred was my brother, I'd go and kill Harold Harefoot and rip his eyes out,' said William, who still couldn't really see what was wrong with that.

'That's the spirit,' said Ralph encouragingly. Then a mischievous, even malicious smirk crossed his much-mocked face. 'So, Your Grace, would you like to hear something very surprising about King Edward and his older brothers?'

'Older brothers?' William asked, his voice rising in surprise. 'But I thought Alfred was his only brother, and he was younger.'

'Alfred was Edward's only full brother and, yes, he was

younger,' Ralph agreed, 'but Edward also had six older half-brothers. They were his father's sons by his first wife, before he married Queen Emma, your great-aunt.'

William took the hint. 'But if they were older, then . . .'

'Exactly, they had a prior claim to the throne of England. One of them, Edmund, actually *was* King of England, if only for a few months. He died. But he had two sons, which means . . .'

'They are his heirs, so . . .'

'So their claim to the throne is at least as good as our cousin Edward's and probably better,' Ralph said. 'So don't you worry about him.'

'Thank you, I won't.' William fell silent.

Ralph could see that the boy was thinking about something, wondering whether to say it or not. 'Is something the matter?' he asked.

William shook his head. 'No . . . well, maybe. I was just thinking, I'm sorry if I laughed at you and called you names. You know, in the past . . .'

'That's all right. I know you've had your share of people being rude about you too, just because your parents weren't married. I know how that feels.'

'People call me "William the Bastard". I hate it.'

Ralph laid a hand on William's shoulder and twisting his face into an affectionate smile said, 'We little bastards had better stick together then, hadn't we?'

'Yes,' William said, 'I suppose so.'

But as he watched him walk away down the hall, William couldn't help thinking that Ralph really did still look like a donkey. And he still didn't feel like his friend.

9

Échauffour, Normandy

Conan of Saint-Briac, a Breton monk, had been sent by his abbot to convey various items of correspondence to his counterpart at the abbey of Saint-Ouen in Rouen. A surprisingly high number of monks had been soldiers before they took orders: often they had spent so many years away on campaign that they had neither families nor homes of their own, so joining a monastery put a roof over their heads. And after so much time spent taking life, many felt the need to get back into God's good books.

Conan was just such a retired fighting man. His route from Brittany to Rouen took him close to Échauffour, and so it was only natural that he should visit Giroie, his old comrade from his soldiering days, who owned most of the land thereabouts. For his part, Giroie considered it his duty to give food and lodging to any passing monk, let alone one he knew as well as Conan.

Giroie had not seen his friend since he had taken holy orders, and it took a few seconds to accustom himself to seeing him riding a donkey rather than a charger, and clad in a monk's simple, rough woollen robe instead of a coat of chain mail. But soldiers, particularly those who had survived into later life, tended to have a strong streak of piety and an even greater sense of gratitude to God for their deliverance from death. So while Giroie was delighted by Conan's presence and slapped him heartily on the back, there was not the slightest trace of mockery in his voice as he said, 'Monastic life seems to suit you, Conan. Must be good for you not wasting all your energy chasing women any more!'

'Not wasting it saving your scraggy old neck, more like,' the monk replied.

'I think you'll find it was mostly me saving yours! Come on, it's dinner time. Dare say you could use a decent meal after a long day in the saddle.'

The two men ate and drank well, then repaired to Giroie's private chamber with another bottle or two of wine with which to wash down their reminiscences. They talked of many battles won and a few that had been lost: old friends who had died and others who still thrived. Then Conan pulled his chair closer to Giroie's and leaned forward to speak in a lower voice, though there was no one but Giroie to hear him.

'One of your boys is in the service of young Ralph de Gacé, isn't he?'

'Yes, my fifth son, Robert. Gacé Castle is just half a day's ride away, as it happens . . . What of it?'

'I'd find him another position if I were you, and soon.'

'And why would that be?'

'Because de Gacé won't be having any more to do with the running of Normandy if our Count Alan has anything to do with it. My abbot is a great friend of Alan's chaplain, and so what I'm about to say comes on very good authority. Apparently Alan has reason to believe that Ralph is in league with Archbishop Mauger and his brother Talou. They want to get rid of William and make Talou the new duke.'

'He's old Duke Richard's legitimate son. He's got as good a right to it as Robert's little bastard.'

'That's not how Alan sees it. He swore to Robert that he would keep William safe. That's what he plans to do. He's raising an army, and as soon as he has a decent number of men marching under his banner, he's heading into Normandy.'

Giroie looked at Conan with an expression of rank scepticism. 'He's invading Normandy? Are you serious? He'd have to be mad. William's other guardians will raise an army of their own to fight him – they'll have no choice. So it will be one guardian against the rest. Mauger and Talou will be pissing themselves laughing. And Donkey-Head will be laughing right alongside them.'

'Not if Alan gets word to William or one of the men close to him that this isn't an invasion at all,' said Conan. 'He'll make it plain that he's marching to William's side to support him against the plotters. As soon as he crosses the border, he plans to spread the word about his true intentions. He's going to tell people: "Stand by me and you stand by Duke William." He's hoping to put on such a show of strength that no one will dare oppose him or the duke. The plotters will be beaten before they've even begun to rebel.'

'Is that the real reason you're going to Rouen?'

Conan nodded. 'Brother Thorold, the duke's tutor and guardian, is a member of our order. I am to pass the message on to someone at the abbey of Saint-Ouen, who'll take it to Thorold.'

'Why not take the message directly to Thorold yourself?'

'Because he doesn't know me or my abbot from Adam.'

'But if you belong to the same order, won't he trust you?'

'Up to a point, but with something this important he'll trust someone he knows even more. My abbot will be believed by the abbot of Saint-Ouen, and the man he sends will be known to Thorold, so that way the information will be taken seriously.'

'But why bother with this performance at all? Why not go straight to the palace and demand an audience with the boy and his guardians?'

'I asked the count that myself.'

'And . . . ?'

'And he told me he feared for my safety. He said that if Ralph or the other plotters heard that Alan had a message for the duke, they'd go to any lengths to stop it getting through.'

Giroie looked utterly unconvinced. 'I'm sorry, but is this one of Alan's jokes? He's always had a strange sense of humour, particularly when he's had a bit to drink.'

'Well, he was stone-cold sober and deadly serious so far as I could tell.'

'In that case, I wish you luck, old friend.' Giroie got to his feet. 'Now, you've got another hard day in front of you and neither of us is young enough any more to spend the whole night drinking and then be fresh as a daisy in the morning. Come with me. I've had a chamber prepared for you, and food set aside for you to take with you when you leave. That should keep you going on your journey.'

Conan smiled and gave Giroie an affectionate pat on the shoulder. 'Thank you. Just make sure you get your boy well away from de Gacé before Alan attacks. Because when that happens, anyone close to those three traitors is going to go down with them. I'm not saying your son will be killed, you understand . . .'

'Of course,' Giroie assured him.

'Just that his reputation will be severely damaged. And that wouldn't be good for you or your family either. But if he's already left de Gacé . . .'

'Then we'll all be better off. I understand completely.'

'Good, then you know what you have to do.'

'Absolutely.'

Brother Conan retired to the chamber Giroie had provided for him. His host closed the door behind him and then returned to his own quarters. Though he had lived in Normandy for many years, he still considered himself a Breton at heart, and he felt a sense of loyalty to Count Alan. He had also pledged his allegiance to Duke William. This quarrel did not threaten the duke directly, since both sides were aiming to control the boy rather than replace him, so the only question worthy of Giroie's consideration was: where did his best interests lie? It took him a while to decide, and when he did, he gave a wry, regretful shake of the head. It was very sad, but there really was no getting away from what had to be done. He went to the chamber where his oldest son was sleeping and shook his shoulder.

'Get up,' he whispered. 'Come with me.'

Arnold got out of bed, wrapped a woollen cloak over his nightshirt and followed his father back to the chamber where he had sat drinking with Conan of Saint-Briac.

'I've got a job for you to do, boy, and it won't be pleasant. That monk you met at dinner, Conan of Briac . . .'

'Nice man,' Arnold nodded.

'Yes, very nice,' Giroie agreed. 'Unfortunately, however, I need you to kill him.'

'Kill him? Why?'

'Because I tell you to. The only thing you need to know is that this is for the good of the family. Take some men, at least half a dozen, because Conan was a damn good soldier and he can still look after himself. Dress in ordinary clothes. No armour, no shields, no emblems of any kind. He'll be heading for the Rouen road; ambush him in the woods between here and Pomont. Make sure there are no witnesses. Got that?'

Arnold swallowed hard, gritted his teeth and then nodded.

'Good. Once he is dead, go straight on to Gacé and find Robert. Tell him to warn de Gacé that Alan of Brittany is planning to march into Normandy at the head of a bloody great army, with the specific intention of making sure that he, Talou and Archbishop Mauger never get anywhere near the ducal throne. So if he and his pals have any intention at all of seizing power, they'd better deal with Alan before he deals with them.'

He looked at his son, who nodded again and said, 'I understand.'

'That's good, but I need to be certain that you've remembered the message, exactly as I told it to you. So we're going to go through it all until you've got it engraved in your head, and then you're going to pick your best men, get them and their horses fed and watered and be out of here before dawn.'

Conan of Saint-Briac died, as planned, the following morning, though he took two of Arnold Fitzgiroie's best men with him as he went. The warning message got through to Ralph de Gacé, who immediately sent two of his fastest riders off to Rouen and the castle of Arques to warn Archbishop Mauger and Talou respectively. They met in Rouen a week later, gathering outside the chapel at the ducal palace one morning after mass, where anyone could see them: just three of the duchy's most influential men having a convivial chat. De Gacé, who had long ago realised that he was far brighter than his two cousins, pointed out that their options were limited. 'We can't start raising an army of our own. That would only attract attention and prove Count Alan's point.'

'So what are we going to do?' Mauger asked, as nervous and twitchy as ever.

'We'll have to remove Alan discreetly, without anyone knowing we've done it.'

'What do you mean, remove?'

De Gacé gave an exasperated sigh. 'What do you think I mean? We'll have to kill him. Or rather I'll have to kill him, because clearly neither of you is capable of doing it.'

'How?'

De Gacé thought for a moment. 'There is one person I might

be able to find to do the job. But if I remove this potentially deadly threat to our plans, I expect some kind of reward.'

Now Talou butted in. 'What did you have in mind?'

De Gacé thought for a moment. 'I want control of the Norman militia and the complete estates of either Brionne or Herfastsson. I'm not fussy.'

'But then you'd be—'

'One of the largest landowners in Normandy, with an army at my beck and call, that's right. But, Cousin Talou, you would be the duke, and of course, Mauger, you would still be archbishop.'

'But you'd . . . well, you'd practically be able to tell us what to do.'

De Gacé smiled. 'What can I say? I'm my father's son . . .'

10

Vaudreuil, Normandy and Alençon

Her first-given name had been Finna. For her trade she called herself Jarl. But there was a secret name that her master had given her and that she held to her heart as her true name. The only other person who knew the name would not say it, for he felt he could not shape the word with the perfection that she deserved, though he could and did write it in liquid Arabic script. This name was Jamila, which meant beautiful, for so she had been as a girl and so she remained as a woman.

Jamila was a loving and dutiful wife to Mahomet, the profoundly deaf Nubian whom she had first met on the road from Damascus to the sea. When she played the role of Jarl, Mahomet acted as her bodyguard, ever obedient to her gestured commands, never uttering a sound for fear that his attempts to articulate might leave him open to mockery and thus dissipate the effect of his presence. She accepted the necessity of this reversal of the proper order, for she was the one who was adept in the poisoner's art while he, whose body was as mighty as his skin was black, intimidated even the most arrogant and warlike of Normans and thus protected her. Still it offended her, and whenever they returned from an encounter with a potential client, or the actual execution of a contract, she was careful to reassure her man of her obedience and respect.

Jamila took pleasure in the simple, repetitive tasks of cooking, cleaning and laundering; tending to the gardens of flowers, herbs and fruits; minding the few animals they kept. All these things brought normality to her life, and she appreciated the moments, even hours, of boredom as the perfect antidote to the violence, fear and abuse that had scarred her early life. It was, in any case, a simple matter to relieve any tedium. All she had to do was think of Mahomet's body lying next to hers, or on top of her, and the way he made her seem so pale and insubstantial that she hardly felt like a physical being at all, but more like a spirit, an accumulation of senses as the smell of him filled her nostrils and the taste of him her mouth, and every part of her body was alive to his slightest touch.

She smiled now at the thought of his love, and then scolded herself for her impiety. She was rolling up the prayer mats after they had both taken part in *salat*, the ritual of prayer that, whenever possible, they performed five times a day. Mahomet had become deaf as the result of a disease contracted in childhood. He had by then already learned the *rak'ah*: the sequence of bowing before God, standing, prostrating, sitting and standing again, along with the words of the prayers that accompanied each posture. Over the years, no longer being able to hear himself, he had lost the ability to say the words clearly, yet Jamila was happy to let him lead *salat*, both because it was proper that he should do so and also because the Lord most high, the most praiseworthy and magnificent, would surely comprehend the sincerity of his faith and hear with perfect clarity the words he was struggling to say.

They lived in the overgrown ruins of an ancient Roman villa, chosen for its remote location in a forest clearing and also because its shape, with the body of the house wrapped around a central courtyard, reminded them of the houses they had both known in Damascus. For many years they had shared the house and its gardens with a handful of acolytes who had assisted Jamila in the cultivation of poisonous plants and their conversion into deadly toxins. Since the death of the archbishop, however, and Jamila's decision to retire from her trade, these followers had left her and, having agreed among themselves to avoid the possibility of direct rivalries, dispersed across the known world: to Cologne, Milan, Léon, Venice and even Byzantium. So now Jamila and Mahomet lived alone, and she no longer had to pretend to be a Christian man but could instead be her true, female, Muslim self.

As she cleaned and tidied the house, Mahomet was elsewhere on the property, engaged in building work. Much of the ruins was still overgrown or even buried. But Mahomet had come across a structure – a floor supported on pillars over a very shallow cellar – that reminded him of the steam baths he had known in Damascus. He had decided to see if he could build a bathhouse of their own, using water diverted from a nearby stream and a fire fed by wood from the forest, for of all the infidel habits that Mahomet and Jamila found offensive, none was worse than their lack of cleanliness.

It made Jamila content to think of Mahomet engaged in his labours while she busied herself with her own. Soon she would take him a drink of hot water infused with herbs, and later she would bring bread and cheese for his midday meal. She had made a small cake, too. There was a boy, a skinny, nimble-footed child as untamed as a forest animal, whom she'd often spotted in the woods near the house, though he had never summoned up the courage to come and talk to her. He looked as though he needed a decent meal, and so if she was ever baking for herself and Mahomet, she always added a little something for her visitor and put it out for him to find, knowing that it would vanish before the day was out.

One of these days I'll persuade that child to come out from the trees and say hello, she thought. It's all a matter of patience and time, and I have plenty of both.

* * *

Ralph de Gacé had never forgotten the discussion about the mysterious figure who undertook murders for money, but neither had he done as much as he'd intended to track the man down. There'd been no immediate need, and he'd been fully occupied building his growing status among Duke William's guardians, who were steadily and gratifyingly coming to see him as an equal. Now, though, he recalled a conversation he'd had with his near neighbour Talvas of Bellême, whose castle at Alençon could be reached in a single day's hard ride from his own estate.

Over dinner in the great hall at Alençon, well over a year after the archbishop's funeral, de Gacé had happened to mention, as no more than a passing remark, Osbern's theory that the old man might have been murdered, possibly by the same killer who had done for Duke Richard III.

Talvas was always entertained by the idea of violent death. 'Now that's an interesting notion!' he said, with unfeigned enthusiasm. 'But before we go any further, can I just ask you: did *you* kill him?'

De Gacé was so surprised by Talvas's question that he had swallowed some wine down the wrong way, coughing and spluttering, showering the table and several of the other guests with wine and spittle. He had required a good while and several hearty slaps on the back before he could finally answer. 'No, of course I didn't! I'd hardly have raised the subject if I had, would I?'

'Probably not, but I had to ask,' Talvas had replied, untroubled by the other man's discomfort. 'Anyone who wanted him dead must have had something to gain from it. Your brothers stood to inherit the family titles and estates, but neither of them has got the balls to kill a chicken for the pot, let alone their own father. So that leaves you, but you say you didn't do it, and oddly enough, I believe you.'

'How very kind . . .'

'As for that sorry excuse for a duke, Richard, if anyone killed him, it was his brother. That pilgrimage Robert went on was the closest thing anyone's ever going to see to a signed confession. Why the hell else would he feel he had to disappear off to Jerusalem?'

'That's true enough. So you don't believe this story of a killer for hire?'

'I didn't say that. I've certainly heard a few stories over the years. He's supposed to be known as the Viper . . .' Talvas had laughed as if at a private joke and went on, 'I can't remember, have you met my daughter Mabel?'

'No. What's that got to do with anything?'

'It's just that I used to tell the children to behave themselves or the Viper would come in the middle of the night and kill them with his venom. My boy Arnulf, who's a great disappointment I'm afraid to say, used to wet the bed with fear. His young brother Oliver wasn't born in those days, so perhaps I should test him now. He'll do well to match his sister, though. Bless her, Mabel is made of sterner stuff. There's a girl a man can be proud of – she absolutely loved the idea of the Viper. She used to make me tell all sorts of tall stories about him. She even tried to poison one of my dogs with a mixture of vinegar and crushed belladonna berries. Christ, that bloody hound was sick. Covered half the castle in its vomit. But it survived, much to Mabel's fury.'

'Delightful, I'm sure,' said de Gacé. 'But do you actually know anything at all about this Viper?'

Talvas had given a dismissive shrug. 'Not much. The story goes that the only way you can get in touch with him is to go to some filthy inn down by the docks in Vaudreuil and ask the old boy who owns it to put you in touch. God knows how he does it, but apparently the Viper gets the message. He's got some

Moor, black as an ebony chess piece and bigger than any other man in Normandy, they say, who guards him. Beyond that, I haven't a clue.' Talvas suddenly grinned. 'Ah, speak of the devil!'

De Gacé turned his head towards where Talvas was looking and saw a dowdy, shabbily dressed woman, who walked with her head held down, only glancing up occasionally to see where she was going, leading two children towards the high table. Only when she came much closer did he recognise her as Talvas's wife, Hildeburg. She stepped up on to the dais and walked towards her husband's place at the centre of the table. As she came closer, de Gacé could see that she was actually shaking with nerves. He had a sudden memory of his own boyhood as the ugly, scrawny butt of everyone's contempt, from the couple who acted as his adoptive parents down to the lowliest servants.

Not wanting to be reminded of those days, he muttered, 'Stupid bitch, she probably deserves it,' and watched as Hildeburg made a jerky, graceless curtsey and said, 'Your children have come to say good night, my lord.'

'Very well.' Talvas had shown her no sign of affection or respect. 'Now get out of here. They can find their own way to their bedchamber.'

'Yes, my lord,' Hildeburg whimpered.

Talvas reached out a hand towards her. He was only stretching for a flagon of wine that was standing on the table, but that single movement was enough to make his wife flinch. De Gacé wondered how many beatings it had taken to break her spirit so totally. By God, Talvas was a hard bastard, he thought admiringly, realising how much he still had to learn.

Then his host turned to him and said, 'These are my children. Arnulf . . .'

A sullen, snot-nosed boy stepped forward, held out his hand and said, as if by rote, 'Good evening, sir.'

De Gacé shook the lad's limp hand.

'And my daughter, Mabel . . .'

The girl who stepped confidently towards de Gacé was as pretty a vision of bouncing golden curls and sweet, smiling lips as anyone could wish to see. She was adorable, with a voice that was as clear and bright as a bell as she said, 'Good evening, Lord de Gacé.'

But when Ralph looked into her eyes, Mabel of Bellême stared right back with a depth of pure, cold evil that pierced him to his very bones and frightened him more profoundly than any man, of any size, carrying any weapon, that he had ever met in his life.

He shuddered at the memory. That girl was surely possessed by demons, and it did him no good at all to think of her. He turned his mind instead to the Viper, and everything that was known about him.

Two days later, de Gacé rode at the head of a small column of armed men into the town of Vaudreuil. It stood at the fork of the rivers Seine and Eure. This position made it a natural trading centre, and its customs post and docks were always busy with boats and barges plying back and forth, cargoes being loaded and unloaded, and boatmen and dockers looking for a drink, a fight, a fuck or all three.

There were three taverns down by the waterfront catering to this rough-and-ready class of customer, and though it was barely an hour or two after breakfast time, there were already plenty of people seeking refreshment. De Gacé led half a dozen of his men into the first establishment and waited until the room had been cleared of drinkers and cheap dockside whores. Then he marched up to the wooden trestle table set up in front of a row of barrels that served as a counter and asked the scarred, shaven-headed bruiser standing behind it, 'Where can I find the Viper?'

'Who's asking?' the innkeeper replied.

'The Duchy of Normandy,' de Gacé replied.

'Duchy my arse. I fought twenty years for old Duke Richard. Me and my mates did all our killing for the Little Cats. Don't see no leopards on any colours here. So tell me who you really are or piss off.'

'Wiger!' de Gacé called out, not taking his eyes off the innkeeper.

One of his men stepped forward carrying a large battleaxe. 'Yes, my lord?'

'Smash that barrel.'

Wiger, who was just as large and almost as ugly as the innkeeper, stood in front of the first barrel, lifted his axe up high and then swung it down with all his strength.

The cooper who had made this particular cask had done a good job. The wood cracked and splintered but did not break. It was not until the fourth swing that Wiger finally smashed through it, sending a flood of mead streaming across the floor and filling the smoky air with the sickly-sweet smell of fermented honey.

Neither the innkeeper nor de Gacé budged as the liquid flowed around and even over their feet.

'Where's the Viper?' de Gacé asked. 'Or do you want my men to smash every single barrel in this stinking dump?'

The innkeeper was breathing heavily, struggling to control his temper. De Gacé decided he needed a little more help making up his mind. 'Wiger!'

The soldier stood by the next barrel and raised his axe. He smashed it down once, twice . . . and then it was the innkeeper rather than the barrel that cracked.

'All right, all right, I'll tell you! Go down the other end of the docks. The place you want has a crescent moon on its sign. But you're too late. The old man who ran the place, the one that knew the Viper, died. His son's taken over, but he won't know where the Viper's hiding. That idiot can't even find his own arse.'

Sure enough, the slack-jawed young man who played host at the Crescent Moon had no idea where the killer could be found. 'I swear our dad didn't tell us nothing!' he pleaded, close to tears. 'He didn't dare, said the Viper would kill him.'

De Gacé was all too depressingly certain that he was telling the truth. But just as he was leading his men out, the landlord of the Crescent Moon suddenly called out, 'Wait! I just remembered something! My old man, he told us, "The Viper'll come slithering out of the forest and across the river and he'll kill us all if he thinks I've crossed him." So that means he must live in the forest but not on this bank of the river, the other one.'

'Which river?' de Gacé asked. 'There are two.'

'Oh, the Seine. When the old man talked about "the river", he meant the big one. He used to say, "The Eure's no more'n a streak of piss."'

'He was quite the orator, your father.'

The young taverner's jaw slackened still further and his brow furrowed as he tried to work out what an orator was. De Gacé ignored him. He stalked from the tavern, calling out to his men, 'Mount up and move out! We're crossing the river, and we're going to catch the Viper.'

11

Eudo the poacher's son was eleven years old. He'd never had a day's education in his life. He'd never even met anyone who could write their own name. But he knew these woods better than anyone, better even than his own father, who was set in his ways and always left his snares in the same old places, even though the animals were learning to avoid the spots where death waited to trap them. There was one place in particular where Eudo liked to go. It was right in the heart of the forest: a series of glades filled with brightly coloured flowers, arranged in a circle around another, bigger opening in the trees where the beautiful lady and the black monster lived in a house of broken-down stones.

This was what Eudo called the magic house, and he had to set out at first light if he wanted to get there and back before sunset, even on a summer's day. But it was always worth the journey. He had never spoken to the beautiful woman, nor even caught her eye, and he'd always hidden as carefully as possible when he came near the house. But she must have known he was there, because he'd once or twice found little presents that she had left out for him: small bread rolls or even a piece of cake, still warm from the oven. It was as if she knew he was coming, even though he hadn't told anyone. That was how he knew she was magic.

It happened that Eudo had visited the house on the same day that Ralph de Gacé had led his men into the taverns on Vaudreuil docks. Sadly for him, he had not found any little gift of food waiting for him when he reached his hiding place. So now, making his way down one of the forester's paths that criss-crossed the woods, and trying to ignore the aching rumbles from his empty stomach, he was so wrapped up in his own hunger that he wasn't paying attention to his surroundings.

Out of nowhere, he heard the sound of horses' hooves beating on the earth, and suddenly half a dozen armed and mounted men appeared just a short way up ahead. If Eudo had been more alert, he would have disappeared into the trees long before the soldiers had spotted him. But his mind was leagues away, his reactions were slow, and already the horsemen were almost on him.

'Hey, you, boy!' one of the men called out.

That did it. Eudo turned and fled. Behind him he heard a shout of 'Stop!' and the next thing he knew an arrow thudded into the trunk of a tree just as he was running past it.

He heard the horseman's voice again. 'The next one goes right through your back.'

Eudo stopped and turned back towards the armed men. As a poacher's son, raised all his life to believe that those in power were a threat to his livelihood and very existence, he assumed that these men were out looking for anyone taking game from forests belonging to the Duke of Normandy himself.

'Please, sir, I've not done anything wrong,' he called out, holding up his hands to show that there was nothing in them.

'I don't care what you've done,' said the horseman, who had one of the strangest faces Eudo had ever seen, with sticking-out teeth and goggly eyes and a nose that looked as long as his horse's. On any other day he'd have looked funny, but not today. 'There's only one thing I want to know, and if you can help me . . .' The horseman rummaged in a purse hanging from his belt, pulled out a small silver coin and held it up so that Eudo could see it. '. . . I'll give you this shiny brand-new penny.

But if you lie to me or deceive me, or try to hide what you know, then I'll stick my sword so deep into your guts that you'll feel like a pig on a spit.'

Eudo didn't know what to say to that. He just stood stock still, hardly daring even to breathe.

'So tell me this, boy,' the horseman went on, 'do you know these woods well?'

Eudo was still completely dumbstruck. He nodded frantically.

'Very well then. I'm looking for a man who lives here, somewhere secret, somewhere only a sneaky, sharp-eyed lad like yourself would know. This man is called the Viper. You ever heard that name, boy?'

Eudo shook his head.

'Speak up!'

'No, sir,' Eudo said. 'I've never heard that name.'

'The Viper has a servant who's as big as a giant and as black as night. I bet you'd be able to spot someone like that if they were in the forest. So have you seen him, this black giant?'

Eudo didn't know what to say. He didn't want to die, but he didn't want to betray the beautiful lady and her monster, either. He darted his head from side to side, looking for a possible escape route, but the horsemen had formed into a ring that almost entirely encircled him.

'You know who I'm talking about, don't you, boy? Don't deny it. I can see it in your face. I bet you know just where to find him, too.'

'No, I don't, sir, honest I don't!' Eudo blurted out. 'Promise!'

The horseman grinned. 'Do you now? Well I don't believe you. I think you're telling lies. And you know what I do to little boys who tell me lies . . .' He whipped his sword out of his scabbard and pointed it directly at Eudo.

Eudo swallowed hard. His eyes filled with tears and his nose began to run.

'What's your name, boy?' the horseman asked, sounding a bit less frightening.

'Eudo, sir,' came the reply.

'Well, Eudo, I made you a promise, and unlike you, I mean it. So I will give you that penny if you just tell me where I can find the giant. Will you tell me?'

'Yes,' said Eudo, and burst out crying. It wasn't for him, or even for the giant. He was crying for the beautiful lady.

A wordless, guttural roar, like the distant sound of a lion at night, but overlaid with a higher pitch of pain and alarm, echoed through the forest to the kitchen where Jamila was working. In the very instant that she heard it, she knew that the sound had been made by Mahomet, and that if he were afraid then it would not be for himself, for she had never once known her man to be scared on his own account. He only felt fear for her.

She dropped the prayer mats, gathered up her skirts and raced across the reed-strewn stone floor to the chest where she kept her knife, a dagger whose needle blade, forged from Toledo steel, made any Norman weapon seem like nothing more than a crude bar of pig iron. It sat in a short scabbard that she belted like a girdle around her waist.

Beside the chest stood a tall wooden store cupboard that was empty save for a few small hessian sacks filled with flour, turnips, cabbages and dried beans. Jamila stepped into the cupboard, lifted her right hand and pressed against a point on the far wall. There was a soft click and a door swung open revealing nothing but darkness beyond. She slipped through into the gloom and closed the door after her, leaving behind an empty room.

12

'Over here, my lord!'

Ralph de Gacé peered down the path that ran away from the building site where the Moor had been working and lost itself in the shadows between the trees. Up ahead, one of his foot soldiers was waving to catch his attention.

'What is it?' he shouted back.

'Some kind of old house, all broken down,' the soldier replied. 'But I can see smoke. Someone's got a fire going.'

De Gacé called out, 'Stay there!' then turned back to the men who were struggling to tie the Moor's outstretched hands to the ends of the heavy wooden yoke that had been placed across his broad shoulders. The Moor was half crippled by the arrow in the front of his right thigh, just above the knee, and his face was slicked with sweat and almost grey with the pain, but he was not uttering a sound. And though two of de Gacé's men were wrestling each of his hands, marvelling as they did so at the contrast between the jet-black skin on the backs of his fingers and the delicate pinky-brown skin on his palms, they could not keep their prisoner still for long enough to pass the ropes around his wrists and tie him to the yoke.

De Gacé gave a sharp, irritable sigh. He dismounted, walked across to the Moor and tilted his head up so that he could look him in the face and smile. Then he grabbed the shaft of the arrow, pushed it deeper into the flesh of the Moor's leg and yanked it up and down.

The Moor emitted an agonised, shuddering groan and sank

to his knees, his head bent down upon his chest. Seeing him finally humbled, his captors set about their task with a burst of new energy and enthusiasm. As de Gacé remounted his horse, another man dropped a noose over the Moor's neck and tightened it so that it prevented him breathing in anything other than shallow, desperate gasps.

'Bring him,' said de Gacé. He wheeled his chestnut stallion and set off down the path at a leisurely walk. Up ahead, the first soldier was waiting by a sharp left-hand turn in the path.

'There, my lord,' he said, pointing ahead of him. 'What did I tell you? A fire!'

The ruins of the villa stretched across a considerable area of the forest floor in a maze of walls, passages, half-demolished rooms, fallen columns and the trees that had grown up through the old mosaic floors and burst through the last few remnants of the tiled roof. Anyone unfamiliar with the place would soon find themselves in a maze, littered with obstructions and dead ends. Jamila, on the other hand, knew every single step, whether in the quantum of sunshine that penetrated the forest canopy or the Stygian gloom of a cloudy winter night. She could race from the secret doorway to any one of half a dozen separate exits into the forest. It would be a few moments' work to escape the crude approach of the knights who came stamping and shouting their way down the winding path she and Mahomet had cut from the ancient bathhouse to the main courtyard. Once free, she could hurry to the graveyard, where a substantial portion of their accumulated gold was cached in a buried coffin, remove enough to keep her for this lifetime and another beyond it, and be gone from Normandy for ever by the time the sun next rose.

But that would mean deserting Mahomet, which was something Jamila could never do. She crouched at one of the observation points littered throughout the ruins, and peered at the entrance to the courtyard. Out of the gloom, no more than twenty paces from where she hid, emerged a foot soldier and then a mounted man – an aristocrat, to judge by the quality and condition of his mount and the richness of his clothing. She kept watching as the man emerged into a patch of watery sunshine and then nodded to herself as she recognised de Gacé. Even with a hood of chain mail over his head and a helmet on top of that, he was unmistakable. Had he made the connection between Jarl the Viper and his own father's death and come looking for revenge, or was the motive for his visit something else entirely?

Her speculation was cut short by the appearance of Mahomet, tethered to a yoke and with a rope around his neck, being led like an animal to slaughter. Jamila cursed the womanly lack of strength that prevented her from drawing back a bow powerful enough to send an arrow through chain mail. Had she been suitably armed, she could have picked off four or five of de Gacé's men before the survivors had time to take their own bows off their shoulders, select their arrows and start looking around for a target. Had they been about to bivouac for the night, she could have slipped through the darkness into their camp and finished the lot of them off with any one of a myriad poisons, aided and abetted by silent stabs from her needle-sharp blade, gently applied to the most vulnerable parts of the human body.

For now, though, there was nothing she could do to save her man except hide and wait and hope.

And then Mahomet cried out. He spoke in Arabic, but not in any form of the language that a citizen of Damascus or Jeddah would have understood, for the words were as malformed as de Gacé's face. But Jamila understood him perfectly and knew that he had said, 'Flee, my beloved! I command you as your husband – run!'

The words were silenced by a grunt of pain as one of de Gacé's men hit Mahomet in the kidneys with the butt of his lance. The other men started mocking him, imitating the garbled, incomprehensible words as if they were nothing more than animal noises.

'Enough!' shouted de Gacé. Then he turned his head towards the centre of the courtyard and called out, 'I come looking for the one that people call Jarl the Viper. I have a proposition to put to him . . .' He sniffed the air like a hunting dog. 'No . . . to you. I know you're here, Viper. I'm certain of it. You wouldn't leave your pet ape here by itself. From what I hear, this creature matters to you; perhaps you even love it as I love my favourite dog. Very well then. I wish to talk business with you. I suspect you may not wish to talk to me, so . . . observe. Serlo!'

Jamila was so outraged by the way this malformed infidel was talking about her husband that she did not immediately realise what was happening.

One of the soldiers had stepped forward. He carried a bow in his right hand and there was a quiver slung over his shoulder. 'The other leg, please,' said de Gacé.

'Yes, my lord.'

Serlo took a dozen long strides away from the knot of men holding Mahomet. Then he turned to face them.

Jamila felt as though an invisible hand had grabbed her throat and started to throttle her. She could not breathe. Her mouth was bone dry. Her pulse raced.

'Observe,' said de Gacé again, in a much more conversational tone, as the bowman took an arrow out of his quiver and laid it on the bow. 'Serlo is one of the finest marksmen in all Normandy,' he went on as the bowstring was drawn back and the arrow aimed.

'No!' Jamila cried, but the sound of her voice was drowned

as Mahomet shouted, 'In the name of God the merciful, flee!'

De Gacé turned to look at the Moor. 'Release him,' he said.

The men holding Mahomet let go of him, and stepped sharply away. At that same instant, Serlo loosed his arrow, and a heartbeat later it buried itself about halfway up Mahomet's left thigh, breaking the bone.

The Moor could not help himself. He let out a high, keening cry of pure agony and collapsed, writhing helplessly on the forest floor.

Jamila had given men poisons that left them racked with unspeakable pain, vomiting blood or suffocated from within. She had stood and watched quite calmly as her victims left this world for the next. But never had she felt even the slightest degree of the anguish that consumed her now. Her man was enduring unspeakable suffering. It was her duty to help him in any way she could. Yet it was also her duty to obey her husband, and he had commanded her to flee. But how could she, if that meant leaving him?

'Serlo can keep shooting,' de Gacé went on. 'He can fill the ape with more arrows than St Sebastian. Perhaps you won't care. In that case, my trip will have been wasted and you will have to hope you aren't burned to death when I put this home of yours, and all the land around it, to the flame. Or you can come and talk, and I will tell you what I want and present you my terms, and if you accept, you will both live.'

Jamila watched Mahomet open his mouth to speak. He was going to tell her, for a final time, to go. She knew it. But when he tried to speak, he could manage nothing more than a pathetic whimper of pain. A mighty giant of a man had been brought down like a felled tree, and it was the sight of him so reduced that made up Jamila's mind.

'I am the one you seek,' she said, emerging from her hiding place. 'I am Jarl the Viper.'

13

De Gacé had been about to laugh, but checked himself just in time. Two women had been spotted going in and out of the rooms in which Jarl the Viper's possible victims had died. But what if they were actually one and the same woman, and she was in fact the killer? Even now, the very notion of a woman hiring herself out as a paid murderess seemed inconceivable. Still, there was no harm in finding out. The one thing that all the descriptions agreed on was that the Viper, if so she was, possessed extraordinary beauty. The tall, slender woman in front of him had a scarf draped over her head and then wound around her face so as to hide much of it from view. And no sooner had she introduced herself than she had lowered her head, not looking him in the eye, but carrying herself modestly and even submissively. That was surely not the way a murderer looked at the world.

'Show yourself. Let me see your face,' de Gacé commanded.

It was only because he was watching her so closely that he noticed the woman glancing towards the wounded Moor, catching his eye and waiting until he had given her a barely perceptible nod before unwinding her scarf and looking directly at de Gacé himself.

De Gacé gasped. The woman who stood before him had long golden hair that spilled around her shoulders and then tumbled down her back and over the breast of her dress. Her forehead was high and smooth; her eyes were a deep cornflower blue, and as she looked at him, there was no fear in them whatever; and her sweet pink lips seemed to be hovering on the edge of a smile. By God, de Gacé thought, if Duke Richard really did fuck this temptress on his last night on earth, he must have died a happy man.

'So, you know what I look like,' the woman said, wrapping her scarf around her head and face again. 'What is the business you wish to discuss?'

De Gacé shook his head. 'First prove to me that you are truly the Viper.'

'Very well. Perhaps your men would like an apple each. If you give me just a short time to prepare, I can bring them a bowl of shiny red fruit, half of them poisoned in a variety of different ways, the other half not. Let them try their luck. If I am not Jarl, and know nothing about poison, they will live and I will die. If I am who I say I am, I will survive and we will do business, but those who choose a poisoned apple will die. You will lose several of your men, and sadly, their deaths will not be pleasant to watch.'

De Gacé did not have to look at his men to know that this was not a suggestion he could accept. 'No,' he replied. 'My men are of use to me. Your ape, however, is not. Poison him.'

The woman nodded, showing no emotion. 'I accept,' she said. 'I shall release him from his suffering. But I need to search among my potions, and they are stored in my workroom. Will you allow me to go into the house and get them?'

'Very well, but I and two of my men will accompany you.'

De Gacé got down from his horse and signalled to a pair of his largest, most intimidating men to follow him, which they did, though the expressions on their faces when their master's back was turned suggested that they would have been much happier charging an army of ten thousand men than entering the lair of this lone sorceress.

* * *

Jamila smiled beneath her scarf as she sensed the unease of the Normans who were following her into the ruined villa. They were right to be frightened. It would be the work of moments to dispose of this misbegotten lord and his two dull-eyed minions and then vanish into the depths of the forest before anyone outside was any the wiser. But her priority, as always, was Mahomet, and for what she had planned she needed a clear head, a sharp eye and a steady hand, which meant no distractions. She led them through the main room, where she and Mahomet spent their days, pausing only to take a key attached to a leather band that hung from a peg on the wall. Then she strode along a series of passages, turning to the left and right so frequently that the men must have lost all sense of their bearings by the time she came to a heavy wooden door criss-crossed by bands of iron. There she inserted her key into the lock, turned it and, with some effort, pushed open the door.

The chamber into which she led de Gacé and the men was unlike any they had ever entered. On the walls there were strange, astonishingly lifelike paintings of naked men and women and mythical creatures – de Gacé, who had been given some education, recognised the bull-headed Minotaur and the half-man, half-horse centaur – disporting themselves in a landscape dotted with buildings more elegant than any in Normandy.

'These paintings are Roman,' said Jamila, seeing his wonder. 'They must have been here for many hundreds of years.'

But de Gacé was not paying attention. He and his two men were looking upwards, mouths open in wonder, at a roof made entirely of glass, fifty or more panes of it set in a wooden frame, through which they could see the sky, the blurred outlines of clouds and the radiance of the sun. They had, of course, seen great windows in churches, and even some that glowed with bright, jewel-like colours. But this was something else entirely, and it meant that the room, though it had solid walls on all four sides, was barely any darker than the world outside. There was no need for the candles or burning torches casting a sputtering orange glow into the gloom that enveloped even the grandest castles or palaces. Everything could be seen perfectly, thanks to daylight alone.

Along one side of the room ran a workbench. On the wall behind it wooden shelves had been erected, and these were filled with glass and pottery containers, each labelled with a script that made de Gacé frown as he looked at it. For though he could not write anything beyond his own crude signature, he knew his letters well enough to see that these were something quite different, something foreign. The equipment on the bench was equally mysterious. De Gacé recognised scales, though they were finer than any he had ever known, and made of a strange shiny material. But he was baffled by the oddly shaped jars and bottles – some of metal, others of glass – that stood on tripods above stone bowls. One of the bowls appeared to contain a small fire, which played on the bottom of the glass bottle perched above it and blackened its base with soot. De Gacé peered more closely and saw a liquid that looked as thick and dark as pitch bubbling and smoking the glass. The bottle had a cork in its neck, though the cork had been pierced by a long, thin glass tube that looped up, across and down in an inverted horseshoe shape. The other end of the tube had also been forced through the cork in the top of a bottle, although this one stood directly on the workbench with no fire beneath it. A liquid was dripping slowly from the end of the glass tube into the second bottle, but this liquid looked as clear and cool as spring water.

'This is witchcraft!' de Gacé snarled.

'You may think so,' Jamila replied, 'but to me it is simply learning. Everything I do now was known to the people who built this house and painted this room. It is simply that so much has been forgotten . . . but not by everyone. Now, let me show you what I can do, and I shall release a dying man from his misery.'

As a young child, Jamila had seen her father killed and her mother raped before her eyes. From that day on, she had possessed the ability to step aside from her emotions and remain entirely calm and detached from what was going on around her. On the night she had killed Duke Richard III, he had treated her as the whore she was pretending to be, using her with crude, drunken coarseness. She had taken her mind elsewhere, so that she could not be degraded or hurt; similarly, when she had ended his life, there was no shred of anger or revenge in her actions, simply the calm concentration on a job well done.

Now, though, as she measured out the opium powder with which she would silence Mahomet's cries of pain and still the suffering in his eyes, even her lifetime of training was barely enough to keep the flood of grief at bay.

This was the same drug, made from her own poppies, that had killed the archbishop. It had never occurred to Jamila that she might ever be required to give it to the one person in all creation whom she loved completely and without reservation. She poured the powder into a small vial of sweet rosehip syrup and then told de Gacé, 'I'm ready. Now I will give this to the Moor . . . unless you would rather one of your men sampled it first?'

'No, that won't be necessary,' said de Gacé.

Jamila could detect the nervousness in his voice. She knew that he must now be thinking of her as a devil in female form. But equally, it was clear that he was in dire need of her services. Why else would he have gone to such lengths to find her? And why else had he let her live once he had seen her laboratory? To an infidel mind she was practising witchcraft, and the penalty for that was death. Yet here she still was, very much alive.

They walked back the way they had come and emerged

into the courtyard again. Mahomet was now lying on his back with the arrows, whose heads were still buried deep within his flesh, sticking up into the air. His wounds had been bleeding profusely, and the lower portions of his baggy *sirwal* leggings were drenched in blood, as was the ground to either side of him. His eyes were closed and he was moaning softly, wordlessly, as if he were lost in pain and hardly aware of anything or anyone else around him.

Jamila had managed to walk through the house in a calm, unhurried fashion, but now she could restrain herself no longer. She ran to Mahomet, crouched down beside him and took out the vial of syrup and opium. She pulled out the cork and then cradled his head in her left arm as she brought the vial to his lips with her right hand. 'Drink, my beloved,' she whispered in Arabic. 'Drink and you will be at peace.'

She poured the syrup into Mahomet's mouth and he swallowed it. His eyelids fluttered open and he looked at her for a moment through his huge, dark, liquid eyes. Then he gave one last, long sigh, and a moment later Jamila's true love lay still and silent in her arms. She bent down and kissed his forehead, then, heedless of the Normans' stares, placed her lips on his before gently resting his head back on the earth.

'Very well,' she said, rising to her feet. 'I have proven myself. What is it you want me to do?'

14

Jamila and de Gacé held their negotiations in private. He explained that he needed Alan of Brittany to die within the next ten days. He told her where she could find him. She assured him that he could consider the job done. That aspect of the conversation took very little time. The more delicate matter was that of their own joint survival.

Each now possessed incriminating knowledge about the other. De Gacé knew that she was Jarl the Viper and had killed both the archbishop and Duke Richard. She knew that he had commissioned the death of one of the duke's guardians and might be expected to kill the rest in due course. It was therefore in both their interests to place as much distance between one another as possible. After some debate and a number of threats, both veiled and blatant, on either side, de Gacé agreed to give Jamila a further ten days, following Alan's death, to pack up her possessions and leave Normandy. She agreed not to kill de Gacé in the meantime. No money changed hands.

When they had finished, they walked back outside and Jamila watched as de Gacé led his men away. She waited to make sure they were not coming back before dashing to Mahomet's side. She had given him a dose of opium calculated to make him unconscious without killing him. But he was so large that the amount required to knock him out might very well, if she had miscalculated even fractionally, be fatal. She placed her fingers to the side of his throat, just beneath his jaw, and felt for the faintest beating of life. When she finally detected it, she slumped for a moment, tears flooding her eyes, but then reminded herself that there was work to be done, and since she could not hope to move Mahomet back into the house, she would have to carry out her tasks out of doors.

Luckily for them both, there were still many hours before sunset. Jamila made a fire and boiled water, for her master in Damascus had taught her that this removed impurities and made water safe to drink and to wash with, no matter how dirty it might be to begin with. She found a clean linen dress and cut its skirt into strips. She fetched vinegar, which she knew aided healing and prevented infection if poured over raw wounds. From her sewing box she extracted her most delicate needle and finest silk thread. Finally she went back to her laboratory, prepared some more opium-laced syrup and collected a set of small knives whose blades were honed to an even greater sharpness than her dagger. She carried everything outside and set it down in an orderly row beside Mahomet, so that every item could swiftly be located when the time came to use it.

Jamila looked at her husband's face. He still seemed completely insensible. When she lifted an eyelid, he gave no sign of any conscious response. Very well, it was time to begin.

First she washed her own hands with some of the boiled water, cleansing herself exactly as if for an act of worship. She cut away the blood-soaked fabric of his *sirwal* so that his legs were revealed. Then she washed the area around each wound so that she could see more clearly the damage the arrows had caused. She poured vinegar over both wounds to cleanse them thoroughly. Mahomet twitched a little and emitted a low, soft sound that was neither a sigh nor a grunt but something in between. This was a good sign. Had he been awake, the stinging of the vinegar on his exposed flesh would have convulsed him in pain. Jamila raised her eyes to the heavens. She called upon God to be merciful and to guide her hand to save the life of this, His true and faithful follower, whose wounds had been inflicted by unbelievers. Then she took out the sharpest of the knives, laid it on Mahomet's right thigh, just where the shaft of the arrow protruded, and made a single, decisive cut down towards the buried arrowhead.

The sun had travelled much of the way towards the western horizon, and Jamila had been obliged to give Mahomet a second, slightly lighter dose of opium, by the time the operation was complete. She had removed the two arrows, stitched and cleaned the wounds and tied the fabric from her dress around each leg to form bandages. While removing the arrow from Mahomet's left thigh, she had seen that the bone was badly cracked and splintered, with fragments floating loose amidst the torn muscles. There was, however, no sign that it had been snapped clean in two, so she removed whatever splinters she could find, then cut straight shafts of newly grown hazel and bound them tightly to the broken leg to help keep it as immobile as possible.

Since there was no hope of getting Mahomet indoors, she pitched a tent around him – the very one in which they had first lain as lovers on their journey from Damascus. There she watched over him through the night. She slept beside him, and just as a new mother wakes at the slightest suggestion of her baby's distress, so it only took the faintest of noises from Mahomet and Jamila was awake and tending to him.

The following day, Jamila unwound the bandages to inspect the injuries and was greeted by the sight of thick yellow-white pus seeping like bloodshot milk curds from the open wounds. With that vile sight came a stomach-churning stench of disease and corruption. She cleaned them with vinegar once again and applied fresh bandages, but by sunset more blood and pus was soaking through the linen, and now beads of sweat were appearing on Mahomet's face as a fever struck him.

For the next night and day, and into the third night, Jamila did her best to nurse Mahomet through the struggle that would determine his life or death. She gave him warm water infused with mint and ginger and even garlic, for its health-giving powers were beyond question. She made brews that were hot with spices and pepper, hoping to induce the sweating that would expel the poisons created by his festering wounds.

Sure enough, there were times when Mahomet was so hot he felt like a glowing slab of iron on the blacksmith's anvil, and the bedding she had placed over and around him was wet with his perspiration. Moments later he would be shivering like a man left naked in the snow, and she would have to cover him with blankets and furs until the burning began again.

Mahomet weakened. Jamila had been unable to get him to eat any food, and he was drinking far less fluid than he was losing, so that on the very rare occasions he urinated, the liquid he produced was as brown as treacle and barely any less thick. By the morning of the fifth day, the heat and the cold seemed to have become one, so that his teeth were chattering even as his skin was roasting. Jamila sat beside him, repeating for hour after hour the simple prayers with which she could help his soul be guided to Paradise: 'There is no God except Allah, and Muhammad, peace be upon Him, is the Messenger of Allah . . . Our Lord! Forgive us our sins and anything we may have done that transgressed our duty. Establish our feet firmly, and help us against those that resist Faith . . . There is no God except Allah . . .'

She was so lost in the constant cycle of prayer that when Mahomet whispered her name, she did not hear it, nor did she see his eyes open or his lips move. It was only when he said, 'Jamila, my love,' a second time that her mouth fell silent and her gaze turned to her husband, and she knew, in that instant, that the fever had broken and Mahomet was going to survive.

During the sixth day, Jamila filled earthenware jugs with boiled water, infusions and a sweet mead brewed from honey that would nourish Mahomet and give him strength. She placed loaves of bread beside him, and finely chopped morsels of freshly cooked chicken. She left empty jars within easy reach for him to piss into, and dug a hole nearby to act as an impromptu latrine, beside which were rags and more water vessels with which to cleanse himself.

Throughout all the time that Mahomet had been sick, Jamila had used any spare moment when he was peacefully asleep to think about the death of Alan of Brittany. She had prepared her disguise and chosen her poison, so when she knew that her husband was safe, it remained only for her to change her clothing from that of a faithful Muslim woman to garments appropriate for a slightly built young man. She kept two horses in a clearing about a hundred paces from the house and had been pleased to discover that if de Gacé had ever come upon the place, which she doubted, he had left the animals alone. That was just as well, for she was going to need both of them in the days to come.

She did not leave Mahomet until she had explained what she had agreed with Ralph de Gacé and received his blessing for the plan she had in mind. By the time they had finished speaking, the sun was setting on that sixth day of the ten that had been allotted her. It would take at least two more days and nights, riding hard, with barely a break for her or her horses, to reach Alan of Brittany's advance. Ralph had told her that the Breton army was encamped outside the walled town of Vimoutiers. She prayed that she would still find them there when she arrived.

Negotiations had dragged on for far too long for Alan's comfort as he tried to persuade the people of Vimoutiers to come over to his side without a fight. Yet he had no choice but to parley. So far as the people of Normandy were concerned, he had invaded their land. If he wished to persuade them that his intentions were honourable, he could not afford the slaughter of innocents that would inevitably follow a full-scale assault.

Then, on the eighth day after Jamila's encounter with Ralph de Gacé, there was a significant development in the talks between the invading army and the local people as the latter finally seemed willing to accept Alan's promises that both their lives and their property would be safe if they opened their gates to his army. Alan felt confident that the issue would be settled to his satisfaction the following day, and he was in fine form as he dined with his most trusted lieutenants. The men were served by young squires, most still a year or two from their first good shave, for whom this was the first taste of being with an army on campaign. Some of the squires were as pretty as girls, and even though they were all red-blooded cocksmen whose taste for female flesh was beyond dispute, still there were plenty of ribald remarks, and Alan himself could not resist slapping the arse of the lad who had been serving him wine all night.

'By Christ, boy, you've a prettier backside than most of the women I've fucked!' he exclaimed, to laughter from his guests and giggles from the boys, including the one who'd been slapped.

Alan got to his feet, swaying somewhat, for he had drunk a very great deal of wine during the course of the evening. 'Here's to arses!' he shouted. Then he raised his goblet and downed its contents in one.

A few seconds later, he started struggling for air. 'I can't breathe!' he gasped. His mouth opened, but he seemed incapable of breathing. He beat his hand against the wooden table. One of the knights dashed to his side and patted him hard on the back, in case he had choked on a particle of food, but it made no difference. His eyes bulged. His face turned puce. His lips took on a blue tinge. As his knights looked on in disbelief, Alan III, Count of Brittany, crashed forward on to the table, gave one last convulsive spasm and died.

For the next few minutes, desperate attempts were made to revive him. He was splashed with water, slapped around the face, shaken back and forth. But there was nothing to be done. In all the chaos, no one noticed the squire with the pretty backside leave the great tent where the dinner was being held, walk calmly across the encampment to where the horses were tethered and then ride, slowly enough to attract no attention, away into the night.

On the nineteenth day of the allotted twenty, Jamila and Mahomet drove their heavily laden cart, pulled by two mighty oxen and trailing a fine pair of horses, across the border of Normandy and into the land of the Franks.

15

Alan's death hit William hard. 'I really liked him,' he told Osbern Herfastsson, soon after the news reached Rouen. 'He was always smiling and telling jokes or doing tricks for me.'

'Aye, he was a cheerful lad. A cheeky little beggar, too, when he was your age.'

'Ralph says he wanted to march on Rouen and take Normandy for himself. Do you think that's what he was doing?'

Osbern looked around. He and William were both mounted, returning to the palace with the rest of the party after a day's hunting with falcons on ducal land north of the city. Their horses were tired and a number of the men were on foot, so they'd been going at walking pace. But now Osbern kicked his horse into a canter and William followed him a short way up the track until the watchful old steward pulled hard on the reins and slowed back down to a walk.

'I didn't want us being overheard,' he said. 'So, you asked if Alan had designs on Normandy. To tell you the truth, I don't know. It's possible, I suppose. There've been plenty of fights between Normandy and Brittany over the years. Your father and Alan went to war not long before your father went off to Jerusalem. Lot of fuss about nothing, if you ask me. Archbishop Robert banged their heads together and told them to stop being so damned stupid.'

'But they must have been friends after that because Papa made Alan one of my guardians,' William pointed out. 'And

Great-Uncle Robert told me that I could trust him. He was sure of it.'

'If that's what he said, then you can believe it. The archbishop was as wise as an owl and as cunning as a fox. He didn't get much wrong.'

'Exactly. So if Alan wasn't coming here to attack us, why was he bringing an army into Normandy?'

'Well, you don't put an army into the field unless you're going to do something with it. So if he didn't plan to attack us, then he must have been coming to defend us. But against what, or who, I couldn't tell you.'

William thought for a moment, his face screwed into a frown of concentration. 'Me neither,' he said eventually. 'But there's another thing: how did he die?'

'I thought you already knew. He had some kind of fit in the middle of a dinner with his officers.'

'Yes, I know that, but how? I mean, he was drinking wine, wasn't he?'

'Yes.'

'And making a toast . . . to arses!' William giggled.

'Now, now, Your Grace. No need to lower the tone.'

'But it is funny, you must admit.'

'A little bit, maybe.'

'More than a little,' William persisted.

Osbern shrugged. 'A little more . . . maybe,' though the smile playing around the corners of his mouth gave a lie to the sternness in his voice.

'Anyway,' William went on, satisfied that he'd won that little battle, 'I think someone could have put something in his wine. Poison, or something.'

Osbern turned away with a sigh, sudden thoughts of dead dukes and archbishops and mysterious women bearing flasks of medicine or wine filling his mind. He gave a little shake of his head to get rid of them, like a dog shaking water from its fur.

'There's been too much talk of poison,' he said. 'People do just die sometimes, you know. Perhaps Alan just had a fit. It happens, you know. Demons in the head. And you're better off dropping dead that way than being half dead, half alive, drooling from the mouth, your face all seized up, hardly able to talk.'

'Urgh, I'd hate that,' William said. But, as Osbern had long since discovered, he was a persistent boy, and once he got an idea into his head, he clung on to it as fiercely as an iron trap on a poacher's leg, and so he came right back to Alan of Brittany. 'I don't understand, Osbern. Why would he just fall down dead if he wasn't poisoned?'

'Look, William, it's not for us to say why God works as He does. All we know is that He has a plan for each of us, and He will take us when He sees fit.'

'So if Alan was poisoned, does that mean God wanted it to happen? That can't be right, because murdering someone is evil, and God doesn't do evil things.'

'First you expect me to be a doctor and now a theologian!' Osbern exclaimed. 'I'm just a humble steward. I leave philosophy to other men.'

'I think Alan was poisoned,' said William decisively. 'I think he was killed by someone who wanted to stop him and his army. Alan was coming to help me and the person who killed him was bad. We should find out who he was and punish him. We should chop his head off, or hang him from a tree. That's what I think.'

Osbern pulled his horse to a halt. 'Look at me, William,' he said. 'And listen very carefully to what I'm about to say. You are the Duke of Normandy. You have countless fields of good, fertile earth where crops will always grow and flourish. You have pastures where fat cows graze. You have fish in your rivers and off your coast. You have tollbooths and customs that even now, when there's disorder and conflict everywhere, still produce rich revenues. You have all these things, and other men will always envy them and want to take them from you. And if they can't do that, then as long as you are a boy and cannot rule for yourself, they will try to rule in your name.'

William said nothing, remembering the archbishop warning him of all the people he could not trust and wondering why his life had to be so full of cruel and frightening things.

'So you will always have enemies,' Osbern went on. 'But on the other hand, you will always have friends, people who love you and care for you. And I promise you, as your cousin and your vassal, that as long as there is breath in my body, I will always be here to protect you. Anyone who wants to get to you will have to get past me first. All right?'

'Yes,' said William. 'Thank you.'

'You're welcome.'

They sat there in silence for a short while as the rest of the hunting party caught up with them. Then Osbern kicked his horse into a walk again and led William back to the palace.

A few weeks later, with a vacancy having been created by the death of Alan of Brittany, Ralph de Gacé found himself promoted to take his place in the innermost circle of the guardians of the Duke of Normandy.

Book Two:
The Women and Their Sons

November 1039–December 1040

1

Trollhättefallen, Norway, and Oxford, England

Two monarchs met a month before Christmas on the banks of the Göta river, at the head of the Troll's Hat falls. The river marked the border between the King of Norway's land on the east bank and Danish territory on the west, though the matter was far from settled and the two monarchs were both backed by large armies. The terrain hereabouts was covered in a forest of pine, spruce and silver birch, so the opposing forces were obliged to pitch their tents between the trees. But at least there was wood aplenty for the campfires, and a good thing too, for there was still a thick blanket of snow on the ground. The air was cold and the wind raw, even at midday, and the sun was hidden behind thick grey cloud in the few hours of daylight before the black shroud of night descended once again.

Both sides had cause to mistrust the other, for a state of mutual antagonism, extending often to war, invasion and even conquest, had existed between their two nations for as long as men could remember. Now, though, both had reason to seek peace. The question was: would they find it?

Harthacnut, King of Denmark, the son of King Canute the Great from his marriage to Emma of Normandy, was standing before a line of stepping stones that stretched across the river to the Norwegian side. Beside him was his first cousin and closest adviser Sven Estridsson. Harthacnut was a strapping, strongly built man and, at the age of twenty-one, still young enough to be able to indulge his hearty appetite for food and drink without detriment to either body or wits. Though he had been born in England and spent his early boyhood there, he had arrived in Denmark when he was eight and stayed there ever since. It never even occurred to him, therefore, to think of himself as anything other than a Dane.

'Is everything prepared?' asked Harthacnut.

'Exactly as you ordered,' Estridsson replied. 'Thirty housecarls – good men, all of them – will come with us. If anything goes wrong, they'll close ranks around us and cover our escape. I've got archers ready to line up along the riverbank, too. If Magnus tries to trick us, they'll make him pay for it.'

'Then give the order for them to take up their positions and we'll go and meet this kid, see what he has to say for himself.'

Harthacnut maintained an air of regal confidence as he marched across the river, but inside he was tense and apprehensive. Even though he had men in front of him and behind, still he was exposed. Beneath him, the stones were slippery with water and slime, and the current foaming between them was swift as the river prepared to hurl itself over the falls. One false step would be as fatal as any Norwegian arrow.

But his feet held their grip and no arrow came. As he stepped on to dry land again, the men ahead moved aside to let him pass, Sven Estridsson came forward to join him and they marched towards the enemy.

'Has that boy even started to shave?' Estridsson said out of the corner of his mouth as they approached King Magnus of Norway.

The king was a lad of fifteen. He was a head shorter than Harthacnut and much more lightly built, with pale blonde hair and a pleasant enough face. There was no sword at his waist, but his hands were resting, waist high, on the handle of a battleaxe whose head was planted on the ground. It was a mighty weapon, but one too large for a boy to wield. In time, Harthacnut thought, Magnus might amount to something, and be man enough to master that axe, but there was no need to fear him just yet.

The men standing on either side of the king, however, were an altogether more serious proposition. Kalv Arneson and Einar 'Strongbow' Eindridesson were nobles who had played the role of kingmaker and, when the mood took them, king-breaker for the best part of twenty years. They had opposed Magnus's father, King Olaf, when it suited them to do so, then masterminded another uprising that put Magnus back on the throne. At times they had supported Canute's campaigns in Norway. At other times they had driven his appointed regents out of the country. Their allegiances were temporary. Their self-interest, however, was unchanging.

Both men were greybeards, and each had more experience in battle, politics and every other aspect of life than all three of the younger men put together. And yet, Harthacnut noticed, Magnus did not so much as glance at them, still less seek their support or encouragement, as he looked the two Danes in the eye. He spoke in the Viking style, as one man to another, with no recourse to titles, as he said, 'Welcome, Harthacnut, and you too, Sven Estridsson. Come . . . a table has been prepared for us. My cooks have roasted an ox and my brewers have prepared fresh mead. Let us eat and drink and talk . . . This way.' He gestured towards the great oak table behind him. 'We thought of putting up a fine tent, befitting a talk between kings, but it is best to do this in the open, so that nothing is hidden and there can be no suspicion of treachery.'

The men took their places: the three Norwegians on one side of the table, the two Danes on the other. Food and drink was served and consumed. Magnus did not down as much of the sweet, deceptively potent mead as Harthacnut, but then few men did. It was the Norwegian, though, who began the negotiation.

'So, Harthacnut, you were the one who asked for this meeting . . . why?'

Harthacnut's mouth was full of ox meat. He took his time chewing, washed the remnant down by emptying his tankard of mead in a single draught, wiped the back of his hand across his mouth and said, 'Because I have better things to do than waste time, men and money on another pointless campaign against Norway. How old were you, Magnus, when my father sent yours into exile in the land of the Rus?'

'I was two. My first memories are all of Novgorod. I don't remember living in Norway before that at all.'

'I thought as much . . . Tell me, did your mother come with you?'

Magnus shook his head. 'No. She was a slave, belonging to my father's wife, Astrid. Hell would freeze over before Astrid would let her come to Novgorod.'

'Have you ever met her, since you came back?'

Magnus shook his head.

'So we know what that war cost you. Now let me tell you what I remember about those days. I was eight, living in England, when my father took me aside and said he was making me his regent in Denmark. I didn't really understand what that meant. I thought he just meant for a short while, you know. So I kissed my mother goodbye on the boat, just before it sailed, and I haven't seen her since that day. We have that much in common, Magnus: we were parted young from our mothers.'

'And our fathers are dead,' said Magnus. 'What sorry fellows we are!' he added with a self-mocking grin, and the atmosphere seemed to become a little more relaxed.

'Anyway,' continued Harthacnut, 'my father became King of

Norway, and then he lost the throne, and won it back, and lost it again.'

More mead had been poured into Harthacnut's tankard while he was talking. He swallowed some down and then said, 'And after all that, after all the pointless, futile bloodshed, and plotting, and changing sides, all those years of total confusion, where are we? Exactly where it started, with a Danish king in Denmark and a Norwegian king in Norway. So my suggestion to you, Magnus, is that we should keep it that way. You are young. You should be able to grow up in peace. Let's make a proper peace, and have done with the fighting.'

'How can I trust you?' Magnus asked. 'How do I know you're not deceiving me? Maybe what you really want is for me to lower my guard and think there's no need to prepare for war . . . and that's when you strike.'

'I say he's scared,' said Strongbow. 'All this talk of history, of fathers and sons, it's just shit. The truth is, if we fight him, he'll lose, and he knows it.'

'Maybe we should fight, Einar Eindridesson, just you and me,' Harthacnut suggested. 'If you stand as King Magnus's champion in a fight to the death, I will fight you. If you win, Magnus can have Denmark. If I win, I take Norway.'

'Harthacnut, be careful, this is the mead talking,' warned Sven Estridsson.

'No it isn't. I can hold my drink and I know what I am saying. This man says I'm a coward, a disgrace to my father. Well in that case, I should be easy to beat. Except that, oh yes, Einar, you're twice my age. And behind your back, people don't call you Strongbow any more. They call you Wobble-gut because of that big fat belly you've acquired since you became the king's right-hand man.'

'I'll fight you, don't you worry, and I'll beat you too,' said

Strongbow. 'I was killing men when you weren't even a gleam in your father's eye.'

'The decision is not yours, old man,' said Harthacnut. 'It's a matter for your king. So, Magnus, will you take my offer of peace, or would you rather stake your crown on a single fight?'

Magnus thought for a moment before he spoke. 'You don't expect me to say yes to that fight, do you, Harthacnut? You don't really want to risk your life, and, there's something else. I don't know for certain, but . . .' Magnus frowned and bit his lip in concentration, suddenly betraying his youth, 'I don't think you want to win the fight, either. I think you're telling the truth that you want to keep things as they are. But I reckon there's something else you're not telling us.'

'If there were, then obviously I'm not going to reveal what it is,' Harthacnut said, with a smile.

'Because you don't want the fight, whatever the outcome, maybe I should accept your challenge,' Magnus went on. 'In Novgorod, I was placed in the care of the Grand Prince Yaroslav the Wise. He taught me that when I was considering what to do, I should always choose the thing my enemy would least like. So that would be the fight.'

For a moment, Harthacnut thought that he really was about to find himself in a fight to the death. But then Magnus said, 'Still, there is a chance that you might win. Einar was a great fighter, but he is old and grey now, and if you beat him, that would be very bad for me. You may not want Norway, Harthacnut, but I do. So I say this. I will accept your call for peace on one condition. If one of us dies without a son to succeed him, then the other can take his kingdom.'

'But you are younger than me,' Harthacnut pointed out. 'You have a greater chance of living longer.'

'You are hardly an old man. You have plenty of time to find

a wife and produce an heir, and if you do, my claim will lapse. In any case, you will be dead, what do you care who rules Denmark?'

Harthacnut laughed. 'Not a jot.'

'So do we have an agreement?'

'Yes, we do. And if you have it drawn up, I'll sign it.'

'Very well, then . . . Please, have some more mead. And more mead for you, too, Einar Strongbow. You look as though you need it.'

News of the agreement spread throughout the camps on both sides of the river, and though there were some who felt deprived of the opportunity for slaughter and booty, there were many more who thanked God that they would be returning home safely to their farms, their fishing boats, their market stalls and their families.

Many hours later, as the Danes staggered back towards their tents, Sven Estridsson stopped, screwing his eyes tight as he attempted to still his swimming brain. 'Wait . . . wait.'

'What is it?' Harthacnut asked.

'This deal . . . you gave Magnus Denmark . . .'

'If I die before him and I don't have a son . . . only if I die.'

'But if you die . . .'

'And I don't have a son.'

'Right . . . if all that happens, *I* want Denmark. Don't want Magnus getting it. Want it for myself.'

Harthacnut put his hands on his friend's shoulders and looked him directly in the eye. 'I told that Norwegian brat he could have the throne. Didn't say he could keep it. You want it, kill him and take it.'

Estridsson thought and nodded. 'Very well . . . One other thing, though. What's the real reason you don't want Norway?'

Harthacnut smiled. 'Simple. All these years my mother has been writing to me, begging me to join her and take England away from Harold fucking Harefoot. I've decided it's time I went and did it.'

'So you want to be King of England, like your father?'

'That's right, Sven . . . that's exactly what I want.'

Christmas came, and New Year too, and then the weeks of feasting gave way to months of cold grey skies, the land rock-hard with frost, when it wasn't deep in snow. In February, two groups of clerics travelled from their respective parishes in Kent to Oxford, for the King of England was residing there and they wished to plead their cases to him. To plead them exhaustively, and at great length . . .

'And so, to conclude, Your Majesty,' said the priest who had been speaking for what seemed an eternity.

The young man with the crown on his head coughed, as he had done repeatedly throughout the monk's speech, reached for his goblet of wine (again, a much-repeated gesture) and muttered, 'About time.'

The priest continued, 'I have demonstrated both by the legal principle of *uti possidetis*, or "as you possess, so you may continue to possess", and by the established weight of precedence in royal judgments on similar issues that the port of Sandwich and the duties raised therefrom are lawfully the property of Christ Church, Canterbury, and that there is no merit to any claim to the contrary, even from an institution as eminent as St Augustine's Abbey. I might also add . . .'

'Must you?'

'. . . that since your gracious father King Canute donated the body of St Mildred to St Augustine's, the revenue generated by the abbey from the pilgrims travelling from all parts of Christendom to visit this famous relic means that the abbey simply does not need the money from Sandwich in the way that our church does. I hope you will recognise the merit in the case that I have put to you and give your judgment accordingly.'

'Go ahead, take it, I couldn't give a damn either way,' slurred Harold Harefoot. 'Stuck inside all day when I could be out hunting. Perfect weather for it, too.'

'What the king means,' said his mother, Elgiva of Northampton, who was seated at his right hand, 'is that he thanks you for your evidence, Father Osmond, and looks forward to hearing the case for St Augustine's prior to making his judgment.'

She spoke in a sharp, decisive voice that cut through Harold's drunken babbling. A portly fifty-year-old man with a ruddy complexion owed in equal parts to fresh English air and strong English mead was sitting to the king's left. He nodded in approval at Elgiva's words and murmured, 'Hear, hear.' Leofric, Earl of Mercia, was the effective ruler of a great swathe of the Midlands, from the Welsh border right across to the Wash. In the months following King Canute's death, he had been the strongest advocate of Harold's claim to the succession, and he remained loyal to both the king and his mother, for all Harold's manifest failings. It was a simple matter of honour: he had pledged himself to Harold Harefoot, and he would not go back on his word.

The fourth member of the council hearing cases in Oxford that day had a rather more flexible, or perhaps just realistic, approach to life. Godwin, Earl of Wessex, was as powerful in the south and west of England as Leofric was in its centre. Now he leaned across to Elgiva and hissed, 'For God's sake, woman, can't you keep your son under control? You worked hard enough to put the crown on his head. It won't stay there much longer if he carries on like this.'

'And who is going to take it off him precisely?' she shot back. 'Make the best of it, Godwin, he's the only king you've got.'

Godwin had to admit that Elgiva might be a conniving termagant, but she was right. Harold was the only man in

England with even a pretence of royal blood in his veins. There had been a time when Emma had the chance to put her son on the throne, and he had done everything he could to help her. But if Harthacnut chose to sit on his arse in Denmark, when England was his for the taking, then he didn't deserve to be king. If that ever changed, Godwin would have to reconsider his position, but for now, he was stuck with Harold. What was it that monk had said, something about 'as you possess'? Well, Harold possessed the throne and would continue to do so until further notice.

Godwin felt the jab of a sharp female elbow in his ribs and was jolted back to the matter at hand: the allocation of the revenues of the port of Sandwich. The abbot of St Augustine's was now stating his case, with just as much long-winded legal nonsense as the man from Christ Church. In his drunken, pig-ignorant way, Harold had actually been right. This was a waste of time, and it would be far simpler if these two greedy, pampered men simply rolled up their sleeves and fought to see who got the damn money, as any real man would.

'. . . and with that, I rest my case,' the abbot eventually said.

Harold was slumped insensible on the table. It was left to Elgiva, who had virtually assumed the role of regent, to thank the two plaintiffs and announce that the council would now be retiring to consider its judgment.

She waited until the warring clerics and their retinues had left the chamber and then shook her son's shoulder. 'Get up, Harold!' she snapped.

The king did not move.

'I said get up!' Elgiva repeated, and then muttered, 'You really are going too far.'

Harold groaned and made a feeble, unsuccessful effort to get to his feet.

Godwin saw that there was nothing for it but to deal with

the king like any other drunk. He stood up, made his way past Elgiva to the throne, grabbed Harold under the armpits and pulled him to his feet. 'Up you get,' he said.

'Unhand the king!' Leofric blustered.

Godwin shrugged and let go. Harold slumped back into his chair and fell forward again on to the table.

'Can you stand, sire?' Leofric asked.

Harold did his best. He pushed his body up from the tabletop and scrabbled for purchase with his feet, but then he was seized by a convulsive bout of coughing and dropped back down again.

Now Elgiva's voice was that of an anxious mother. 'Harold . . . ?'

Godwin sighed. Protocol be damned, the drunken sot wasn't going to get up by himself. He lifted the king's upper body off the table again, taking the weight of it in one arm as he pressed his other hand against Harold's brow. It was burning hot, and wet with sweat. It wasn't alcohol that had done that to him.

'He's got a fever,' Godwin said. 'We'd better get him to his bed.'

Then he looked down at the table and saw, glinting back up at him, the reflective crimson surface of a drop of blood, about as wide as a silver penny piece. Harold was very ill indeed, or perhaps someone had poisoned him. Either way, thought Godwin, it could soon be time to start looking for another king.

2

The North Sea

It had taken Harthacnut three months to send word to his sea captains and bring them all together in one place. Finally he could begin the voyage that he planned would end in the reclaiming of the English throne as his father's rightful heir. He sailed from Roskilde, north through the Øresund straits, across the shallow, treacherous waters that separated the Danish heartlands from his territories on the southern shorelines of Sweden and Norway, then around the Jutland peninsula and into the North Sea. Behind his flagship stretched more than sixty ships, a fleet as large as any that had been assembled since the days when the Danes were the most feared of all the Viking raiders who preyed upon the east coast of England, from the holy island of Lindisfarne in the north right down to the Kentish ports in the south.

Harthacnut, however, was not going to raid or pillage, but to recover what was rightfully his. To that end, as the fleet sailed down the west coast of Denmark, he ordered the bulk of his ships to go no further, but to anchor in the sheltered waters of the Heligoland Bight, while he went ahead to Bruges to see his mother. She knew England, its people and the nobles who would have to be won over, whether by the strength of his claim or the brute force of arms. He was all too aware that he could not afford to fail. As he told Sven Estridsson: 'My half-brother Alfred failed to unseat Harold, and ended up dumped in the Ely marshes with his eyes gouged out. I won't make the same mistakes he did. If anyone ends up dead, it will be Harold, not me.'

Harthacnut left Estridsson in the still waters, awaiting his signal to sail for England, while his flagship and the small flotilla accompanying it made for the open sea. Now they were a few leagues off the Frisian coast, and the last rays of the sun were narrow shafts of gleaming gold against the massed ranks of grey and black thunderclouds that were bearing down out of the north-west, all the way from Greenland and the icy wastelands of the far north.

The cloud mass marching across the sky looked as solid and overwhelming as an avalanche. Harthacnut had seafaring in his blood and had been accustomed since he was a little boy to rough seas, crashing waves and whipping winds that lashed the salt spray like a whip against his skin, yet he had never seen anything quite like this.

'Thor's hammer is hard at work tonight,' said his skipper, Rörik Ingesson, for a century or more of Christianity had merely overlaid the myths and legends with which Norsemen had been raised since time out of mind, like flimsy clothes over a strong, healthy body.

The wind seemed to rise suddenly and the sun disappeared completely behind the clouds. As rain began to fall, and lightning bolts flashed white light across the dark skies, the banshee scream of the wind in the rigging blended in a deafening cacophony with the pounding rumble of oncoming thunder. Harthacnut had to shout to make himself heard. 'So what are you going to do?'

Ingesson was a massive man, barrel-chested and thick-bearded. Aboard his own ship he did not bow his head or bend his knee to any man, no matter what their rank. He saw no need to reply to his king, but instead shouted out, 'Lower the sail and bind it tight! Stow the oars and make sure they're properly tied down! Anything else that's loose, stow it or tie it. Helmsman, keep the wind at your back!'

The crew, a mongrel band of Danes, Saxons, Icelanders and island men from Shetland and Orkney, busied themselves with his orders. To an untrained eye, their movements as they dashed about the long, slender ship might have seemed chaotic. But Ingesson knew what he was watching, and he satisfied himself that all was being done as he would like before he turned back to Harthacnut and said, 'There's only one thing to do: run with the storm as best we can.' He looked up at the sky. 'That wind's going to drive us down towards the coast. You know as well as I do what the waters off Frisia and Holland are like. If we're lucky, we'll find a safe anchorage. If we're not, we'll hit a sandbank and founder, and we'll all be thanking Thor in person for the storm.'

'Then I shall pray to God Almighty to deliver us from the old gods' evil.'

'Pray to whoever you like, sire. None of them'll be able to hear you.'

Then the full force of the storm hit, and Harthacnut understood why his forefathers had worshipped a storm god wielding a war hammer, for this was a brutal, punishing, battering blow. The wind tore at the mast, whistling and screaming as it sought to grip the slender shaft of pine and rip it from its mount. The waves picked up the ship and hurled it down into the depths of the ocean. They threw themselves over the gunwales and crashed on to the deck, drenching the ship and everyone on it in freezing water. Harthacnut found a good strong rope and clung to it with all his might. His palms were rubbed raw and bloody. He lost all feeling in his frozen fingers. He was no longer a king bound on a great enterprise, but simply a weak and helpless mortal, no better than any other and no more powerful in the face of forces entirely beyond his command.

Somehow, amidst the chaos, Rörik Ingesson was able to keep his wits about him. He prowled the boat from stem to stern, delivering an encouraging slap on the back here, a growl of displeasure there, or joining the men in their unceasing struggle against the elements. He was with a gang of men using wooden buckets to gather up the water that was steadily accumulating within the open hull when the ship suddenly lurched around, so that instead of running with the wave, it had slewed side-on. Harthacnut looked around and saw that the great steering oar, with which all longboats were guided, had been wrenched from the helmsman's hands by the sheer power of wind and water pushing against it, so that it was pointing out to the side of the boat rather than trailing behind it. The helmsman was desperately trying to regain control, but the oar refused to respond, no matter how hard he tried to pull it round and turn the ship back into line with the wind.

The ship was perched on the crest of a massive wave. Below it the water fell away like a precipitous hillside, and Harthacnut could not stop himself from shouting out in alarm, for they had ridden over the top of the wave and were now sliding down that black mass of furious water, plunging helplessly to the bottom. A figure raced down the deck, hurdling the oarsmen's benches as he dashed towards the stern. It was Rörik. He grabbed the terror-stricken helmsman and threw him so hard out of the way that he crashed into the gunwale on the far side of the boat, only saving himself from toppling into the raging sea by grabbing a rope and hanging on for dear life.

Rörik wasn't watching his crewman's struggles. He had clasped the steering oar in his huge hands and was throwing himself into battle against the gods of the storm and the sea. Harthacnut could not see the veins standing out like thick cords on Rörik's neck and forehead, but somehow he could almost feel the strain of the effort his captain was making, the tearing pain in the muscles of his arms, back and thighs; could almost hear the curses Rörik was shouting into the howling wind and stinging rain as he defied the elements to do their worst.

But still they were sliding to the bottom of the watery ravine, and still the ship was side-on to the fall, her mast swinging in an arc from the sky down towards the sea as the hull rolled over.

And still Rörik could not bring the oar round.

Harthacnut was struggling to keep his balance as the wooden deck tilted over, further and further. 'Come on!' he screamed at Rörik, though his captain could not hear him.

The roll became even more pronounced.

Harthacnut watched in impotent terror as seawater poured over the side of the submerged gunwales and flooded into the boat. It was only a matter of seconds before the ship capsized and they were all drowned as the wave crashed down upon them.

And then he felt something beneath his feet, as though the whole hull was shuddering and groaning. He looked back at Rörik and saw that the captain had somehow managed to bring the steering oar back under control. But the ship, half filled with water and as beaten down by the sheer effort of staying afloat as any of the men inside it, couldn't seem to find the means to respond.

Now the look on Rörik's face changed. He was no longer screaming at his nemesis, but coaxing the ship he loved, pleading with it, charming it, begging it to heed his commands. And slowly it responded.

Harthacnut watched as the bow swung round just a little. But they were almost at the bottom of the wave. High above their heads, a great overhang of water was blotting out the sky as it curled and foamed.

'Turn!' he screamed. 'In the name of God, turn!'

And the ship did turn. The bow picked up pace as it swung

around, and the mast came back up towards the vertical. The ship was almost straight, almost upright . . .

And then it reached the bottom of the wave, and everything that was above it, a great mountain of icy water, crashed down.

Harthacnut had taken as deep a breath as he could when he saw that the sky had completely disappeared behind the wave. But the sheer weight of the impact drove all the air from his lungs. Down and down the ship kept going, deeper and deeper into the water. Every instinct told him to let go of the rope to which he was clinging and try to kick for the surface, but he forced himself to hold on, for he knew that it would be impossible to tell which way was up in the maelstrom of churning water. And even if he did, by some miracle, make it to the surface, he had no hope of surviving as a man alone on the ocean. For better or worse, he had to stay with the ship.

But the vessel was still diving down and Harthacnut's lungs were screaming for air, and now the voices in his head were begging him to do the natural thing: to breathe out the last gasps of stale gas and then breathe in and fill his chest with clean, fresh air. But there was no air, just water. He forced himself to keep his mouth shut, but the pain was unbearable and the need to breathe an insatiable craving, and it took every last shred of his willpower to do nothing, to have faith, to pray for deliverance and believe that it would be granted.

And then the descent stopped. An instant later, the ship started rising again, back up through the freezing wet blackness, and the water seemed to slide away as the wave completed its passage overhead, and the tip of the mast poked through the surface of the North Sea and kept going, and suddenly the longboat popped back up on to the surface. Rörik was still at the helm, a look of mad, berserker triumph on his face. Harthacnut was still hanging on to his rope, and his mouth was wide open as he sucked rain-drenched air into his lungs. All around him men were coughing and spluttering and pulling themselves to their feet. And then Harthacnut realised that the wind had dropped a little and the waves, though far from calm, were no longer quite so mountainous.

Rörik ordered the sail to be unfurled just enough to get the ship moving so that he could steer properly, and he guided it into the partial shelter of a coastal inlet. He ordered the anchor to be dropped and then, once the ship had come to rest, called for food and drink to be distributed to his crew. Harthacnut made do with the same stale, salt-water-soaked bread and smoked fish as everyone else, then collapsed exhausted on to the sodden deck: just one more body among many.

He woke to the first light of dawn as the sun rose into cold blue skies, casting a burning path of light across a sea as flat and smooth as glass from Constantinople. He counted nine other boats bobbing on the water close by. Three had clearly been dismasted, and all were visibly battered to a greater or lesser degree, yet all had survived.

It seemed to Harthacnut that his expedition had been tested with brutal severity, yet it and he had passed that test. God had brought him safe through the storm, and that surely was a sign of His favour.

'How soon can you be ready to sail?' he asked Rörik Ingesson.

'Ready now,' said the captain. 'The day I'm not'll be the day they put me and my ship on the pyre and burn us both.'

'Then set a course for Bruges. Any of the others that are fit to sail can come with us. The rest can make their repairs and join us later.'

More than three years had passed since the messenger had arrived at Harthacnut's court bearing a letter from his mother begging him to come to her aid. He'd kept her waiting long enough. It was time she received his answer.

3

Oxford and Coventry

Harold Harefoot lay in bed, feebly coughing his lifeblood away, his body racked with pain, his skin hot and feverish. Leofric spoke to one of the monks attending to the king and satisfied himself that His Majesty was sure to be dead by morning. Since there was nothing to be done and Leofric had vital interests to attend to, he decided to be on his way.

Godwin rushed out after him into the corridor.

'You can't go – not now!' he hissed.

'I most certainly can,' Leofric replied, wishing that just for one instant Godwin could allow himself to be guided by something other than his insatiable ambition. 'I have matters of my own to deal with.'

Godwin looked at him with the suspicion that hung around him like mist on a mountaintop. 'What kind of matters?' he asked.

'The kind that are none of your damn business!' Leofric snapped. 'Not everyone spends their entire lives thinking about their self-advancement, you know. Some of us have other things on our minds than conspiring over the fate of the crown.'

Godwin said nothing.

Leofric laughed. 'You took that to mean the exact opposite of what I said, didn't you? I can see it on your face. You think that conspiracy is precisely what I have on my mind. Well I won't waste my time trying to prove you wrong. My view of the succession, if you must have it, is that there is no rush. The country has been governed perfectly well by a council acting on behalf of a king who might as well not have been there. By tomorrow morning, he *won't* be there. No one will notice the difference for a good while yet.'

'Someone has to be king,' Godwin insisted.

'Don't be tempted to think that someone is you, Wessex. I will tolerate you as my rival, but not as my monarch.'

'So who will you tolerate?'

'I have yet to decide. We can reconvene in due course and discuss who has the best claim on the throne. Until then, I'd rather be left in peace.'

Godwin said nothing, but clearly he had not been mollified.

Leofric gave a frustrated sigh. 'If you absolutely have to communicate with me, I will be at Coventry. Send a messenger there.'

'Coventry?' Godwin frowned. 'Where's that?'

'North of Warwick, barely an hour's ride. Not much of a place. There are about seventy families there, most of them tenants of mine, and an old convent that Canute's men razed to the ground the year he became king.'

'But there's something there that's more important to you than the death of the king.'

Leofric shrugged and let a moment's silence fall. 'Now, if you'll excuse me, I'll be off,' and he walked past Godwin and away down the passage without saying another word.

Godwin spent the next few hours pacing up and down the chamber where the king lay, trying to work out what Leofric was up to. His restlessness disturbed Elgiva, who left, telling him that she was going outside, and damn the weather, but would be back soon. 'Stay with my boy,' she pleaded. 'Stay in his hour of need.'

'Don't worry, I'll stay here for him,' Godwin assured her,

and he might actually have done so had a messenger not burst into the chamber and, still breathless from his journey, gasped, 'I must speak to you, my lord!'

'How dare you? Can't you see that the king is gravely ill?'

'But my lord, the lady Gytha commanded me that I must speak to you the moment I saw you.'

Godwin fell silent. His wife Gytha understood power politics and the cold, ruthless calculations that it demanded as well as any woman in Christendom. If she wanted him to hear something, it had to be important. 'Come with me,' he said and led the messenger out of the chamber.

'Godwin?' croaked Harold.

But the earl paid him no heed as the bedchamber door slammed shut behind him.

'What is it, then?' he asked, when he and the messenger were alone.

'My lady Gytha wishes you to know that she has heard from a Danish merchant to whom she was selling a dozen female slaves – at a good price, she said – that King Harthacnut of Denmark has set sail with a huge fleet, bound for England.'

That complacent old fool, Leofric! Godwin thought. Of course Harthacnut was bound to make a move. There was not a second to waste.

'When will the Danes reach our shores?' he asked.

'I do not know, my lord,' the messenger replied. 'It seems the king is not coming directly to England, but going first to Flanders to meet his mother.'

Godwin felt the first shock of alarm recede a little within him. 'He can't possibly know . . .' he muttered to himself.

'I'm sorry, my lord?'

'Nothing . . . Let me think.'

Godwin paced the corridor, trying to keep his thoughts as measured as his footsteps. There had not been time for the news that Harold was ill to reach Denmark, still less that he was dying. That mean that Harthacnut had struck lucky. He had finally answered his mother's call just at the point when the throne was about to fall empty. The question was: how should Godwin respond?

His half-brother died because of me, he reminded himself . . . but Harthacnut never even met Alfred; why would he care about that? Because Emma will ram it down his throat and tell him to take his revenge for her sake.

Godwin needed to make it worth Emma's while to put her anger and grief to one side. He thought a moment longer. Yes, I can do that . . . but I'll need Leofric.

He turned back to the messenger. 'Thank my lady for telling me about Harthacnut. Inform her that I am going to meet Leofric of Mercia at a village called Coventry, north of Warwick. Got that?'

'Yes, my lord.'

'And one other thing. Lady Gytha and I are constructing a ship, intended for our own use. Would you please tell my lady that she may be as lavish as she wishes when commissioning the gold work. When I am done, we shall not have any difficulty affording it.'

The storm that hit the North Sea with such untamed savagery had fallen upon Oxford too. It was more than matched by Elgiva's rage. In the middle of the night, driven half mad by maternal grief and frustrated ambition, she walked outside into the rain, the wind and the lightning and screamed at the heavens. For Harold's life was ebbing away while he was barely a full-grown man, just as his elder brother Sweyn's had done four years earlier. And as heartbroken as she was to be losing her boy, she was equally enraged by the realisation that her power in the land would perish along with him. She had no more pieces left on the chessboard, but Emma still had two to play: Harthacnut and Edward.

Damn her! Damn her to hell!

Elgiva walked back inside the royal residence. It was a solid place, built of stone and strong enough to withstand a small-scale assault, though it was neither large enough to be classed as a proper castle nor luxurious enough to be called a palace. Still, it was grander and better staffed than any house Elgiva had known before she caught Canute's eye, and she had little chance of living in anything half as nice once her connection to the throne was gone.

But maybe, even now, there was hope. Godwin had toyed with the suspicion that Harold might have been poisoned, but although Elgiva was cynical enough to suspect foul play in most circumstances, she could not detect it in this one. The question one always had to ask was *Cui bono?* Who stands to gain? There was only one person who would benefit sufficiently from Harold's death to make it worth their while to kill him, and that was Emma. But she was in Flanders and had no ally in England willing to commit murder on her behalf. In any case, it wasn't her style. For all her hunger for power, Emma lacked that final touch of ruthlessness necessary to seize it. Elgiva had no such scruples. That was why it was her son who had inherited Canute's kingdom, and not Emma's.

So Harold's affliction was a matter of sickness, and that was a mysterious internal combat between a man and the invisible demons that assailed him. Sometimes God saw fit to cast the demons out and the sufferer lived. But He might equally well decide that the time had come to call a soul from this world to the next, in which case all the poultices, leeches and herbal concoctions administered to the patient would make no difference. If God had decided to take Harold from her, there was nothing to be done but pray for the poor, drunken, useless lad's soul. But there was still a chance that the Father might show mercy, and Elgiva paused for a minute to finger the rosary that hung around her neck and pray for her son's deliverance.

Alas, her prayers were in vain. When she returned to the chamber where Harold lay, she found a priest saying prayers over his body. And then Elgiva's knees gave way and she fell to the floor, sobbing. Her son had died and she had not been there to comfort him in those final moments, any more than she had comforted his brother. She had failed them both, and for the first time in her adult life she found herself wondering whether she had done the right thing, working so hard to drag herself from provincial nonentity to lie in the bed of a king and stand beside a nation's throne. Perhaps she would have been better off staying where she was, marrying a local nobleman – for her father was a respected landowner and would have given her a decent enough dowry to make her worth marrying (her looks and healthy carnal appetites had always been enough to get her bedded) – and settling down to life in the shires.

But that had not been her fate, nor had she wished it to be, and it was too late to start complaining now. She pulled herself to her feet. She needed to talk to Godwin. He would have good, sound advice about how she should position herself to survive the next few months. Even if she was no longer queen mother, she still had the fortune and landholdings she had amassed over the years as Canute's mistress. Emma would not have forgotten the way Elgiva and Harold had stripped her of much of her fortune (though God knows it had been so vast that even a fraction of it was enough to make her rich). She would want her revenge, but Godwin would know how to outwit her.

Elgiva stalked the residence trying to find her ally, even looking in the kitchens and stables before she accepted he was gone.

Of course he's left; how could I ever have been foolish enough to believe he'd stay? she told herself, shaking her head at her own naivety. Godwin had grown up in the reign of King Ethelred. When Ethelred had been defeated, he had made himself the indispensable servant of his conqueror, Canute, winning his earldom and helping Emma run the country when Canute was engaged elsewhere in his empire. Then Canute died, so Godwin had dropped Emma and taken his place alongside Elgiva as the power behind Harold's throne.

'And now you've gone to find your next master, haven't you?' Elgiva muttered. Oh yes, Godwin of Wessex would do very nicely for himself, whichever of Emma's boys took the crown, but he'd have no more time for Elgiva of Northampton.

Why would you? she thought, bitterly. I've run out of sons.

Leofric and a handful of his retainers had ridden through the storm to Banbury, slept there and then headed on to Coventry, where he and his men passed another night. Now he was standing in the ruins of the old convent chapel. An altar had been erected there, two of his tenant farmers drafted as witnesses and his personal priest summoned to read the rites. For today was Leofric, Earl of Mercia's wedding day. To his great surprise and overwhelming delight, for he had thought that such happiness could never again enter his life, he had fallen in love with the widow of a local landowner, and she with him. As he looked on her lovely, gentle face and thought of the body that lay hidden beneath her wedding gown, a paradise that would be his to plunder when he took her to bed this night, his heart and manhood both swelled. He pledged himself to her, and she to him, and then both of them joined in a shared vow: that they would give thanks to God for their love by funding the building of a new monastery on the site of the convent, whose future prosperity would be guaranteed by the rents and tithes from local estates donated by the newly married couple. It was a magnificent act of charity, and both the vicar and the witnesses were effusive in their praise for the plans.

The congratulations, however, were disturbed by the clattering of horses' hooves on stone. Leofric turned to see a dozen men-at-arms with a familiar figure at their head. There were shouts and curses as his own men drew their swords and hurried to their master's side. Leofric held up a hand to calm them, then looked up at Godwin. 'So now you know my business. This is my wedding day.'

For once, Godwin was at a loss for words. 'I . . . I . . . I apologise, Leofric, and to you, my lady. I had no idea . . .'

He dismounted and walked towards Leofric, his hand outstretched. 'Many congratulations. Please forgive me.' He gave a nod of the head to the bride.

Leofric seemed content that his honour had been satisfied. 'Godwin,' he said, 'may I present my wife Godiva, the new Countess of Mercia. My dearest, this is Godwin, Earl of Wessex.'

'I am honoured to meet you, my lord,' she said, in a soft, low voice.

'The honour is entirely mine, Lady Godiva,' said Godwin, taking her hand while making no effort whatever to hide the frank appreciation with which his eyes were taking in her beauty. 'But now, I must beg your forgiveness too. I must speak with your husband. It is a matter of the gravest importance.'

Godwin drew Leofric to one side and told him the news that Harthacnut was en route to Bruges to rendezvous with his mother. 'We both stand to lose by this,' he pointed out. 'Emma wants my balls on a plate for handing her boy Alfred over to Harold.'

'Well I had nothing to do with that sordid business,' said

Leofric. 'I was away on the Welsh marches, keeping that savage Gruffydd ap Llywelyn at bay.'

'I understand that, and the price you have paid to keep our western border safe,' said Godwin sympathetically, for he knew that barely six months had passed since Leofric's brother Edwin had died fighting the Welsh. 'But Emma has been away. She neither knows nor cares about any of that. The only thought that will be in her head is that you allied with Elgiva to promote Harold's claim to the throne over Harthacnut's.'

'Harold was in the damn country!' Leofric protested. 'For all I knew, Harthacnut might have been an even greater monarch than his father, but he was in Denmark and we needed a King of England. What else was I supposed to do?'

'I take your point. In fact, I made it, repeatedly, to Emma at the time. But it means nothing now because Harthacnut is not in Denmark. He's on his way to Flanders and from there he'll come to England with an army at his back. What chance do we have of raising an English army to face him when he gets here?'

'None,' said Leofric bluntly.

'I agree. And if he becomes king by conquest, then you and I can expect to have our titles, our lands and probably our lives taken from us. You're a lucky old dog, Leofric. You've found yourself a beautiful young wife. Do you want to make a widow of her so soon after the wedding?'

'Of course not!'

'Then we have to find a way to win Harthacnut and Emma over, so that they see us as allies not enemies.'

'How in God's name do you propose to do that?'

'I'm not yet sure,' said Godwin. 'But one thing I do know. If we are to have any chance at all, we have to get to Harthacnut before he sets foot on English soil.'

'Will he speak to us?'

'It's more a matter of "Will she let him speak to us?"'

Godwin said. He paused for a moment, lost in thought, and then smiled. 'You know, I may have a way past Emma. From what I hear, Harthacnut's closest friend is my wife's nephew, Sven Estridsson. He may be able to make his young master see sense. In any case, we must leave at once.'

'But my wedding night . . .' Leofric protested, appalled at the sacrifice he was being asked to make.

Godwin gave him a sympathetic shrug. 'I would feel the same way if I were in your shoes,' he said. 'But think of how many more nights will be yours to enjoy if we manage to pacify our new king and king mother.'

Leofric thought for a moment, shaking his head. Then he gave a long, regretful sigh and walked back to his wife. 'My dear, there's been a change of plan . . .'

4

Bruges

A tall, broad-shouldered man stood outside the door of one of the Flemish capital's most imposing houses. His hair and beard were a reddish golden colour, as were his eyebrows, which seemed fixed in a permanent frown, for his forehead was strong, his brow heavy and his blue eyes slightly sunken. His complexion looked ruddy and healthy enough, and it would have taken close examination to see the network of veins that was just becoming visible on his cheeks: the sign of a heavy drinker.

He knocked once, hard, and a few moments later the door opened and a woman peered round it to see who was standing there. She had to tilt her head up to look at the man as he told her, 'Please fetch Queen Emma. Tell her that her son is here.'

The woman scurried away at once, thrilled by what she had heard, for she knew that the queen had spent many months hoping for her son to pay her a visit. With each passing day, Her Majesty's melancholy had deepened, and her staff had begun to fear for her well-being. But this good news seemed to lift Queen Emma instantly from gloom to manic excitement, for she did not instruct her servant to let the visitor in but flew past her in a whirl of woollen skirts and linen veil.

The visitor, who had been expecting to see the servant return, was surprised to be greeted by a tall woman who still possessed the faded remnants of what had been a spectacular, regal beauty. 'Mother?' he asked, uncertainly, for he had not seen Queen Emma since he was a small boy.

She screwed up her eyes and held a hand horizontally to her forehead, for the sun was shining upon the house and casting a golden aura around the visitor while leaving his face in deep shade. 'Alfred, is that you?' she asked. 'Oh, my darling boy, you came back to me, my darling, darling boy.'

As she took him in her arms, the visitor spoke in a puzzled, hurt tone. 'No, Mother, it's me: Harthacnut.'

When Count Baldwin, the ruler of Flanders, heard about Harthacnut's arrival in Bruges, he at once sent word to Emma's house insisting that the king should be a guest at his castle and offering him the use of the chamber in which King Henry of France had once stayed. Emma understood that this was as much a command as an invitation. She might want to keep the son she had not seen in thirteen years under her own roof, but a visit by a reigning monarch was a significant event, and Baldwin would naturally want to be seen to be a good host.

'I hope you have a hearty appetite,' Emma said to Harthacnut. 'He will want to lay on a great feast for you, and the Flemish love their food.'

'Oh you need not worry about that, Mother,' her son replied. 'I'll match them course for course and tankard for tankard. And I'll be the last one standing.'

As one night followed another, with a more splendid spread on each occasion, Harthacnut's ability to down his food and hold his drink greatly impressed his fellow diners. He seemed to them to be a hearty, good-humoured young man, and this, combined with the reputation for grace and charity that his mother had already established, made him a popular addition to Bruges society.

When Godwin, Leofric and their men arrived in the city, they immediately made their way to the castle to pay their respects to

Baldwin. The throne of England lacked an occupant, and such a vacancy was liable to make men greedy and reckless. Godwin wanted a king on that seat as soon as possible, and what was more, a king he could rely upon to heed, or preferably obey, his counsel. He had spent the past three reigns placing himself at the heart of the kingdom's affairs. Now he planned to surround himself with his sons, so that it mattered not who supposedly ruled the country; the Godwin clan would always remain in power.

If Leofric sensed, let alone feared, Godwin's ambitions, he gave no sign of it. He had other things on his mind. 'I reckon we sell 'em our wool too cheap,' he said, looking around at the magnificent town houses owned by the city's wool merchants, weavers and tailors. 'This lot live better than we do, that's for sure.'

Not better than me, thought Godwin, but he took Leofric's point. 'They're certainly making handsome profits, that's for sure. And it's your sheep and mine that are earning them. But we're not here to haggle over wool prices. Let's just make our introductions, and remember, there's no need to bow and scrape. A Flemish count is no more noble than a good English earl, and I don't care how fancy his city is, we've both got more land than he has.'

'And land is what matters,' Leofric agreed.

When the time came for their interview with Count Baldwin, the three men therefore greeted one another with respect, but without deference on either side.

'You're very welcome to stay here, and of course I would be honoured if you ate at my table,' Baldwin said. 'May I ask what brings you to Bruges?'

'We're here to talk to Harthacnut of Denmark,' said Leofric. 'We heard he had come here to, ah . . . to visit his mother.'

Baldwin smiled at the Englishman's clumsy, very Saxon attempt at subtlety.

'We recently heard of the death of King Harold. Naturally I offered King Harthacnut my deepest condolences at the passing of his half-brother. He seems to have taken the loss very well, I must say.'

'I'm sure he did,' said Godwin, 'and you will not need me to tell you why. Can you tell us where we might find him?'

'Yes, of course . . . There is an enclosed herb garden within the castle walls of which the king's mother, Lady Emma, is very fond, though it's rather bare at this time of year. I believe you'll find the two of them there. One of the servants can show you the way.'

They were shown to a wooden door, set into a high brick wall. Godwin opened it and led the way into the garden. Emma was standing just a few paces away and saw them at once.

'Godwin,' she said, flatly.

'My lady.'

'And Leofric, too. It's not often I've seen you two on the same side.'

She turned her head to look at a man a short distance beyond her. He was bent over an earthenware pot in which a thyme bush was growing, with his back towards them. 'There are two men here from England,' she said. 'I expect they've come to see you.'

'Your Majesty . . .' Godwin began, as the man straightened up, for there was only one person this could be. Then he stopped dead as for the first time he saw Harthacnut's face.

A smile that seemed almost triumphant flickered briefly on Emma's face. 'You see it, don't you, the resemblance? I knew I was right! The last time I saw Alfred, he was a very small boy, but a mother always knows.' She stepped close to Godwin. 'You must feel like you've just seen a ghost,' she whispered.

Godwin swallowed hard and went on, 'Your Majesty, I am Godwin, Earl of Wessex, and this is Leofric, Earl of Mercia.'

'Good day to you both,' Harthacnut replied. 'You look familiar to me, Godwin, from when I was a boy. Didn't you fight alongside my father in Denmark?'

'I did, sire. Your father was a great man and it was my honour to serve him. And if you'll forgive me, I remember you too, when you were that boy.'

Harthacnut grinned. 'You showed me your sword once. It still had bloodstains on it from the last battle you'd fought. I thought that was the most exciting thing I'd ever seen in my life.'

'I remember the occasion well,' Godwin said, though in truth he had nothing but the dimmest memories of a small, flaxen-haired boy getting under the soldiers' feet as his father insisted on taking him on campaign.

'Earl Godwin agrees with me that you look just like Alfred,' Emma said. 'Isn't that so, Godwin?'

'I really couldn't tell, my lady. I'm not that good at faces.'

'Come now, you know exactly what I mean. You saw Alfred in my son's face, and I pray for your sake that you felt even a shred of guilt or remorse when you thought of him, for I fear for your soul if you did not.' She looked again at Harthacnut. 'Earl Godwin helped murder your half-brother.' She frowned. 'I've probably told you that already . . .'

'I'm sure we all regret the fate that befell Alfred Atheling . . .' Leofric said, then fell silent as he realised that no one was paying any attention to him.

Things were not going the way Godwin had planned. He had expected that his part in Alfred's death would be an issue between him and Emma, but he had not anticipated that she would be so changed by grief that her once effortlessly regal demeanour would have become so brittle. He had a very strong sense that there were raging pent-up demons in her just waiting to be let loose. He looked across at Harthacnut, who was frowning, clearly displeased that his mother had been made unhappy. So now, though he was talking to Emma, Godwin aimed his words at the Danish king.

'I am truly sorry that Alfred died in the way he did. But he had been banished from England for life, and suddenly there he was, landing on the Kent coast with several ships filled with armed men. Any king would have seen him as a threat.'

That much was straightforward enough. No one could deny it. Godwin should have stopped there, he knew he should, and yet he could not prevent himself from adding, 'You must have known that, Emma, but you begged him to come to you anyway. His blood is on your hands too.'

The blood drained from Emma's face and she gave a little gasp of pain, almost as if she had been struck. At once, Harthacnut leaped to her defence.

'How dare you talk to my mother like that?' he snarled at Godwin. 'Is this your way of attempting to win my favour – accusing my mother of killing her own son?'

There was nothing to be gained by grovelling now, Godwin decided. He stood tall and looked Harthacnut straight in the eye. 'No, I'm not accusing anyone of anything. I'm simply being honest.'

'We had no idea that Harold could be so wantonly cruel,' Leofric said. 'He was an ignorant oaf, of course, that was obvious. But I for one had not understood that he was also a monster.'

'Nor had I,' said Godwin, grateful now for Leofric's support. 'If the king had asked me, I would have told him to imprison Alfred but to make sure he was well treated. He would have been a useful hostage, a bargaining chip in any negotiation with Normandy or even Denmark. Instead—'

'The boy was an idiot and his head was filled with malevolent demons, that's perfectly clear,' Leofric interrupted. 'But he's dead now, so there's no point going on about what did or did not happen in the past. We're here to talk about the future, and to offer you, King Harthacnut, the throne of England.'

The Earl of Mercia might not have been a subtle man, but there were times when his bluntness was more effective than any cleverly worded diplomacy, and this was one of them. All thought of Alfred was driven from everyone's minds. Even Emma's face suddenly snapped back to its usual cool composure.

Harthacnut was the first to react. 'Thank you, Earl Leofric, but why should I wait for you to offer me the throne when I can just go and take it for myself?'

'Because our offer gives you legitimacy. The English nobility choose their king – that's our custom. Of course, a king can seize the realm by conquest. But it's an exceptional man who can do that and then win the country over to his side.'

'My father did exactly that.'

'Yes, but he did not have to be asked to do it by his mother,' said Godwin. He suddenly felt very strongly that the crown should not be handed to Harthacnut on a plate. If he, Leofric and the other nobles were to have any power under this new king, then he had to feel beholden to them. He also had to respect them as men whose loyalty and respect needed to be earned. Godwin had thrown down a challenge. Now it was up to Harthacnut to respond.

For a moment it looked as though that response would be an outburst of rage. Godwin let his right hand hover over the pommel of his sword, just in case Harthacnut should go as far as violence. But the Dane controlled his temper and very calmly said, 'It's a foolish man who insults his future king.'

'It is an even more foolish man who chooses a king without testing his mettle first. If Earl Leofric and I are to go back and tell the English nobility that you should be their king, then I for one need to know that I am not saddling them with another

Harold Harefoot. From that, all else follows. If the people see that their lords have welcomed you, they will accept you far more readily than if you have laid waste to their farms and razed their towns to the ground. That is one reason why you should not take England by conquest. The other is purely practical: why shed a drop of blood, or pay a single soldier's wage, or risk defeat if you do not have to?'

'There is no risk. You would not defeat me,' Harthacnut said.

Godwin shrugged. 'Possibly not, but can you be certain? Far better to win everything without fighting a single battle.'

'And what do you expect in return?'

'Nothing.'

'Really? Nothing at all?'

'We simply want English customs to be respected and things to stay as they are,' said Leofric. 'Let us keep what we already have: our titles, our estates and the proper influence on the governance of the realm that has always been afforded to men of senior rank.'

Harthacnut shot a look at his mother. Godwin could see that he was desperate to ask her advice but clearly feared to do so in front of men who had already called him a mummy's boy. It was time to throw him a bone. 'What do you think, Emma?' Godwin asked. 'Is our offer a fair one?'

He knew that Emma would happily see him dead, that she would dance on his grave, that it would claw at her guts every time she saw him sitting on the king's council, or feasting at his high table. But he also knew what her reply would be.

'Yes,' she said, 'it is fair.'

For as Godwin well knew, Emma of Normandy had lived too long and suffered too much to let anything come between her and a return to power. Having twice been a king's consort, she would now be the king mother. She would place her signature on Harthacnut's decrees, just as she had done on Ethelred's and Canute's. She would take back the estates and gold and jewellery that Harold and Elgiva had seized when they ruled the land. She would endow monasteries and convents, and bask in the prestige that her acts of philanthropy would bestow upon her.

Now that the principal issue had been settled, conversation became more relaxed as they discussed the practical details of Harthacnut's arrival in England. This, it transpired, would take longer than Godwin or Leofric had imagined.

'I won't conquer England, but neither will I arrive unprotected,' Harthacnut insisted. 'My fleet will bring me to England, my men will accompany me on the march to London, and the people of England will pay the cost of maintaining my army in peacetime, or face the ruination that they would cause in war.'

'Are you sure that's wise?' Leofric asked. 'You will lose much goodwill if your very first act is to levy a tax.'

'Better than losing my life, as my half-brother did.'

'But sire . . .'

Godwin could see that Leofric was about to embark on his version of a debate, which was to repeat the same point again and again until his opponent agreed with him, if only to shut him up. He motioned to Emma to walk with him a little further into the garden. She followed him, but Godwin was painfully aware of the simmering tension within her. She might have accepted his presence as a necessary element in making Harthacnut king of England, but she was clearly a long way from forgiving him. Still, there were matters that had to be discussed.

'Your boy seems a strapping lad. Does he have a bride yet?'

'Not that I know of,' Emma replied grudgingly.

'Don't you think it's time that he did?'

'Once he is settled in England, yes.'

'We'll need an heir. Harold only cared about hunting and drinking. If he ever did take a woman to bed, he wasn't able to impregnate her. We don't want that happening again.'

'Give the boy time, Godwin. His father died before he could find him a suitable match. I was cut off for him from the time he was a small boy, so I couldn't help. Now that he has England, he'll be as good a match as any in Christendom. There'll be no shortage of kings and princes offering up their daughters. We'll find a girl to be his brood mare, don't you worry.'

'Make sure you do. I wouldn't want to see you driven out of England again, for want of a boy to wear the crown.'

'Wouldn't you now?' Emma looked Godwin up and down as if measuring him for his shroud. 'You're full of yourself, aren't you, Godwin? You think you can keep playing your little game and moving the pieces on the board, but it never occurs to you that you're just a piece in the game, too. And remember this: the knight and the castle are both strong. But neither is as mighty as the queen.'

5

Rouen

William's education, such as it was, had taken place at the ducal palace with two other boys connected to the House of Normandy. One was his closest friend William Fitzosbern, or 'Fitz' as William called him, the son of Osbern Herfastsson. The other was Guy of Burgundy, the younger son of Reginald, Count of Burgundy. His mother Alice had been the daughter of Duke Richard II, and had died when Guy was still a very small boy. His father, perhaps in consideration of his wife's heritage, or simply as a means of placing a piece of his own in the great game being played to gain control of the duchy, sent Guy to Normandy as the ward of his cousin, Gilbert of Brionne.

In any group of three children, one is likely to be the outsider, and so it was here, for Guy had never been as close to either of the two Williams as they were to each other. Still, there were some things on which they were all agreed. None of them, for example, had any enthusiasm for the Latin grammar that Brother Thorold tried to ram down their throats. But all three were equally happy when they could hurtle out of their classroom, through the palace's halls, along its corridors and cloisters and out into the stable yard, where they were given their lessons with the swords and bows that any Norman nobleman was obliged to master if he wished to shine as a huntsman or a warrior. So while Brother Thorold's greatest problem was keeping his pupils awake, their master-at-arms, Turkill, a leathery old veteran of the Norman militia, whose broken nose and scarred face testified to his presence on many a battlefield, was more concerned about calming them down.

Today they were working with swords. It was Turkill's habit to give them a decent period of supervised instruction and practice, followed by a series of fights in which they tried out what he had taught them on each other. True, the blades were made of wood rather than tempered steel, but that didn't stop the boys setting about one another with ferocious, bloodthirsty zeal.

The first bout was between William and Fitz. They had been fighting one another since they were barely more than toddlers, competing with that special intensity that boys reserve for their brothers and best friends. There was nothing to choose between the two of them, for each always knew exactly what the other was about to do.

'Concentrate, Fitz, come on!' Turkill shouted. 'You've got to pay attention all the time. How many times have I told you? It only takes a second to die! And William, vary your attack! You're too predictable.'

The old soldier was leaning on a hitching rail on one side of the yard. Next to him stood Osbern. The ducal council was in session, but he had taken a break to come and watch his son in action.

'You've got a good lad there, Osbern,' Turkill said. 'He'll go far, mark my words.'

'God willing.'

'Any news from the council?'

'Just the usual . . . Barons building castles without permission from the duchy, trying to take other men's land, going on raids, stealing property, raping women. Half the duchy's going up in flames if you believe what people are saying. Bishops complaining their estates are being wrecked. Farmers saying they won't be able to get their crops in if it's not safe to go outside.'

Turkill spat on the ground in front of him. 'This is what you get when there isn't a duke – I mean a strong, fully grown man – to keep everyone in order. I reckon this boy's got it in him. But will he get the chance, eh?'

'He will if I've got anything to do with it.'

Turkill turned his attention back to the boys. 'Right, that's enough! Now, Guy, were you paying attention to your pals' scrap?'

Guy was leaning against a wall several paces away. 'Of course,' he said, with a casual, almost dismissive shrug.

'Then please be good enough to tell me who you think won, and why. And stand up straight while you're doing it.'

William and Fitz both tensed as they waited to hear the verdict.

'Well, it was a close contest,' Guy said. 'Mostly because neither of them fought with any real style.'

'Hey! That's not true!' William protested.

'There's no need for that tone, Guy,' Turkill warned him. 'Just stick to the facts and tell me what you saw.'

'Very well, then, I saw William doing what he always does, which is just swinging his sword like a battleaxe, hoping he'd hit something but not really caring what it was. Fitzosbern isn't as strong as William but he did try to be a bit more clever, even if he wasn't always paying attention. So I give it to Fitzosbern.'

Again William complained. 'That's not fair! I hit Fitz much more often than he hit me.'

'No you didn't!' Fitz exclaimed.

'Enough!' Turkill shouted. 'Right, William, if you don't like Guy's decision, now's your chance to do something about it. You and him are up next.'

He glanced at Osbern. 'You staying for this?'

'Yes. I think the council has an interest in knowing how well our duke is progressing.'

'In other words, you've an excuse for staying out here a bit longer. Let's see if the boy makes it worth your while.'

William was still only twelve. Though he was well built and strong for his age, he was a shade smaller than Guy, who was already fourteen and had started to grow into his adult shape. He had a naturally athletic build, with broad shoulders that tapered to a lean waist and long legs. He was quick and light on his feet, and even though the longsword could never be described as a weapon that demanded subtlety or guile – for that one required a light-bladed scimitar such as the Moors wielded – still Guy was able to dart forward, launch a flurry of blows at William and then spring back, so that William's counter-thrusts hit nothing but thin air.

As ever, the two boys kept up a running, bantering commentary, though the atmosphere was becoming less light-hearted with every blow that Guy struck, and every taunt that he aimed at William.

'That Burgundian dances as prettily as a girl,' said Turkill, as Guy planted another pair of stinging blows on William's arms while escaping untouched himself.

Osbern looked distinctly unimpressed. 'You can't prance around like that on the battlefield. My money's on the duke . . . I never saw a lad who was readier for a fight.'

'Aye, he'll be right in the thick of it, every time. His men'll love him for that.'

Osbern grimaced. 'If he doesn't get himself killed first.'

'Well, no need to worry about that just yet.'

William hadn't been able to lay a single blow on Guy. The older boy moved so quickly that he could get inside William's defences and hit him before William could react at all. So far, Guy had only been striking him on his shoulders, arms and hands, but for all that it was made of wood, the sword was still hard enough to hurt, particularly when Guy hit him with the side of the blade. Three or four times William had wanted to cry out in pain, but each time he'd managed to stop himself. He wasn't going to give Guy that satisfaction, not when he already had that smug, superior look on his face, as if there was something special about being able to beat a smaller, younger boy.

There was more to it than that, though. As William grew older, he had come to understand that beneath Guy's friendship lay a streak of bitter resentment. William might be the Duke of Normandy, the son of the previous duke, directly descended from Rollo, the Viking raider who had founded the Norman dynasty, yet he was illegitimate, and as far as Guy was concerned, that made him unworthy to rule Normandy.

Only recently, Guy had raised the issue in the course of a scripture lesson, asking Brother Thorold, 'God wants men and women to marry before they have children, isn't that right?'

Thorold had of course understood at once what lay behind the apparently innocent question, and had seen from the red flush of anger and embarrassment colouring William's face that he knew what his classmate was up to as well. But as a man of the cloth, he had no option but to answer, 'Ideally, Guy, yes, He does. But He loves all of us equally, for we are all made in His image, no matter what our parentage.'

'Yes, but only the children of married parents are truly legitimate in the eyes of the Church,' Guy had persisted.

'Yes, I suppose so.'

'Doesn't that mean that a son isn't really his father's heir if his father and mother weren't married?'

'That's quite enough, Guy,' Thorold had snapped. 'Even if what you say is true, it is wrong to say things that are spiteful or malicious – wrong in God's eyes – and you would do well to remember that. You should also bear in mind that your grandfather, Duke Richard the Fearless, was not married to the late, beloved Lady Gunnor when your mother Alice was born. Nor were Richard the Fearless's parents married, for that matter. It is not something to celebrate, but one cannot ignore the fact that for generations, the dukes of Normandy have been the sons of concubines. Your argument, followed to its logical conclusion, robs you and every other living member of the House of Normandy of any claim to the duchy. Is that the point you were trying to make?'

'No,' Guy admitted. But even if he had lost the argument in class, still he clung to his conviction that by being the son of married parents, he was better than William, who was not. And the more he tried to rub it in, the more William felt the sting of being a bastard, felt his anger building inside him and grew ever more determined to face down and defeat anyone who threw that indignity in his face. So now, on the practice ground, he took Guy's blows without wincing or flinching, he controlled the rage that was building inside him, keeping it well hidden, and steadily he realised that he was getting his eye in. He could see Guy coming and anticipate what he was going to do.

As Guy attacked him again, William was about to parry his thrust but then stopped himself. No, he'd take another hit – it was only one more bruise, and that would soon heal – and let Guy believe that he was still incapable of serious resistance. And this time, when the sword smacked against his shoulder, William did wince and give a little cry of 'Ow!' – not too loudly, for the last thing he wanted was for Turkill to step in and stop the fight, but just enough to convince Guy that he was suffering.

Guy grinned. 'Do you want your mummy, cry-baby?' he taunted.

Then he attacked again, taking two quick, skipping steps towards William, up on his toes, with all his weight and momentum moving forwards. But this time, when Guy swung his sword, William wasn't there. Almost without Guy realising what was happening, William had stepped just enough to his left to evade the charge, so that Guy's sword flayed at thin air, and the lack of the usual solid contact caused him to lose his balance and stumble slightly.

That in turn made him reach out to steady himself, and in so doing he left his lower chest and belly exposed.

William put every bit of strength he had into his arms and shoulders as he brought his sword backhanded, edge-on, underneath Guy's flailing arms and straight into his stomach. The blow hit Guy just below the diaphragm, punching him harder than any fist had ever done, doubling him up and leaving him winded and gasping for air. He dropped his sword and hugged himself, moaning softly from the pain of the blow.

'Got you!' William exulted.

A couple of men-at-arms looking down from the castle walls cheered the blow, and Guy glanced up and shot them a murderous look.

'Right, lads . . .' said Turkill, pushing himself off the rail.

He was about to make his way into the centre of the yard, to talk to the two boys about what had just happened, for neither of them could afford to be caught the way Guy had just been, but Osbern put out a hand to stop him.

'Wait,' he said. 'I want to see what happens next.'

William was standing, sword still in hand, watching to see what Guy would do.

Guy straightened up, obviously still hurt, and staggered towards him. Somehow he managed to summon up something approaching a smile and even a chuckle as he said, 'Well done, Will . . . Your Grace . . . you really got me there. God above, I can barely walk . . .'

William relaxed and dropped his guard, grinning at his triumph.

Guy reached out with his right arm and laid it on William's shoulder, as if for support. Because he was still not standing straight, his head was level with William's, almost touching, and no one could hear what he said as he whispered, 'Have some of this, you little bastard.'

His swung his knee hard into William's crotch, catching him completely unawares. Now it was the duke who was doubled up in pain and Guy who was smirking.

Osbern could see that William was trying as hard as he could not to cry, visibly determined not to give Guy that satisfaction.

'Now?' Turkill asked.

'Wait,' Osbern replied.

It was then that William launched himself head first at Guy, as fast and true as a flaming arrow, tackling him around the waist and knocking him backwards on to the bare dirt floor of the yard.

Guy was left lying on his back, with William on top of him, raining down punches, so that he had to cross his arms above his face to stop himself being pummelled.

'Don't call me that!' William shouted.

'Bastard, bastard!' Guy replied in a singsong voice, laughing now because William simply wasn't strong enough to break down his defences and hurt him.

'Now,' said Osbern, 'I've seen enough. I have a meeting of the council to attend.'

As the steward strode away, Turkill made for the middle of the yard. 'Right, boys, that's enough,' he called out as he walked towards them. 'Get up, dust ourselves down, shake hands and then be friends again. I don't want any hard feelings.'

The two boys did as they were told, but their handshake was grudging, with sulky looks and muttered curses.

'Moody little beggars, aren't you?' Turkill said. 'But you can forget about that now, because we've got work to do. Guy, don't you dare let anyone under your guard like that again. If that had been a real sword, he'd have gutted you like a fish.'

'Ha!' said William.

'Don't you look so pleased with yourself, Your Grace,' Turkill said. 'If Guy had been using a real sword, he'd have chopped your arms clean off before you laid a finger on him.'

'Now who's laughing?' sneered Guy.

'Enough! Both of you! Pick up your swords and pay attention. It's time we got back to work.'

'I hear there was a bit of a scrap between Duke William and my ward in the stable yard this morning,' said Gilbert of Brionne as he and Osbern chatted over goblets of wine that evening. The formal business of the ducal council had been dealt with, and now its members were ranged around the table, some standing, others leaning back in their chairs as they chatted to one another.

'Yes,' said Osbern thoughtfully. 'I think we should keep an eye on those two. I don't want it getting serious.'

Gilbert had been brought up in the same military tradition as every other male member of the House of Normandy, and could wield a sword as well as anyone, but he was a kindly, gentle soul at heart. 'Oh, I'm sure we've no need to worry,' he said. 'You know what boys are like. One minute they're at each other's throats, the next they're the best of friends again.'

'Hmm . . .' Osbern took another sip of his drink. This was probably not the time to tell Brionne what he really thought of his ward. In any case, Brionne was already changing the subject. 'I must apologise to you all,' he said, so that everyone present could hear him, 'but I won't be able to attend our next meeting.'

'Why's that?' asked Ralph de Gacé, who had poured himself a drink and joined their conversation. 'Don't say you'll be enjoying yourself while we're trying to keep the duchy in one piece!'

Brionne laughed politely. 'Well, I won't be out hunting or

feasting, if that's what you mean, but I think it might be pleasurable in another way.'

'How so?'

'An old soldier of mine, Herluin of Le Bec, has set up a small monastery in a village called Bec Hellouin. It's no distance at all from Brionne, an hour's ride, if that. Naturally I said I'd be his patron, so I helped to fund the buildings and put up a small church.'

'How very generous,' said Ralph, 'and, if you don't mind me saying so, how characteristic of your good nature.'

'I'm sure you're being far too kind,' said Brionne, clearly delighted by the compliment. 'The church is really nothing special, but Herluin is a remarkable fellow, almost saintly in his way, and he's doing good work helping the poor and the sick. The local folk think he's a real saint, and I can see why. I'm sure Our Lord and Saviour must be looking down on him with great favour. Anyway, the church is being dedicated next week, and of course it's my duty to be there for the ceremony, but also my great pleasure. I'm sure it will be a most enjoyable occasion.'

Ralph, who had been listening attentively, asked, 'What day exactly is this dedication? I should like to send a gift of some kind, a cross or a psalter perhaps. It certainly sounds like a deserving cause.'

Osbern looked on in surprise tinged with something close to respect. He'd looked on de Gacé with intense suspicion when he'd first joined the council, and initially everything he'd seen of him had suggested that he was as ugly on the inside as he looked on the outside. But since Alan of Brittany's death, he had offered only sensible and just advice, and here he was showing interest in Brionne's obscure rural monastery and offering to donate to its church.

Perhaps Osbern had been unfair. Could it be that now that

de Gacé had finally been allowed to join the innermost circles from which he had always been excluded, he had mellowed a little and acquired a degree of polish or even, dare one say, charm?

Stranger things have happened, Osbern said to himself as they walked towards the great hall for dinner. Though not many.

During dinner, Ralph de Gacé had a message sent to one of his men, who was gorging himself – for he was twice the size of any ordinary man, with an appetite to match – at one of the long tables set aside for the council members' servants and men-at-arms. Three hours later, as the rest of the palace was settling down to sleep, Ralph met the man in a deserted cloister. 'Now listen very carefully,' he began. 'I have a job for you. And it must be carried out exactly as I tell you . . .'

6

The road to Bec Hellouin

Odo the Fat's nickname did scant justice to his corpulence. He sat astride his horse like a huge sack of turnips perched on a cottage roof. The gown he wore beneath his coat of chain mail would have served as a decent-sized tent for any soldier on campaign, and yet it bulged from the rolls of flesh that pressed against it. With such a weight to bear, it was no surprise that Odo's horse was of much greater than average size. Its massive shoulders and haunches were more akin to those of an ox and, perhaps disgruntled by the great weight it had to bear, it looked out at the world with an air of sullen resentment that was a fit match for the malice in Odo's own eyes.

Other, happier folk might have had a smile on their face, for this was the balmiest of spring mornings. The sun was hinting at a lovely day to come. The grass was fresh with dew, and there were still a few wisps of mist drifting through the trees that lined the riverbanks. In the forest through which Odo was now riding, the tracks were dry beneath his horse's hooves and the air was filled with the scents of wild herbs. Somewhere in the distance, a pigeon cooed. At once Odo threw away the uneaten remnants of the pastry with which he had been staving off the hunger pangs that were apt to afflict him between breakfast and lunch, and turned to the younger, much thinner man next to him. His mouth was still full, but he stopped chewing so as to hear the bird more clearly.

'He's on his way, two men with him,' he said. 'You know what you have to do?'

'Of course.'

'Remember what the man said. They all die. No survivors, no witnesses.'

Robert Fitzgiroie nodded, then wheeled his horse away from Odo. Up ahead, the path curved and was lost behind the trees that grew on either side. There were another two mounted men-at-arms and six foot soldiers standing cold and wet in the drizzle that had been falling all morning. Half of them marched off in Fitzgiroie's wake.

Odo watched until they were swallowed up by the woods. Then he turned in his saddle and gestured at the trees on the inside of the bend. 'We'll wait over there,' he said to the other soldier on horseback, in a voice that was barely louder than a whisper. 'You other men, take up your positions beside the path. Walk softly. Don't say a word. Don't let them know we're here. If anyone makes a sound and I can't kill Brionne, I'll kill them instead.'

The men took Odo's words just as seriously as he'd intended. They knew that for all his gross corpulence, he remained a deadly fighter, nimble as a dancer and strong as a bear. Many an adversary had thrust at his body with sword or lance, thinking it far too big a target to miss, only to find themselves hitting nothing and realising, a heartbeat later, that the only blood to be shed would be theirs. So his threats were heeded, and as the men moved into position, the only sounds to be heard were the exhalation of the horses and the gentle pattering of the raindrops on the trees.

Gilbert, Count of Eu and Brionne, great-grandson of the first Duke William of Normandy and cousin of the second, was enjoying the easy journey from his castle to the village of Bec

Hellouin, and happily anticipating the dedication ceremony for the new church. Even walking, a horse could comfortably cover the ground in under an hour. So there was no need to hurry, and Gilbert was engaged in a leisurely conversation with two lesser noblemen who were his friends and allies: Wakelin of Pont-Echanfroi and Fulk Fitzgiroie, whose younger brother Robert was, at this precise moment, leading his men through the forest in the opposite direction, barely a stone's throw away.

'So, I hear Duke William and Guy of Burgundy have been fighting again,' Wakelin said to Brionne.

'Oh, it's nothing to worry about,' the count replied. 'You know what boys are like. They're family, known each other all their lives. One minute they're at each other's throats, the next they're the best of friends.'

'Mind you, I'd be curious to know who'd come out on top if they ever did have a proper scrap,' Wakelin went on. 'Burgundy's the older by what, eighteen months or so?'

'A little less.'

'Either way, I think William's still his match.'

'He's got the hotter temper, too,' said Fulk. 'I never saw a lad who was readier for a fight, anywhere, any time. You only have to look at that mop of ginger hair blazing away on his head, and you know what kind of a character he's going to be.'

'Now, now,' Brionne chided him, though his tone was light-hearted. 'That's our duke you're talking about . . . Look, they're both my cousins and they've both been entrusted to my care. So I'm not going to show either of them any favour, even if I do have to remind Guy from time to time who it is he's trying to hit. I don't mind a couple of lads having a scrap; in fact it's good for them. But I'm not standing for anything more serious than that.'

'Ha!' Fulk exclaimed. 'Maybe you should tell Guy that if he

harms a hair on William's head, you'll have him executed for treason.'

'Don't, please. I spend my whole life trying to stop my relations from conspiring against their duke.'

'That's what you get when the duchy's ruled by a bastard whose dad isn't around to look after him.'

'Enough!' snapped Brionne. 'I think you'd be well advised to change your tone, or—'

'Listen!' hissed Wakelin, cutting the count short. 'I think I heard something. A horse . . . very close by.'

The three men stopped and looked around them. For a moment total silence fell upon the forest path. Then there was a single rasping shout of 'Now!' from up ahead, and a gigantic figure mounted on a monstrous horse smashed through the screen of trees and came charging towards them. For a second it seemed to Brionne as if this solitary giant were their only enemy, but then more men ran at the three riders from either side of the track, shouting incoherently as they came. And then there was another cry from behind them and the trap snapped shut.

Robert Fitzgiroie urged his charger into a canter and then a gallop. He had miscalculated slightly and come out on to the path further behind the count and his two companions than he had planned. So now he had ground to make up if he was to do his fair share of the fighting and earn the reward that would be his if he dealt the fatal blow to Brionne.

He could see Odo using his sword like a bludgeon, trying to smash his way through Brionne's desperate defence by sheer power, his blade hammering down again and again against the other man's sword. The two men who'd been riding with the count were twisting their mounts this way and that as they tried to avoid the foot soldiers' weapons. Fitzgiroie rode past them with barely a glance, his attention entirely focused on the struggle between Odo and Brionne. But then he heard a shout of 'Robert! Thank God!'

Fitzgiroie brought his horse to a skidding halt at the sound of Fulk's voice. Of course he knew that his elder brother was part of Brionne's household: the Fitzgiroie children, brothers and sisters alike, were scattered across half the major families in Normandy as loyal soldiers or wives. But he and Fulk had not spoken in years. There'd been no reason to think he'd be with the count today. 'Odo, you bastard!' he shouted. 'My brother! You didn't tell me!'

'Kill . . . him . . .' gasped Odo, heaving for breath as he kept up his unrelenting assault. 'Or . . . by God . . . I'll kill you.'

Robert turned his horse. He caught Fulk's eye. They both knew the rules drummed into them by their father from their earliest days: 'You will serve our family best by serving other, more powerful families first. Your loyalty is therefore to the house you serve. If that should mean that one day you have to fight your own flesh and blood, so be it. May the stronger man win. That way the family will grow stronger.'

Robert had his master. Fulk had his. Now they would fight to see whose would prevail.

Robert turned his horse until he faced his brother directly. Then he rode straight at him.

Odo could feel Brionne's parries weakening with every swing of his blade, but his own strength was ebbing too. At the start of a fight, his sheer bulk provided him with crushing force, but with every passing second, it became more of a weakness, weighing him down and exhausting him. Brionne was close to his fiftieth year. The very fact that he had survived this long proved that his courtly demeanour hid the mind and courage of a true warrior. If he could just hang on long enough, he might yet carry the day. There was a glint in Brionne's eyes and renewed vigour in his defence. He dug his spurs into his horse's flanks and barged against Odo's much bigger mount, changing the momentum of the fight so that it was he who was on the offensive and Odo who was forced to defend.

Odo suddenly felt afraid. He was a bully. So long as his targets were outnumbered and helpless, he felt nothing but pleasure at the thought of seeing them suffer. Once they were fighting back, he was a great deal less enthusiastic. Brionne was striking first to one side then the other, forcing Odo to twist and dodge, using up his energy. Odo's breathing had become ever more laboured. The air was rasping in his throat and he was wheezing like a blacksmith's bellows. His heart was pounding so hard he feared his ribs could not withstand the battering. The sweat was pouring down his face, into his eyes, drenching his back and his armpits. His lungs were burning and his sword felt so heavy it might as well have been forged from lead rather than steel.

He could not hold out much longer. Brionne stabbed directly at him, and Odo was only able to deflect rather than block the blow, which pierced the chain mail on the side of his chest, just below his left arm, and cut a clean slice through his fat-backed skin. He howled with pain and alarm, but his voice was drowned by the high-pitched whinny of Brionne's horse.

One of the foot soldiers, seeing how the struggle between the two mounted men had swung from his master to his enemy, had stepped aside from the attack on Wakelin and Fulk and swung his sword, two-handed, at one of the horse's hind legs. It carved a terrible wound through the lean flesh and gristly tendons just above the animal's hock, smashing so hard into the bone beneath that the blade became stuck. The wounded leg gave way, ripping the sword from the soldier's grasp, and the horse fell to the ground in agony.

Brionne dropped with his mount and crashed to earth with

a blow that broke his own leg, sent his sword flying from his hand and trapped him beneath the agonised, writhing beast.

A vicious smile rippled across Odo's flabby cheeks. Still gasping for air, he steadied his own horse, then dismounted and, taking care not to be struck by a stray hoof, made his way around to where Brionne lay, wounded and defenceless – just the way that Odo liked his enemies.

The fat man's first instinct was to take his time, savour his task and dismember Brionne piece by piece, taking care to keep him alive as long as possible. But time was pressing. The struggle between the Fitzgiroie brothers was still unresolved, and though both Wakelin and his horse were bleeding from multiple wounds, they were still fighting on in a flurry of sword strokes and flailing hooves.

The job had to be done quickly.

Odo stepped up to Brionne and placed a single huge foot on his chest, then leaned forward, putting all his weight on that foot and driving the breath from Brionne's lungs. He grasped the hilt of his sword in both hands, with the blade pointing straight down, and looked Brionne in the eye for a moment. Neither man said a word. Then Odo raised his arms up high, paused for a moment to gather his breath and check his aim, and drove the sword down, stabbing Brionne just at the point where his neck joined his torso, severing his windpipe and gullet and striking so deep that his head was all but cut off.

The job was done. Now all that remained was the tidying-up.

'Help me up,' Odo wheezed at the foot soldier as he walked back to his horse. He remounted with a graceless, laboured series of movements, assisted by several desperate heaves on the soldier's part, then turned his attention to Wakelin and Fulk Fitzgiroie.

In trying to evade the knot of foot soldiers who had gathered around him, Wakelin had inadvertently turned his horse so that he had his back to the rest of the battle. Odo grinned once again. He had a tactic that had served him well on many similar occasions, and now he put it to use again by simply charging at Wakelin's undefended left flank, barging into him and knocking him right out of his saddle.

Wakelin was agile. He fell on his feet, with his sword still in his hand. But, having set out on a peaceful ride without any real expectation of combat, he had no shield to protect him. The six foot soldiers surrounded him like dogs around a wild boar. As individuals, none would have stood a chance against their prey, but together they had more than enough power to prevail.

Odo turned towards the Fitzgiroies. He could see two things at once: first, that Robert was a better swordsman than his more peaceable elder brother, and second that he was showing a distressing squeamishness about applying his superiority to the full and bringing the struggle to its natural, fatal conclusion. Odo sighed. Why did he have to do everything?

He wheeled his horse until he was behind Fulk, then, while the other man was fully occupied fending off his brother, dug his spurs in, raced forward and swung his sword so that the length of the blade cut right across Fulk's back. It was enough of a blow to kill him, but not straight away. Fulk was shouting out in pain, crying for his mother, who was Robert's mother too, pleading for the mercy of a swift death. One last blow was required.

'Do it,' said Odo.

'I can't,' Fitzgiroie protested.

'For God's sake,' Fulk pleaded.

'You heard him,' said Odo.

Now that their other two targets were dead, the foot soldiers, seeing no further need to take part in the battle themselves, had gathered in a semicircle, like spectators at a mystery play.

'Go on, kill 'im!' one of them shouted, to raucous cheers from his comrades.

There was a mocking sneer in Odo's voice as he asked Fitzgiroie, 'Are you really that much of a coward?'

Fitzgiroie looked around at the men, at Odo and finally at his brother. He took a couple of deep breaths, muttered, 'Forgive me, brother, and may God forgive me too,' and drove his sword deep into Fulk's chest, passing between two ribs and piercing his heart.

The ambush was over. Brionne and his two companions were dead.

'Well done, men,' said Odo to the foot soldiers. 'We've carried out our orders and you all did your jobs to the full.' He pointed to the man who had crippled Brionne's horse and added, 'You . . . Rest assured, what you did won't be forgotten.'

The man grinned as his pals slapped him on the back and informed him that he'd be buying the drinks that night.

'Get hold of your brother's mount, and Wakelin's,' Odo told Fitzgiroie. 'We'll take those, and I'll have first pick.' He looked across to Brionne's horse, which was still struggling to right itself, though its strength was fading.

'Do any of you men know anything about butchery?' he asked.

'I do,' one of them volunteered. 'My uncle was a slaughterman. He taught me how to cut up a pig. A horse can't be that different.'

'Fair enough. Carve some decent joints off that nag and we'll all eat well tonight.'

7

Rouen

Two days later, Odo brought news of the murders to Ralph de Gacé. 'Well done,' Ralph said. 'You have done me a great service. Was Fitzgiroie much help to you?'

'Not a lot. I had to see to Brionne myself. Then I sent Wakelin flying from his horse and let the foot soldiers finish him off. After that I turned my attention to Fulk Fitzgiroie and crippled him. His brother killed him in the end, but I had to make him do it.'

'So you don't think he's much of a soldier?'

'No.'

'I see . . . Still, he may have other uses.' Ralph took the purse from his belt and held it out. 'This is for you. Decide for yourself what share to give your men. But be sure to give them something of your own free will, or they may take it from you by force.'

'Yes, my lord.'

'Very well, off you go.'

A short while later, Ralph addressed William and his fellow members of the council. 'I have terrible news to report,' he told them, making sure to arrange his features into a suitably shocked and horrified expression. 'Count Gilbert has been murdered.'

There were exclamations of grief and surprise, and then Osbern said, 'Do you have any idea what happened or who is responsible?'

'He was riding from Brionne to Bec Hellouin with Wakelin

and Fulk Fitzgiroie. It seems Fitzgiroie was the real target. Gilbert's death was just bad luck.'

'But who'd want to kill Fitzgiroie? He's never struck me as a man with deadly enemies.'

'Evidently they exist, and in his own family too. Fitzgiroie's killer was his brother Robert. I am ashamed to say that this man has been in my service for the past few years. I admit I had no idea he was capable of such a crime.'

'I'm sure that no one here blames you for what he has done,' said Osbern, to general murmurs of agreement.

'That's very good of you, Herfastsson, but I can't help feeling responsible. Rest assured, I have given strict orders that he's to be hunted down and brought to justice. He has committed an unforgivable act of fratricide. He must be made to pay for it.'

Osbern nodded. 'I agree. And I commend you for the way you've dealt with this tragic event. You've done well.'

Ralph gave a modest, suitably sombre nod of the head. 'It is, as always, my pleasure, as well as my duty, to be of service.'

Only when the meeting was over and Ralph had left the chamber could he relax, and then the mask of sorrow disappeared, to be replaced by a toothy grin of unrestrained, even gleeful delight.

William had liked Gilbert of Brionne very much, and was devastated by the loss of yet another of the men he'd counted on for love and guidance. But to his amazement, Guy of Burgundy, who had owed so much to Gilbert, wasn't at all saddened by his murder. He wasn't even angry that Gilbert had only died because he'd been caught up in a fight between two of Giroie's sons. Instead, when he met William after the funeral, he was smirking, puffed up, almost crowing with pride.

'He left me everything, did you know that? Good old Cousin Gilbert, he had no sons of his own to inherit his property, so he gave it all to me. Brionne Castle is mine now, and so's Vernon Castle. After all, Gilbert held two titles, so of course he had two castles, and two great estates. And now the land, the villages and manor houses, the peasants, the soldiers, the pretty young women just waiting to catch their lord and master's eye . . . they're all mine. What do you make of that?'

'I don't know,' William said. 'You're very lucky, I suppose. But Gilbert was a really good man. Aren't you sorry he's gone? I am.'

'Sorry? What, sorry to be rich? Sorry to have two castles filled with soldiers? You don't have any of that.'

'Yes I do. I'm the duke. Of course I have castles and soldiers and stuff.'

'But they belong to Normandy, not you, not personally.' Guy smiled. 'I think I'm more powerful than you. And I'm a descendant of old Duke Richard, a legitimate descendant. Not like you . . . William the Bastard.'

'Don't call me that!' said William, and the two of them started fighting again. This time, though, it didn't feel like a game. It felt like Guy really meant it, almost as if they were fighting for their lives, like real soldiers in battle.

It took Osbern to separate them, but as the steward glared from one boy to the other, William suddenly noticed that Guy was almost looking him in the eye. And then he heard Guy say, 'That's the last time you lay a hand on me, Osbern Herfastsson. I'm not a child any more. I'm not spending another day in Brother Thorold's schoolroom. I'm going to my castle – MY castle – and no one is going to tell me what to do. Not you . . . not him,' he pointed at William, 'no one!'

'Arrogant, jumped-up brat . . .' Osbern muttered as Guy stalked away. He turned to William, as if to say something, but then stopped himself: why trouble the boy now with things he could do nothing about? There would be time enough to tell him all he needed to know. But Osbern thought the words, nonetheless: watch young Burgundy, William. Watch him like a hawk. For one day trouble will come your way. And when it does, that haughty pup will have something to do with it.

8

Winchester, Thorney Island and London, England

'But that ship was meant for us!' shouted Gytha. 'We planned it – you and me. My God, the months I spent supervising the craftsmen. And the trouble and expense we went to. A golden dragon's head at the bow, and a scale golden tail at the stern. Actual jewels for the beast's eyes. And now you've given it to the king . . . and his bloody mother!'

'What else could I do?' Godwin pleaded, following in his wife's furious footsteps while she stormed around their house in Winchester as if she were one of her Viking ancestors, bent on ransacking the place. 'That damn woman wanted revenge for Alfred. If she could have had me executed or banished, believe me, she would have done. Of course, once I'd sworn on oath that I was acting on Harold's orders, which I was, she couldn't get me for murder. But I'd still had a hand in Alfred's death, I couldn't deny that. So I had to pay restitution and—'

'And you gave them that ship, and eighty men, with all their armour. You didn't even ask me first!'

'There wasn't time, and—'

'And nothing! You seem to forget, Godwin, that my money helped pay for that boat, just as much as yours.'

'What else was I supposed to do – hand over half our estates?'

'I don't know. But if you'd come to me and talked about it, maybe we could have thought of something together, the way we usually do.'

'You're probably right, dearest.' For the first time, Gytha

looked mollified. So much so that Godwin felt emboldened to point out that he shouldn't have to shoulder all the blame for their loss. 'Of course, my dear, some might say that you bear some responsibility for what's happened. After all, it was you that said I should make myself indispensable to Queen Emma. Do you remember? It was Christmas Day, and you said—'

'Get out!' Gytha drew her substantial frame up to its full height and, looking more terrifying than any warrior Godwin had ever confronted in battle, yelled again, 'Get out!'

Two weeks later, Godwin's troubles with women still weren't over. He was standing in the graveyard of St Peter's Abbey on Thorney Island, a few miles upstream of London, where the Tyburn river flowed into the Thames. The island was a delightful spot. Fishermen cast their nets by the riverbank for the salmon that thronged the local waters, while farmers worked the green fields. The last white sprays of hawthorn blossom could still be seen along hedgerows where the wild roses were blooming and a myriad wild flowers glowed in yellow, red, pink and blue.

Godwin, however, was in no mood to appreciate the glories of nature. He had come to the graveyard, under protest, to witness an exhumation. For this was where Harold Harefoot's body had been brought for its burial, and now it was going to be dug up, by order of the man who had replaced Harold as king.

Harthacnut had insisted that Godwin should witness the occasion. 'Look upon the body of the man you once obeyed, and repent of what he made you do,' he had said, though Godwin knew the words really came from Emma. She had never left Harthacnut's side during the hearing into Alfred's death, whispering in his ear from the first moment of the proceedings to the last. She was here at the exhumation, too, although her presence was entirely voluntary.

'Hurry up! Get him out of there!' The queen did not so much give the order as shriek it. There was something about the way she paced back and forth beside the open grave, muttering to herself, that alarmed the diggers. They feared she was possessed by demons that might at any moment be loosed upon them, or that her next words would be an evil spell that might drive them mad, cover them in boils or strike them down with a deadly fever.

And so they dug until they hit the wooden lid of King Harold's coffin. Then they worked even harder to clear the earth around the casket so that ropes could be passed under it. More men hauled away until the coffin was lifted clear of the grave and then swung across on to the grass verge. The diggers all crossed themselves, and one or two muttered prayers, for the exhumation of a king's body was a wicked act in many men's eyes, and none wanted to be damned for it. Even Queen Emma stopped her pacing and stood silent as the lid was prised open and the body revealed.

Harold had been embalmed, and so his body and face, though blackened, were reasonably intact, and the smell of decay and putrefaction, though pronounced, was not overpowering. Certainly it was not enough to deter Emma, who walked across to the coffin and peered inside.

'Murderer,' she spat, then turned to Godwin and said, 'Come over here. See what's become of your master.'

'I serve the king . . . whoever he may be,' said Godwin as he walked across and gave the body a cursory glance. He had seen plenty of corpses in his time, many in a much worse state than this. If Emma had hoped to shock him, she had failed.

There was one last interested party who wished to see the body. His name was Thrond, he was built like an ox that stood on two legs rather than four, and he carried a long-handled axe, for his profession was executioner.

As he looked inside the coffin, the sunshine glistening on his shaven scalp, he said nothing, nor was there any sort of expression on his bearded face to indicate what, if anything, he was thinking. The workers stayed well clear of him, and though the queen commanded, 'Well then, load it on to the cart,' none dared approach until the giant had finished his examination, grunted wordlessly and stepped away.

Only then was the coffin lifted on to an ox cart. Emma stepped into the royal carriage, and a troop of mounted soldiers, fully armed and armoured in chain-mail coats and steel helmets, formed up into a column and led the carriage, followed by the cart, away from the abbey and along the track that led towards London.

A wooden platform with an executioner's block upon it had been erected on the open ground in front of St Paul's Cathedral, and a great crowd had gathered – most coming from the city itself, others crossing London Bridge from the settlement at Southwark on the Thames' southern bank. As yet, however, the identity of the man who would meet his end had not been announced, and rumours swept to and fro among the people like a changing breeze across a cornfield. Some said it was a notorious murderer, others that it was a rebellious nobleman, or a Welsh prince captured in battle. The gossip only heightened the people's anticipation, and the roaring trade in mead, ale and wine done by the city's taverns – for it was a warm day, and men were thirsty – only fuelled expectations still further.

At last came news of an armed column approaching from the west and passing through one of the gates in the massive Roman walls. Queen Emma herself was said to be riding in a carriage, surrounded by the king's troops and accompanied by Godwin of Wessex. The people knew and loved Emma of Normandy and rejoiced at her presence, but their mood soured when they learned that her son, King Harthacnut, had joined the procession at the city gate.

Just days had passed since word had gone out that Harthacnut was demanding the huge sum of twenty-one thousand pounds in silver from the people of England as payment for his army. Older folk, remembering the Danegeld – the tribute paid to Viking invaders to make them go away – muttered that there was no difference between this Dane and his forebears.

Now trumpets were blaring in the distance, followed by the clopping of hooves and jangling of chain mail as the leading soldiers cleared a path through the crowd for the column behind them. The riders, the carriage and the cart made their way towards the platform, and the spectators nudged one another and asked, 'Which one's the king?' for he had not yet made a public appearance in the city, and the soldiers were forming a solid wall of steel around the members of the royal party.

Finally the procession reached the foot of the platform. Emma's carriage was placed side-on, and a curtain drawn so that its solitary passenger could witness the execution.

A lone voice cried, 'Come out, Queen Emma! Show us your face!' but the mood had turned sombre and the crowd was strangely quiet as a coffin was lifted from the ox cart and carried up the steps to the top of the platform by four men. They were clearly straining under the weight of it, which meant that there must be a body inside. But how could that be? And where was the condemned man whom they'd all come to see die?

There was a ripple of applause as a huge man wielding a battleaxe stepped up on to the platform, following the coffin, and stood beside the block. One or two particularly well-informed onlookers whispered to those standing next to them, 'That's Thrond. He's the king's executioner, come with him all the way from Denmark.'

Then the soldiers cleared and a tall, strongly built man

followed the executioner up the steps. The sun, which had been behind a bank of white clouds, suddenly came out, and its rays struck the gold diadem that encircled the man's red hair. This was the king, but he received none of the massed cheering that would have greeted his father, Canute, just a few shouts of encouragement and rather more of abuse, but mostly silence. If anything, there were more cheers for Godwin.

Next, two soldiers marched to the coffin and took their places next to it, one on either side. The king gave an order, and they reached down into the coffin and pulled out a body, clad in tattered rags and black with rot, holding it upright for all the world to see. A few women in the crowd screamed in horror. Another, right at the front and thus just a few paces away from the body, fainted at the sight of it.

The king stepped forward. 'Behold the body of Harold Harefoot, my father's bastard son and former King of England.'

A gasp went up from the crowd, and people started backing away from the stage.

'He stands accused of the murder of my brother, Alfred the Atheling, prince of England, son of King Ethelred and my own mother Queen Emma. Let it be known that when Alfred came in peace to England, with the sole purpose of visiting the mother he had not seen in twenty years, he was seized, without due cause, by Godwin of Wessex and taken in chains to Harold, who, with his own hands, holding his own knife, cut out his eyes and commanded him to be taken to the marshes of Ely, there to be left so that his body would never be found again.'

There were murmurs of assent in the crowd, for many knew of Alfred's murder and some even saw him as a sort of martyr.

'Dunno why he's suddenly so fond of Alfred,' one cynic announced to his neighbours. 'He never even met him. Harold was much more his brother than Alfred. They were both Canute's lads, weren't they?'

But he was told to shut up: the king was still talking.

'Monks from the abbey of Ely, out fishing in the marshes, found Alfred, still alive, but on the point of death, and took him back to the abbey. There they cared for him with kindness and mercy. Yet God Almighty saw fit to release Alfred from his suffering and called on him to join the company of angels in heaven.

'And thus, by his death, was Harold Harefoot made a murderer. And though he escaped justice in life, he will not do so in death. For no man, not even a king, is so mighty that he is above the law. The law demands that just as Harold mutilated my brother, so he too must be broken. And so I sentence him to be beheaded before you all, so that it may be seen that as long as I am king, no wrongdoer will escape justice, whoever he may be.'

The soldiers dragged the body across the platform and laid it down with its head on the block.

Thrond took his place, his legs set apart to give himself the strongest foundation as he lifted his axe and swung it over his shoulder so that it lay vertically, pointing downwards against his spine. Then he heaved his shoulders and pulled the axe up, its blade catching the sun for an instant as it described a perfect arc through the air, over Thrond's head and down towards the block.

The axe cut through Harold Harefoot's decomposed neck as if it were nothing more than a twig. The force of the impact was so great that Harold's head was propelled forward off the block and on to the platform, where it bounced across the wooden boards until it came to rest at Harthacnut's feet.

Any normal execution was greeted with a great cheer when the moment of death came, for there was nothing that a great mass of people enjoyed more than the sensation of staying alive when another member of mankind was not. But this time the silence persisted, so that the repeated impact of the skull against the boards could quite clearly be heard.

Harthacnut kicked the head in the direction of his soldiers. 'Take it away, and the body too,' he ordered, his voice loud and his diction clear. 'Throw them in the nearest sewer. He was filth, and to filth he should return.'

Still the silence persisted, though Godwin could feel the tension and anger that underpinned it.

Then a single voice called out, 'Booooo!' And suddenly the call was taken up, and from every corner of the crowd, the sound of jeering and catcalls rang forth, so that when Harthacnut descended the platform, it was as if all the people of England were joining together in a single, overpowering chorus of disdain.

As Godwin followed his monarch down the steps, his mind was seized by a question that might once have seemed absurd, but now was all too potent: have I just replaced a bad king with one who is even worse?

9

Normandy

Roger de Tosny fought because he had long since forgotten how to live in peace. He drank because he no longer knew what it was to be sober. Had his wife lived long enough to welcome him home, he might have settled down with her to a quiet, contented old age, but she had died, and besides, who could find contentment or calm with Normandy the way it was now?

So now Roger would die, for it was clear that his adversaries were not about to offer him quarter. And his sons, Helbert and Heliband, would die with him, for they had gone into battle beside him and could expect no more mercy than him at its conclusion. Roger looked at them now, both of them bloodied; Helbert's face battered and swollen, one eye closed and his nose smashed; Heliband with his right arm hanging broken and useless, trying to get used to the feel of his sword in his left hand, his reins tied to his wooden saddle for he had no other way to hold them. He remembered them as boys, running around the farmyard; their squeals of delight and the indignant squawks of the chickens they were chasing. He saw them as youngsters getting their first taste of battle in skirmishes with the Moors on the parched farmlands north of Zamora, where the sweat turned the dust into mud on their faces – mud that cracked as they grinned with the sheer exhilaration that comes with a battle fought, and won, and survived. And now he saw them as they were: two men in their thirties who looked old and tired beyond their years, their eyes dulled, the certainty of death hanging over them like the shrouds in which he and they would soon be wrapped.

Tosny had set out two weeks ago with a simple plan. He and his men would ride west from his wooden castle, which stood by the banks of the Seine downstream from Rouen. They would fight and steal and burn and rape until they had amassed enough booty to help pay for his castle keep to be rebuilt in stone – the one idea in Tosny's life that came even close to a long-term ambition – and then they'd turn round and go back home again. It wasn't an original or even an unusual plan. The absence of an adult Duke of Normandy, strong in mind and body alike and willing to make an example of anyone who crossed him, had led to a period of near anarchy that the murder of Alan of Brittany six months earlier had only deepened. Some lords felt free to take whatever they wanted, whether they had a right to it or not. Others, knowing that they could expect no protection from the duke, took the law into their own hands and fought back. And that was what had happened here. Two other barons, Roger de Beaumont and Hugh de Grandesmil, had pooled their manpower and raced to cut Tosny off before he could reach the safety of his stockade. He and his men had been outnumbered. Just as significantly, they had also been exhausted, hung-over and beset with fevers, bruises and festering sores. The result could be seen in the dead bodies of their own men strewn around Tosny and his sons, and the bloodied swords of their opponents.

The light was failing now, for it was November, a time when darkness fell all too soon, yet there was time enough for matters to be settled before the day's end, and no chance of escape under cover of night. A cold drizzle had begun to fall, and Tosny had to wipe the water away from his eyes with the back of his hand. He shivered, and told himself it was just the damp and the chill.

By Christ, I'd give anything for one last skinful of wine, he thought. But the last of the wine had long since been drunk, and now his throat was as parched as his head was sore. And none of it mattered in any case.

Tosny and his sons were trapped with their backs to a hillock whose slope was steep enough to block their way and make flight impossible. Their enemies were now arrayed in a semicircle around them, completing the trap.

There were about thirty of them, he reckoned: far too many to kill. He had one chance in a thousand of escaping with his life, and that only if he could somehow get to Beaumont and Grandesmil and kill them. That might be enough to make their followers turn and run. It would have been a tough enough ask if his sons were in full fighting fettle. In their current state, it was virtually impossible. But perhaps he could turn that to his advantage. His position was so obviously hopeless, there was one thing no one would expect him to do.

Tosny dug his spurs into his horse's flanks, and as the beast shot forward, he shouted out, 'Charge, my boys, charge!'

Muddy clods of earth flew from the ground as the charger galloped into battle. Tosny did not wait to see if his lead was followed, but rode directly at Grandesmil, a greater warrior by far than Beaumont and thus the one to target first. Two men stood in his way. One fell beneath his horse, screaming as his bones snapped under the iron-shod hooves, and the second was cut down with a single scything blow from Tosny's sword. Their deaths, however, had bought Grandesmil the few seconds he needed to draw his sword and pull his own horse out of the direct line of the charge.

To stop himself riding beyond Grandesmil, Tosny had to pull hard on the reins, slowing his mount to barely walking pace before turning to face his opponent. He cursed under his breath. He had hoped to smash into Grandesmil before he could react and cut him down as quickly as the men defending him. Now it would be an even fight, and that would make a difficult task well-nigh impossible, for Grandesmil had men to help him, men who could swarm all over Tosny like rats over a corpse.

In desperation, he put all his energy into one frantic, reckless assault, caring nothing for self-defence, thinking only of plunging his sword into Grandesmil's body.

And he succeeded. With his arm fully outstretched, he broke through Grandesmil's guard and jabbed the point of his blade into the other man's body, striking between the waist and the ribs and cutting deep into his defenceless belly.

As he withdrew his blade so that he could strike again, Grandesmil cried out in pain and dropped his sword. But before Tosny could deliver the killing blow, he felt rough hands grabbing his legs and heard his horse whinny in pain as it was attacked by half a dozen swords and axes. As the animal fell, Tosny tried to keep his balance, but now there were men pulling at his arms and body, dragging him from his saddle. He cast one last look around him, searching for his sons. He caught a brief glimpse of Heliband's riderless horse, and saw a knot of men clustered around a single opponent whom he realised must be Helbert.

He gasped with the shock of the pain as the first blade cut into him. Then there came another, and another: so many that it became impossible to distinguish one wound from another as the agony deepened.

And then, in the stopped beat of a sundered heart, it was over.

The anarchy and violence that poisoned relations between houses wormed its way within them too. In Alençon, William Talvas of Bêlleme came to the conclusion that he was tired of oppressing, bullying and humiliating his wife Hildeburg. He felt the need to kill her, too, and ordered William Fitzgiroie to do the job.

Fitzgiroie refused.

'What do you mean?' Talvas asked. 'I'm telling you to kill that useless bitch. I have no further need of her.'

'Then divorce her. Send her to a nunnery. Do whatever you want, but don't ask me to murder her.'

'Why not? You've killed plenty of men in your time.'

'Yes, that's right. I've killed fighting men, who could look after themselves. But killing a defenceless woman is a sin against God. It means damnation for eternity. I won't do it.'

Fitzgiroie tensed as he waited for Talvas's response. He looked around to see how many other men there were who could be ordered to seize him. He did not care. Better to die now and have at least a hope of redemption than live to a hundred and face burning and torture without end. But Talvas just nodded thoughtfully, said, 'I see,' and walked away to find someone else with fewer scruples.

Hildeburg died that Sunday, killed by three armed men as she walked to Sunday mass. They carried out the attack on the steps beneath the open door of the largest church in Alençon, in full view of the other members of the congregation. The killers' faces were not covered and their identities were well known, but Talvas was in charge of administering justice in Bellême, and he was hardly going to arrest his own men.

As a vassal of the Duke of Normandy, Talvas should have felt the force of ducal retribution for his lawlessness. But the duke was still a boy, and the man in charge of the Norman militia, the only force powerful enough to march on Alençon and arrest Talvas, was Ralph de Gacé, who was both a neighbour and a close friend of the accused, and had no interest in bringing him to justice. So Hildeburg's death went unpunished and unavenged, and Normandy slipped that little bit further towards the abyss.

For his part, Talvas found that his children took very different views of their mother's slaughter. His son Arnulf was furious, cursing his father, lashing out at him with his fists – surprisingly powerfully, Talvas noted, as the lad's punches connected with the arms he had raised to protect his face. Arnulf was so indignant, and so insistent that he would see his father rot in hell for what he had done, that Talvas seriously considered killing him too, before making do with thrashing him to within an inch of his life.

Mabel, however, took a very different line. She was fascinated by the murder, listening with a look of feline contentment on her face as Talvas told her why he had decided that her mother had to die, how he had planned the attack and whom he had chosen to carry it out. Above all, she revelled in every detail of the actual violence itself, and when her father had given his first account, she made it plain that it had been lacking in one essential detail.

'Tell me about the blood, Father,' she said, in a purring voice that another girl her age might use to persuade her doting parent to give her more pocket money or a dress she particularly craved. And then she repeated, for emphasis, 'Tell me about the blood.'

10

Rouen

Osbern Herfastsson slammed his fist into the council table. 'This has got to stop!' he shouted. News of the deaths of Tosny and his two sons had just reached the ducal palace in Rouen. Grandesmil, too, had died of his wounds. 'Tosny was a good man,' Osbern went on, as much to himself as to Duke William sitting next to him, the other councillors on either side of them, and the man who sat opposite, his wrists and ankles chained, looking at the others with stony, narrow-eyed malevolence. 'He shouldn't have gone like that. Killed by the Moors, that would have been an honourable death. But this way? Fighting Normans, men from good families he'd known all his life . . . We have to put an end to it.'

'But how?' asked William. 'If men want to kill each other, what can we do to stop them?'

Good question, thought Osbern, looking at William. A couple of months had passed since his thirteenth birthday. He seemed to grow a little taller every day, and a dusting of ginger hair was appearing on his chin and top lip. Yet the journey to manhood was still a long way from completion. His voice, for example, had not yet broken. He spoke at a lower pitch, but it was only by a conscious effort, and when he laughed – not often enough for a lad his age – he still emitted a high-pitched girlish giggle. Still, he had a sharp enough mind and he wasn't too far away from having the physical presence to go with it. If only Osbern could keep the duchy together long enough for William to reach an age when he could impose his will upon it, then all might yet be well.

To do that, however, he had to deal with men like the one who sat chained before the council today. Roger Montgomery was a baron whose wanton disorder had been so egregious that it could not be ignored or excused. As commander of the Norman militia, Ralph de Gacé had been sent to arrest him. He had avoided a direct confrontation with Montgomery and his considerable private army, preferring to use spies to uncover the wanted man's personal indiscretions and take him unawares when he was in bed with a concubine. It was not the most honourable of arrests, but, as de Gacé had pointed out, 'Not a drop of blood was spilled. Semen, perhaps, but not blood.'

'Roger Montgomery,' Osbern said, addressing the prisoner in a voice still simmering with anger. 'You owe everything you have to the good favour of our late, lamented Duke Robert. He made you Viscount of the Hiémois, a title that had once been his own, did he not?'

Montgomery shrugged dismissively.

'Did he?' asked William. 'Did my father give you that title?'

'Yes, what of it?'

'You were more than just a loyal subject to Robert. He considered you a friend,' Osbern continued. 'He gave you a place on his council. You signed your name as witness to his charters. More than that, the duke was a cousin to your wife Josseline. You were family.'

'Everyone in the duchy who matters is family if you go back far enough,' Montgomery said. 'Doesn't stop them fighting one another.' Now he looked at William. 'Did your dad ever tell you how he fought his own brother. Killed him, too, some said.'

'He did not!' William said, jumping to his feet, his voice rising with furious indignation. 'Take that back, right now!'

'Or what?' Montgomery sneered.

'Or I'll kill you.'

This time William's voice was low and steady, and every man who heard it knew that he meant what he said. His hand was on his sword.

Montgomery's face lost all its arrogance. 'Very well,' he said. 'I take it back. Your father did not kill his brother.'

William said nothing. He looked at Montgomery, who edged backwards, sitting deeper in his chair as if put on the defensive by the sheer force of the boy's personality.

Finally the duke sat down. 'Very well,' he said. 'Osbern, continue with your questions.'

'We have established that you had no cause to feel anything but loyalty and gratitude to Duke Robert. If you had any decency in you at all, you would have honoured his memory by supporting his son. Instead, you have spent the past five years engaged in larceny, violence and insurrection.'

'I reject that accusation. Your Grace.' Montgomery looked at William. 'It is just gossip and slander.'

'Really?' Osbern placed both his elbows on the table and leaned forward. 'Do you deny that you seized woodland belonging to the abbey of Jumièges and took the revenues from a market held by the abbey?'

'The woodland and the market were both within my estates. The abbey had no right to either.'

'Yet you were forced to pay restitution.'

'Wrongly.'

'Now we come to the present matter. You have been accused of plotting rebellion against Duke William—'

'I have done no such thing!'

'You have increased your lands by the seizure of farms and villages that lie within the ducal estates. If you take the duke's land by force, what is that if not insurrection?'

'It's the way the world is,' said Montgomery. 'It's happening right across Normandy. You know as well as I do, Osbern.'

'You killed three knights who were the duke's sworn vassals. Again, if you hurt them, you defy him.'

'They were defying me. They were on my land. I have a right to defend myself.'

'They fled to the safety of a church, a sacred place. You burned it down.'

'They were up in the damn clock tower, shooting arrows at me and my sons. What the hell was I supposed to do? Let my boys be used for target practice.'

'They were the ones who were defending themselves from attack, not you,' Osbern said.

Now Montgomery leaned forward. 'We can prattle away like old women at their weaving, but we all know the truth of the matter. What I did was no different from what men up and down the duchy are doing. Take that old drunk Tosny. He died trying to make himself richer. I didn't. That's the only difference. Am I to be punished just because I fight better than other men?'

'No, you're to be punished because men like you should not be fighting at all,' William answered. 'When I am older, I will put an end to it. People will see what happens to anyone who disobeys me, and they will think twice before they do anything to anger me.'

'Let the council do that for you, Your Grace,' said Osbern. 'With your permission, we will put this traitor to death. The sight of his head on the end of a spike will make men stop and think all right.'

'You can't put me to death,' Montgomery said. 'This isn't a proper trial. I have the right to defend myself if my neck is at stake.'

'He's right, Herfastsson,' said Ralph de Gacé, in a way that made Osbern wonder whose side he was really on. His own, of course, who else?

'Is there any other punishment we can impose?' William asked.

'Yes, Your Grace,' said Osbern. 'Banishment.'

'How long?' asked Montgomery, evidently preparing to haggle over the term.

'Life.'

'Life?' Montgomery looked aghast. 'No one gets banished for life. Three years, five years, maybe. But life? Forget it, I won't go.'

'Life, and the loss of your titles. Your castle will be torn down and you will forfeit all your estates—'

'No! You can't do that! What about my sons?'

'All your estates,' Osbern repeated, 'excepting only your home villages of Saint-Germain-de-Montgomery and Sainte-Foy-de-Montgomery. They will provide land and a modest living for your sons. But you and your wife must be out of the duchy within thirty days, or you will be executed – and I won't need a court to hear your case if you've tried to escape fair punishment.'

Montgomery looked at Osbern. 'You bastard, Herfastsson. I won't let you get away with this. As God is my witness, I'll even the score between us. Now get these chains off me so I can go and tell my family what you've done to us.'

'No,' said Osbern. 'You will remain here, under lock and key, until it's time for you to leave the duchy. It's for your own safety. After all, if you're here, you can't do anything that might get you killed. Take him away.'

Montgomery was led away screaming blue murder. Osbern watched him go, and so did not see the half-smile on de Gacé's face as he watched the disgraced nobleman being brought low. In any case, the steward was more concerned by the duke's two uncles, Mauger and Talou. He could tell that they were uneasy about the severity of Montgomery's punishment.

'I'm not convinced this is a good idea,' said Mauger, his face twitching as always and his shoulders giving a series of sharp little jerks.

'On the contrary,' said Osbern. 'It will serve as a warning and make men think twice before they do anything wrong.'

'It might just as easily make them feel sorry for Montgomery and think he's been hard done by,' Mauger countered. 'The next thing you know we'd have a rebellion on our hands, and what good would that do us, eh?'

'Well for one thing,' said Osbern, 'at least we'd know our enemies.'

The men who had attended the council dispersed until only Osbern and William were left. Osbern got up and made ready to leave, but William stayed in his chair, leaning forward with his elbows on the table and his chin resting on his clenched fists.

'Are you coming, William?' Osbern asked.

'I was just thinking about something.'

'Can I help?'

'Yes . . . I was thinking about the argument that started all this, Montgomery and the monks at Jumièges arguing about the woods and the market that they said he'd taken from him.'

'What about it?'

'Well, there wasn't a way to prove who owned what things. Even though he lost the judgement, Montgomery still thinks he was right.'

'Don't you pay any attention to Montgomery. He always thinks he's right! Anyway, there are ways to know who owns what. There are deeds and charters that set it all out.'

'Who has them?'

'Whoever owns the land.'

'Or says they own it,' William pointed out. 'But we don't know, do we? And we should. I think it would be better if every duke or king knew exactly what was in his kingdom or his duchy, and who owned it. What's the name of that book that merchants keep showing all the money they've made from selling things and spent on buying things?'

'A ledger?'

'Right . . . so I should have a great big ledger, with everything in Normandy written down. It would say that there was a market at this particular place, and how big this market was, and who had the right to take money from it, and things like that. And then if there was an argument about the market, I could just look it up in the ledger – well, a monk could find it for me, because I wouldn't know where to look – and there would be the answer that would sort out the argument.'

'It would have to be a very big book,' Osbern chuckled. 'Just think of how long it would take to find every house, and farm, and woodland, grazing land, tradesmen's workshops, fishing rights, market rights, customs rights . . . you'd need an army of clerks to do that. And by the time they'd finished, lots of things would have changed and they'd have to start all over again. I mean, every time someone died, they'd have to take a note of who'd inherited his property. They'd be working from now till doomsday and they'd never be finished!'

William could not think of an answer to that, so he gave a cross little grunt, said, 'Well, I still think it's a good idea, anyway,' and got up from the table. 'I've got a lesson with Brother Thorold,' he said, and stalked off towards the schoolroom.

Only when he was climbing the stairs did he suddenly think: what if everyone who owned anything had to declare it themselves? That way they would do half the work and that would solve the problem. A moment later, an objection popped into his mind: what if two people both declared the same thing? How would you know which one was right?

William sighed. He'd argued himself into a corner. But then, as was his habit, he simply cut through his own objections by sheer force of will.

I don't care. I think it's a good idea. And one day I'm going to do it.

11

Rouen and Saint-Germain-de-Montgomery, Normandy

Whenever Duke William was in residence in Rouen, Brother Thorold made his way every morning from the abbey of Saint-Ouen to the ducal palace to teach his young master. He was in the habit of stopping on his way at a bakery, whose patron, Tallifer Pie-Man, was happy to exchange the prayers that Thorold promised to offer up on his behalf (and did so, for he was a man of his word) for one of the piping-hot meat pies that had made his name.

'I've got a nice bit of mutton for you today, Brother Thorold,' said Tallifer proudly one morning, presenting his latest offering. 'That'll keep you warm on a cold winter's day.'

'Thank you so much,' Brother Thorold replied, rubbing his hands together and stamping the snow off his sandal-shod feet. He blew hot breath into his cupped palms and gave an appreciative 'Mmm . . .' as the baker cracked open the thick pastry crust revealing the treasure within. The savoury smell of mutton in a rich onion gravy filled Thorold's nostrils.

The baker handed him a knife and a warm piece of crusty fresh bread. 'There you are, Brother. That should be worth a benediction or two, eh?'

'Indeed it should. God will not forget the kindness you have shown a humble servant of His faith when the time comes for you to present yourself before Him in heaven.'

He stabbed a piece of meat with the knife and lifted it to his mouth. A long, slow bake had left it tender and moist, while the gravy was rich and spicy. 'You have surpassed yourself, Tallifer,' Thorold said, dabbing his bread into the pie to mop up even more of the delicious juices. 'This is nothing short of a triumph.'

'Just remember to tell everyone at the palace how much you enjoyed it,' Tallifer said. 'I'd be happy to make His Grace the duke one too. A growing lad needs plenty of meat to feed him.'

'Very true . . . very true,' Thorold agreed, though he could barely speak for all the food in his mouth.

In due course the pie's contents were consumed, leaving nothing but the pastry. No one of any substance ever ate this thick, flavourless crust, but plenty of the gravy had seeped into it, and there were little scraps of meat and shiny slivers of onion scattered across its surface.

'That will make a fine meal for a lucky beggar boy or two,' Thorold said. The donation of his leftover pastry to the poor was almost as important a part of his daily ritual as the eating of the pie itself, and there was always a knot of small children waiting for him to emerge from the back door of the bakery into the refuse-strewn alleyway that ran behind it.

'I'll say!' Tallifer agreed, breaking the pastry into pieces and wrapping it in a scrap of old cloth. He handed the small parcel to Thorold and then moved aside to let the monk pass him and walk through the shop and the family's one-roomed home behind it.

Thorold stepped out into the alleyway expecting to be assailed at once by grasping little hands trying to get at his parcel of scraps, and plaintive, high-pitched cries of 'Me! Me!'

But there were no children waiting for him, not one. He stopped, frowned in puzzlement and looked around.

The alley was empty. It was a dead end, and there was only one way in or out, but the light from the entrance was blocked by what looked to Thorold, whose sight was not as sharp as it had been in his youth, like a huge dark shadow.

Then the shadow moved.

Thorold felt a sudden stab of fear. His pulse raced.

The shadow was looming larger now as it came towards him, and Thorold heard the slapping of boots on the slushy ground, and the panting of breath. Then he made out the swollen features and cold, piggy eyes of the biggest man he had ever seen, holding a sword whose length matched his giant proportions.

Thorold opened his mouth to shout out in alarm, but terror clamped his throat and no sound came out.

A second later, Odo the Fat drove his blade point-first into Brother Thorold's chest, skewering his heart just as Thorold had skewered that piece of meat just a few minutes earlier. And in that moment, the third of William of Normandy's guardians died.

Ralph de Gacé was feeling particularly pleased with himself as he rode into the village of Saint-Germain-de-Montgomery. It was a very long time since anyone had called him Donkey-Head. These days men looked at him more in fear than contempt, for many suspected that he was in some way responsible for the deaths of the men who stood between him and Duke William, though no one could produce any evidence, let alone proof. In the case of both Alan of Brittany and Gilbert of Brionne, he had been nowhere near the killings, as many a witness could testify. Now, if all had gone according to plan, Brother Thorold should have died in Rouen just as Ralph made his way to the abbey of Jumièges to conduct a straightforward piece of business on Duke William's behalf.

With Roger Montgomery now exiled to Paris, some of his former lands had been given to the abbey in recognition of the wrongs it had suffered at his hands. That being the case, it was perfectly natural that Ralph, as Duke William's representative, should stop along the way at the village where Montgomery's sons had made their home. After all, William had no quarrel with them and wished to make sure they had not been excessively harmed by their family's fall from grace.

Ralph stopped in the village to ask for directions. 'Go to the church, my lord, and look for the track that leads uphill,' a woodsman leading a cart piled high with logs told him. 'Bad Roger's boys are at the end of it. Mind, it's not the kind of place they're used to.'

All the colour had been leeched from the landscape as Ralph rode on. The ground was covered by a blanket of snow, the skeletal trees were black, and smoke drifted upwards from the village houses in charcoal plumes against a dove-grey sky. Sure enough, there was the church, and beyond it a path, muddied by horses' footsteps, leading up a hill topped by a crude wooden stockade that could not offer any but the most token obstacle to any determined attacker.

There were no guards at the open gate. Within the fence stood a barn, its doors hanging open to reveal a few bales of rotting hay within. The solitary horse whose head poked out of the stable next to the barn looked hungry and unkempt, while the chickens that pecked miserably at the frozen earth had muddy, bedraggled feathers. The house at the centre of the compound was little bigger than a farmer's cottage, though as he stepped inside, Ralph had a strong suspicion that he would find it far less tidy and well-maintained than any dwelling cared for by a self-respecting farmer's wife.

He was delighted to see that the reality was even more depressing than he had anticipated. The air was rank with the smoke from a smouldering, untended fire, mixed with the sweat, shit and stinking feet of young men forced to fend for themselves. Only one of the Montgomerys could be seen through the fog, a lad just a few years shy of twenty, by Ralph's estimation. He had the haughty, disdainful expression of one born to lord it over his fellow men, though his unshaven face, his filthy clothes and his matted hair were little better than a beggar's.

'Who are you?' he asked.

'Ralph de Gacé, councillor to Duke William of Normandy.' Ralph noted with satisfaction how the lad bristled at the very mention of the duke's name.

'Are you the one they call Donkey-Head?' The question was delivered with sullen contempt.

'I'm the one they used to call that. Not any more. Not by anyone who has any sense. And you are?'

'William Montgomery. What's it to you?'

'Nothing . . . aside from the fact that I'm concerned for your well-being. This place needs a good clean. Can't you afford a housekeeper?'

'We don't have any money. That bastard William took it all. I thought he was our friend. Got that wrong, didn't I?'

'Yes . . . but not the way you think. Duke William isn't responsible for your present situation. It was Osbern Herfastsson, the duke's steward, who delivered the verdict against your father. I was there; I saw him with my own eyes, heard him with my own ears.'

William Montgomery grunted.

'Where are your brothers?' Ralph asked.

'Out hunting. I couldn't go. My horse is lame.'

'And half starved. When did your animals last get a decent meal?'

'The same time any of us did . . . ages ago. I can't even remember when.'

'Hmm . . . I'm very sorry to hear that. I might be able to help you buy some food, but first I want to ask you a question: what do you think your father would want you to do?'

'What do you mean?'

'Well, he's in exile in Paris. You and your brothers are living in worse conditions than most of the peasants round here. Meanwhile, Osbern Herfastsson, the man responsible for your suffering, is the duke's steward, his senior councillor, the master of estates and castles scattered all over Normandy. What would your father want you to do about that?'

Montgomery looked at Ralph suspiciously. 'Is this some kind of a trick?'

'I don't understand. What do you mean?'

'Are you trying to trick me into saying something against Osbern, just so you can have another excuse to persecute us?'

'Absolutely not. That's the last thing on my mind. I just asked you a question, that's all. How you choose to answer is entirely your business. If it's any help, I can tell you that if someone had sent *my* father into exile, I'd not have stood by and let them get away with it. But perhaps you're different. I apologise, it's none of my business . . .'

Ralph turned away and stepped towards the door. He took one pace . . . two . . . three . . .

'Wait!' said William Montgomery. 'Don't go. You said you were going to give us some money.'

'Then I asked you to answer a question. But you didn't, so why should I give you anything?'

'I'll tell you, I promise!'

'So . . . ?'

'I think . . .' Montgomery looked at Ralph, still not entirely sure if he could trust him. But then desperation got the better of discretion. 'I think he'd want us to take revenge on Osbern for ruining our lives.' He stopped, not daring to say anything else until he saw Ralph's reaction.

'I think you're right,' said Ralph. 'I'm certain that's exactly what your father would want, and if you and your brothers have any pride left whatsoever, you should surely act on his wishes.'

'But how? We can't just walk into the palace and kill him, can we?'

Ralph shrugged. 'I don't know. Sometimes the simplest plan is the best. But I agree it's risky. Personally, I don't have anything against Osbern. There's no reason why I should wish him harm. But if I did, I think I'd wait till the duke is travelling around Normandy. Osbern always goes with him. They stay at barons' castles or the duke's own properties, and even though they have guards, they're still more vulnerable than they are in Rouen. I mean, just as an example, they're going to be in Vaudreuil in about three weeks' time. That would be somewhere you could try attacking Osbern, particularly if you knew someone who could get you into the castle.'

'But Vaudreuil's on the other side of Normandy,' Montgomery whined. 'We don't know anyone there!'

'Don't you?' asked Ralph, looking him straight in the eye. 'Are you sure?'

Montgomery looked back at him, not quite understanding what he meant. Ralph waited until the penny dropped and Montgomery said, 'Oh, you mean . . . ?'

'Exactly. Talk to your brothers. Think about what you want to do. And think about where your truest loyalties lie.'

'What loyalties?'

Ralph sighed. The boy really was remarkably dense. 'I mean that every man has a duty to God, and to his master here on earth, which in our case is the duke. But is there any loyalty stronger than the blood ties between a family? Is there any duty more sacred than a son's respect for his father's wishes? I don't know about you, but I would have done anything for my father . . . absolutely anything.' He smiled at William. 'Here,' he said, 'take this.'

He held out his hand, fist clenched, then opened it to reveal five silver pennies – enough to keep them in food and animal feed for weeks. He waited for Montgomery to take the money, and when he did, Ralph smiled broadly and slapped him on the shoulder. 'Good lad. Talk to your brothers. I'll be back in five days' time to hear what you decide.'

Then he got back on his horse and rode out of the compound, down the hill and along the track that led to Jumièges with joy in his heart. For he knew that he was close, oh so close, to the fulfilment of all his plans.

12

'I hate funerals,' said William, standing by the grave into which Brother Thorold's coffin had just been lowered.

'Me too,' said his best friend, Fitz. 'It's fine for the grown-ups. They can drink wine and mead afterwards to cheer them up. We just have to stand around feeling bored.'

'I never liked Brother Thorold when he was alive. I mean, he was all right, but he made us work too hard and he got so cross whenever I got something wrong. But now that he's dead, I actually miss him.'

'So do I. The new monk they sent to teach us is rubbish. At least Thorold had a few good stories, even if he did tell them again and again, but this one . . .'

'And he's got such a stupid voice,' said William. 'He sounds like he needs to blow his nose all the time. He goes, "Dow, boys, can you tell be duh dames of all the twelve aposs . . . aposs . . . aaaaa-tishoo!"'

Fitz burst out laughing at William's impersonation, and the two boys spent the next couple of minutes trying to outdo one another in the accuracy and outrageousness of their mockery.

Then they heard Fitz's father, Osbern Herfastsson, calling them to follow him back into the abbey of Saint-Ouen, where the abbot was proposing to hold what he described as 'a modest repast, as befits an institution dedicated to poverty and simplicity', in honour of his former brother monk.

William suddenly felt sad. It was the kind of winter's day

when there was barely any light in the flat grey sky, the cold and damp in the air seemed to seep into the bones and the golden warmth of summer was an eternity away. 'I feel like I've spent the whole year going to funerals,' he said.

'Me too,' Fitz agreed.

'I used to have four guardians, and now three of them have been killed.'

William stopped walking. Fitz went on a couple of paces before he realised that his friend wasn't with him, then turned around to see what had stopped him.

'Can I tell you a secret?' William asked.

'What sort of secret?'

'A really important one. But if I tell you, you have to swear on the Holy Bible that you'll never tell anyone.'

'I swear.'

'Promise?'

'Yes!' said Fitz impatiently. 'I told you, I swear on the Holy Bible not to tell anyone. All right?'

William nodded, but said nothing, still trying to find the courage and the right words.

'Well, what is it?' Fitz asked.

William kicked a stone that was lying at his feet and watched it skitter away across the dirty yellow-green grass.

'I'm scared.' The words hung in the air between them, then William hurriedly added, 'I'm not a coward, I promise.'

'Of course you're not,' Fitz assured him. 'But why are you scared?'

'Because of all my guardians dying. First Alan, then Gilbert, now Thorold. I feel like there's someone out there trying to get me, and he's getting closer and closer.'

'But you don't know that anyone killed Count Alan. He just dropped down dead. That might have been a demon inside him. And Count Gilbert was only killed because he got mixed up in a fight between the Fitzgiroies. No one planned to kill him.'

'I don't believe that,' said William. 'I think someone is trying to kill all my guardians.'

'I hope not. One of your guardians is my father.'

The two boys looked at one another, both horrified by the prospect of Osbern dying, neither knowing what to say. Finally William blurted, 'Well anyway, I'm frightened that one day he's going to try and kill me too.'

'Why would he do that?'

'So that he can become Duke of Normandy, of course.'

'But if someone became duke because he'd killed lots of people, then no one would follow him.'

'Not necessarily. Not if they didn't know that he was a murderer.'

Fitz looked as if his head was spinning, trying to follow William's logic. 'Well I don't know about that,' he said. 'But I know my father would never let anyone hurt you. And I know what he'd say if he was standing here, right now, instead of staring at us from over there.'

'What would he say?'

'He'd say that a man must never show his fear. He always says that to me. He says that all men are frightened sometimes and there's no shame in that. But you must never, ever show it because then your enemies will think that you are weak and it will make them believe that they can beat you.'

'Maybe whoever's killing my guardians *can* beat me.'

'Or maybe not . . . But whatever happens, you mustn't make them feel like they're winning. Because then they'll be all confident and sure of themselves, and you'll be all miserable and sorry for yourself, and of course then they *will* win. That's why Dad says never, ever to show it.'

William nodded thoughtfully. 'I wish I had a dad to tell me things like that.'

Fitz nodded understandingly. Then he said, 'Let's go and get some food.'

William's unhappiness vanished in an instant, as he grinned and slapped Fitz on the back. 'Good idea. I'm starving!'

William Montgomery did not tell his brothers about the visit from Ralph de Gacé. So far as he was concerned, this was his chance to make his name in his own right and earn his father's respect in a way that none of the others would be able to match. So when the fifth day came, he found an excuse to get out of the house by himself, took up a position in the churchyard from which he could see everyone come and go, and waited for de Gacé to arrive.

The sun was beginning to sink towards the west and Montgomery was freezing cold and damp down to the very marrow before he saw the ducal councillor riding into the village from the direction of Jumièges. He went out on to the track to meet him, but de Gacé did not seem pleased to be accosted in this way. He looked around with darting, nervous eyes to see if anyone was watching them. Only when he was satisfied that no eyes were upon them did he ask, 'Is there anyone in the church?'

'No, there won't be anyone around until the priest comes for vespers.'

'Very well, go inside. I'll meet you in a few minutes.'

It was barely any warmer within the church than it had been outside. The thick walls provided shelter from the cutting wind and snow flurries, but the stone seemed to exude an even deeper chill than the open air, and Montgomery shivered as he sat in the family pew, drawing his cloak tighter around him as he tried to keep the cold at bay.

There was a sudden draught and a dusting of snowflakes on the air as the main door opened and de Gacé came in.

'Where are the rest of you?' he asked.

'They're not coming. I was the only one had the balls for it.'

'You're telling me that you told them there was a chance to avenge your father and they said no?'

Montgomery did his best to hold his ground. 'If you don't believe me, ask them!' he insisted, praying that Donkey-Head would do no such thing.

De Gacé gave one of his twisted, toothy smiles. 'Don't worry, I won't. Though I know what they would say if I did, and I'm glad of it. You're prepared to lie in the service of your ambition. For a scheme such as this, that counts as an advantage. Now, pay attention. I am going to tell you what you need to know, and everything – including your life – depends upon you remembering every word.'

13

Vaudreuil, Normandy

If there was one thing that his short life had taught William, Duke of Normandy, it was that love brought him pain. He loved his mother, but his father had sent her away – for her own good, he said, though William had not understood how that could be – and though he had seen her many times since, still the shock of seeing her leave, that terrible sense of abandonment as her carriage had clattered away through the gates of the palace at Rouen, had stayed with him ever since.

Then his father had left him too, gone on a pilgrimage to Jerusalem from which he had never returned. William had ridden with Papa to Paris to swear fealty to King Henry of France. The king himself had explained what that meant, telling him, 'You must do me service if I call on you. But I have to look after you too. So if you ever have serious trouble and no one can help you in Normandy, I will do what I can to solve your problems, or defeat your enemies.'

William had understood that his father was doing his best to protect him. But the only reason he was doing that was because he was going away. The following morning, William had been packed off back to Rouen, while his father set off on the long journey to Jerusalem. 'Don't worry, Will, I'll come back,' he'd said.

William had begged him, 'Please don't go, Papa,' and all the way to Rouen, three days on the road, he'd been hoping and praying that his father would think about what he'd said to him, change his mind and come home again to be with him. But Papa had gone to Jerusalem and died on the journey home, so far away that William would never even be able to visit his grave. He did his best not to think about things like that. But there were nights when he just couldn't help it, and dreams when his father would come back to visit him and it would seem so real he could hardly believe that Papa would not be there when he awoke. When morning came, William would have to clamp his jaw, and frown and be rude to everyone, just so they didn't know that what he really wanted to do was run to his mother and cry. But how could he run to her when she lived in Conteville with her husband Herluin and William's two brothers, and he was in Rouen or wherever he happened to be travelling in the duchy? And so William retreated further into his shell, ever more convinced that only a fool let himself feel anything for anyone.

The only man who came even close to understanding William's true feelings was Osbern Herfastsson. William trusted him completely and without reservation. Osbern had been part of his life for as long as he could remember, first as his father's steward and then his own. He was absolutely loyal and never, under any circumstances, took anyone's side against William. But if he thought William had made a mistake, he would never be too shy or cowardly to tell him so, in private, when nobody else could hear.

'You are my duke and I will always obey you,' he would say, 'but you're also my whippersnapper young cousin. I knew your father and your uncle, and your grandfather before them. I loved and served them all and I know they'd want me to teach you all the things they can't, and to put you right if you've got something wrong.'

William always argued his corner, but secretly he was glad that Osbern loved him enough to put him in his place when he deserved it. When they spent time away from Rouen, Osbern would always sleep in William's room to guard him. In all the nights he'd done that, no one had ever tried to do anything bad, but William still kept Osbern there because he liked nothing better than lying in bed listening to the old man's stories of days gone by. More than anything, he enjoyed the tales about the battles Osbern had fought alongside Duke Richard the Good when they'd both been young men. He would lie in bed, drifting off to sleep to the comforting sound of Osbern's voice spinning the same old yarns for the umpteenth time, constantly repeating the lessons about how Duke Richard had arranged his troops to trick the enemy, or draw them into a trap, or prevent the opposing general from doing what he wanted. Osbern would recite the speeches Richard had given to his men on the eve of battle, or describe how the old duke had plunged into the thick of the fighting to show both his men and the enemy that he was afraid of nothing. And with every retelling, those lessons would become just a little more deeply and firmly lodged in William's mind, so that without even knowing it, he was receiving an education in strategy, campaigning and leadership that would stay with him all his life.

Even now, though William was far from a small boy any more, he still looked forward to Osbern's storytelling last thing at night. Lying beneath his woollen blankets in the ducal bedchamber at the castle of Vaudreuil, with a fur throw laid on top of them to keep out the midwinter cold, he watched Osbern clamber into his own bed, and as he did so, he was struck by a thought that had never occurred to him before. As a small boy, he had thought of Osbern as ancient: his hair had always been thin on top, his face lined and his beard grizzled. But at the same time he had still seemed strong and solid, like a towering oak, its size and might undiminished by age. Now, for the first time, William saw that just as he himself was on the verge of becoming a grown man, so Osbern was close to being an old one. His skin was sagging and his body softening, so that his chest, which had once been broad and muscular, now looked pendulous and womanly. As he lifted his arms above his head to let his nightshirt fall down around him, he winced, struck by a twinge from his back, and he got into bed somewhat gingerly, as if fearing another aching joint.

His voice, however, was as deep and reassuring as ever. 'Did I ever tell you the story of how your grandfather and I went to fight the Burgundians for old King Robert of France?'

'I don't think so, Cousin Osbern,' said William, for though he had heard the tale a myriad times before, it suited them both to pretend that each new retelling was the first.

'Well,' Osbern began, 'it all started when Henry the Venerable, Duke of Burgundy, died without a son of his own. Now Henry had married a woman called Gerberga of Mâcon, who was the widow of King Adalbert of Italy. She had a son by Adalbert called Otto-William, and Henry adopted him and made him his heir. But of course, Otto-William had none of Henry's blood in him . . .'

'Can you miss out this bit and go straight to the battles?' asked William.

'No, I can't,' Osbern said. 'The story doesn't make any sense unless you know why the war began, and anyway, you need to know how all the great families of Christendom are related, because you're going to have to deal with them, and you'll have to find a wife from one of them.'

'But I don't want a wife.'

'Not now you don't, but you will. How else will you have a son to follow you if you can't find a nice girl to be his mother, eh? Anyway, when Henry of Burgundy died, Otto-William claimed his title, and there it might have ended except that King Robert of France said that Burgundy should belong to him, because Henry had been his uncle on his father's side and so he was Henry's closest blood relative. And blood, he said, was what counted. So he went to war against Otto-William to see who would be Duke of Burgundy. Your grandfather supported King Robert of France because he was Robert's vassal, and also they were cousins, so there was a blood connection there too. So off we all went, a mighty army of Normans, to join the French and fight the Burgundians. Well . . .'

Osbern settled into his tale, but long before he reached the battle scene that William had been pleading for, he realised that his young master had fallen fast asleep. He kept talking for a little while longer, as was his custom. He told himself it was just to make sure that the boy really was properly asleep and wouldn't wake up the moment he stopped, but the truth was that it was as comforting for him to tell his stories as it was for William to hear them. Soon, though, Osbern felt his own eyelids drooping, and a short while later his voice fell quiet, he rolled over on his side and a moment later his snores were echoing softly around the otherwise silent bedchamber.

14

The castle at Vaudreuil was little more than a stone keep atop a defensive mound, with a wooden stockade at the bottom enclosing a flat area on which stood stables, barns containing supplies for both men and animals, a smithy, a well and a vegetable garden. It had been a bitter experience for William Montgomery riding into it, for it was all too reminiscent of his father's castle before it had been put to the torch by a troop of men from the Norman militia, leaving nothing but a blackened, burned-out shell. Three of de Gacé's men rode alongside him, there both to protect him and also to dissuade him from changing his mind and backing out of the assassination.

None of them wore any colours to signify their allegiance, nor did they give their true identities. Instead they told the guards at the gate that they were pilgrims, on the road to Chartres to pay homage to the *sancta camisa*, the robe worn by the Virgin Mary herself when she gave birth to Christ. No one thought twice about four tough-looking military types undertaking such a journey: with all the blood on their hands, soldiers had more need than most for the absolution from sin that a pilgrimage could provide.

They ate in the great hall, keeping well clear of the ducal party and sitting among the everyday inhabitants of the castle and any other passing travellers who had found hospitality there. Montgomery barely touched his bowl of thick, meaty stew, and only nibbled at the bread that came with it. His thoughts were all directed towards the high table, where Duke

William sat with Osbern Herfastsson at his right hand. William had grown tremendously since Montgomery had last seen him. How old is he now? he wondered. Thirteen? Fourteen? Either way, I bloody hope he doesn't wake up while I'm in there. I'm not fighting him if I can avoid it. Herfastsson was a big man, but from the way he moved and the fact that he sometimes had to lean across the table to hear what the men near him were saying, Montgomery could see that time was catching up with him.

'He's old and slow and weak,' he said to no one in particular. 'I can do this, I know I can.'

His words were overheard by one of de Gacé's men. 'Have you ever done anything like it before, boy?' he asked.

'You mean . . . ?' Montgomery glanced around, not wanting to say the words out loud. The man just looked at him, biding his time. 'Well . . . no, no I haven't,' he finally admitted. 'But I'm sure I can.'

'We'll see, won't we?' the man said. 'But it's not easy, specially the first time. Not easy at all.'

Those words lodged in Montgomery's mind through the rest of dinner and then as he and the other men in the great hall bedded down for the night. As he lay awake waiting for everyone else to fall asleep, he tried to empty his mind of the voices of doubt and fear that were slowly creeping into it. He felt slightly nauseous. He needed to piss. He couldn't slow his heart, which was now beating so hard and so quickly that he felt as though the whole hall must be echoing to its drumming. He remembered what his swordmaster used to say, back in the days when his family was rich enough to hire such a man: 'Relax, breathe deeply, rid your mind of any distractions and concentrate only on the matter in hand.'

He waited until all the shuffling and farting and yawning of men settling down to sleep had subsided, then waited again until the fire that warmed the hall had burned down almost to its embers. Then, very slowly, he got to his feet, wrapping his cloak around his shoulders to hide the lower part of his face, and started to tiptoe between the slumbering bodies of men and dogs strewn among the rushes. A few times he accidentally brushed against one of the huddled figures, and on one heart-stopping occasion a man mumbled, 'What, what?' only to fall straight back to sleep as Montgomery went on his way.

He came to the deep shadow in the wall indicating the arch at the foot of the stairs to the first floor. The torches that had earlier illuminated the winding stone stairway had all gone out, and Montgomery had to climb up in the pitch black, feeling his way with his outstretched fingers. His shoulders brushed against the walls and he had to bow his head to avoid knocking it on the low ceiling. He felt cramped, hemmed in and weighed down by the immense weight of the stone all around him, and something close to panic started to set in as the stairs went on and on without him ever seeming to reach the top.

And then the tips of his fingers on his right hand, which had been brushing against raw stone, suddenly had nothing beneath them but air, and he realised that he'd reached the archway that led to the ducal bedchamber.

The space on the first floor was subdivided into separate rooms by wooden walls, with a narrow passage running between them. De Gacé had told Montgomery that the chamber he wanted was at the end of the passage on the right-hand side, and here at least there was some faint illumination, enough to show him the way, provided by the guttering flame from a candle in a sconce on the wall. He tried to keep his hand from shaking as he lifted the handle that operated the latch and slowly opened the door.

The hinges creaked.

Montgomery stopped dead, not daring even to breathe as he waited for a reaction. But all he could hear was the snuffling sound of an old man's sleep.

'There are two beds in the chamber,' de Gacé had said. 'A low, simple one nearer the door and a big, heavy, decorated one beyond it. Osbern sleeps in the smaller bed. William sleeps in the bigger one. Kill Osbern, but don't you dare harm a hair on the duke's head. I want him alive and well. Do I make myself clear?'

'Yes, I get it,' Montgomery had replied, and as his eyes adjusted to the dim reddish light from a smouldering brazier on the far side of the room, he saw that everything was exactly as de Gacé had said. There in front of him, so close that he could almost reach out and touch it, was the bed containing Osbern Herfastsson, and beyond it the shadowy bulk of a bed befitting a Norman duke.

Now that he was in the room, Montgomery wasn't too worried about disturbing William. If the duke was anything like Montgomery and his brothers, he slept so deeply the hounds of hell couldn't wake him. Even so, he wanted to make the killing as quick and quiet as possible.

'Don't mess about,' one of de Gacé's men had told him as they were riding to Vaudreuil. 'Put your left hand against the old man's mouth, palm over his lips, fingers tight against his nose. Clamp down hard and press your fingers tight so he can't breathe and can't make a sound. Then you take the knife in your right hand and cut his throat, one slice, left to right, deep as you can go.'

'One slice, yes . . .' Montgomery had said, feeling unnerved by the thought.

'Keep your other hand on his mouth till he stops struggling,' the man had continued, 'then drop the knife and get out, nice and easy. If you panic, or try to go too fast, you'll start tripping over yourself, and you don't want to be falling downstairs and breaking your neck, do you?'

'Er . . . no . . . no I don't.'

'Right, so get out and make your way to the gatehouse. We'll be waiting there with horses ready to go.'

'What about the sentries at the gate?'

'We'll deal with them. And don't you worry about us doing our job. It's not the first time for any of us.'

The act of killing had sounded bad enough just listening to the man's description. But now that Montgomery was here, standing over Osbern Herfastsson, the idea of killing a defenceless man as he slept, without a fight or even an argument to get his temper up, was more than he could handle.

He stood for what seemed like an age, trying to make himself do the deed. Twice he gripped his dagger in his right hand and reached his left towards Osbern, but then withdrew it before it touched the old man's bristly face. He remained there, paralysed and uncertain, not knowing what to do. He couldn't just go back to the hall as if nothing had happened. He knew de Gacé would never let him get away with that. But equally he couldn't—

'Papa!'

Montgomery was jolted from his endlessly spinning thoughts by the sound of William's voice.

'Papa, is that you?'

Now what do I do? Montgomery thought desperately, offering up a silent prayer that the duke was talking in his sleep.

He waited. Nothing happened. William was sleeping. Montgomery was safe. But he couldn't wait any longer. Before he had the chance to stop himself, he reached down and slammed the palm of his hand against Osbern's mouth.

He hadn't really thought about what Osbern would do at that point. He'd been too busy trying to cope with the idea of cutting the steward's throat, like a slaughterman killing a pig.

The old man writhed convulsively. He arched his back, kicked his legs and waved his arms, trying to knock Montgomery's hand away. The attempt almost succeeded too, for Osbern was still surprisingly powerful. But Montgomery kept his grip on the steward's mouth and nose, even as he felt Osbern's jaw working up and down as he gasped for air, trying to bite the hand that was suffocating him.

Now kill him! Stab the old bastard and kill him! The thought was like a clarion call in Montgomery's mind . . . but how? Osbern's neck wasn't exposed. The clear expanse of defenceless white skin that he'd been expecting simply wasn't there, and he couldn't seem to work his dagger between Osbern's heaving chest and his chin. The old man's clenched hands had found their range too and were pounding away at Montgomery's shoulders, and even his ears, so it was all he could do to keep his grip and stop himself crying out in pain.

The struggle carried on in silence, like the mime show of an evil clown. And still Montgomery hadn't inflicted so much as a scratch on Osbern's throat.

Well, to hell with that. The kicking of Osbern's legs had sent his blankets flying off the bed, uncovering his body. His nightshirt had ridden up, revealing his wrinkled old balls and shrivelled penis. One more convulsive kick sent the material even higher, and now Montgomery could see his stomach.

He needed no second invitation. He drove his dagger deep into Osbern's guts, stabbing him again and again until his belly had disappeared beneath a slick dark coating of blood.

Osbern's hands reached down, desperately trying to protect his torn body, and that left his neck exposed. Montgomery didn't slice across it as he had been told; he simply drove the point of his blade into the side of Osbern's neck, just below the corner of his jaw.

As he withdrew the blade, a sudden eruption of blood burst from Osbern's neck, covering Montgomery's arms almost up to his shoulders and even sending a fine shower of droplets across his face. The steward's body slumped into the absolute stillness of death and Montgomery stepped back in shock at the sheer horror of what had just happened. His fingers lost their grip on his knife, which fell with a clatter to the floor, and he had to press a gory hand against his own mouth to stop himself from throwing up, though the taste of Osbern's blood on his tongue only made his retching worse.

Damn it! Damn this blood! he cursed. Why did no one tell me that a man held so much blood?

15

William could no longer remember his father's face when he was awake. But in his dreams he saw him, or a man he knew to be him, and the sight gave him comfort until the point in the dream when his father went away. And then it was always the same. The part of his mind that could think, even as he slept, would fight to stay in the dream and try with all its might to keep Papa in sight.

He had been trying to stop his father from leaving when the clattering noise, coming from somewhere outside his head, intruded on the dissolving tatters of his dream. He fought to stay asleep, but a deeper, more powerful instinct denied him the escape of oblivion. He could sense danger close at hand, and he woke, propping himself on his elbows, rubbing the sleep from his eyes and looking around the room.

It took him a moment or two to find his bearings and focus on the scene playing out before him in the half-light. A man whose face he thought he recognised was standing by Osbern's bed. There was a knife in his hand, and a dark, glossy liquid that gleamed wherever it caught the flickering glow from the brazier was pooled at his feet, spattered across his body and face and splashed over the wall behind the bed.

With what seemed like aching slowness, William's mind made sense of what his eyes were seeing. The man was one of the Montgomery brothers – his namesake, William – and . . . *No, it can't be! It's not possible!* . . . Osbern was lying still, covered in the black oil, which William now saw was blood. Montgomery had killed him.

He opened his mouth to shout for help, but no sound came out of it. The shock of what he was seeing seemed to have gripped him by the throat so that he could hardly breathe.

Montgomery seemed to be as dazed as William. He was looking around as if he could not see properly. He caught William's eye, and for an instant the two of them were trapped by one another's stares, neither able to act.

And then the spell broke and suddenly William was leaping from the bed, screaming, 'No! No! No!' and rushing towards Osbern's broken body.

Montgomery lifted his knife and pointed it at the onrushing boy. He might have killed him too, for William wasn't going to stop and would have run straight on to the blade.

But Montgomery did not even try to hold his ground.

Instead he croaked, 'I'm sorry,' in a desperate, broken voice, then turned on his heel and fled the room.

William barely saw him go. He reached the bed and looked down in horror at Osbern's half-naked corpse. The wounds to his stomach had torn his flesh asunder, and something that looked like a vile blood-covered worm had burst from his gut and was lying partly coiled on his pallid skin.

The face that had always been so full of life, so reassuring a sight for William whenever he was in need of comfort or advice, was frozen in a contorted rictus of pain and terror.

William was thirteen years old. This was the first time he had seen the corpse of a man killed in an act of frenzied violence, let alone that of a man he deeply loved. He wanted to be sick. He wanted to cry. He wanted to run – to Osbern, who else? – for protection. Or failing that to throw himself on the body and order it back to life. I'm the duke, he thought frantically. He has to do what I say!

And then he realised that yes, he *was* the duke, and he remembered what Fitz had said, repeating Osbern's own words: *Never, ever show your enemies that you're scared.* He swore to himself that he would not let himself scream, or cry, or show any sign of weakness. He wouldn't let anyone think he was beaten. He refused to give them that comfort.

He took a deep breath, ignoring the stench now rising from Osbern's punctured bowels, pulled himself together and ran from the room. And as he ran he did not scream, but shouted, as deeply as his voice would allow: 'Guards! Guards!'

There was no response. He ran down the stairs to the great hall, where sleeping bodies, huddled under their blankets like butterflies in their cocoons, were slowly stirring. 'Get up, all of you! Osbern the Steward has been killed by William Montgomery! Catch him – catch him now!'

But Montgomery had run too fast and his accomplices had done their work too well. By the time the castle's inhabitants were awake and ready to hunt for him, he was long gone and two unsuspecting sentries were lying dead at the castle gate.

De Gacé had no intention of being convicted for this murder any more than the others. He was his father's son, and just as the archbishop would have done, he had planned for every eventuality. Ideally the Montgomery boy would have been killed while trying to murder Osbern, or after he had done so, thereby preventing him from squealing. If he had been taken alive – unlikely, for the urge to avenge Herfastsson would surely overpower whoever captured him – de Gacé had men ready to kill him as soon as possible.

As it was, Montgomery had managed to escape the castle before anyone could lay a finger on him. Clearly the boy had discovered hidden resources that neither he nor de Gacé had known existed. But it was of no account. Ralph had told his men to take Montgomery to a farmhouse a few leagues from the castle and wait there until they received word from him that the hunt for the killer had calmed down enough for them to complete their escape.

Naturally, as the duke's councillor and head of the Norman militia, de Gacé made his way to Vaudreuil to supervise the search for the killer and ensure that the duke was safe. At the castle he met Barnon of Glos, Osbern's estate manager, who had come to collect his master's body and begin the business of putting his affairs in order. Barnon was a man in his master's image: tough, honest, decent, and not one to cross.

'I've just had to take Osbern's son into the castle chapel to see his dad's body,' he said to de Gacé when they met at Vaudreuil. 'Poor lad, he was in bits. I'd like to get my hands on the bastard who did this. I brought a dozen of my best men with me just in case anyone finds him. And if they do, I'll tell you this, my lord, there won't be any need for a trial.'

'The law must take its course,' de Gacé said, testing the water.

'You don't really believe that, do you? A man like Osbern Herfastsson murdered in cold blood in front of the duke, and you'd give William Montgomery the benefit of a trial?'

'Well it's my duty to maintain law and order on the duke's behalf. It's not an easy job, the way things are at the moment.' He paused. 'But of course I understand how devastated you are by this cowardly murder; we all are. Osbern Herfastsson served the House of Normandy for more years than most people have been alive. So I'll make you this promise, Barnon . . . I have men all over the duchy searching for Montgomery. If they find him, I will give you the task of apprehending him. And if he happens to resist when you seize him, of course you will have to defend yourself . . . won't you?'

Barnon nodded his head, 'Aye, that I will. Thank you, my lord.'

De Gacé waited another two days before he raced through the castle asking everyone he met where he might find Barnon of Glos. When he finally ran into him, he took a moment to gather his breath before gasping, 'Excuse me, but I thought you should know this at once. William Montgomery has been found.'

'Where is he?'

'Gone to ground in a farmhouse. I'll get you the exact directions. But he's not alone, he has three accomplices.' De Gacé paused, then asked, 'You say you have a dozen men?'

'That's right,' Barnon said.

'Then take them all with you. These fugitives are cornered rats. If they should try to fight, you need to be sure of exterminating them all.'

Within the hour, Barnon and his men were on their way. De Gacé watched them go with joy and exhilaration in his heart. It was a pity that three of his men would have to die. But they were by no means the best he had, and their loss was a small price to pay for their silence. There wasn't a man in Normandy who wouldn't understand why William Montgomery had murdered Osbern Herfastsson, nor would any but a Montgomery fail to applaud Barnon of Glos for avenging his master.

That Osbern's death had left Ralph de Gacé as the last remaining guardian and closest councillor to Duke William was, of course, nothing but the purest coincidence.

Book Three: Trial by Combat, Trial by Ordeal

September 1041–January 1045

1

Winchester

'Your Majesty,' said Leofric, his voice slurred by all the drink that had been consumed during the course of a royal dinner, held in the great hall of Winchester Palace, that was prodigious even by Harthacnut's standards of consumption. 'I wonder, Your Majesty, if I might . . . possibly . . . if you would be so kind as to hear me . . . beg your indulgence for . . . for . . . ah—'

'Come on, old fellow, spit it out!' Harthacnut interrupted. 'How can I be indulgent if you won't tell me who to indulge, eh?'

Sven Estridsson and the other toadies and hangers-on that had come with the king from Denmark all laughed uproariously at this splendid example of regal wit. Godwin, meanwhile, just winced. He could tell that Leofric was about to talk his way into trouble and was too far gone to know it. If he'd kept his wits about him, he would have remembered that Harthacnut was a bullying drunk, who liked to use his own extraordinary capacity for drink as a weapon. He would insist that his courtiers match him drink for drink, and though this demand was dressed up as good fellowship and even generosity – for it was, after all, the king who had supplied the wine or mead that was being consumed – it was actually a means of imposing his will, for the more incapacitated his guests became, the more he would taunt them for their weakness, as if a man's worth could be measured by his thirst.

Leofric had been a man of healthy appetites in his time, but not on Harthacnut's scale; besides, he was well past the age when a man started losing his ability to drink all night and then be up at dawn to go hunting or warmongering.

'I think the Earl of Mercia is tiring, sire,' said Godwin, trying to get Leofric off the hook on which he was impaling himself. 'It's his age, no doubt. Why don't I escort him to his chamber, just to make sure he doesn't get lost on the way?'

'Tiring . . . really?' replied Harthacnut. 'What do you say to that, Mercia? Are you too exhausted to ask for my favour?'

'Certainly not!' Leofric insisted, to cheers from the Danish sycophants. 'Never heard such nonsense, Godwin. I'm as wide awake as . . . as . . . well, I'm wide awake, anyway.'

'If you say so,' Godwin sighed. 'I was trying to help, you old fool,' he muttered under his breath.

'Excellent!' crowed Harthacnut. 'The Earl of Mercia's eye is bright. His wits are sharp. Here! Charge your cup and wet your throat before you speak . . . No, I insist.'

Leofric struggled through yet another drink and then, with red wine dribbling down his silvery beard, said, 'It's about . . . about the people of Worcester, Your Majesty.'

Oh God, thought Godwin. Not this. Anything but this . . .

'What about them?' asked the king. 'Apart from the fact that they're refusing to pay their taxes?'

'Well, that's just it,' said Leofric. 'Many of the people simply cannot afford the tax. They found it hard enough to pay their share of the money for your fleet last year. Now they're being asked to pay again and . . . well, they just can't.'

'You care about Worcester, do you?'

'Oh yes, sire. It's in the heart of Mercia, so it's my land. It's also a family matter. You see, the townsfolk come from an ancient tribe called the Hwicce. And my family originally came from the same tribe, so I'm honour-bound to defend them.'

'Huh!' grunted the king. 'Tell me, do these . . . what did

you say they were called?'

'Hwicce, sire.'

'Yes, well, do they believe that England should be defended against its enemies?'

'Absolutely, Your Majesty, they certainly do.'

'So they would agree that I was right to build more ships for the English navy?'

'Well, yes, but what I think, ah, confuses them is that they thought they were paying for a navy last time.'

'They were, but that was *my* navy, the one that brought me here from . . . where did I come from, Leofric?'

The king spoke with exaggerated calm, like a teacher talking to a particularly dim pupil.

'Bruges, sire.'

Harthacnut rolled his eyes, to titters from his friends. 'Before that.'

'Oh, yes, Denmark.'

'That's right, so what nationality were my ships?'

'Er . . . Danish?'

'Exactly. There were sixty Danish ships, and one day they and their men will go back to Denmark. Now I'm building thirty English ships – which is not enough, not nearly, but it will have to do for now – so that if someone else tries to invade, we have some way of defending ourselves. And ships have to be paid for. Do the Hwicces of Worcester understand that?'

'Well, yes, sire, but—'

'But nothing!' Harthacnut slammed his fist down on the table. 'The English must pay their taxes. I don't care what they think. I don't care whether they can afford it. I need that tax and they must pay it. Do I make myself clear, Leofric?'

'Yes, sire.'

For a brief moment Godwin relaxed, thinking it was over. Leofric would be sent off to find the money, and once he'd been gone two or three weeks, something or someone else would have occupied the king's attention. But then he saw Harthacnut's eyes turning towards him and heard the king say, 'So, Godwin, did you know that Leofric was about to plead on behalf of tax-evaders?'

'No, Your Majesty.'

'I find that hard to believe. You clearly knew something was up.'

'I, ah . . .' Godwin searched desperately for a form of words that would get himself out of trouble without dropping Leofric even deeper into it. The task was not helped by the fact that his own wits were dulled by the effect of the night's overindulgence. Then inspiration struck. 'You're absolutely right, sire. I was afraid . . . afraid that Leofric was about to launch into one of his stories about the old days. Excuse me, Mercia, but they really can be arse-achingly dull.'

That got a laugh out of the Estridsson contingent. Godwin shot Sven a furious look: *You're supposed to be Gytha's nephew, you little shit. That makes us family. Try acting like it for once.* Harthacnut, however, remained unamused. 'Good try, but I am not as easily fooled as some of my friends. I think you knew he was about to say something that would anger me, even if I am prepared to believe that you did not know exactly what it would be. Am I right?'

'Yes, Your Majesty.'

'So, Godwin, tell me, what would my father have done, confronted by an entire city refusing to pay a tax imposed by royal decree.'

'Well, Your Majesty, your father was a great man, much loved by his people for his fairness and kindness—'

'Horse-shit. My father was as hard as nails. He ruled an empire that straddled the North Sea like a giant's footsteps. True, he was fair. Those who did their duty and served him well would be properly rewarded. But God forbid that a man should betray him, or fail him, or disobey him, for then that man's life was forfeit. Is that not so?'

Godwin nodded. 'Yes, Your Majesty.'

'And have the people of Worcester disobeyed me?'

'Yes.'

'Thank you. I have been disobeyed and betrayed, and if I let this pass without taking action, men all over the country will know that my word carries no weight and my commands are just so much hot air.'

'But sire,' Leofric begged, 'they have no money, they cannot afford to—'

'Nonsense! When my father became king, he levied a tax three times greater than the one I raised last year. The English found a way to pay him then, yes, even the ancient Hwicce from Worcester. They could pay me now; they just choose not to. So what then shall I do?'

The question was rhetorical; even Leofric, drunk as he was, understood that. Godwin waited to see what his delinquent sot of a monarch would decide. Just then, Sven Estridsson leaned over and whispered something in the king's ear.

Harthacnut's eyes widened. His face, already flushed and sweaty from his excessive consumption, turned a darker shade of puce. His breathing grew more laboured, and with spittle gathering in a white foam at the corners of his mouth, he shouted at Leofric, 'Is this true? Is . . . this . . . true?'

'Is what true, Your Majesty?'

'*Is what true?*' Harthacnut repeated in a mocking singsong voice. 'Don't give me that shit. You know perfectly well what I'm talking about. Is it true that your treacherous kinfolk in Worcester killed two of my tax-collectors?'

Leofric desperately tried to evade the issue. 'I can't be sure of that, sire. I mean, I didn't see any bodies or anything.'

'The hell you didn't! You knew about this, didn't you?'

Leofric's shoulders slumped in surrender. 'Yes, Your Majesty.'

Harthacnut nodded with slow deliberation. 'Very well, then, I have made my decision. I condemn Worcester to harrying.'

A look of absolute horror spread across the earl's face. The king had just ordered the destruction of the entire city. 'No, sire, please . . . I beg—'

'You beg in vain. That is the punishment I have chosen for Worcester. And *your* punishment is that you will carry it out.'

Godwin was shocked. 'Your Majesty, are you sure this is wise? To ask a man to slaughter his own people, and burn down buildings within his own earldom . . . Your father would not have done that.'

Harthacnut nodded thoughtfully. 'Yes, I see that . . . Father might well have been concerned that his orders would not be obeyed.'

'Exactly, sire.'

'In that case, Godwin, since Worcester is very definitely not in *your* earldom, you had better accompany Leofric and ensure that my instructions are carried out to the letter. I want Worcester razed to the ground. I want it reduced to ashes. I want the streets to run with its inhabitants' blood. And if you do not obey my orders, I remind you both that I still have those sixty Danish ships, each one of them fully crewed by fighting men . . . oh, and the ship you were so kind as to give me, Godwin. And I will not hesitate to turn them loose against anyone who crosses me.'

2

Worcester and Winchester

Three whole days had passed since the harrying of Worcester had begun: three days and nights of murder, rape, looting, demolition and arson. Now the flames rising into the night sky cast a glow like the fires of hell itself over the city and illuminated the torment of a screaming woman lying trapped beneath a fallen beam. Her hips had been smashed by the impact of the massive shaft of oak that had once supported the roof of the house where she served as some kind of menial scullion. Now she lay immobile, howling in agony, with the crushed remains of her dead child in her arms.

Her ear-splitting screeches cut through Godwin's aching head like a skewer through his brain. He was drunk – very, very drunk, far more so than at any of Harthacnut's feasts, so that it was a struggle just to stay in the saddle, even when his horse was still – and his discomfort was made worse by the smoke in the air, which made his eyes smart and irritated his throat and chest so that he kept coughing: dry, rasping hacks that only made his head hurt even more.

'For God's sake, someone shut her up!' he shouted, not aiming the request at anyone in particular, let alone expecting to be obeyed.

The Saviour did not hear his words, but Satan must have done, because out of the smoke there emerged a man-at-arms, as ugly a brute as Godwin had ever clapped eyes on. His nose was caved in, and the sword that had split it had left its mark in the vivid scar that slashed across his face. His eyes were piggy, his gaping mouth was almost toothless and there were two large, swollen warts on his chin.

Compared to the dog that was straining at the leash in his hand, however, the man-at-arms was a paragon of masculine good looks. It was some kind of nightmarish mongrel, the spawn of beasts specifically chosen for their absence of any redeeming features by a breeder for whom viciousness, malice and an absolute refusal to be tamed were all considered virtues.

The man walked down the desolate street with a terrible, implacable certainty, and it seemed to Godwin as though the air somehow chilled for a moment as he passed. The earl was, in theory, this man's commander – though he could not recall having seen him or the dog before – yet he did not dare utter a word, either of command or reproach. He just stood mutely as the man walked to within a few paces of the wounded woman, stopped and then loosed his dog.

The beast crossed the ground in the blink of an eye, sank its teeth into the woman's throat and shook its head from side to side. When it pulled away, its maw was full of skin, flesh and gristle. It swallowed the grisly mouthful, then bent its head again towards its prey. It soon lighted upon a far more enticing dish.

As the dog began to tear at the dead child, emitting rumbling growls and snuffles of appreciation and wagging its stubby tail, while its master looked on as emotionless as before, Godwin felt nausea rising in his throat. He pulled on his horse's reins and, desperately fighting the urge to vomit, spurred his mount into a trot, then a canter and finally a gallop. He tore through the burning city, past the piled mounds of corpses and the drunken, blood-spattered soldiers – for no half-decent man could undertake such a task if he was sober; past the burned-out shells of looted taverns; past the ruins of the modest buildings where the town's tradesmen and their families had lived and worked; past the roofless, smoke-blackened church that should have been spared but simply fell victim to flames that could no longer be controlled; past the remnants of what had started the week as a peaceful Mercian town, and out into the meadows beyond.

Only then did he dismount, bend double and heave the contents of his guts out on to the fresh green grass. As he straightened up, wiping his hands across his face, he heard the sound of footsteps, accompanied by heavy, almost convulsive breathing.

He drew his sword and sprang around to face this new threat.

It was Leofric, stumbling blindly, head in his hands, sobbing helplessly. Godwin went to him and put his arms around him, holding him tight and murmuring reassurance in a tone he'd only ever used before with a crying woman. But Leofric was unmanned by shame and grief, and so, Godwin realised, was he. Soon tears were pouring down his face too, so that he could not talk, and they both stood weeping while the waters of the River Severn rolled by, heedless of what was happening on its banks, and the birds in the trees sang on, indifferent to human stupidity.

They had both stopped crying, though neither had said a word, when one of Godwin's men approached them. 'My lords,' he began, 'it's about the townspeople. A lot of them got away. They've gone to an island in the middle of the river – Bevere Island, it's called. What do you want us to do about them?'

'I don't know,' said Leofric. 'Go away.'

Godwin patted his fellow earl on the back. 'Don't worry,' he said. 'I'll deal with this.' He glanced at the messenger. 'Let's leave his lordship be, eh? Walk with me a while.'

They stepped down towards the river's edge. 'John, isn't it?' Godwin said.

'That's right, my lord. John of Saltwich, they call me, for that's where I come from.'

'Very well then, John of Saltwich, tell me where this island lies.'

'Oh, you can't see it from here, my lord; it's a way upstream.'

'So it's not within the boundary of Worcester?'

'No, my lord, not by quite a way.'

'Then we shall let it be. The king ordered us to harry Worcester. I was there myself when he gave the order. He said nothing about any islands, and therefore if we were to attack an island, we would be disobeying a royal command. And we wouldn't want to do that, would we, John?'

'No, my lord.'

Godwin heard the relief in the man's voice and sympathised. 'Tell me,' he said, 'have St Peter's Priory and the cathedral church survived?'

'I believe so, yes.'

'Thank God for that,' said Godwin. 'We can only hope that earns us some forgiveness when the Day of Judgement comes.'

The king was drunk when he heard the news that Worcester had been destroyed. He greeted Godwin and Leofric's report with a burst of manic laughter that caused him to swallow some food the wrong way and cough violently. His courtiers hung back, unwilling to help for fear that any vigorous action towards the royal body, such as slapping him on the back, might be seen as an act of treasonable violence. Eventually Harthacnut recovered his breath, but the very act of prolonged coughing had unsettled his stomach, with the result that he vomited a great flood of vinous purple-red effluent all over the banqueting table.

No one thought it amusing. Godwin saw that even Sven Estridsson and the other Danes were looking on in silent disgust. If Harthacnut was losing their allegiance, his position was parlous indeed. And then there was the question of his health. The king was growing fat. His breath was laboured, his complexion mottled, his mind almost permanently befuddled.

If he carries on like this, he'll soon be dead, Godwin thought. And then what?

He walked across to Estridsson's place at the table and leaned down to speak in his ear. 'A word if you please, nephew.'

Sven glanced across at Harthacnut, for it was the height of bad manners to leave the table before the king.

'Don't worry. He won't notice,' said Godwin.

He led Estridsson away until they were standing by the wall behind the high table. 'You were at that meeting with Magnus of Norway, the one where he signed the peace treaty with His Pie-Eyed Majesty over there.'

Estridsson nodded.

'Am I right in thinking that one of the clauses in the agreement was that whoever died first, the other would inherit his kingdom?'

'Yes,' Estridsson agreed.

'Now tell me, did that clause apply to the kingdom His Majesty ruled then – that is to say, Denmark? Or did it apply to any kingdom he might rule at any time?'

'Well I think we all understood that His Majesty was only talking about Denmark.'

'I'm sure you did understand that, my boy. But were there specific words, written in black ink on white parchment, that very clearly said that Magnus could have Denmark but not England?'

Estridsson frowned. 'I'm not sure. I mean, I'm not that good with writing. Leave it to the monks.'

'Look over there, young Sven. Look at the man who signed

that godforsaken treaty. Now, I don't know King Magnus, but my guess is he's probably in better health than our monarch currently is.'

'Well, he's younger than Harthacnut, certainly.'

'And does he eat and drink every night to the point where he's sick, or passes out, or both?'

'Probably not.'

'So we have a problem, don't we? The King of England is sickening fast, and there's another king over the water who has what he doubtless believes to be a very good claim on the throne. Now, Magnus will go for Denmark first. It's closer. His claim there is iron-clad, and he won't want to strike for England if it leaves Norway exposed to attack from Denmark while he's gone. So he'll sort that out first and then come for us.'

'So what should we do?'

Godwin shrugged. 'I don't give a fuck what Magnus does to Denmark. With respect to my dear Danish wife, it's none of my damn business. But I care very much about England, and my personal slice of it, and I don't want it being taken from me by a bunch of Norwegians. So the best thing you can do for yourself, and for your Aunt Gytha and me, is to take your mates and all their ships, and piss off back to Denmark. Harthacnut signed that treaty. You didn't. And you're a nephew of Canute the Great, so your claim to the Danish throne is better than Magnus's, treaty or no treaty.'

Estridsson nodded. 'You know, Harthacnut said that if Magnus had the throne of Denmark, I should just kill him and take it for myself.'

'Then there's one thing, at least, that he and I agree on.' Godwin moved to walk away, paused, and then turned back to Estridsson. 'When the king said that to you, about taking Denmark . . . was he drunk at the time?'

'Yes,' said Sven Estridsson, 'very.'

'Still, I think you'd be wise to heed what he said. Denmark is yours for the taking. If you've got the balls for it.'

'You're right, Uncle. I'll start making arrangements at once.'

You do that, thought Godwin. He was relieved to discover that Sven didn't seem to have the limitless, insatiable hunger for more that marks out the truly ambitious. The boy seemed more than satisfied with the idea of seizing Denmark. Yet there was a bigger prize for the taking, if he had the nerve to seize it. Sven's father had been Gytha's brother Ulf. But his mother Estrid was Canute's sister. That made him the late king's nephew too, giving him a strong claim to England's crown as well as Denmark's. Godwin smiled to himself: thank you for not noticing that, Sven, my lad. Because you're not the man I have in mind for this job.

3

Winchester and Rouen

Godwin went straight from the great hall, where the palace servants were now trying to lift Harthacnut to his feet and get him to his bedchamber, to the treasury, where he knew that Emma and the noble ladies who attended upon her would be gathered. The elixir of power had worked its magic on the dowager queen. Godwin had been shocked, as well as surprised, by the signs of fragility, brittleness and even mania he had observed in Emma when he had first set eyes upon her in Bruges. Her condition had worsened still further on that ghastly day when Harold Harefoot's body had been exhumed and decapitated. But the restoration of her status had brought with it a steady recovery of her old qualities of strength, determination and a sharp, invigorating dash of sheer malice.

The first evidence of her return to form had been the humbling of her old rival, Harefoot's mother Elgiva. As was frequently the case with women of high rank who had outlived the men from whom their power derived, Elgiva had been sent to pass the rest of her days as a nun – in a convent chosen specially for its remote location and modest accommodation. At Emma's request, the mother superior kept her fully informed about the activities of the newly renamed Sister Magdalena as she accustomed herself to a life of strict poverty, chastity, obedience and prayer. The queen particularly enjoyed the reports that described occasions on which Sister Magdalena had been obliged to undertake acts of contrition in penance for trifling misdeeds. She had at first been unwilling to accept the disciplines of monastic life, but any residual haughtiness was being expunged from her personality in a most satisfactory fashion.

With two of her enemies disposed of, the queen had devoted all her energies to reassembling the huge fortune, acquired while she was consort to Ethelred and Canute, that Harefoot and Elgiva had taken from her when they were in power. Having retrieved all they had appropriated, and added to it the considerable quantity of gold, jewellery, illuminated manuscripts and holy relics – including a bone from the arm of St Augustine and the skull of St Ouen – that she had been able to take with her to Bruges, she was now the mistress of one of the greatest hoards in all Christendom, and it was her pleasure to visit the treasury with her most favoured ladies-in-waiting to sort through the piles of coins and objects so that it could all be recorded and stored as efficiently as possible.

When Godwin arrived at the treasury, however, he was surprised to discover that Emma was accompanied not by her ladies-in-waiting, but by Aelfwine, Bishop of Winchester.

'I need to talk to Her Majesty,' he said. 'In private.'

The bishop glanced at Emma, received a fractional nod of the head that signalled her assent, and left the room.

'Strange place to meet a priest,' Godwin said. 'But then, greed is a deadly sin. Was he taking your confession?'

'Mind your tongue, Godwin,' Emma replied. 'Remember that my son is king. One word from him would finish you for ever.'

'One word of scandal might finish you too. Might I ask what the bishop was doing here?'

'The same as he has done for many years, giving me wise counsel and honest friendship. There is nothing whatever scandalous about that. So . . . why are *you* here?'

'To save that son of yours. You realise, don't you, that he's doomed?'

'I realise no such thing.'

'For God's sake, open your eyes. He's losing the country, if he ever had it at all. He's barely been here a year and already the people have had to pay for his fleet, and now there's this Worcester nightmare. The whole of Mercia will know about that now, and it won't be long till the story's reached every corner of England. The reality was bad enough; God only knows how it will sound by the time it's been told and retold, and exaggerated a little more each time.'

'All kings do that kind of thing. Canute was no angel.'

'Yes, but he was a conqueror, a leader, a real man. People couldn't help but admire him. His son is a bully; that's not the same thing at all. And he's drinking himself to death. You've got to stop him.'

Emma seemed to shrink before Godwin's eyes, her defiance vanishing like mist burned off by the rising sun. 'Do you think I haven't tried? I'm his mother, Godwin. I notice everything about him. How he looks, how he talks, what he does . . . But I can't stop him. I wasn't there, you see, when he was a boy. By the time he was eight, he was gone. So he didn't grow up with me looking after him, nursing him when he was sick, congratulating him when he did well, ticking him off when he did wrong. He's not used to being obedient to me. He has no reason to care about my opinion of him. He knows that I'm his mother. But he doesn't feel it, deep down, the way a son should. But then none of my children do . . . They were all taken away from me. Every one of them . . .'

Emma paused for a moment, lost in thought, then looked at Godwin with eyes suffused by an overwhelming air of loss and melancholy. There were, he now realised, limits to what even power could achieve. Emma's separation from her children was the one wound that nothing would ever heal.

'My little Gunhilda died, did you know that?'

'No, Your Majesty.' Godwin felt he owed her that honour, that acknowledgement at least. 'I did not. Might I ask . . . ?'

'It was three years ago. She was on campaign with Henry. He was in southern Italy, sorting out some dispute or other, and she went with him because she wanted to show that she was worthy to be his empress. Fever broke out in the army. It took half the soldiers and . . . and it took my little girl.'

Godwin recalled a day fifteen years ago, maybe more. He had been a young man, still flushed with the power that had been bestowed on him with the earldom of Wessex, glorying in his position as Canute's most trusted English subordinate. The king had pointed to his two children, Harthacnut and Gunhilda, who were playing some childish game or other while Emma – and by God she had been a sight to behold in those days – looked on. Harthacnut must have been six or seven, his sister a couple of years younger.

'See those two kids of mine?' Canute had said, glowing with paternal pride. 'Well, that little boy is going to be ruling Denmark soon. I'm going to take him back there and make him my regent, help him understand what it means to be a king. And she . . .' he nodded at Gunhilda, 'my pretty little princess, well, today I have just concluded an agreement with an ambassador from the court of the Holy Roman Emperor himself. Conrad has agreed to betroth his eldest son and heir, Henry of Germany, to Gunhilda. We'll be sending her off to live at the imperial court. Do you understand what this means, Godwin?'

'Well, it's a very fine match, sire.'

'It's more than that, Godwin, it's my legacy. Just think of it! When I'm gone, my son will rule over my empire in England, Scotland, Norway, Sweden and Denmark. And his sister will be the Holy Roman Empress, wife to the ruler of all Germany, the Low Countries, Burgundy and Italy. Together they will hold Christendom in their hands . . .'

But now Canute was gone, his son was a wreck and his daughter was dead.

'I'm so sorry,' Godwin said, and meant it.

Emma nodded in acknowledgement. 'I envy you, Godwin,' she said. 'What is it you have now, six sons?'

'Seven . . . and four daughters.'

A wry smile hovered around the corners of Emma's mouth. 'Poor Gytha, she must be exhausted.'

'She thrives on it.'

'And they all still live with you?'

'For the moment. It's time my eldest, Sweyn, had some responsibility. He's headstrong, impetuous . . . It's time he became a man.'

'He's young, he'll learn.' Emma paused. Godwin saw the conscious effort it took for her to drag herself away from her sorrow before she straightened her spine, tilted her head back to its old, regal haughtiness and said, 'So, we have a problem with Harthacnut?'

'Yes.'

'I assume you have a solution in mind. I've never known you be without one.'

Godwin nodded. 'Hmm . . . possibly.'

'Well?'

'The king has no heir and, since he has no queen, no immediate prospect of producing one.'

'Even if he had a wife, he'd be in no fit state to bed her.'

'Probably not. So we need someone that the people will accept, the nobility and the common folk alike. He has to have an indisputable claim to the throne and he has to be English, or at least someone who can be presented as English, so that if

Magnus of Norway ever lands on the coast of Yorkshire and marches south, claiming the crown for himself, England will rally behind our man.'

'Ah, yes . . . I can see where this is taking you, Godwin,' Emma said. 'The difficulty is, the man you're thinking of has good reason to hate you.'

'Yes . . . he does.'

'Well let me tell you, he's not too fond of me either. So that leaves us both in a pickle, doesn't it? What do we do?'

'There's only one thing we can do: show a united front. We make it perfectly clear that we are the reason he's back in England and that he is in our debt. And we speak with one voice.'

'You've made an offer like that to me before,' Emma said.

'I know.'

'And you didn't keep your word.'

'You didn't persuade your son to come to England.'

'But this time I will, is that what you're thinking?'

'Yes.'

'And so this time I can trust you.'

'Absolutely.'

'It seems to me that I have no choice.'

'Neither of us does.'

'Well then,' said Emma, 'you'd better fetch me a monk. It seems I have a letter to write.'

'How long do you think they'll keep the boy alive?' the self-styled King Edward of England asked.

His closest friend, Robert Champart, abbot of Jumièges, looked across the great hall of the ducal palace at Rouen to the table at which Duke William was sitting, flanked by his uncles Archbishop Mauger of Rouen and William Talou, Count of Arques, and his cousin Ralph de Gacé.

'What an interesting question!' Champart replied with effete, acidic relish. 'Well now, let's see . . . At first glance, I'd say that our bastard duke is lucky to be alive at all, let alone be in possession of his title. He's illegitimate, his father only became duke because he killed his own brother—'

'One can't be sure of that.'

'My dear Edward, what a simple, honest English soul you hide behind your Norman facade. When two brothers go to war, and one of them dies suddenly, for no good reason, and the other then takes his dukedom, I think it's reasonable to assume that the new duke was responsible for the passing of the old. Still, that does at least show a ruthless streak, which is no bad thing in a ruler. But as I was saying . . . the boy's father was a murderer, his mother is a peasant—'

'Oh come now, Bishop, that's the Viscountess of Conteville you're talking about,' said Edward in mock outrage.

'Yes, and the stink of the tannery still wafts around her wherever she goes.' Champart wrinkled his nose in distaste. 'But listen to me prattling away like an old woman, and I still haven't answered your question. So, will the boy live? Hmm, let me ponder for a moment . . . Well, there's one thing I can tell you. Master William is lucky in his enemies.'

'Ooh, I like that. How clever you are, Champart! Tell me more.'

'Well, let's consider them one by one. First, we can eliminate Mauger from our calculations. In the first place, he has nothing to gain by William's death, since he's already Archbishop of Rouen and can neither rise any higher in the Church nor take the title of duke himself.'

'And in the second place?'

'He's quite, quite mad!' The two men laughed gleefully. 'No, I'm being serious,' Champart snickered. 'He's a very strange young man. He's going to have a hard enough time holding on to his archbishopric without worrying about anything else.'

'So what about the other two?'

'Well, poor Ralph is blessed with much of his father's talent – the more duplicitous, conspiratorial, malevolent aspects of it, anyway. He certainly has a hunger for power, and talk about ruthless . . . he's been absolutely savage the way he's got rid of everyone who ever stood between him and William.'

'But . . . ?'

'But he looks like a donkey! . . . No, Edward, stop laughing! People will wonder what's so funny, and that's dangerous. Anyway, I'm telling the simple truth. No man who looks like Ralph can hope to rule Normandy – not if he's a usurper, anyway. Deep down I think he knows it too. So that leaves Talou . . .'

'Ah, but Ralph would never let him kill William, would he?' Edward said. 'I mean, if Talou took over, what need would he have of Ralph? None at all – in fact he'd want him out of the way: dead, or at the very least exiled.'

'Exactly, so there's a stalemate. Meanwhile, let me ask you a question. Of all the men seated at that council table, who looks most like a duke?'

Edward cast his eyes back and forth along the line of dignitaries, and each time they came to rest in the centre of the line. 'William,' he said. 'It's that little bastard William.'

'Remarkable, isn't it? The boy is what, fourteen, maybe fifteen now?'

'Something like that.'

'He has nothing but bad blood in his veins, and yet, just look at him. He's already as big and strong-looking as any other man there. And though he's not handsome exactly, there's just something about him, an air of leadership, of dominance. I hate to say this, but it's really quite attractive. I mean, in the sense that men will follow him and women will want to bed him.'

'Oh yes, I understand exactly what you mean,' said Edward. 'You wouldn't want to cross him either, would you?' A memory came to him of a conversation with William years earlier: of his unbroken voice calmly, but with an undercurrent of genuine relish, describing how, if Harold Harefoot had blinded *his* brother, he would have ripped out Harefoot's eyes in return.

'He's always had a vengeful nature,' Edward said. 'In fact, the more I look at him, the more I'm inclined to think that it's not a matter of when Ralph, Mauger and Talou will get rid of William, but when he will dispose of them.'

As Edward and Champart had been talking, another man had been making his way through the mass of litigants, supplicants, courtiers and servants thronging the hall. From time to time he had stopped to ask a question, but no one had given him an answer until at last someone pointed him in Edward's direction. Now he pushed his way through the last few people until he came to his quarry, whereupon he bowed low and said, 'Your Majesty, I bring news from your mother in England.'

Edward was suitably gratified by the show of obeisance, but less impressed by the reason for it. He gave an irritable sigh as he took the rolled parchment and broke open the wax seal. His eyes scanned the message, carelessly at first and then with increasing absorption, and as he read, his mood visibly changed. He stood taller, with his shoulders square and his sullen pout transformed into a beaming smile.

'My,' said Champart, 'someone's had good news.'

'Indeed I have, my dearest bishop, indeed I have!' Edward enthused. 'You know, this is truly an extraordinary moment, one that I've waited for all my life. I always knew it would come, but I'll admit there were times when doubts crept in. But now . . . now . . .'

'Oh Edward,' said Champart. 'Have they . . . ?'

'Yes, old friend, my people have called for me. And I am bound for England.'

4

Alençon, in the county of Bellême

'You can't do this!' William Talvas of Bellême screamed at his son. 'You can't kick me out of my own property. I'm your father, damn you. Show me some respect!'

Arnulf of Bellême laughed. 'Show you respect? What have you ever done to deserve that? When have you ever respected anyone in your whole rotten, poisonous life?'

'By God, I'll not let you get away with this. I'll . . . I'll . . .'

'You'll what?' asked Arnulf, and Bellême was uncomfortably aware that though his son had barely a hair on his chin, he was now a head taller than him. 'If you had a sword and I just picked up a knife from the dinner table, I'd still beat you. But you wouldn't pick up a sword, would you? You're too much of a stinking coward. You showed the whole world that. And why should any man fight for you when you won't fight for yourself?'

Talvas cursed the fates that had led him to this humiliation. He cursed his second wife, Rohais, who now stood beside his son, urging him on, supporting that rebellious brat against his own father. It was her fault, all of this, Talvas now realised. If she hadn't been such a Jezebel, seducing him with female trickery and witchcraft, he never would have wanted to marry her and none of this would have happened. Or maybe William Fitzgiroie was to blame. If he hadn't let those men hang Walter Sors and his ill-begotten sons, or refused a perfectly reasonable request to kill that pathetic slut Hildeburg, everything would have turned out perfectly.

What people never seemed to understand, Talvas now realised, was that he had a right to expect things to work out as he wished. He deserved that. So, for example, the problem with his brother Robert's death was not that he had died. As that oaf Giroie had pointed out all those years ago, that had been to Talvas's advantage. The point was that he had not died in a way that Talvas had controlled. Things had not been done properly.

The same with Hildeburg. What damn right did William Fitzgiroie have to place the needs of his immortal soul – which was surely going to burn anyway – ahead of Talvas's desire to see his wife killed in a location and manner of his choosing? All Fitzgiroie had to do was say yes, and then there would have been no need to punish him. And Talvas's wedding could have gone ahead in peace, and nothing would have happened . . .

'Don't go to Talvas's wedding,' Ralph Fitzgiroie had said. The fifth-born Giroie son had been the one sent to make the family's peace with God. He was a monk, complete with shaven pate, or tonsure, and plain brown habit, and was known for two characteristics above all. The first was his fondness for strapping chain mail over his monk's robes and joining in any fight he could find. This had led to his somewhat cumbersome nickname of Ralph the Ill-Tonsured, the point being that he really wasn't cut out for a life of contemplative religious devotion.

He was also known as Ralph the Clerk, for he possessed remarkable intelligence, in both the intellectual and military sense. Brother Ralph seemed to know everything, be it about theology, philosophy or history on the one hand, or everyday gossip and rumour – who was doing what to whom and why – on the other. And now he had information he wanted to share.

'I'm telling you, William, Talvas is after you. He still blames you for his brother's death, and he's never forgiven you for refusing to kill Hildeburg, either.'

'Don't be ridiculous, Ralph,' said his brother, laughing at the very idea. 'I don't know where you got this from, but for once in your life you're wrong. Talvas hardly objected at all when I said I wouldn't do it. He just nodded and went off to find someone else.'

'He didn't scream or shout, you mean? He just stood there quietly?'

'Exactly.'

'Well then, it must have been really serious. He was putting a little note against your name, marking you down for vengeance.'

'For Christ's sake, that's just absurd!'

'No it isn't. You're in danger. Don't go to the wedding. I mean it.'

William went anyway. He took a dozen armed men with him to Alençon, but he attended the wedding itself and the celebrations afterwards alone and unarmed. So he had no way of defending himself when Talvas had him seized and locked away. The day after the wedding, Talvas went out hunting. While he was gone, his men, acting on his orders, blinded William Fitzgiroie with a red-hot poker, then cut off his ears and his nose.

Somehow he survived his ordeal, though he was left horribly mutilated. Luckily for Talvas, Giroie himself was now dead, for the retribution he would have exacted for his son's ordeal would have involved Talvas being chopped, very slowly, into little pieces amidst the corpses of his family and the charred ruins of his lands. There were, however, still enough Giroie brothers alive to take immediate and only marginally less savage revenge. They rode through the county of Bellême sacking, looting and razing Talvas's farms, manors, granaries and storehouses. Finally they came to Alençon itself, where they stood outside the castle gates and taunted Talvas, mocking him and challenging him to take on any one of them in combat to the death.

Talvas refused. In his mind, he was, as always, playing the long game. He could always rebuild anything the Giroie clan had burned down and replace what they had stolen. But he could not get another life. The whole point about castles was that one was safe inside them. Only an idiot would voluntarily leave that protection and risk his neck in a fight.

That, though, was not the way the rest of the world saw it. By maiming William Fitzgiroie, an entirely blameless wedding guest who had served him loyally and accepted his hospitality in good faith, Talvas had finally gone too far. The fearsome reputation that he had spent a lifetime building up was instantly and irrevocably destroyed. He had brought shame on himself and, by extension, on the House of Bellême and all who served in it.

Arnulf was his father's son. He had been taught from earliest childhood that the only thing to do when confronted by weakness was to exploit it and crush it. He had watched as his father, knowing that Hildeburg was both physically and emotionally fragile, had beaten her down and eventually killed her. Why? Because he could.

And now that Talvas was weak and there for the taking, Arnulf had turned on him and had him expelled from his own castle, thrown out on to the streets of Alençon like a common vagrant, condemned to spend the rest of his days wandering through Normandy begging for shelter and a bite to eat wherever he could find it.

Arnulf had, however, bargained without one surprise. He had thought that his sister Mabel, a girl who loved nothing more than to see cruelty being done to others, would relish her father's downfall. Instead, she told her maid to pack one trunk with her finest robes and another with blankets and furs, and send them both down to the stables to be mounted on a donkey's back. She gathered up the jewels and money she had inherited from her mother and put them in a chest that she hugged to her body like a mother with a newborn babe.

Then she went to Talvas as he stood hunched and shivering in the cold air of the castle yard. 'Don't worry, Papa. I am coming with you. I'll make sure you're all right. As for you, Arnulf, I will never forget what you did here today.'

Her voice rose and her cold, beautiful eyes looked around at the soldiers, servants, priests and townspeople who had been drawn to witness the spectacle of Talvas's expulsion. 'I curse you, Arnulf,' she cried, 'here and now, before everyone present. You will never know another day's peace, nor a night's good rest. For you will know that your doom is approaching and that of the three of us, it is you who will die first. And die in screaming agony, too.'

So saying, she grabbed the rope attached to the donkey's halter and led it out of the castle, her eyes flashing, her head held high and her father following meekly in her wake.

A league or two down the road, she turned to Talvas and said, 'Papa?'

'Yes, my dear,' he replied, oddly conscious that his daughter seemed somehow to have taken charge of events.

'Do you remember the stories you used to tell me about the Viper, that man who was a deadly poisoner?'

'Yes . . .' Talvas paused, wondering if he dared go on. Ralph de Gacé had told him something once, in strictest confidence, insisting that he should never tell anyone. But that had been many years ago, and besides, having been so publicly humiliated, he wanted to impress his daughter. So he added, 'Except that the Viper was not a man.'

Mabel stopped dead in her tracks, eyes alive with curiosity. 'What do you mean?'

Talvas was delighted. 'The Viper was a woman,' he said,

relishing the look of wonderment and delight suffusing Mabel's face. 'Ralph de Gacé found her and assured me that she was extraordinarily beautiful, and that her skill as a poisoner was worthy of a sorceress.'

'Where did he find her?'

'I don't know for sure. But I do remember him asking me all about her, years ago. I told him that there was only one way to get in touch with her, and that was to go to an inn by the docks at Vaudreuil.'

'Then that is where we are going!' said Mabel.

'But dearest, Vaudreuil is several days' walk from here. And there's no guarantee that the inn will still be there, or that she is even alive any more. I haven't heard anything about her in years.'

'I don't care. We are going to Vaudreuil. Someone there will know something. They will lead us to someone else. No matter how long it takes, or how far we have to go, we are going to find the Viper!' With that, Mabel strode away.

Talvas stood where he was for a while, wondering what to do next. It didn't take him long to realise that he had no choice. He was penniless, homeless and entirely dependent upon his daughter. 'Wait for me!' he cried, and set off down the road after her.

5

Lambeth, England

Edward had been back in England for nine months, accompanied by a number of Norman knights who hoped that by showing loyalty to him, they might be able to acquire land and titles, and also by Champart, to whom he had promised the bishopric of London once the current incumbent died. Harthacnut was not troubled by Edward's presence, for he simply did not see him as a threat. One look at his half-brother told him that he would have a hard time seizing a bread roll from a hungry child, let alone a kingdom from its king.

It actually suited Edward to be thought of as harmless, because it meant he had no need to make a secret of his intentions. It delighted him to know how angry his very public support for Champart's cause made Godwin, who wanted to strengthen his own position by putting supporters into key positions in the Church. Patronage was the key to maintaining control of England. The greater a man's capacity to dole out favours to his friends, the more friends he acquired, the more loyal they became and the greater the influence he could exert on them and through them.

No one, of course, could exert more power than the king, yet Edward saw no need to usurp the throne, even had he been capable of doing so. He knew that if anything ever happened to Harthacnut, he'd be the most obvious successor. Even so, he could not guarantee his ascension to the throne, and there lay

Godwin's great strength, as he had reminded Edward on more than one occasion.

The crown of England could not be bestowed upon a monarch without the approval of a gathering of nobles known as the Witenagemot. Godwin had more influence over the Witenagemot than anyone else in the land, and thus Edward would never be crowned without his help. Or perhaps he would never be crowned at all. Harthacnut was fifteen years his junior after all, and frequently boasted of his iron constitution. Edward was disgusted by the king's gluttony and limitless thirst, and could see the toll his lifestyle was taking as Harthacnut became fatter and meaner. But he was not convinced by Godwin's belief that the king was putting his life in danger. A lot more time and overindulgence would surely have to pass before that . . . wouldn't it?

But then, thought Edward, just look at the boorish pig right now. It was a glorious early summer's day, and the court had assembled at a manor house in Lambeth, a marshy stretch of land that lay along the south bank of the River Thames, across the water from London. There they were celebrating the marriage of two of the horde of Danish immigrants who had come to England when Canute became king. The groom, Tofi the Proud, had been Canute's standard-bearer, and had therefore stood alongside the king in battle, a fact that had been brought up again and again throughout the day, much to Edward's chagrin, since some of those battles had been fought, victoriously, against his father Ethelred. Tofi's bride, Gytha, was the daughter of an East Anglian landowner, Osgod Clapa, who had, Edward presumed, either stolen the land from its rightful Saxon owners or been given it by Canute after he had seized it. In either case, it just added to the general bitterness of the day, so far as Edward was concerned. But he was the king's half-brother and second only to him in all the land, so it was beholden on him to attend the marriage of two of his more important subjects.

The service had taken place and the wedding feast was almost over when Harthacnut rose, unsteadily and with considerable difficulty, to make a speech in honour of the bride and groom. He had, of course, stuffed himself with the richest foods on the table, washed down by flagons of wine.

'My lords, ladies, friends . . . enemies,' he grinned as he got his first laugh, 'it is time to charge your vessels and drink a toast to the bride and groom. Oh, wait . . . I can't charge my vessel. It's already full . . . Huh! That won't do. Better empty it so I can fill it up again.'

There were a few laughs and incoherent shouts from around the hall, and then a single voice, very clear, called out from the back, 'Go on, Your Majesty, down it in one!'

That set off a round of applause and more shouts of encouragement. Swaying a little, so that he had to reach out and grab the top of his gilded chair for support, Harthacnut raised a pewter tankard that looked big enough to hold an entire bottle of wine. 'Drink this?' he asked.

The revellers cheered.

'In one, single draught?'

They cheered again, even more loudly.

'Are you sure?'

Now the entire hall echoed to the sound of shouts and applause.

'Very well then.' Harthacnut held the tankard up in front of his face, so everyone could see it, and called out, 'Are you ready?'

Someone started banging the table in a steady beat, like a drummer setting times for a warship's oarsmen, chanting, 'Drink! Drink! Drink! Drink!' All around the other guests joined in the banging and chanting.

Harthacnut took a deep breath, then put the tankard to his

mouth and started drinking. His thick throat vibrated with every swallow. Rivulets of purple wine stained his red-gold beard as it dribbled down from the tankard.

'Drink! Drink! Drink! Drink!'

Harthacnut threw his head back further, tilting the tankard ever more steeply to his face. Edward, sitting in a place of honour at the top table, looked on in disgusted fascination as sweat poured off the king's forehead. It seemed to be taking forever, as though the vessel were enchanted, constantly refilling no matter how hard Harthacnut tried to empty it. But then, quite suddenly, he stopped, took the tankard from his mouth and held it out upside down, so that everyone could see it was empty.

The roar that rose from the room filled with Norsemen and Saxons was enough to make the timbers shake. Harthacnut nodded his head, his face wreathed in a triumphant smirk. Still holding the tankard, he wiped the back of his hand across his mouth. Then he slammed the pewter vessel down on the table and waved a serving girl over to refill it, giving her a regal slap on her behind for her troubles. Finally he raised his tankard one more time and said, 'I give you a—'

His face seemed to collapse before the wedding party's very eyes. His right eye dropped, and the right side of his mouth twisted downwards in a grotesque, frozen grimace. His arms fell to his sides and dangled there, like puppet limbs whose strings had been cut. For a few seconds he tried to speak, but he could make no sound, and then he fell, as straight and sturdy as a felled oak, face first on to the tabletop.

A sudden, absolute silence fell upon the hall as Harthacnut lay there quite motionless, not breathing. Then the bride screamed and the same awful realisation struck every man and woman at once: the king was dead.

* * *

'He was poisoned,' said Edward, as he and Godwin rode in the column wending its way through the marshes en route to Winchester, with the carriage carrying the king's body bringing up the rear. 'This reminds me very strongly of the death of my cousin Alan of Brittany, a couple of years ago. He dropped dead at a banquet too, very similar circumstances, though he was on campaign, dining with his officers. It's always been my belief that Ralph de Gacé, my uncle Robert's bastard son planned the whole thing. I'm absolutely certain he set out to kill everyone between him and that other little bastard, William of Normandy. Succeeded, too.'

Godwin looked across at the man he might soon make into a king. It was hard to see any obvious reason why England should wish Edward to rule her. True, he had one major advantage over his immediate predecessors: he could always be counted upon to be sober. And he obviously had some kind of survival instinct that had kept him alive and well when so many around him were dying. But in other respects he was a disappointment. All those years in Normandy had robbed him of the sheen of wealth and sophistication that he would have acquired had he grown up as a prince in England. His clothes, for example, were the shabby hand-me-downs of a poor relation with no land or wealth of his own.

Not that Edward seemed to care. He'd managed to persuade himself that material display of any kind was sinful. Well, perhaps that went down well with monks and nuns – though they always managed to look after themselves very nicely, in Godwin's experience – but the people expected to be ruled by someone who looked like a proper king. And the nobles expected a man who could think like a king. Now Godwin set about testing Edward, to see whether he could fulfil that requirement.

'So you say Ralph killed Brittany because he had something to gain by it?' he asked.

'Of course, why else would he do it?'

'I don't know . . . hatred, revenge, sheer bloody-minded malice.'

'I don't think so,' Edward said. 'Alan was quite popular among the Normans, and I have no reason to think that Ralph disliked him on a personal level. Of course, I considered him to be a profoundly vulgar and immoral character. He was responsible enough in his role as Count of Brittany, I suppose, but the things he cared about most were hunting and fornicating.'

'Most men, not to mention most women, would think well of him for that.'

'Well I am glad I am not like other men, then.'

'Quite so . . .' Godwin murmured. 'If I follow your logic correctly, whoever murdered Harthacnut, if indeed he was murdered, did it because he sought to gain by the death. Is that right?'

'Yes, I would say so.'

'But the person who stood to gain most was you. After all, you can now claim the crown itself. What greater prize is there than that? So did you have King Harthacnut killed?'

Too late, Edward realised that Godwin had been leading him to this conclusion all along. 'Of course not!' he blustered. 'The very suggestion is . . . why, it's outrageous, and deeply defamatory. I insist you withdraw it at once!'

'With pleasure,' said Godwin. 'I am perfectly content to believe that Harthacnut died from a surfeit of food and drink. Everyone who was there will believe that too, whether it's true or not, because they saw Harthacnut drink the entire contents of his tankard before he suffered his fatal seizure, and they will reason that if he had been poisoned, he'd have felt the effects after the very first swallow. He certainly wouldn't have kept on drinking. So that won't be an issue. The real question is: who will be the next king?'

'But surely . . .' There was sudden bemusement in Edward's voice. 'I mean to say . . . surely I'm going to be the next king. I should have been king these past twenty-six years.'

'That may be true, but you weren't. Canute and his line were. And the only surviving male relative of Canute is young Sven Estridsson, my nephew by marriage . . . My dear wife will certainly be pressing his case, I can assure you.'

'You won't be swayed by your wife, will you?' asked Edward, who found the very idea of having a wife, let alone listening to her, hard to comprehend.

'If I know what's good for me, I'll certainly have to let her have her say, yes. Then you must consider the Danish settlers, who control so much of the country these days. You saw plenty of them at that wedding. They were still loyal to Harthacnut and they'll naturally look to Estridsson to carry on the line.'

'But the people will want a true Englishman, born in this country. They will rally to me.'

'They can do all they like, but none of them have a vote in the Witenagemot. That is where your fate will be decided.'

'You must get me the crown, Godwin. You must!'

'It's not my business to "get" it for anyone,' said Godwin, wondering if Edward could possibly believe that. 'It is for my fellow nobles to decide. Of course, I am the senior earl of England, so I suppose I carry a certain influence.'

'Then for God's sake use it!' Edward cried, his voice rising to a pitch of near desperation.

'Hmm . . . I suppose it would be perfectly reasonable of me to point out that Sven is in Denmark and we don't want to hang around for another half-year to see whether he will return to England. We wasted long enough waiting for Harthacnut in the months after Canute's death. We don't want to go through that again, particularly with Magnus of Norway poised to try to enforce his claim.'

'What claim has Magnus got? He has no blood tie to Canute's house or mine.'

'No, but he has a treaty signed by Harthacnut, while drunk, as usual, saying that Magnus would be his heir if he died without a son of his own.'

'But I heard that just applied to Denmark.'

'That's a matter of debate. Either way, it certainly gives Magnus an excuse to launch an invasion. But it also means we need a king to lead us against Magnus.'

'I see . . .' Edward suddenly sounded less enthusiastic.

'Not all kings have to be warriors. Of course it's best if the men can see their monarch in the heart of the battle. That was always Canute's style. And I saw your father in the thick of the fighting on more than one occasion. A figurehead, there on the day of the battle, might well be enough . . . maybe the odd skirmish or two.'

'And you could persuade the Witenagemot to accept me . . . if Sven stays in Denmark?'

'Yes, I believe so. But I would hope that you would show regal generosity to one who has served your cause so well. I feel certain that Sven would wish to show his gratitude if I were to decide that I owed it to my family connections to support him. As I said, he is my nephew. It would only be natural.'

'What do you want?' Edward asked, all business now.

'I have seven sons, fine young men every one of them. The two oldest, Sweyn and Harold, are of an age now when they need something to do, and somewhere to do it. I was thinking that Sweyn could have some of the land between my earldom of Wessex and Leofric's territories in Mercia. I was thinking Berkshire, which borders Oxfordshire, which in turn is neighbours with Gloucestershire, from which his land could run north-west to Herefordshire and south-west to Somerset.'

'That's five counties!'

'Oh, you sound surprised. Too few?'

'No, most certainly not. And what do you expect me to give Harold?'

'East Anglia. Harold's a born warrior. If Magnus or anyone else lands anywhere south of the Wash, Harold will see them off. And if they land north of the Wash, Harold will wait till they reach his land and destroy them there.'

'Well, that sounds promising. So your price is those two earldoms, then?'

'And one other thing . . . My eldest daughter, Edith, is a lovely girl. God knows where she got it from, because no one would call her mother beautiful, and I've never been known for my good looks either. But she's a stunning lass, and educated, too. She can read and write as well as a monk. She writes Latin prose and poems and I'm sure they're damn good, though I can't understand a word of them. And if her own dam's anything to go by, she'll have no trouble giving you fine, healthy sons on a yearly basis.'

'So . . . what? You wish me to find her a husband?'

'No, I wish you to *be* her husband. Take it from me, you won't find a better wife anywhere.'

'Wife?' said Edward, as the blood drained from his face.

'Yes. We've had two kings die without an heir to succeed them. We can't afford a third.'

Edward swallowed hard, breathed deeply and sat up straight in his saddle. 'Very well, I accept your terms. Your sons shall have their earldoms and your daughter shall have me for a husband.'

'In that case, sire,' Godwin said, 'I will be honoured to make you my king.'

6

Rouen

Across the water in Normandy, the man whom Edward had rightly deduced to have plotted the killings that robbed William of his guardians was enjoying the fruits of his machinations. Ralph de Gacé was the unofficial but universally acknowledged power in the land. And like all wise leaders, he took care to make occasional, but very visible, gestures of goodwill to the people on whose support his position depended.

On this occasion, for example, a troupe of travelling entertainers had arrived in Rouen – a minstrel, a bawdy comic poet, an animal trainer with his dancing bear, a quartet of acrobats (including a pair of particularly comely maidens) and a strongman – and Ralph had invited them to perform for the court in the great hall of the ducal palace one night after dinner. Of course, William still sat at the centre of the high table, but it was Ralph who stood up when the tables had been cleared of food and made a short speech welcoming 'the jongleurs, tumblers, wild animals . . . and of course that charming bear', inviting them to display their skills and encouraging the audience to applaud them warmly.

Tables were pushed aside to create space for the performers, who duly displayed their skills and, in the case of the two maidens, far more of their ripe young bodies than any respectable woman would ever dare reveal. Ralph led the applause. Talou volunteered when the magician asked for someone to come forward from the audience, and was amazed to discover that three gold coins had been removed from his purse – which remained at all times hanging from his belt, in full public view – and replaced by three slices of carrot.

William, meanwhile, found himself rendered mute and invisible, as if he were not actually there. The one time Ralph de Gacé spoke to him was when he leaned over just before the poet was about to start his epic tale of the love affair between Samson and Delilah and said, 'It's getting late, William, everyone's had a great deal to drink and if I know anything about wandering poets, things are about to get rowdy. Perhaps it might be best if you retired.'

'No,' said William, and glared at de Gacé, daring him to try to overrule him.

'Very well, as you wish,' and de Gacé turned back towards the poet and with a jaunty wave of the hand signalled that he should begin.

Sure enough, the poem was scabrously filthy, shockingly blasphemous and wildly funny. It brought the house down, and William was lifted from his bad mood, laughing along with everyone else and banging the table with the flat of his hand as he joined in the calls of 'More! More!'

Yet he still felt more like an anonymous guest than the master of the house, and the frustration ate at him. He wanted to impose himself upon events in some way, to be seen as a duke rather than a mere adolescent. And then he saw his opportunity.

Having bent iron bars, lifted great barrels of wine and bitten through thick leather belts, the strongman, who called himself Brutus the Great, had sat himself down at one end of a long table and placed a gold coin in front of him, promising the coin to anyone who could beat him at arm wrestling. He was a giant of a man, dressed only in breeches so that everyone could see that he had arms thicker than any normal man's thighs, a torso like a castle keep, great slabs of tightly bunched muscle and a back that was almost as thickly covered in wiry black hair as the bear's.

'Roll up, roll up!' Brutus shouted. 'And I'll even let the other man push first.'

One after another, the heftiest members of the household, from the sergeant of the guard to the palace blacksmith, duly stepped forward to the raucous cheers of their friends. With crushing inevitability, every single contender had his arm forced down and his knuckles slammed against the tabletop as the suddenly mocking jeers of the crowd echoed from the hall's high stone walls.

Finally, after a dozen men or more had walked back from the table rubbing their biceps or nursing their crushed right hands, there came a point when no one else was willing to put himself through such obvious and futile torture.

'Come on!' Brutus encouraged them. 'There must be one more man here brave enough to try his luck!'

Clearly there wasn't, because an embarrassed silence, punctuated by coughs and shuffling feet, descended on the hall. Having been so willing to make themselves the centre of attention and admiration before, neither de Gacé nor Talou felt any need to make a spectacle of themselves again.

'Very well then,' said Brutus, with a shake of his head. He picked up the coin in one of his huge furry paws and was about to get up from the table when William rose to his feet.

All eyes turned towards the duke, who had presumably stood to congratulate the strongman and commiserate with his victims. But those were not William's intentions.

'I'll take you on, Master Brutus. Why don't you try your luck with me?' he called out, loud enough for everyone in the hall to hear.

A great burst of laughter and applause broke out. The lad

had a nerve. Three months shy of his fifteenth birthday, and he was challenging a mighty strongman. 'Go easy on him, he's only a lad!' someone called out, and Brutus grinned and called back, 'Don't you worry. I'll send him away in one piece!'

As William pushed back his chair, about to step down from the dais, de Gacé reached up and grabbed his sleeve. 'Don't!' he hissed. 'You'll only make a fool of yourself!'

William brushed the hand away and marched towards the strongman.

'The pup looks like he means business,' Talou muttered to de Gacé, and William's face did indeed bear the fixed, tight-jawed determination of a warrior going into battle, rather than the cheeky grin of a young lad trying his luck.

Brutus, however, was all smiles as he placed his elbow on the table. 'Sit down here, my lord, and let's see what you're made of.'

William said nothing. He betrayed not a flicker of emotion as he fixed his eyes on the strongman and let his hand be swallowed up in his massive fist.

'Ready?' Brutus asked.

William nodded. He felt the strongman's grip tighten around his hand and almost winced in pain. He did his very best to push, but the other man's arm did not budge. A force more powerful than any he had ever known bore down upon his arm as Brutus took the strain and pushed back so hard it felt as if one of the mighty stone pillars that supported the great hall's gallery had fallen down upon him. William did his best to resist, but it was impossible. He was on the point of conceding defeat when, as if by magic, Brutus gave way and William felt his hand forcing the other man's down until it touched the table.

He had won.

'Well I never!' Brutus shouted as wild applause broke out around them. 'Your young master's my master too.'

Still William said nothing. His expression did not change. He waited until the noise had died down, then raised a hand for silence and, being sure to make himself heard by everyone, said, 'Do it again, strongman. And this time give it your best.'

There were gasps of astonishment all around, followed by a hum of excited chatter.

'Are you sure about this, my lord?' Brutus asked, speaking low enough to make it a private conversation.

'Yes.'

'You're going to regret it, but no matter,' Brutus said. He stood up, and intoned in his thunderous voice, 'Let all here bear witness, I am obeying the duke's command.'

Every man there, William included, knew what that meant.

Brutus sat back down, put his elbow on the table once again and looked at William. 'This is going to hurt,' he said.

Brutus the Great had never lost a fight or a trial of strength in his life, and he wasn't about to start now. He took another look at Duke William of Normandy, forgetting his rank and considering him dispassionately as an opponent. He was a well-made boy, no doubt about that, and strapping for his age, but still just a boy for all that. He'd been on the point of defeat first time around, before Brutus had pretended to surrender. It would be no trouble to finish him off in an instant this time, without damaging anything other than his lordly pride.

And that was important, because Brutus had no intention of causing injury. Damn the duke's command – that would be forgotten soon enough if William of Normandy was lying on the ground screaming in pain and crying out for his mummy.

Brutus grabbed hold of William's hand. 'Go ahead,' he said. 'Whenever you're ready.'

The boy pushed. It felt no stronger to Brutus than a gentle breeze against his skin. He squeezed the duke's fist, hard enough to hurt but not to harm. The pain alone was enough to beat most men. It distracted them, sapped their will, and then their arms gave way. One little shove should do it . . .

William did not give way.

He was hurting, he had to be, Brutus was sure of it. But he wasn't letting it show.

Brutus was impressed. The lad was tougher than he'd expected. He waited a bit longer, not trying any harder, just so that the duke could enjoy the shouts of encouragement from his people. He had already lasted longer than anyone but the blacksmith: they had good reason to be impressed.

Now the time had come to end it. Brutus squeezed a little harder, feeling the bones in William's hand being crushed together beneath his grip. He had been doing this for long enough to know that anyone he ever faced was in screaming agony at this point. Usually they would shout out in pain and beat their spare hand against the table to try and keep themselves from conceding.

But still William was silent. Still his eyes were fixed on Brutus. The veins were standing out on his forehead. His face was flushed scarlet. His skin was lathered in sweat, but he wasn't giving way.

By now, the great hall was in uproar. It was clear to everyone that this was a real contest, a fight to the finish, and that somehow their boy, their duke, was matching the man-mountain. But it couldn't go on much longer, surely . . . could it?

Brutus pushed harder. He knew how strong he was. He knew that William was not remotely as physically powerful as him. By now the muscles in his arm must be pressed far beyond their limits. They would be screaming at him for release, they had to be.

So all that was keeping the boy in the contest was willpower, a blunt refusal to surrender under any circumstances. Brutus suddenly understood that for all his own visible strength, for all his bulging muscles, he was facing someone with an invisible power that was greater than any he had ever encountered.

Oh, he could still win the bout all right. He could crush Duke William's hand like a rotten apple in his fist and rip his arm right off his shoulder. But it would take that before the boy would give in.

So now what did he do? He could not injure the Duke of Normandy beyond repair. He was under orders not to fake his own defeat. That left just one alternative.

Brutus let go of William's hand, and as the boy slumped back on the wooden bench, flat out, completely spent, the strongman got up, towering over every other man in the hall. 'Hear this, people of Normandy!' he boomed. 'I, Brutus the Great, am the strongest man alive. I have never in all my days been beaten. I was not beaten tonight. But neither could I beat the man I was wrestling. My lord, I salute you!'

He gave a deep, respectful bow and held out his hand.

Finding some last, hidden reserves of energy, William struggled to his feet and shook Brutus's hand in a gesture of mutual respect.

Barely aware of the hubbub around him or the slaps on the back from everyone he passed, aching in every fibre of his being, William staggered back to the high table. He looked at Ralph de Gacé. 'Now I'll go to bed,' he said.

7

Winchester

It was customary, indeed compulsory, for any powerful man who wished to benefit from the accession of a new king to present him with a gift to mark his coronation. Godwin may have muttered to his wife Gytha, 'If we keep having new kings this often, I'm going to end up a pauper,' but he and his family stood to gain an enormous amount from the reign of King Edward, and so his gift was suitably generous.

It was a ship, just as he had given to Harthacnut, but this one was even more magnificent. The hull was twice as long and the golden dragon at the bow correspondingly larger, with a three-pronged tongue of red-painted flame blazing from its mouth, while a golden lion roared defiance from the stern. The sail was dyed purple, the colour of emperors and kings, and embroidered with Edward's lineage, stretching back through his father and a line of kings to Alfred the Great himself. On it, too, were scenes from the great sea battles fought by the kings of England against those who would invade their country. 'I'm hoping,' said Godwin to Gytha, 'that it may encourage him to go to sea himself if Magnus's ships are ever sighted off our shores.'

For her part, Gytha was assembling the trousseau that would form a part of Edith's dowry when the time came for her to become Edward's queen. Traders from Constantinople and the Arab-ruled lands of southern Spain furnished the Godwins with finely patterned carpets and hangings, while the fabric merchants of Flanders sold many a bolt of wool and linen from which the royal couple's clothes and bedcovers would be made.

Yet Edward was no ordinary king. He had little interest in display or finery. For all that he had spent his whole life craving his coronation, when the event took place at Winchester Cathedral almost a year after Harthacnut's death, he seemed strangely uneasy on the throne. As the crown was placed upon his head and he held the jewel- and pearl-encrusted golden orb and sceptre that symbolised his kingship, he wore a look of discomfort rather than joy.

Nor were his priorities those that Godwin had expected. Edward showed little interest in the news from Scandinavia, where Magnus of Norway had successfully claimed Denmark and given Sven Estridsson his own earldom in Jutland, thereby securing his loyalty, for now at any rate, and freeing Magnus for an assault on England that he could launch at any moment. He sanctioned the continuation of the warship-building programme that Harthacnut had begun, but he did so with an almost total lack of interest. His real concern was much more personal.

'I want my mother brought low,' he told a gathering of his three most powerful nobles: Godwin, Leofric and Siward of Northumbria, a dark, brooding presence as imposing as a mountain crag. 'I want her titles, her money and her possessions taken from her. She must be banished from the palace, stuck in a convent or a hovel. Find me a way to destroy her.'

It was not a new request. Ever since Edward's coronation, his court had come to understand that the single biggest influence upon their new monarch's thoughts, words and actions was his detestation of his mother, Emma. Week by week, month by month, the king brooded, doing nothing yet growing more bitter, until everyone around him became caught up in the poisonous atmosphere, waiting in scarcely bearable tension for the hatred to be turned into some kind of action.

'Do you want her killed, sire?' Godwin asked, again not for the first time. 'It could be arranged if you did.'

Godwin had no personal desire to harm a woman he had known for his entire adult life. He was just desperate to get Edward to do something, anything, to rid himself of his obsession, so that they could all get on with the proper business of ruling the kingdom of England.

'No,' Edward replied. 'I want her kept alive. Let her grow old and grey, so that she has year after year of miserable poverty, stripped of all her possessions and power, knowing that I have done this to her.'

Siward gave a contemptuous grunt. 'Why the bloody hell are we still bothering with this when Magnus is on his way?'

'I don't need to give you my reasons, I just want you to obey my commands,' Edward shot back. 'But since you ask, it is very simple. My mother abandoned me.'

'And your brother and sister,' Godwin murmured, as if prompting Edward.

'Yes, yes, and them too,' the king said impatiently. 'She chose to spread her legs for Canute rather than look after her own children, because she cared more for being a queen than being my mother. And then after all those years, when Canute was dead and we finally became useful to her, it was Alfred she loved, not I, and it's Alfred she still mourns.'

'You must be careful, sire,' said Leofric. 'Rightly or wrongly, the queen is very popular among the people. She has allies in the clergy, too. In Canute's time she was famed for the generosity of her donations to cathedrals and monasteries. Those acts of charity haven't been forgotten.'

'Then I shall appoint new bishops and archbishops who don't remember what happened in the past but care only for the present and the future.'

Godwin had only half his mind engaged in Edward's embittered ranting. For the most part, he was thinking about Emma. At one time or another he had been both her closest political friend and her most bitter enemy. What would he be now? He bore her no personal malice, and it hardly seemed fair that, having asked for her cooperation in bringing Edward to England in the first place, he would now help the king to bring her down. She would expect him to defend her, and she had every right to do so. But from Godwin's point of view, fairness didn't come into it. He dealt in expediency. His consistent, unflinching aim was to maintain his position and his family's long-term legacy. At any one time, the king, whoever he might be, was the man best placed to help him achieve those goals, so Godwin's first loyalty was to him. And all this talk about clergymen had given him an idea.

'I think I can help you, sire,' he said. 'Her Majesty—'

'Don't call her that!' Edward snapped.

'Very well, your mother is close to Bishop Aelfwine, here in Winchester.'

'Go on . . .'

'One night, before your blessed return to England, I found them together in the palace treasury. No one else was present.'

'Were they conspiring?' Edward asked eagerly.

'They were certainly engaged in, ah, intimate conversation.'

'Intimate? Were they fornicating?'

'They were fully dressed when I saw them. What had happened before, or might have happened if I had not intruded upon them, I can't say.'

'Is Winchester one of the dioceses to which my mother made donations?'

'Yes, Your Majesty, she gave a magnificent cross to the New Minster. I think I'm right in saying that it contains at least fifteen pounds of gold and hundreds of pounds of silver.

The jewels mounted upon it are worth a fortune in themselves.'

The king looked far from impressed. 'That sounds less like generosity than vainglorious profligacy, intended not to honour God Almighty but to burnish my mother's reputation. It seems to me that this, ah, union between my promiscuous slut of a mother and a sinful, oath-breaking bishop affords me the opportunity to serve two ends at once, since I now have good reason to punish my mother and replace the bishop.'

'You do, sire, but only if you have evidence to support your accusations,' Leofric pointed out. 'If you do not, you will succeed only in uniting the people and the clergy against you.'

'Then get me the evidence,' said the king.

Winchester was the principal city of Wessex and thus in Godwin's earldom. It fell to him, therefore, to find the evidence that would prove an illicit carnal union between Queen Emma and Bishop Aelfwine. He did not suppose for a single second that the two had ever been together when they were not fully dressed and standing or sitting at a suitably modest distance from one another. But that was not the point. He had a task to fulfil, and it was a matter of necessity and also personal pride that he should accomplish it.

His first thought was to speak to Emma's ladies-in-waiting, but it immediately struck him that this was almost certain to prove counter-productive: none of them were likely to betray their mistress, and all would immediately go to her and warn her what he was up to. Instead he went to the palace chamberlain and said that he wished to interview a number of servants, for reasons he was not at present at liberty to reveal.

This was puzzling enough to the chamberlain, for men of Godwin's stature did not normally trouble themselves with menials, and he was even more bemused when Godwin stressed that he particularly wanted to talk to anyone known for their surliness, discontent or treacherous personality.

'But those are all faults,' the chamberlain said.

'On the contrary,' Godwin replied. 'For the task I have in mind, they are all virtues.'

The chamberlain asked, as firmly as he dared, whether he might be allowed a few days before attending to the matter. St Andrew's Day was approaching, one of the great days in the Christian calendar, and it was his job to make sure that the feast that marked the occasion was of properly regal standards. Every hour, carts were arriving at the palace gates laden with carcasses of oxen, sheep and pigs, chickens and geese by the score and eels by the barrel, along with sacks of flour and earthenware jars filled with honey, all bound for the palace storerooms and from there to the cooks' fires.

'The men and women I want will by their very nature contribute little to your work,' Godwin observed. 'Attend to it at once.'

The chamberlain assumed that Godwin was looking for spies of some kind, but knew better than to question him any further. So it was that a stream of resentful, deceitful ne'er-do-wells made their slovenly way to the chamber where Godwin was conducting his interviews. Since none of them could be relied upon to be remotely discreet, Godwin reckoned he had a single day at most before word got back to Emma. In the end, however, he had not even had his lunch by the time he found what he wanted.

Her name was Mildred. She was lank-haired and long-nosed, and her face was liberally scattered with pustules, several of which were bleeding and seeping from having been squeezed. So when she told Godwin that she had once been Emma's personal maid, he refused to believe her and told her to stop telling such obvious lies.

'Weren't a lie!' she protested. 'They sent me to work for her when that Harefoot become king. I seen her with nothing on, seen her dirty hose an' all.'

'Where was she living when you were her maid, then?'

'Not in her old chambers, that's for sure. Harefoot's ma . . . wossername?'

'Elgiva.'

'That's the one . . . she kicked 'Er Majesty out of her old royal bedchamber, stuck her in a right hole.'

That was true enough. Edward wasn't the first to try humbling Emma. The first thing her old adversary Elgiva of Northampton had done when her boy Harold became king was to strip Emma of all the marks and privileges of royalty. Replacing her personal attendants and staff with this ugly, slovenly scullion would have given Elgiva particular satisfaction – as it would have pleased Emma, he knew, had their positions been reversed.

'I see,' Godwin said. 'Let's suppose you're telling the truth. Answer me this: did you see anyone going to the chamber to visit Her Majesty, anyone unusual, I mean?'

Mildred didn't have to think. 'Yeah, I did, and I told me dad and me mam about it soon as I next seen 'em. Just ask 'em, they'll tell you.'

'What did you tell them?'

'Why, I told 'em about that dirty old Bishop Aelfwine, going in and out of 'Er Majesty's chamber at all hours of the night . . . and dressed up like a common priest, like he didn't want to be recognised.'

'When was this?'

'It was twice. Once was quite soon after the real king died . . .'

'You mean Canute?'

'Yeah, when they was still all arguing about who was going

to be king, though Harefoot was acting like he was already.'

'And the second time?'

'It was later, just before 'Er Majesty went away across the water.'

'What did you see?'

'I told you. I saw the bishop. I could see he'd been doing summink he oughtn't, 'cos 'e was coming out the chamber, like . . .' She darted her head from left to right, like someone guilty checking to see if they had been spotted.

'What was he wearing?'

'He had a cloak on with a hood right up over his head.'

'So how do you know it was him?'

'He was holding a candle, wasn't 'e? And I could see he wasn't wearing no bishop's clothes, just one of them brown things like what monks wear.'

'And what time was this?'

'Proper late it was. I know 'cos I'd taken 'Er Majesty a bowl of broth for her supper, but that was hours before I saw the bishop and I was just on me way to bed.'

'And Her Majesty left the palace soon afterwards, you say?'

'Yeah, wasn't but a few days later. I go in one morning and – poof! – she was gone. Didn't think she'd be coming back again neither, but she did.'

'Thank you,' said Godwin. 'That was very useful. You may go now, but before you do, mark this. If I hear any word, from anyone, about our conversation, I will assume you were the source of the gossip. And I will cut out your tongue and brand your face with a red-hot iron. Do you understand?'

Mildred nodded frantically, then snivelled, 'I won't tell no one, not even me mam, I swear I won't.'

'Make sure you don't, or you'll never say another word as long as you live.'

The girl left the room weeping piteously and shaking with

fear, leaving Godwin pondering her evidence. From the timing of events it was clear to him what had happened. Aelfwine had been on her side in the battle with Harold and Elgiva. Doubtless he had run errands for her. The two of them had conspired in a way that might have amounted to treachery against Harold but was of no bearing at all so far as Edward was concerned. Godwin knew that. But he also knew that the tale Mildred had told sounded very much like a man visiting a woman's chamber for an illicit assignation. And that was just what the king wanted to hear.

For a man who never appeared to indulge in carnal activity himself, Edward was obsessed by the possibility of it in others and, as Godwin had anticipated, seized upon the servant's evidence like a starving dog being thrown a juicy red steak. He insisted on her repeating her account for him. At first, she refused.

'He said I shouldn't talk to no one, Your Majesty, or else he'd cut me tongue out and brand me face.'

'Well I'll do that if you don't talk to me,' said Edward.

Mildred looked completely flummoxed and started sobbing again.

'For God's sake, woman, stop howling!' the king commanded.

'It's all right, you can tell His Majesty what you told me,' Godwin said.

'You won't cut me tongue and stick hot pokers on me face?'

'It might improve your looks, girl,' shouted Siward of Northumbria, bursting out in laughter at his own wit.

So Mildred told her story once again and received a silver penny from the king for her pains. Edward was delighted. 'I've got her!' he told his senior earls. 'The devious old bitch won't wriggle out of this snare!' He looked around. 'Master Chamberlain, can you tell me where my mother can be found?'

'I believe she is in the solar with her ladies, sire.'

'Very well then . . . Godwin! Leofric! Siward! You're coming with me.'

'Where to, sire?' Leofric asked.

'Why, to the solar, of course. I'm going to arrest my mother.'

8

A convent outside Winchester, and the city itself

Oh, the irony of it, Emma thought. Not long ago, she had been wallowing in the humiliation that Elgiva was suffering as a lowly nun. Now here she was herself in a convent, but her status was even lower than Elgiva's, for she was not even a nun. She was very clearly a prisoner.

Stripped of her treasure, her servants and even her title, she had been locked in a penitent's cell, from which she was released twice a day to perform her ablutions and stroll awhile – always under close supervision – in the convent cloisters. She was not allowed to communicate with any of the nuns, all of whom were under strict instructions not to talk to her. Once again she had been struck down, and by her own son. The injustice of the situation, and Edward's sheer ingratitude, was all but overwhelming. Yet her absolute conviction that she was in the right gave Emma strength and imbued her with a stubborn determination not to be beaten by her whey-faced coward of a son.

A number of weeks passed, and then, without any warning, Emma was summoned to see the mother superior. The nun was standing just inside the convent gates talking to a young nobleman Emma recognised as one of Edward's closest allies, Ralph of Mantes. Ralph was Edward's nephew, the son of his sister Goda. He was also, therefore, Emma's grandson. She had heard a little about him from the occasional letters she received from Goda, but they had only met once or twice at court, and she barely knew him.

Ralph was well built and handsome enough, but he seemed nervous. 'I've c-come to take you to, er, Winchester, G-grandmother,' he stammered.

'Am I to be my own grandson's prisoner?' she asked.

'Oh n-no, no . . . er, not at all. I was hoping you might come of your own free will and, er, give me your w-word that you will not try to escape.'

Emma looked at the half-dozen mounted soldiers Ralph had brought with him. 'My dear boy, I am an elderly woman armed with nothing more than my wits and what's left of my charm. I hardly think I could get away from you and your men, do you?'

Ralph agreed that this was unlikely, and so Emma was helped up into the open ox cart in which she was to be carried back to Winchester. 'Ride alongside me awhile, boy . . . please,' she said.

'I'm not sure if I'm allowed to do that,' Ralph replied.

'Would the king really forbid a man to talk to his grandmother?'

'I suppose not.'

So Ralph fell into line, riding his horse at a walk beside the ox cart while Emma questioned him as gently as possible, so as not to frighten him into silence. She learned that her possessions had been seized by the king, and that Aelfwine had been stripped of his bishopric and all his personal estates.

'Why did they punish him?' she asked, in genuine puzzlement.

'Because of the a-a . . . the adultery, Grandmother,' Ralph replied.

Emma burst out laughing and kept on going until the tears ran down her face, while Ralph looked on with an expression of clueless panic.

'W-what's so funny?' he asked eventually.

Emma had to make an effort to pull herself together before

she replied. 'Because the very idea of me wishing to have carnal knowledge of that man is completely ridiculous. Bishop Aelfwine is a very old, very loyal and very dear friend of mine. But he is hardly the kind of man I would take to bed, even if I wished to take any man to bed, which at my age I most certainly do not.'

'I don't understand. The k-king himself has accused you. Robert Champart, the new Bishop of London, will prosecute you on Edward's behalf.'

'I'm sure he will . . . and find me guilty if he possibly can. Well, I know I'm telling the truth, and I will put my trust in God to know that and protect me.'

On arrival in Winchester, Emma was kept for a night in a locked and guarded cell beneath the palace before being taken to the great hall, which was packed with a huge crowd of onlookers, all agog to see the trial of a queen.

A dais had been erected at one end of the room and the council table placed upon it. Behind it sat Champart, the king, Godwin, Leofric and Siward.

Mildred, who had been dressed and groomed to lend her appearance some semblance at least of respectability, gave her evidence.

Someone's been coaching you, thought Emma, for the girl spoke far more fluently than she would ever have managed if her words were all her own, and her account had been embellished with rhetorical flourishes – a vivid description of the guilt on Aelfwine's face; a hint that his cassock bore unseemly stains – that added spice to her tale.

For her part, Emma was entitled to be defended by the testimony of character witnesses who would swear to her chastity. But she had been given neither the time nor the means to find someone willing to speak on her behalf, even had there been anyone willing to risk the king's anger, which she doubted.

It was not long before Champart rose to give his verdict. 'Emma of Normandy, you have been charged with the crime of fornication with a priest. The evidence against you, given by an eyewitness, has been heard by everyone present here today. Since you deny the charge, but have no witnesses of your own, the case will be decided by a trial by ordeal. If God knows you to be innocent, He will ensure your survival. If you are guilty, He will see to it that you die.'

Emma felt her insides quail, and it took every scrap of the self-control learned over decades as a duke's daughter, royal consort and dowager queen not to let the terror show on her face as Champart went on, 'As one who once held royal rank, you may choose the ordeal that you will undergo: trial by water, or trial by fire. Which will it be?'

Emma could not swim. If thrown into water, she would drown. She had seen a drowned corpse and it had not been a pretty sight. If she perished in flames, however, she might be burned away altogether, leaving no trace behind. Of the two outcomes, the latter was marginally the less terrible.

She looked Champart straight in the eye and said, loudly and clearly enough for all to hear, 'I choose trial by fire, sure in the knowledge that I will survive, for God knows that I am innocent.'

'Very well,' said Champart. 'The trial will be held one week from today. A fire will be laid in the cathedral here in Winchester. It will be ten paces long, and you will walk over the embers, taking five paces for your sake and five for Aelfwine, who once was bishop here. If you do not complete the walk, the verdict will be guilty. If you do complete the walk but there is any burn, or wound, or even a single blister upon your feet, then you will be found guilty. The penalty for guilt will be death, both for you and for Aelfwine.'

There was a gasp from the onlookers crammed into the hall,

followed by a few shouts of disapproval and a loud hum of conversation. Wounds suffered in an ordeal were not normally deemed a sign of guilt. It was left to God to determine whether the accused recovered, and if they did, that was taken as proof of innocence. But to walk across burning embers without so much as a blister, well, that would take a miracle.

'Do you have any final requests?' Champart asked once the hubbub had subsided.

'Yes,' Emma replied. 'I wish to spend the night before the trial keeping vigil by the tomb of St Swithun in the cathedral crypt, so that he may hear my prayers and make my case with God.'

The crowd liked that. Such a sign of faith showed that Emma's reputation as a truly devout Christian was well deserved. As a bishop, Champart could hardly deny a request for the chance to pray. 'Very well then,' he said. 'At sunset on the eve of the trial, you will be taken from your cell to the crypt and you may pray there, under guard, until sunrise. Then you will be held in captivity until the time for your trial comes. And may God have mercy on your soul.'

9

On the afternoon of the day preceding Queen Emma's ordeal (for so the people still called her, for all that the king had decreed otherwise), the roads, tracks and footpaths leading into Winchester began to fill up with travellers, all converging on the Old Minster. Men and women, young and old, fit and ailing, they came as if on a pilgrimage, by the score, by the hundred and then by the thousand, so that every tavern and outbuilding was filled, every scrap of common land packed with people come to witness the following day's events.

Edward was not pleased, for it was apparent to anyone who walked among the crowds that they had not come to jeer and mock his mother, but to show their love and support for her in her time of trial.

'Do not trouble yourself, Your Majesty,' Champart assured him. 'She will die on the fire and be consumed in flames and it will be all the better that so many people should be present to see it, for it will prove that she is guilty and God's judgement will be seen by all.'

'But what if she does not die?' Edward asked.

'Calm yourself, Your Majesty.' Champart leaned forward and spoke softly in the king's ear, as if offering him a private, priestly benediction. 'Edward, dearest, don't be afraid. The bitch will die. No one can walk through fire and come out unscathed the other side. No one.'

The king's shoulders slumped, though whether it was from relief or despair, none could say. 'I suppose so,' he said.

By sunset, the cathedral and the yard outside were full to bursting and echoing with the noise of conversation, laughter, argument and general hubbub. But all noise ceased as word spread that Queen Emma was being led to spend the night in prayer by St Swithun's tomb. She was tall enough that her white linen headdress could clearly be seen between the steel helmets of the soldiers guarding her, and the weight of the silence of so many souls and the intensity of so many staring eyes all concentrated on the same point seemed to burden the very air itself as she walked through the yard, into the cathedral and down the stone steps to the crypt. Even when she had disappeared completely from view and people felt able to talk again, they did so in hushed voices, as if unwilling to disturb the vigil taking place beneath their feet.

Though her faith had sometimes been tested to the limit, Emma's devotion to God had never been a matter of show. She truly believed in His power and His mercy alike, and did all she could to praise and glorify His name. But God had made her road a hard one. Both her husbands and three of her five children had died before her. Now another of her children was seeking to have his own mother put to death. She prayed to St Swithun to intercede on her behalf. She prayed to God and Jesus to guide her and give her strength in her time of trial. And she prayed to the Blessed Virgin Mary to take pity on another mother who had known the pain of losing the sons she loved.

Late in the night, when the torches rammed into iron sconces on the stone walls of the crypt had burned down almost to extinction, and Emma was lost in a daze, halfway between wakefulness and sleep, she thought she heard a voice in her ear and saw the figure of St Swithun himself walking towards her. 'Do not be afraid, my child,' he said. 'Walk steadily over the fire, as if on soft green grass. Look neither to the left nor the right, but straight ahead. Walk towards the light and God will walk beside you.'

Was it a dream, or had the saint really spoken to her? Emma did not know, but a sense of calm, of warmth spread through her, and she felt sure that all would be well.

The king's men had set slabs of paving stone over the floor of the cathedral's aisle, so that it would not be damaged by the fire. Then a local blacksmith, skilled in the art of creating a fire hot enough to melt iron itself, laid a thick bed of charcoal over wooden kindling. Long before dawn, he lit the kindling, then he and his apprentices tended the fire as lovingly as a mother with her child, fanning the flames with their leather bellows to make it burn hotter, then letting them subside so that what was left was a path of glowing red-hot embers, running along the aisle towards the great west door of the cathedral.

The sun had not yet risen in the east when Robert Champart, Bishop of London, came to inspect the site of the ordeal. He seemed shocked to discover that the flames were not rising high into the air as he had pictured them doing. The blacksmith, who had anticipated this possibility, assured him that he would not be disappointed. 'Watch, Your Grace,' he said, and took a slug of pig iron and placed it in the embers. He and his apprentices then worked the fire around it with their bellows, and Champart's eyes lit up as he saw the iron growing red hot and then white with blazing heat.

'Show the people,' he said.

The blacksmith used a pair of tongs to lift the iron out of the fire, then held it up so that the people clustered at that end of the cathedral could see it. There was a gasp as they understood that this was the fire over which their beloved Queen Emma would soon be walking.

The blacksmith was unmoved. To him this was simply a job

of work, but he was showman enough to want to prove his point even more powerfully. He placed the white-hot slug on his anvil, then picked up his hammer and beat down upon the end of the piece of iron, stretching and flattening it. The sound of the hammering echoed through the cavernous building like a demonic answer to the cathedral bells. When he was done, the blacksmith held up the steel, which had been transformed into a crude but vicious-looking blade. 'There you are, Bishop. If the flames don't kill her, that will.'

Champart went off to take matins, the first service of the day, at the palace chapel with a spring in his step. 'I've been to see the fire,' he told Edward afterwards. 'I think you will be very pleased indeed with its heat.'

Emma was led from the crypt to a vestry, where she was given the use of a chamber pot and then provided with a simple breakfast of bread and water. It was a chilly morning, with an early winter frost lying white on the cathedral roof and making the ground hard and cold beneath the feet of the crowds surrounding the great church like a besieging army. Emma shivered as she ate her meagre breakfast and offered up one last prayer to God: 'Dear Lord, do not cause me to shiver when I face my ordeal. I would not have the people believe that it was fear that made me tremble.' A few moments later, she was led out into the main body of the cathedral to face her fate.

Edward, her own son, whom she had carried in her belly and whose blood-smeared newborn face she could see as clearly now as she had on the day he was born, was seated on a platform, raised above everyone else. He did not give his mother so much as a glance as she was led past him, and she kept her eyes looking straight ahead of her, for that was what the saint had commanded and she was damned if she was going to be seen begging her ungrateful offspring for mercy.

Champart was waiting in the pulpit and Emma was taken to stand before him, looking up at him while he gazed down on her from on high as if he were a deity himself. 'You know the crimes of which you are accused,' he said, speaking as loudly as if he were giving a sermon so that all might hear what he said. 'You are an adulteress and a fornicator, no better than a common whore. Do you repent of your crimes and beg God for forgiveness, or do you still deny your guilt?'

'I deny it,' Emma replied, as strongly and clearly as she could. 'For I am innocent, and God knows it.'

The words and the manner in which they were spoken acted on the crowd like an archer loosing his bowstring. It was as if all the tension and trepidation that had grown within the multitude through the hours of the night was suddenly set free, and a great roar of defiance went up from the thousands inside and then outside the cathedral. Emma felt her people's support lifting her like a wave, so that she hardly heard Champart shout, 'Take her to the fire!' nor felt the floor beneath her feet as she was led to the ordeal.

No need to worry about shivering, she thought as she finally stood before the fire, for the heat that rose from the glowing coals was enough to make the skin on her face feel scorched just from standing beside it. She knew that the distance she had to cover was the length of ten male paces, and her stride was not much shorter than a man's. Yet it seemed to stretch before her like a road a thousand leagues long, running all the way to the horizon.

Fear seized her, clawed at her guts and gripped her throat so that she could hardly breathe. She felt a warm trickle down the inside of her leg and thanked the Lord for the long dress that hid the humiliation from her people and her enemies. She fixed her gaze straight ahead. Far away in the distance, beyond the fire, there was light. The doors of the cathedral had been opened, for the king, confident in what Champart had told him, had decided that he wanted the crowds outside to be able to see his mother burn. But in her state of fear and confusion, Emma did not see a door, with a cathedral yard outside. She simply saw a square of light, and the saint's words echoed in her mind: 'Walk towards the light and God will walk beside you.'

The warm, comforting certainty that the vision had given her came back to her now, calming her fears and giving her the courage to lift up her skirts, walk towards the fire and, without the slightest hesitation, step on to it.

She did not hear the gasps as she took her first two paces upon the embers, whose red glow could clearly be seen beneath her feet, while small flames flickered and danced around the hem of her robe.

But neither did she feel the fire.

There was no agony, no sweet, sickly smell of burning flesh, no screams of torment coming from her mouth.

She simply walked as gracefully and regally down the embers as she had done on the day she had walked down that very aisle when she became King Canute's wife and queen. She walked as if there were sweet-scented flowers strewn before her, rather than blazing coals.

She took three steps, four, five . . . and as she walked, the certainty spread through the host of onlookers that she was going to survive, and the mood of all but a very few of the people turned from apprehension to optimism and then to wild joy. She took eight, nine, ten, eleven and finally a twelfth pace, and then she stepped down from the fire on to the cool limestone slabs with which the cathedral was floored . . .

. . . and kept on walking, hardly conscious that there was anything different beneath her feet. For she was walking towards the light, just as the saint had told her to do.

Emma of Normandy, dowager Queen of England, walked

through the doors of Winchester Cathedral and stood at the top of the stone steps that led down to the yard, where all her people could see her, and applaud her, and bathe her in their love. For she had been confronted with an ordeal, and she had turned it into a triumph.

10

Conteville and Rouen, Normandy

William had often been told the story of how his parents had met. He could recite it all by heart: how Robert, the rebellious younger son of the late Duke of Normandy, had seized the castle of Falaise against his older brother's wishes; how he and his best friend Herluin had been returning to the castle from a hunting trip when they saw three young maidens dancing in a clearing in the woods; how they'd both fallen in love at first sight with one of the girls – an angel in a dark blue cloak with hair as golden red as the autumn leaves on the trees all around them. Robert had talked to the girl and asked her to come to the castle that night. He had told her to use the postern gate, a half-hidden entrance behind the keep, for that way she would not be seen. But Herleva had defied him and insisted on walking through the main gate itself, for she refused to act as though she had something to be ashamed of, and her spirit had won Robert's heart as much as her beauty and he had led her through the great hall, packed with guests, men-at-arms and castle staff, to a seat at his high table.

'By God, William, you should have seen your mother that night,' Herluin would say if he was telling the tale. 'She was magnificent! She may only have been a humble tanner's lass, but she walked with her head up and her eyes surveying the room as proudly as a duchess.'

Herleva's version of a young girl's first entrance into an aristocratic household was rather different. 'Oh, I was so scared, you can't imagine!' she told her son. 'All those people were staring at me, and I could feel their eyes like a hundred pinpricks on my body. My knees were shaking so badly I could barely put one foot in front of the other. But your father was so kind. He took my hand in his, reassured me and gave me strength. I had been dizzy with excitement ever since I'd first seen him. But it was then that I really fell in love.'

It was at this point that William invariably stopped listening, and if either his mother or his stepfather ever tried to suggest that his parents had conceived him that very night, he would clamp his hands over his ears and shout at them to stop.

If truth be told, he had little interest in sentimental nonsense about seeing girls and falling in love. He liked the part of the story that only Herluin could tell, for it concerned what had happened earlier that same day, before the two young men came across the dancing girls.

Robert and Herluin, along with some other young noblemen and their retainers, had been out hunting for boar in the forests around Falaise. They had come across a magnificent specimen, a giant with razor-sharp tusks, and had chased it through the trees. 'He was a cunning old beast, you could tell,' Herluin had told William, 'and I dare say he'd have got away from our hounds. But although boars are big, and fierce, with extremely sharp hearing and noses as sensitive as a dog's, they have one big disadvantage. They can hardly see at all. They're like an old man who has to screw up his eyes just to see his food at dinner, so although they run very fast, they find it surprisingly hard to see where they're going.

'And this turned out to be a very serious problem. For in these woods was a great hole in the ground so large and so deep that the local people used to call it the Mouth of Hell. Plenty of horsemen, out riding at night or in bad weather, had fallen in there over the years and killed themselves.

'Well, the boar was in a terrible panic, being chased by our hounds, and he couldn't see very well, so he crashed through the undergrowth and went straight over the side of the Mouth of Hell. He should have been killed, but a tree growing out of the side of the hole broke his fall. So there we were, up at the top, and there he was, halfway down. Most people would have just cursed their luck at losing such a prize and ridden away. But not your father, oh no. He saw a narrow path clinging to the side of the rock, barely wide enough for a man to walk down. It made me dizzy just to look at it, and the dogs felt the same way, because they really didn't want to set foot on it. But your father was determined to go down and kill that boar, just him and a couple of dogs, Bloodfang and Snow. And by God, he did it, too. He trapped the boar against the side of the hole, so that it had no choice but to charge him, and when it did, he just stood there, not flinching at all as the great beast came right at him, and speared it with his lance. But that wasn't enough to kill it, so Robert chased after it, jumped on its back and cut its throat with his knife. He was still on top of the boar when it collapsed and died. It was quite incredible, the bravest thing I'd ever seen.'

William loved thinking about his father standing his ground as the great boar charged. He'd only been a very young man at the time, in his eighteenth or nineteenth year by Herluin's reckoning. Of course, when William had first heard the story, he'd only been a very small boy himself, so eighteen seemed impossibly old and grown-up. But now he was sixteen, only two years younger than his father had been.

'Am I as big as Papa was when you met him?' he'd asked his mother recently.

She'd smiled and said, 'Well, I have to tilt my head up almost as far to look you in the eye as I had to do with him, so you can't be very much shorter. He was broader in the shoulder than you are, but that's just age. All boys fill out as they become men. But I think you've got a bigger build than him. You're sturdier, more solid, more like your uncle Richard in that respect, though not like him in any other way, thank the Lord, because he was a vile man.'

'So do you think I could kill a boar, the way Papa did?'

Herleva's good humour vanished from her face. 'No, I most certainly do not. And don't you dare try. Do you hear me?'

William had said nothing. He hated being told about things he couldn't do, and if anyone else tried it, he would tell them that he was the duke and could do whatever he liked. But his mother was different. She was the only person in all Normandy that he felt he ought to obey, and he didn't like upsetting her because that only upset him too. Even so, he really wanted to kill his first boar, and do it single-handed, the way his father had done.

Herleva let him stew for a few seconds, then she took his hand in hers and spoke more gently. 'Really, my darling, I'm serious. Your father was brave and impetuous, and I loved that because I loved him. But the truth is, what he did was crazy. He could have killed himself. Nine times out of ten he would have done. And in the end, he went on that pilgrimage, which was another mad idea, in my opinion, and it did kill him. I don't want to lose you. I know there will be times when you have to go into battle; that's your duty, and I won't try to stop you. I'll just be like all the other mothers, praying to God every night to bring my boy back to me safe and sound. But promise me, William, that you won't go looking for danger. Believe me, it will come looking for you often enough.'

William had nodded sullenly and muttered, 'All right.'

William returned to Rouen, where he stayed for the next few months. Then news came that an ambitious baron, Thurstan the

Dane, Viscount of Avranches and Exmes, had taken advantage of the chaos that still gripped Normandy to seize Falaise Castle with more than a hundred armed men. The steward of the castle was William's grandfather Fulbert, who had been given the job by Duke Robert, for it was not fitting for his heir's grandfather to remain a mere tanner. It was not clear whether Thurstan had taken Fulbert and his wife Doda prisoner or was allowing them to continue with their duties as before. The couple were both now approaching their sixtieth year and were thus quite elderly, so their health was a matter of some concern to anyone who cared about them.

'I want to come with you!' William had said when Ralph de Gacé immediately declared that he was summoning the Norman militia to go to Falaise and lay siege to the castle.

'I don't think that would be a good idea, Your Grace,' Ralph had said, in that way he had that sounded fawning but felt incredibly condescending, in fact insulting, to William's ears.

'Why not?' William replied. 'I'm sixteen now. That's old enough to go on my first campaign. Falaise is a ducal castle, so it's my property. And it's where I was born, so I want to get it back. And . . .' he was rattling out his arguments one after another in a continuous stream so that Ralph had no chance to contradict him, 'my grandparents might be in danger and I want to know if they're all right.'

He was sure that he'd made a convincing case, but Ralph just ignored it all. 'I'm sorry, Your Grace,' he said, 'but sieges are hazardous in the extreme. Not only do they involve all the normal dangers of war, but also illnesses and fevers of all kinds, which kill even more men than swords and arrows. No, I'm sorry, but it's just too great a risk. Do you not agree, cousins?'

Ralph had addressed those words to Archbishop Mauger and his brother Talou, Count of Arques, who were also sitting in council. As always, Mauger was twitching with nerves, while

Talou just looked sullen and bored, but both were happy to agree with Ralph, if only because they took pleasure in any opportunity to do the precise opposite of what William wanted.

'This may take several weeks, even months to sort out,' Ralph said. 'I won't even be at the siege myself for much of the time. I mean, once the noose has been drawn around a castle, there's really nothing to do but wait until the men inside are finally strangled.'

'They aren't strangled,' William snapped. 'They die of hunger or thirst. Everyone knows that.'

'It was just a figure of speech . . . Your Grace. Look, why don't you go and visit your mother and half-brothers at Conteville? You haven't seen them for a while, and I'm sure your mother is missing you.'

William had continued to protest, but it hadn't done him any good. Ralph had assembled the militia and led them off down the road going south to Falaise, while he had been sent west to Conteville. And of course it had been great to see Mama, and he always liked spending time with Odo and Robert, but he was still seething about the way Ralph had treated him, and it cast a cloud over everything he did.

11

Conteville

Herluin waited three days for the black mood that was now hanging over the whole family to dissipate, but when William's air of resentful gloom remained as deep as ever, he reached a decision. 'Right, boys, I'm going to take you all hunting. Some of the farmers are complaining that there's a boar in the woods up by Saint-Pierre-du-Val. Apparently he's coming out at night and digging up their turnips. I think it's time we went and dealt with him, don't you?'

That had cheered William up all right. He and his brothers talked of nothing else for the rest of the day, and leaped from their beds when they were woken before dawn to get ready for the hunt. The only person not thrilled by the prospect of fresh boar meat for dinner was Herleva. She had caught William just as he was heading out to the stables and made him promise, on his word of honour, not to do anything stupid, and on absolutely no account whatsoever to try to kill the boar by himself.

William had promised. But as they rode out, he became more and more cross about being forced yet again to turn his back on glory. The way a man made his name was by his feats of hunting and fighting, everyone knew that. But how could he make his name if people kept stopping him from doing the very things on which his reputation depended?

He looked down at the Alaunts, pure white hunting dogs who were nothing but muscle, fur and bone, with teeth that sliced into their quarry and clung to them as cruelly as any iron trap. They looked as pent-up and bad-tempered as he felt, growling at their handlers and snapping at each other as they criss-crossed the land where the boar had been foraging, searching for his scent.

Then suddenly they were racing across the fields, barking and yelping with excitement as they went, with the mounted hunters hot on their trail. William's mood had changed as swiftly as the dogs'. He was completely caught up in the thrill of the chase, determined to take the shortest, quickest route across country, no matter how high the hedges or how wide the ditches his mount had to jump. His father had put him on his first pony when he was barely old enough to walk, and he had spent his entire life with the finest stables in the duchy at his disposal. So it was no wonder that he was a magnificent horseman, and thus no surprise that when the dogs found the boar and cornered it, William was the first hunter on the scene, a long way ahead of the rest.

He looked down from his saddle at the beast, barely thirty paces away, grunting, pawing the earth and readying itself for the fight. He grinned with delight at the size of it. That thing must weigh as much as two men – maybe three, he estimated. *I bet it's even bigger than the one Papa killed!*

Just to wound such a magnificent creature would require a nimble horse, a first-class rider and some brilliant spear work. For a lad of sixteen it would be a feat that would earn him the respect and envy of all his peers. But William hardly considered that possibility for an instant. In fact, he barely thought about anything at all, and certainly not the solemn promise he had made to his mother, as he sprang down from the saddle, took his spear in both hands and held it out in front of him, advancing on the boar while the dogs growled and flashed their teeth at the quarry, their hackles raised, just waiting for his command.

William knew how his father had set up his kill. He had taken up a position, set himself to aim the tip of his spear at the centre of the boar's chest, and then let the force of its charge do the work, so that the hurtling beast impaled itself on a virtually motionless spear.

For years, William had dreamed of doing exactly the same thing. Now his chance had come. But the boar did not play its allotted role in the drama. Instead of hesitating and giving William time to set himself, it charged at once, its spindly legs powered by the huge bunched muscles in its shoulders and haunches and the mighty heart beating within its barrel chest.

Robert of Normandy had told Herluin how time had seemed to slow down as his boar came at him, and his vision had become so sharp that he could distinguish individual hairs on the animal's coat and flecks of spittle in its mouth.

But for William, taken by surprise before he could steady his mind and senses, as well as his body, there was none of that. He was overwhelmed by the size of the animal; the pace at which it came towards him, far faster than any running man; and the size and deadly sharpness of its tusks. All these sensations came to him in a single indistinct blur, and he panicked and hurled his spear. It glanced off the boar's flank, scarcely even grazing it, not slowing it or diverting it in any way as it ran inexorably towards him.

William's head was filled with the shriek of the animal's outraged squeal, the thunder of its charge, the smell of it, the sight of it, all jumbled and twirling in his mind so that for a second he was as immobile as a frightened rabbit.

The boar was almost on him when finally, with barely a heartbeat to spare, he threw himself to one side, out of its path.

If the animal could have kept running, all would have been well. But the ring of dogs blocked its path with their snarls, their bristling fur and their drooling teeth. Now the boar was as panicked as William. It came to a skidding halt, turned, caught the scent of the fallen boy and charged again towards that.

William was lying on the ground, half winded. There was no way on earth that he could evade the boar a second time.

His fingers scrabbled for the dagger that hung from his belt, as if that could defend him against a creature that was so much bigger, faster and stronger than him. His mind was suddenly quite calm as the thought came to him that he was done for. And now that sense his father had described – the slowing-down of time itself, the extreme acuity of vision – finally fell upon him as he waited for the impact of the boar's racing body against his, and the stab of its tusks through his skin.

His concentration was so totally focused on the one animal that he barely even heard the thunder of the other huntsmen's horses across the ground, was unaware of the shouts and blaring horns, did not see the dogs spring forward at their masters' commands.

All he knew was that one moment the boar was heading towards him, and the next it had turned and dashed away in a completely different direction, pursued by hounds and horsemen as it went.

But one man had not followed the pack. Herluin remained, sitting atop his mount, blocking out the sunlight so that he cast a shadow right across the ground where William was struggling to his feet.

'How dare you?' he rasped, in a voice William had never heard from him before. 'How dare you break your word to your mother? Have you no respect for her at all. By God, if you were not my duke, I'd give you a thrashing you'd never forget.'

William walked shamefaced to fetch his own horse and mount it while Herluin glared at him.

'Come here,' Herluin commanded him, and William obeyed. His stepfather had begun to sound a little more like his normal kindly self. 'Don't you realise that you can't go around acting like a fool? You're too important. This whole duchy is sliding into anarchy and you are the only person who can bring back peace and order. Your people need you. You're their only hope. You're the Duke of Normandy, William. You have to start acting like it.'

'How can I?' William replied, almost crying with pent-up frustration. 'How am I supposed to be a proper duke when Ralph and Mauger and Talou won't let me? They're supposed to be my guardians and advisers, but they don't behave like that. They go around like they're the real dukes and I'm just this . . . this . . . this little boy that has to do whatever they tell him.'

Herluin nodded. William had made a fair point. 'Listen,' he said, 'there's no need to tell your mother about what happened today. No point in worrying her unnecessarily. I'll tell Odo and Robert to keep their mouths shut too. But if you ever try anything like that again . . .'

'I won't. I promise.'

'Good. Now we must decide what to do about your self-appointed guardians. You're quite right to dislike them. They're all as poisonous as vipers, if you ask me, and I wouldn't trust any of them further than I could throw them. I think this is something we can discuss with your mother. She's been dealing with dukes and their problems since she was barely older than you are now. Let's hear what she has to say.'

'You need a powerful friend,' Herleva said, as the three of them talked after supper. 'Someone you can turn to who has nothing to do with those three weasels. As long as you're weak and you've not got anywhere else to go, they can control you. But if you had an ally, that would make them think twice.'

'Yes, but who?' William asked.

'How about King Henry of France?' Herluin suggested. 'He is your liege lord, after all. If you need his help, he's bound to provide it.'

'Yes, but William can't go to him too often,' Herleva objected. 'It has to be for something really important, if his life or his dukedom are threatened. Things aren't that bad yet.'

'Mama's right,' William said. 'Anyway, the king is angry with Normandy because the fighting here is spilling on to his lands. I can't see him wanting to help me.'

'I know just the man!' said Herleva, her face lighting up with the pleasure of finding a solution to such a tricky problem. 'You should go and see Baldwin of Flanders.'

Herluin looked sceptical. 'Really?'

'Yes, he's perfect!' Herleva insisted. 'Think about it. William, you want someone who's powerful but who has no desire to grab Normandy for himself, otherwise he'll just use you and you'll be even worse off than you are already. That exactly describes Baldwin. He's completely secure on his throne, incredibly well-connected—'

'How?' asked William.

'Because his wife Adela is King Henry's sister.'

'And Flanders owes its allegiance to the Holy Roman Empire, so he's close to the emperor, too,' Herluin pointed out.

'Yes, but how do I know he'll want to help me?' William asked.

'You don't,' said Herleva. 'But Baldwin's late father was married to your aunt Eleanor. Adela was married to your uncle Richard. And your great-aunt Emma lived in Bruges for years after Canute died. So you're practically family. And as it happens, I knew Adela years ago. Robert took me to the wedding when she married Richard. You remember, Herluin? She was such a shy, mousy little thing, even younger than I was, and Richard was so beastly to her that I felt sorry for her, even though she was the daughter of the King of France. And then, when Richard died, she stayed with us in Rouen for a while and it was Robert who helped arrange the marriage to Baldwin. I really liked her. She was very clever and a lovely girl once you got to know her – far too good for Richard.'

Herleva fell silent, clearly contemplating what she was about to say next. 'You know, I think that conniving murderer Ralph de Gacé—' she began.

'That's a bit strong,' Herluin said. 'There's been no proof against him.'

'Yes, that's because he's sneaky and always manages to keep his hands clean, but don't tell me that he didn't have something to do with Alan, Gilbert and Osbern's deaths – and all of them far finer, kinder men than he will ever be, too. Anyway, as I was saying, Ralph thinks he's done something clever by sending you here while he demonstrates who's really in charge by going to Falaise to deal with Thurstan. He's not paying attention to what you're doing now because he doesn't think there's any need to. So you can go to Bruges without him being any the wiser.'

'That's a very good point, William,' said Herluin. 'Ralph would never let you go to another court by yourself. He'd see right away why that would be good for you and bad for him. You should definitely go.'

'I can't just turn up and say, "Hello, I'm William of Normandy, I want to speak to Count Baldwin", can I?' William said.

'I don't see why not,' his mother replied. 'You're a duke, my darling. That makes you Baldwin's equal, at the very least. But just to make sure, I'm going to call a monk over tomorrow and he can write me a letter of introduction for you to give to Countess Adela. If you have her on your side, Baldwin will be all ears.'

'But how can you write to the King of France's daughter?'

'Because I am a viscountess, and the mother of a duke. I can write to whoever I please.' Herleva stopped, frowned and looked at her husband. 'What's the matter, Herluin? Why are you looking at me like that?'

Herluin was smiling in wonderment. 'Nothing's the matter, my love. Nothing at all. I'm just looking at you and asking myself how the simple girl I saw dancing in that clearing grew up to become the great lady who can call herself the equal of Adela of France. And yet you don't look a day older or the slightest bit less beautiful than you did then. I can't believe how lucky I am to have you.'

'You are being very foolish indeed, my lord,' said Herleva, though even her son could see that she didn't really think that at all.

William could tell what was coming next. 'I'm going,' he said, and left the room before his embarrassment could become even more acute than it already was.

12

Bruges

It was not the luxury of Count Baldwin's court at Bruges that surprised William, rich though it was. The House of Normandy too had fine tapestries, silken rugs and golden ornaments aplenty. What was unexpected was the sight of the count and countess sitting side by side on golden thrones to greet him upon his arrival at their palace.

To be sure, Baldwin's throne was larger than Adela's, as befitted both his greater size and his status as the ruler of the county of Flanders. William made sure to pay his respects to the count first before greeting his wife and handing her the scroll on which his mother's letter was inscribed. Still, there was no doubt that Baldwin ruled alongside his wife, sought her counsel and took her opinions seriously.

'Remember,' Herleva had told William, 'Adela may not be as big or strong as Baldwin, but she is more than his match in wisdom and learning. I've heard that she corresponds with scholars across Christendom, in her own hand.'

William had been impressed by that, even if he was puzzled as to why anyone would bother writing letters themselves if they had monks and priests at their disposal. He was struck, too, by the cool way Adela looked him up and down, assessing him as calmly and shrewdly as if she were selecting a joint of meat from a butcher's market stall.

His initial interview with the couple was brief and, once the formal greetings had been completed, consisted of little more than pleasantries. William had, of course, been trained from earliest boyhood to conduct himself properly in august company. But he was no fonder of small talk than any other sixteen-year-old boy and was grateful for the presence of Herluin, who had escorted him to Bruges with a company of Conteville men, and who was now able to keep the conversation moving along when William could not think of anything to say beyond basic answers to the count and countess's questions.

Finally Count Baldwin indicated that their audience was over, and William was unable to suppress a heartfelt sigh of relief. He was just about to leave when Countess Adela gave a little wave of her hand to indicate he should approach her chair. 'I shall read your mother's letter as soon as I am able. Then you will sit next to me at dinner and we will discuss what she has to say.'

William nodded and made his way out of the council chamber. As he did so, a girl ran past him in a blur of energy. He half turned to watch her, and as he did, she stopped and turned back towards him. Their eyes met. He saw a girl who was no bigger than a child of eight or nine, but who somehow looked at him in a way that suggested she was rather older than that. Either way, William wasn't interested. He grunted a rudimentary greeting then loped away out of the chamber. The girl stood watching him for a few more seconds. Then her mother's voice called out, 'Don't just stand there all day, Matilda!' and she picked up her feet and sped towards the countess's throne.

'Your parents were both very kind to me, William,' said Countess Adela at dinner that night, waving away the servant offering her another slice of roast pork. William, who was used to the rough-hewn slabs, chunks and knobbles of flesh that were hacked from the joint by Norman cooks, thought the quantities served at the court of Flanders pitifully inadequate, and was desperately staring at the man who had been shooed away by Adela in the hope that he would turn back and make him the same offer the countess had just spurned.

Having received no response to her remark, Adela looked at William, saw his desperation and swiftly ordered that the boy's trencher should be topped up with meat and plentiful supplies of gravy. She let him gorge himself for a while without intruding upon him with further conversation, for it gave her time to ponder the immediate impression he had given her when they'd met earlier in the day.

He was gauche, that much was indisputable. His conversational skills were minimal and he had the table manners of, well, a Norman. But for all that, the boy had something that many other more polished young men of royal or aristocratic blood lacked: an unmistakable animal energy. Everything about him, even the desperation with which he'd gazed at the departing salver piled with meat, suggested that this was a young man fuelled by hunger. He'll spend his entire life wanting more, she told herself. She had never seen William fight, but she would bet her entire fortune that if he hadn't yet dipped his sword in another man's blood, it wouldn't be long before he did.

As she thought about William, Adela remembered his father. When she had first set eyes on Robert of Normandy, he could only have been a couple of years older than his son was now, but he was much more of a young man, filled with a boundless self-confidence verging on arrogance, offset by his ready smile and effortless charm. How she had pitied herself at her own wedding feast, being married off to his surly, wine-sodden oaf of an older brother, Richard. And how she had envied Herleva, common though she was, who had basked in the love that shone from Robert like the dazzling light of the summer sun.

William lacked that joyful, ebullient streak that had made

Robert so attractive. He was by no means bad-looking, and he did not strike her as mean-spirited or malevolent, but he was contained, watchful, well armoured against the hurt that the world could inflict on more open souls. But then, when she considered all that had happened to him in his short life: his mother taken from him, his father dead, his guardians murdered – one of them, it was said, before his very eyes – she suspected that he would always be prey to suspicion, find it hard to trust and, once crossed, never rest until he was avenged.

Still, as she had said, his parents had been very kind to her, and so Adela persisted in her attempts to engage this gauche young man in conversation.

'So . . . you have a problem with your guardians, is that right?'

'Yes.'

She waited to see whether he would add to that comment, and saw that nothing else would be forthcoming. She reminded herself that he was, after all, just an adolescent male sitting next to a woman twice his age whom he'd only just met, and realised she would have to draw him out of his shell a little.

'I gather that the one causing you the most trouble is Archbishop Robert's son, Ralph. I remember his father well enough. He married me to your late uncle Richard.'

'My father didn't kill his brother,' William snapped, his whole body tensing as if for a fight, before she could say another word. Interesting, thought Adela, the way he jumps to his father's defence. Not for the first time, I'll be bound.

'He would only have my thanks if he had done,' she replied, and watched William's shoulders relax. Good. She'd won a little of his trust.

'So, this Ralph . . . I hear people call him Donkey-Head, is that right?'

William managed something close to a smile. 'Yes . . . but

not when he can hear them. They're too frightened to say it to his face.'

'And are you frightened of him?'

For the first time, William looked her right in the eye. 'I'm not frightened of anyone.'

Plenty of boys his age would say a thing like that, but most would simply be puffing themselves up to look bigger and tougher than they really were. But William meant it, and spoke as if there were not the slightest doubt that he was telling the truth.

'So, if you are standing next to Ralph, are you as tall as him? Could you look him in the eye?'

William thought for a moment, then nodded. 'Uh-huh.'

'And are you as strong as him? Let's say you arm-wrestled with him, who would win?'

'Oh, me, easily,' William said at once. 'Ralph's all skinny and weak.'

'And you'd beat him if you had a sword fight?'

'Definitely.'

'So now we have established that he is less physically powerful than you. And he cannot match you for rank, because you are the Duke of Normandy and he is your vassal. So do you know the only reason why he still has any control over you?'

William frowned. 'Er . . . no.'

'Because you're both used to him being in charge. You've actually outgrown the need for him. But neither one of you realises it.'

'Oh . . .' said William thoughtfully. 'But how do I do anything about that? I mean, I can't just go up to him and say, "I'm in charge now."'

'Well, you could, actually, but I'm not sure it would be the cleverest approach. The best thing would be to do something that showed Ralph, and everyone else, that you had earned the right to be in charge. If you really want to persuade people, deeds almost always work better than words. But what can you do? That's the question.'

There was one very obvious thing, but Adela wasn't going to say it. Let the boy get there himself. Silence fell on their stretch of the table as William pondered. Then his face lit up. 'I can take Falaise Castle! I know that Ralph doesn't think it will fall quickly. He's expecting it to take months. He won't even be there half the time, he told me so himself.'

'Well done, Your Grace, that would be an excellent way of showing people you deserve to rule the duchy yourself, without any guardians. But why would you be able to take the castle if Ralph cannot? After all, you're stronger than him, but you're not strong enough to tear down the walls. And even if you're a better fighter than him, you can't fight everyone there yourself.'

'No,' William agreed, warming to the conversation now that it was touching on a subject that really interested him, 'but Ralph wasn't born at the castle. He hasn't heard stories about it all his life, and his grandparents aren't inside it. That's why he can't get into the castle. But I can.'

'How, exactly, might I ask?'

'I'll tell you,' said William, and proceeded to do just that. By the time he had finished, Adela realised that she had underestimated the shrewd intelligence and driving ambition that lay beneath William's unprepossessing exterior.

'He carries within him the possibility of greatness,' she told her husband when they lay in bed together that night. 'Perhaps you might consider giving him a small company of men to take with him to Falaise. Twenty, maybe, or even thirty – enough to put him in our debt, but not so many that we are at all weakened.'

Baldwin laughed affectionately. '"Might consider" indeed! There's no might about it. You demand that I should pack some of my men off to Normandy with this young pup, and I happen to think you are right. Tell me, is William betrothed to anyone yet?'

'I don't think so. I can write to his mother and ask her, if you like.'

'Yes, why don't you. After all, here we are with a daughter who will one day be in need of a husband. And there, just across our border, is an apparently brilliant young Duke of Normandy who will soon be in need of a wife. Might it not make sense to join the two needs in a single marriage?'

'How clever you are, my lord,' said Adela, who had come to precisely the same conclusion a few hours earlier. 'I think it would indeed make a great deal of sense. I can't imagine why I didn't think of it myself.'

13

Falaise, Normandy

It took more than a week to march down through Flanders and Normandy to Falaise. William used the time to quiz Herluin about every detail of the castle's architecture and defences. He could not have had a better adviser, for Herluin had been in the castle when Duke Richard went there to tame his rebellious brother, and had helped Robert prepare for the siege they both knew was coming and fought alongside him for four long, hungry months. Now he and William took the rough idea that William had described to Countess Adela and went over it time and time again, trying to think of every possible eventuality, anything that might go wrong, until they had refined it into a detailed plan that stood some chance of success.

Anyone who lacked William's absolute faith in his own ability to achieve his ends might have considered that the odds were against him. For one thing, he had first to persuade both Ralph de Gacé and Thurstan the Dane to do precisely what he wanted, the moment he asked. He decided that this task would only be half as difficult if he simply ignored Ralph and any objections he might have.

'He won't like that,' Herluin said.

'Maybe,' said William, 'but he's going to have to get used to it. That's why I'm doing all this.'

So it was that having arrived at Ralph's tent, which stood amidst the stinking mire of human excrement, rotting food and filthy men that any besieger's encampment very rapidly became,

William only gave him the most cursory of greetings before walking straight back out again.

'Hey! Where are you going?' Ralph shouted, before adding, 'Your Grace.'

'To see my grandparents,' William replied.

On the way from Bruges, he had ordered one of the Flemish soldiers, who had once been apprenticed to his father, a master tailor, to make a fine white flag of truce. Now he handed Herluin his sword, took the flag and rode alone through the Norman lines and up the path that twisted back and forth along the side of the bluff on which the castle stood, up to the main gate.

There he called out, 'I am William, Duke of Normandy. I wish to speak to Thurstan the Dane.'

Men on both sides of the castle walls stood and watched as William sat quite still and apparently untroubled by the fact that he was in easy range of any bowman who might decide to defy his white flag and fire an arrow into his heart.

'The lad's got guts, I'll say that for him,' one Norman militiaman said to his mate.

'Or he's too stupid to know what he's doing.'

'The way he rode his horse up there, cool as you like, I reckon he knows exactly what he's doing.'

'So what *is* he doing, then?'

'Ah, yeah, well, you got me there. I haven't got a fucking clue.'

A short while passed, and then Thurstan appeared behind the gatehouse battlements.

'Here I am,' he called down. 'What do you want, boy?'

William ignored the insult. 'I want you to bring my grandparents, Fulbert the Steward and his wife Doda, through the gates, so that I may see them and be reassured that they have been well treated. I give you my word of honour that you will not be harmed.'

'And why should I do that?'

'Because you are my vassal and have sworn a solemn oath to obey me. Or do your vows mean nothing to you? Is your word no more valuable than your piss?'

'Do not provoke me, Duke, or one of my archers may forget that flag you hold in your hand.'

'Do not defy me, Viscount. Not if you wish me to show mercy when all this is over.'

Thurstan the Dane was now struck by the same realisation as Adela of Flanders: that William was not bluffing or blustering, but meant precisely what he said.

'What if I do come down? How do I know you won't trick me?' he asked.

'I am alone. I am unarmed. What could I possibly do?' William suddenly sounded much more like a boy again.

Silence fell as Thurstan considered his position, then he spoke again. 'Your grandparents have been well treated. I shall bring them down to you and then you will know that I am a man of my word. I swear to you now that no harm will befall Fulbert or Doda through any action of mine or my men's. And I will promise you something else as well, William, Duke of Normandy. You will never, ever set foot in this castle, not as long as I have breath in my body.'

That show of defiance brought a ragged cheer from Thurstan's men, ranged along the battlements. Their leader disappeared, and a short while later, the castle gates creaked open a fraction and a man with thinning grey hair and his equally silver-haired wife walked out, followed by Thurstan, who was mounted on his favourite warhorse. He paused near the gate, evidently not wishing to be any more exposed to possible attack than was absolutely necessary, while Fulbert and Doda walked on until they were standing a few steps from William's horse.

'There,' Thurstan called out. 'You've seen them. They're

alive. I kept my word. Now I'm taking them back in.'

William's voice took on a more plaintive, boyish note as he replied, 'Please, Viscount Thurstan, may I have a few words with them? I may never have another chance. I mean, look how old they are. They might not survive a long siege.'

'Don't you worry about us, Will, we can manage!' Fulbert said.

William cursed under his breath. If his grandfather carried on like that, his plan to retake the castle would be over before it had even begun.

'That's very brave of you, Grandpa,' he said. 'But God will call you and Grandma when He sees fit, and I may not have the chance to talk with you before then.' He looked over towards Thurstan, 'Please, my lord, just a few minutes . . . We need to be on good terms when this is over, you and me. And I will always look on you with favour if you show me kindness now.'

'Ha! Why should I care about your favour?' Thurstan was feeling confident. He'd managed the situation well. No one could say that he had been cruel or unreasonable. But he'd not let himself be fooled by William. 'The way things are going in Normandy, you'll be dead before these old codgers.'

'In that case we really do need to talk, so they can say goodbye to me.'

Thurstan laughed. 'You've got a nerve, Duke, I'll give you that. Very well, you can have your talk. But be quick about it. And don't even think of whispering any plots in their ears. Whatever you've got to say, I want to hear it.'

William dismounted and walked across to Fulbert and Doda. He embraced them both and said, 'Mother sends her love. I was with her just recently, and she told me all about the first time she came here, the night Papa asked her to come and see him.'

'Oh, what a happy night that was,' Fulbert said.

'Really? That wasn't what she told me. She said you were furious when she said she was going to ride right in through the main gate, where everyone could see her.'

'Well, yes, I was a bit cross, I suppose.'

'Don't listen to a word he says, Will,' Doda piped up, sensing that her grandson wasn't pleased with what her husband was saying, even if she did not know why. 'He was a lot more than a bit cross. He was raging.'

'That's right,' William said, 'and Papa must have been surprised, too, because he'd told her to sneak in, you know, in secret. Because of course he thought it would be better for her the other way, not doing it how she did. You know, for her reputation and stuff.'

'Oh yes, that's right, he said she should come in by—' Fulbert began, and now Doda saw what William was driving at, and slapped her husband hard on the back so that the rest of his sentence was drowned by splutters and gasps for breath.

'There you go, my dearest!' she said. 'Poor old boy, he gets these coughing fits sometimes. But you're quite right, Will, I know exactly what you mean.'

'Is it really true that Mama and Papa only met that morning?' William went on, doing everything he could to sound as little like a conniving duke and as much like an innocent boy as possible. 'Did he really ask her to come here that very same night?'

'Oh yes. He didn't hang around, your father. He knew what he wanted.'

William nodded. 'I'm a bit like that, I think. If I see something I want, I don't like to wait. So if I was like Papa, and I'd seen a girl – I mean, I haven't seen a girl I want—'

'Then you're a late developer!' someone shouted from the gatehouse.

'But if I did,' William ploughed on, 'I'd think, why wait? Why not do it tonight?'

'I wouldn't go telling your granny something like that,' Thurstan said. 'The poor old woman might die of shock, isn't that right, madam?'

'Don't you worry, Viscount, I've had two boys of my own, there's nothing I haven't heard. Anyway, William, I know just what you're trying to say, even if nobody else does. Come here and give your old granny a hug.'

William hung back a second, then went across and let his grandmother hug him, not having to feign his embarrassment as soldiers on both sides laughed, made exaggerated 'Aaahhh . . .' sounds or simply shouted abuse. But as she took him in her arms, Doda, knowing that William's taller body hid her from Thurstan's view, whispered, 'I understand. Midnight. Just knock.'

Then she pushed him away and glared at the soldiers all around, and waved her fist at them as she shouted, 'You should be ashamed of yourselves. What would your own mothers and grandmothers think, seeing you mocking a boy just for giving his old gran a nice hug and a kiss, eh?'

Someone shouted, 'That's right, Gran, you tell 'em!' and then another wag added, 'Oi, Grandad, can't you control your missus?' and that set off another wave of shouts, cheers and jeers so that it hardly seemed like a siege at all and more like a town square on market day.

William went almost unnoticed as he slipped back to the besiegers' lines. Behind him, Thurstan the Dane led Fulbert and Doda back into the castle, surrounded by an iron wall of his men's shields, and the gates slammed shut behind them.

William dismounted, handed his horse to a groom and went straight to de Gacé, who was standing with a small knot of his senior officers, all of whom had the common characteristic of being his most devoted hangers-on. William felt a shiver down his spine as he saw Odo the Fat looming in the background. There was something about the man. He wasn't frightening exactly, but it made William's skin crawl just to look at him.

'Well I hope you're satisfied, Your Grace,' de Gacé said. 'I must ask you not to take action on your own again like that. With respect, this is not an arm-wrestling bout against a gypsy strongman. This is war. And you are not ready to make decisions without my approval.'

'*With respect*, de Gacé, I am the Duke of Normandy. My decisions are my business and my commands will be obeyed. I want a strong force of men assembled at midnight tonight, ready to storm the main gate of the castle. But do it discreetly. I do not want the sentries on the walls thinking that anything special is going on.'

De Gacé rolled his eyes, not bothering to hide his impatience.

'May I ask why you are issuing this order?'

'Because shortly after midnight, the gates will swing open and the castle will be ours for the taking.'

'And this will suddenly happen, will it, after we've been here a month with not the faintest sign of a victory?'

'Yes,' said William.

'How, exactly?'

'I cannot tell you. It's a secret. But the gates will open, you have my word on it.'

Behind William, one of de Gacé's henchmen whispered to another, 'And we're supposed to believe this child who's never shed a drop of another man's blood . . .' But his voice carried further than he intended, right to William's ears.

William spun round, drawing his sword as he went. Its point was at the man's throat before he had a chance to lay a hand on the hilt of his own blade.

'One more word, and the very first blood I shed will be yours.'

The issuing of a threat is a risky business. Too many men offer hostages to fortune by making promises they cannot or will not keep. Other men sense it and defy them, and once a threat has been faced down, the one who made it is lost.

But there was no defiance now, for there was something about William that told every man there that he was completely serious. Young, inexperienced and callow though he might be, still he carried an air of genuine menace.

The man held up both hands in front of him beseechingly. 'I'm . . . I'm very sorry, Your Grace. I meant no offence, I swear.'

William looked him in the eye, lowered his blade and turned back to de Gacé. 'Be ready at midnight. You give me your men, I'll give you the castle.'

De Gacé laughed. 'That sounds like a rare bargain.'

'So I have your word you will be there?'

'Of course, Your Grace. You have given an order. What can I do but obey it?'

William looked at him. He didn't like or trust Donkey-Head, as he still thought of him, but the man had given his word, in front of witnesses. How could he go back on it?

'Very well,' he said. 'Just make sure you're there.'

With that, he walked away. His tent had already been erected, and he went straight to it. When he got there, he turned to Herluin. 'Have any of your men done any poaching?'

Herluin looked puzzled for a moment, then he smiled. 'I should think so. Wherever there's good hunting country, there'll be men stealing the game. But none of them'll admit to it. Poaching's a hanging offence.'

'Tell your men from me that I'm declaring an amnesty. I need the three best poachers you've got. There'll be ten silver pennies for any of them that do their duty. And their families get the money if they die doing it.'

'That's a fine reward,' Herluin said.

'They'll earn it.'

Herluin nodded. He paused for a moment, wondering whether he should share the words that were in his mind, then said, 'Listen, William, I watched your father become a man right before my eyes. And looking at you now, it's just the same. I bet he's up there right now, looking down and saying, "That's my boy!"'

William didn't know what to say. He found himself blinking fast and biting his lip to stop himself from crying. Herluin saw it, and patted him on the shoulder. 'Don't you worry, I'll go and get you three fine rascals. And then you can tell me what we're going to do with them.'

By the time Herluin returned to the tent, William had pulled himself together. Sure enough, his stepfather had found three thoroughly disreputable-looking individuals. They were all wiry, tough and tanned as brown as William's boot leather, with the darting eyes of those who were constantly on the lookout for prey to hunt, and human predators who might be hunting them.

'Right, what's your name?' William asked, addressing the biggest of the trio, and looking him right in the eye, for he was just as tall.

'Martin,' the man answered.

'You address the duke as "Your Grace",' Herluin said.

'Oh, yeah, right . . . My name's Martin, Yer Grace.'

'So, Martin, I made a promise to my lord of de Gacé that I would give him the castle.'

'Yeah, I had heard that . . . Yer Grace. Some of the lads was talking about it.'

'News travels fast in an army encampment,' Herluin said.

'Clearly,' William said. 'Well, I meant it. I'm going to get that castle, but I need you three men, and you, Count Herluin, to help me do it.' He looked at Herluin. 'Do you think you would still know your way around the castle?'

'I should think so, if it hasn't been changed too much.'

'And you know how to get to the postern gate?'

'Well, I'm not as nimble as I was when your father and I fought Duke Richard here, and my eyesight isn't what it was then either, especially at night. But even so, yes, I can get you there. Or I could, anyway, if there weren't lookouts up on the battlements.'

'Well, that's why I asked you to get me three fine poachers. Gentlemen, the postern gate is at the rear of the castle keep. There is, or at least was, a narrow track running around the foot of the wall from the postern to the path that leads down from the main gate. As soon as it gets dark, I want you three to go out there and work out the best way to get on to that path and along to the gate without being spotted.'

'Just to make it trickier,' added Herluin, with the calm, studious air of a teacher gently pointing out the flaws in one of his favourite pupils' argument, 'the gate is sited where the bluff is steepest, pretty much a sheer rock face, in fact. The whole point is that you can't get to it unless you go along the path, right under the nose of anyone up on the battlements.'

'Well, we have to get to it by midnight,' said William. 'My grandmother's expecting me, and I don't want to keep her waiting.'

14

The moon was almost full, but thick cloud had covered it for most of the night. The darkness had hidden the three poachers as they led William round the face of the bluff upon which Falaise Castle stood to the foot of the precipice beneath the postern gate. William's heart sank as he looked up at the rock face that rose almost vertically, pitch black and featureless, like an extension of the castle wall above it.

'We can't get up that!' he whispered to Martin.

The poacher tapped the side of his nose, then put his finger to his lips to indicate silence before waving to William and Herluin to follow him for another half-dozen paces. He pointed at the rock, stepped towards it with his two comrades . . .

. . . and disappeared.

William gasped. His night vision was excellent, but he simply could not see where the three men had gone. And then, without any sound or warning, Martin was back, gesturing at William and Herluin to follow him into the blackness. William flinched, expecting at any moment to hit solid rock, but he found that he could take two steps into the rock face before he ran into Martin, who had come to a stop just ahead of him.

'Can you see anything?' Martin whispered, so softly that William could barely hear him.

He looked around. Slowly his eyes adjusted to the even greater darkness, and he began to see that they were standing within a deep fissure that ran up through the rock. They had walked in through an opening no wider than a door, and he could reach out and touch the walls on either side. He heard Herluin mutter, 'Mother of God' beneath his breath just behind him, and he could well understand his stepfather's alarm, for the crack was narrower than the most cramped castle staircase, and the rock bore down oppressively without even a torch to lift the darkness.

'Where are the others?' William asked Martin.

'Already gone up. It's easy. No different to climbing a cliff for gull's eggs. Just follow me.'

Martin turned to the rock and began making his way up. William saw how he used his legs to brace himself either side of the crack, while his hands searched for tiny outcrops or horizontal fissures that would give his fingers something to cling to as he pulled himself up. The poacher seemed to have a steady rhythm and pattern to his movements, and the speed and apparent ease with which he moved persuaded William that it really shouldn't be that difficult.

He reached up, grabbed the first handhold he had seen Martin use, placed his left boot against the side wall, pulled up with his hands and scrabbled for purchase with his right foot. He and his companions had come out without helmets, shields or chain mail, to save weight and cut down noise, but even that wasn't enough to help him now. His fingers ached as the full weight of his body dragged against them, and his right foot swung and kicked against the rock but could find no resting place. His protesting hands gave up the unequal struggle and lost their grip, and he fell back down to the ground, bumping and bruising his forearms, shins and chest bone against the rock as he went, and cursing as he ended up in a crumpled heap on the ground.

He felt Herluin's hand grip his upper arm, helping him to his feet, and then heard his voice say, 'Go ahead without me. I'll only slow you down. Besides, there's another job I can do for you. One that will serve you better.'

With that, he was gone. William hissed, 'Come back!' but it did no good. He could not believe it. All his life Herluin had been held up to him as the epitome of a loyal, brave friend. His father had told him endless stories about their adventures together, and everything he had seen on his visits to Conteville had only served to reinforce that glowing image. How could he run away now, of all times?

'Hurry up, Yer Grace. Cloud's thinning.'

The sound of Martin's voice brought William back to the here and now. He looked up at the tiny sliver of sky visible at the top of the crack. Sure enough, it looked paler, and now there were very faint patches of light and blue-black shadow picking out the features on the rock around him. That would make it easier for him to climb, but also for the sentries to see movement beneath them. For if the rocks could cast shadows, so would people, and theirs would move, catching any watching eyes as they went.

William threw himself at the rock again. This time he tried to copy the scuttling rhythm of hand and foot movements that he had seen Martin employ, and although his was a very clumsy version of the poacher's technique, his feet still scrabbling for grip and his fingers rubbed raw by the rock, still he managed to make his way up until another hand grabbed him by the scruff of the neck and virtually pulled him the final few feet up to the narrow grassy ledge, just below the top of the precipice, along which the track ran, where Martin and his two companions were crouched waiting for him.

'Where's Lord Herluin?' Martin asked.

'Gone back,' William replied.

The poacher nodded as if the news did not surprise him. By now, William too had come to understand why his stepfather might have thought himself more of a hindrance than a help. But then another thought struck him. Herluin was the only one of them who knew his way around the castle. What were they going to do without him?

He felt a tap on his shoulder. Martin was pointing upwards. The glowing silver moon was just showing its face beyond the veil of cloud. The poacher tapped him again, this time to show him that he had a small rock in his hand. He indicated that he was about to throw the rock in one direction. Then he pointed at William and gestured in the opposite direction.

William nodded.

Martin drew back his arm and threw the rock down the path. In the silence of the night, the sound of it clattering along the stony earth seemed like a company of horsemen riding up to the castle.

Even before the noise had died away, William had pulled himself over the top of the precipice on to the track and sprung to his feet. Above him he could hear two men's voices shouting.

'Did you hear that?'

'Where'd it come from?'

'Over there!'

William raced along the track, almost running on tiptoe as he tried not to make the slightest sound.

'Nah! Can't see nothing. Must've been an animal,' said one of the voices as William reached the gate, which was really more of a door inset into a stone arch, and squeezed himself right up against it. Now he faced a new problem. How did he knock on the wooden door loudly enough to be heard by his grandmother, even assuming that she was there, but not so loudly that the sentries would hear? He tried once, barely touching the wood at all, but nothing happened. Then he had a second go, a little more firmly this time.

Still nothing happened.

William stood there, his heart thumping so loudly he feared that that alone would be enough to give him away. He took a deep breath, raised his fist and was about to risk everything with a proper, loud knock when he saw the door move a fraction, very slowly, and then a bit more, until he could just see the very vague outline of a human head poking out from behind it, and a nervous high-pitched voice whispered, 'William?'

'Yes, it's me,' William replied as the door opened and he darted through it to be greeted by his grandmother's relieved embrace.

'I'm so glad to see you,' she said. 'I've been waiting here for ages, thought you'd never come.' She paused and stepped back from his arms. 'Are you by yourself?'

William realised he hadn't heard the other three follow him up from the ledge. He felt a momentary start of panic, and then, without the slightest advance sign of their coming, there they were, slipping through the gate as noiselessly as wraiths.

'This is all of us,' he said. 'Now, Granny, it's time we went to the gatehouse. Herluin told me the way.'

'Well, it's changed a bit since your father's day. But just follow me and I'll get you there in no time.'

'Why aren't the men ready? The castle gates will be open soon!' Herluin glared in furious desperation at the men languidly draped around Ralph de Gacé's tent – a far larger, more well-appointed one than that allocated to the Duke of Normandy.

'Oh for heaven's sake, Conteville, do stop this nonsense,' said de Gacé. 'Sit down, relax, have some wine. There was some excellent roast beef around earlier. I'm sure one of the squires will get you some if you ask them.'

'I couldn't give a damn about wine or beef! William of Normandy – your duke, whose vassal you are – is almost certainly inside the castle by now. He will find a way to open the main gates, and when he does, he'll be expecting his men to come charging through them.'

De Gacé gave a noisy, irritated sigh. 'Look, I've had about enough of this nonsense. That little bastard is sixteen years old. He's never so much as seen a battlefield, and now he thinks he can single-handedly break the siege of a castle held by one of the duchy's greatest warriors. It's absurd!'

'Just how legitimate are *you*, de Gacé?' Herluin asked, his voice tight with the effort of controlling his temper. 'And how long is the honour roll of your victories? You know, I'm beginning to wonder whether you actually want William to succeed. It might show you up if he did. Much handier if he should die tragically, taking a foolish risk, nothing you could do about it . . .'

'Are you insinuating that I would betray the duke?'

'I'm not insinuating anything. You are the one who is refusing to go to his aid. Others can draw their own conclusions. I have better things to do.'

With that, Herluin turned on his heel and stalked out of the tent. He had just made an enemy of the man commanding the troops on whom William's survival relied. Now it was up to him to do the job, or tell Herleva that her firstborn was dead and he had done nothing to save him.

Well, he had the remaining men from Conteville. They at least would follow him. After that, God alone knew, and He would decide what all their fates would be.

Doda led William and his three companions along a circuitous route that took them through the storerooms at the foot of the keep and round the back of the stables. The castle lay as still and noiseless as if it were deserted, with only the snorting of a wakeful horse to break the silence. Finally, as they stood in the shadow cast by the barn where the animals' feed was stored, there was no more cover, just thirty paces of open ground between them and the back of the gate, which stood within an arch flanked by stone towers.

'How do we get across that?' William whispered to Martin.

The poacher grinned. 'Wait, pray . . . and run like hell.' He looked up at the sky. Another bank of clouds was scudding across the heavens towards the moon. In a matter of minutes its light would be extinguished. William was thankful for the oncoming darkness, but it would still not be enough to save them if any of the eyes up on the battlements, currently looking out towards the enemy, should glance inwards at the castle itself. And yet they were so close now that as he watched the clouds approaching the moon, skirting around it like a suitor sidling up to a beautiful girl, he found himself gripped by a feeling he'd never known before. He was apprehensive, he had to admit it, about all the things that might go wrong, and even a little afraid of what might happen to him – he was suddenly very aware that this was not a game, not a training session, and that his life itself was at stake. But that fear was far outweighed by anticipation and even excitement about what was soon to happen. This was his chance to make his name in the way that counted above all others: victory in battle. Right now, as he stood in the shadows waiting for his moment, he was still the boy duke, the bastard duke, the ruler of a duchy in name alone. But if he took this castle, everything would be different. He was sure of it.

The clouds swathed the moon and hid it away. Darkness fell. It was time.

'Go!' hissed Martin, and they started running, darting across the muddy yard. William felt even more exposed than he had done dashing along the track to the postern gate. His back seemed to itch, as if expecting at any second the piercing agony of an arrow or crossbow bolt between the shoulders, though it would be a rare archer indeed who could hit a moving target at the dead of night.

And then they were there, breathless but alive in the lee of the gateway, and Martin was pointing his men to the far end of the heavy oak beam that sat between two iron brackets and kept the gate closed.

William looked around. There was an open arch at the foot of one of the towers, with a stair beyond it that led up to the battlements. He waited for a moment, half expecting someone to emerge from the arch and ask them what they were doing. But no one came, so he stood beside Martin and grabbed their end of the beam, lifting it up and back over the top of the brackets, and then, very gently, noiselessly, down to the ground.

The gates, loosened from the beam's grip, creaked on their hinges as they swung ajar. Now the four men pulled them wider until the gateway was a void through which William could see the night sky. The moon had come out again. Stars dusted the heavens. Any second now, a cheer would go up from the Norman lines, and de Gacé would lead the charge up the path and into the castle.

But there was no cheer. There was nothing but silence. And then shouts from above them.

'The gates! They're open!'

'What the hell?'

'Look, down there . . . See? Open!'

'Well go and bloody close the fuckers then!'

There were sounds of running footsteps now, orders being given to fighting men, soldiers racing to the gates. But they came from the battlements.

Where William had expected to see a column of his men, bearing the golden leopards on their shields, charging to join him, there was nothing.

He ran through the gates on to the path beyond and shouted out into the night.

'Men of Normandy! This is William, your duke! The gates are open and the castle is ours!'

It was meant to be a warrior's battle cry. But it sounded more like the high-pitched screeching of a child.

And still nobody came.

15

Herluin had gone to rouse his own men and those that Baldwin had provided, but the ones who had ridden from Bruges were tired from long days in the saddle, and those who had walked were footsore. And while they had heard hours ago that Duke William had promised to take the castle, and even borrowed three of their number to help him do it, they didn't quite believe – any more than de Gacé, or any other man in the camp – that the boy really meant it. They thought he was playing at soldiers, and had gone to sleep without giving the matter any serious thought at all.

But now their lord was pulling the blankets off their sleeping bodies, kicking them as they lay on the ground and shouting at them to get up. And though they loved Herluin as a good and just master, and were normally willing to obey him, still his words didn't really register with them as he shouted, 'Get up! Now! Your duke needs you! His life is in danger unless you get up now!'

The sound of Herluin's voice carried to the men clustered around the nearest campfire, and to one set of ears at least it brought back memories from many years earlier. One fifteen-year veteran of the Norman militia, a towering mass of muscle, rose to his feet, rubbed the sleep from his eyes and walked across to where Herluin was desperately trying to get his men to put on their padded leather jerkins and chain-mail coats, stick helmets on their heads, pick up their swords, bows and shields and follow him up to the castle.

'My lord,' the man said, 'can I help?'

Herluin turned and looked up at the giant standing before him.

'I'm John,' the man said. 'The blacksmith's son. From the siege.'

Herluin looked at him, frowned, recalled a boy of twelve or thirteen who'd spent his time atop the highest tower of Falaise Castle, for he'd had the sharpest young eyes of any of them. Now here was this titan who was, no doubt about it, built just like a blacksmith. And then a look crossed the titan's face, an expression of well-meaning, almost innocent eagerness to please, and Herluin at once saw the face of the boy in the man he'd become.

'By God, so you are,' he said. 'And yes, you can help. William of Normandy is in the castle. He is planning to open the gates. And he needs us to be there when he does.'

John had known William's father, Duke Robert. He'd been little more than a lad himself when he took the castle and held it against his own brother. But he'd been a fine leader, always putting himself where the fighting was thickest, never asking anyone to do anything he would not. If Duke Robert's lad was in danger, then John knew where his duty lay.

'Count on me, my lord,' he said, and moments later, his voice was added to the growing clamour as he bellowed, 'Right, you lot, up! Boots on, helmets on! Shields! Swords! Now!'

Herluin thought of running to get his horse, but it would need to be found amidst a hundred other men's mounts, untethered and saddled, and by the time he'd done that, the battle would be lost. So he just shouted, 'To me, men of Conteville! For William, Normandy . . . and glory!'

Then he ran towards the castle, hardly daring to look behind him for fear that nobody was following.

* * *

'Run!' said Martin. 'Run for the lines and we will hold them at bay.'

'No,' said William, knowing that the poacher was offering to sacrifice his life for him. 'I will stay here and fight.'

'But Your Grace—'

'Thank you, Martin,' William said, quite calmly, though the sound of footsteps racing down from the tower was growing ever louder. 'I understand. But I'd rather fight and die like a man than run like a little boy.'

Martin grinned and slapped him on the shoulder. 'Well said.' Then he drew a long, wicked-looking dagger from his belt and took up position to one side of the arch that led to the stairs.

The first of the castle defenders appeared. He looked aghast for a second as he saw three armed men in a semicircle opposite him, then Martin stepped out from his hiding place, clamped a hand across the defender's face, pulled his head back and sliced his knife across his exposed throat.

The second man rushed out, stumbling over the first one's body, and suddenly William was transported back to the stable yard at the palace in Rouen. For it was just like watching Guy of Burgundy lose his balance in their training fight as the man threw out his arms, rendering both his shield and sword entirely useless and exposing his stomach. William didn't think. He simply reacted, and the sword in his hand almost moved of its own accord as it swung sideways across the man's belly and deep into his flesh. But this time his victim was not just winded, he was doubled over, screaming, as blood poured from under his clothes, and it was as much to silence him as anything that William pulled his sword free and then swung it again, bringing it down in a vertical arc on to the back of the wounded man's neck, almost severing his head from his body with the force of the death blow.

I've just killed a man, he thought, but there was no time to think about that, because a third man had emerged from the tower, seen what had happened and promptly turned tail and run back the way he had come.

'Get him!' William shouted, and one of the poachers dashed past him, leaped over the dead bodies and darted up into the blackness of the stairwell. Seconds later, there was a muffled cry and then the crashing of a chain-mail-clad body falling back down the stairs, closely followed by the poacher, bearing a broad grin and a bloody blade.

William felt a surge of elation course through him. They had survived! But then he heard a voice mutter, 'Shit!' and Martin was saying, 'Look . . . the keep.' He looked across the castle yard, past the outbuildings and up the slope that led to the castle. The main door of the keep was open. Men were pouring out of it and running down the slope, heading towards the gate. There must have been forty or more, with Thurstan the Dane at their head, all of them shouting and screaming war cries.

And they were coming straight for the sixteen-year-old lad and the three country criminals huddled by the open gate.

'We can still run,' Martin shouted, trying to make himself heard over the noise of the oncoming enemy. 'You stood your ground and you fought. No one can deny it.'

'No!' replied William. 'I won't run.' But inside he knew he was being a fool. There was nothing to be gained by staying, no glory to be won by dying. Anyone with a shred of good sense would get out while they still had the chance. But still he could not make himself do it.

'If you won't go, we will,' Martin said. 'We've done our duty. Come on, lads . . .'

The poachers' leader took one last look at Thurstan and his men, who were now barely twenty paces away, then turned to go . . . and gasped. 'By God . . . they're coming. They're finally bloody coming!'

William turned his head to see what Martin was talking about, and now it was his turn to be amazed. For there, at the top of the path, no further away in one direction than Thurstan was in the other, was Herluin, running towards the gate with the men of Conteville and the Flanders contingent behind him. Beyond them was a huge soldier, bearing the largest war axe William had ever seen, with more men behind him. All the way down the path, right back to the lines, some in tens and twenties, others in twos and threes, or simply running by themselves, the Normans were coming to rescue their duke.

William took the first backward step he had made all evening, away from Thurstan's men towards his own. He looked at them and shouted, 'I am William of Normandy!'

They answered him with a roar, and suddenly they were all around him, like a wave surging around a rock, and William turned and ran with them, through the gate, into the castle yard and straight to the heart of the battle.

Thurstan the Dane had seen that his cause was hopeless and thrown down his sword. William accepted his surrender and that of his men, but on one condition: Thurstan had to get down on one knee and pledge his solemn allegiance, as a vassal, in front of both his and William's forces, for the men of Normandy were William's now, and his alone. Once that had been done, William marched up the steps into the keep and from there to the great hall, where he solemnly reclaimed his castle. Herluin found him there amidst the hubbub and said, 'I'm sorry I left you. But I knew that de Gacé would let you down.'

'Thank you,' William said, embracing his stepfather, grateful beyond words to Herluin for what he had done, and a little ashamed for ever doubting his loyalty.

'There's someone here who wants to meet you,' said Herluin, and William had a sensation he had not been used to over the past year or so: looking up into another man's eyes. 'This is John. He and I are old comrades.'

'I was here during the siege, Your Grace,' said John. 'I was only a boy then, younger than you are now, so I couldn't fight. But it was my honour and privilege to watch your father lead us through that siege – half starved we all were by the end of it, isn't that so, Lord Herluin?'

'Indeed it is,' Herluin said.

'And it's my honour and privilege to fight alongside you now, Your Grace. You're a proper chip off the old block, you are.'

William grinned. That was twice in one evening he'd been compared to his father, and it meant as much coming from this common soldier, whom he'd never met before, as it did from the man he'd known all his life. 'Thank you very much, John,' he said. 'It's my honour to have you beside me in battle.'

A huge smile spread across John's face, and he leaned forward towards William. 'I'll tell you another thing,' he said. 'I was right here in this hall the night your mother, the Lady Herleva, came here for the very first time. Let God strike me down if I tell a lie, she was the most beautiful girl I ever saw, and—'

But he never finished his sentence, for another voice interrupted him. 'Excuse me, Your Grace, but I came to pay you my compliments.'

It was Ralph de Gacé, and now a hush fell on the room, for every man in it knew that de Gacé had not come to the duke's aid.

'Did you now?' said William. He stood there bloodied, his coat torn from the fight, and it was impossible not to see that he was taller than the man who was supposed to be his guardian;

that his shoulders were broader and his face that of a duke, not a donkey. 'Well, I'm afraid to say that, not for the first time, you arrived too late. I have just been paid a fine compliment by my comrade John, who helped me when you did not, and fought for me when you stood idle. I have thanked him from the bottom of my heart for what he said, for I respect him and value his opinion. You, on the other hand, I do not respect, and I have no interest in anything you may have to say. So, John, you were about to tell me about my mother.'

John opened his mouth to speak, but once again, he could not tell his story, for his voice was drowned in the sound of cheering and shouts of acclamation. For the first time in his life, William had tasted victory. And having sampled it once, he knew deep in his heart that he would crave that sweet fruit for ever.

16

Winchester, and the Viscounty of Narbonne

More than a year had passed since Emma's triumphant vindication. Edward had been given no option but to reinstate her as dowager queen, and in a church, with God's evident blessing, to boot. Her name now appeared on royal charters, first in line below the king's, as it had done on Ethelred's, Canute's and Harthacnut's charters too. Edward, meanwhile, had found another woman to trouble him, for he was betrothed to marry Edith, daughter of Earl Godwin of Wessex, and there came a point when their marriage could be delayed no longer.

It was a winter wedding, with the weather as cold as King Edward's heart. For Godwin, however, this was a joyous occasion, the culmination of many long years of working, fighting and scheming for his own advancement and that of his children. His oldest sons, Sweyn and Harold, already had their earldoms, as Edward had promised. Now the last of the three payments due for his service in putting Edward on the throne would be made in full, and he was in high spirits as he and Gytha welcomed their guests to the ceremony. This would be both a wedding and a coronation, as Edith would receive a golden crown as well as a ring. By the morrow's end, Godwin's daughter would be honoured as Queen of England.

No wonder then that he greeted Earl Leofric with a sly dig in the ribs and pulled him aside, while Godiva chatted to Gytha, to ask, 'Is it true? Did that wife of yours really ride through

Coventry stark naked? By Christ, man, why didn't you tell me it was happening?'

'Do we have to talk about it?' Leofric muttered. 'It was a private matter, and the sooner it's forgotten the better.'

Godwin laughed. 'Fat chance of that! I'm not sure how an old man like you did it, but you bagged the most beautiful woman in England. You can't blame any red-blooded fellow for stirring at the thought of her bare legs astride a stallion.'

'For heaven's sake, Godwin, that's my wife you're talking about! And we're in a church.'

'Yes, but this is a wedding. It's the joining of a man and a woman. What's that about if not lust? Look, I won't say another word, but first, just tell me . . . why did she do it?'

Leofric gave the sigh of a man resigning himself to a lifetime of telling the same story. 'It all started with a tax that the people didn't want to pay . . .'

'My oath, Leofric, don't even say that. Brings back memories of Worcester.'

'It was nothing like that! I need money for this convent we're building at Coventry, and I thought I'd institute a toll on horses passing through the town, because many more people are visiting just to see how the building work's going. But the local people didn't like it because they were frightened it would drive away trade, and Godiva, bless her – she's a lovely, kind soul – took pity on them. She said Jesus would not approve of us, who have so much, taking money from others who have so little.'

'By God, it's a good thing she doesn't rule England. The king would be penniless!'

'Well, quite . . . she just doesn't understand that some things have to be done, even if one doesn't like it. She insisted we had to carry out an act of penance. I said I damn well wouldn't do it, but she did: she rode through the town, which isn't far because it's a very small little place . . . but she wasn't completely naked. She wore the sleeveless shift she normally wears beneath her dress, and although it's not exactly modest – her arms were bare, and her lower legs, and her head – she absolutely was not naked!'

'Maybe not,' said Godwin. 'But the story sounds better that way, you must admit.'

Before Leofric could reply, Gytha had appeared beside them. The two men were the most senior nobles in England, but Godwin's wife was not a woman to bother with formalities. 'You two are worse than a pair of old women,' she said, taking Godwin's arm. 'Come . . . our daughter needs her parents to send her on her way.'

When he saw Edith in her wedding dress, Godwin had to discreetly wipe away a tear of paternal pride. His little girl had grown up to be a woman fit for any king, and if Edward were anything but a king, she'd be far too good for him.

When the time came for the ceremony itself, Edith carried herself with regal grace, and many a member of the congregation felt that Edward was more fortunate to be getting her than she was to be getting a crown, though she wore the jewelled gold diadem that was placed upon her brow as though she'd been born to it.

Even Edward could not help but notice his new bride's effortless assumption of royalty, and the way she mixed the charm and happiness of a new bride with the superiority of a queen as she greeted the noblemen and women who crowded round after the ceremony to offer their congratulations. As they bowed and curtseyed and called her 'Your Majesty', a casual observer might have taken her for a young woman who had been greeted this way all her life, and it emboldened Edward to say, 'Follow me, my dear,' and, for the first time, enter into the crowd to seek out a particular person, rather than waiting for them to come to him. As they walked together, he said,

'Remember, you are above all other women in England . . . all of them. And they must never forget it.'

'Yes, sire,' said Edith, who had already learned that her husband expected her to show him just as much deference as any other of his subjects would do. Then Edward found his intended target, and she understood why he had made a point of stressing her superiority to the rest of her sex.

'This is my mother, Emma of Normandy,' he said. 'Mother, this is Queen Edith of England.'

For a fraction of a second, neither woman said anything, or moved a muscle. Then, with visible effort, for she was far from a young woman, Emma bent her knee and lowered her head as she said, 'Your Majesty . . .'

'Lady Emma,' replied Edith with gracious condescension.

For a moment Edward felt something that might almost have been described as love for his wife. And for the very first time, he wondered why he had not married her much sooner, or why he had somehow not until now understood what his marriage meant for his mother. If there was a real queen in England, a wife to the king, then there was no need for a dowager queen any more, no need for Emma to sign charters, or maintain quarters in the palace. He could pack her off to the country to live on a distant estate, or send her back to that convent to spend the rest of her days in humble prayer, and she could not possibly have any cause to complain.

A great smile crossed his face, and Edith smiled too, because Edward had not seemed particularly pleased by anything she had done before then, and she had been worried that she might have been failing him in some way.

As another group of well-wishers came up to talk to them, Edward whispered in her ear, 'Would you please take care of these people yourself? I need to have a word with your father.'

'Of course, sire,' Edith said, and put particular effort into being even more charming than usual, to the delight of everyone she met.

Edward found Godwin in the centre of a crowd of back-slapping noblemen, all simultaneously telling him how pleased they were for him and how beautiful his daughter looked while, Edward felt sure, being consumed with bitter envy for the earl's good fortune. Well, that was about to change.

'Might I have a word with my new father-in-law?' he said, doing his best to sound convivial.

The nobles all laughed dutifully and vanished back into the crowd.

'How can I be of service, Your Majesty?' asked Godwin.

'There is nothing you need do . . . or can do, come to that,' Edward said. 'I just came to inform you that I will not be sharing a bed with your daughter tonight, nor indeed at any point in the rest of our lives. She will remain my wife. She will be my queen. But I will never fornicate with her, and you will never have a royal grandson. That is all.'

Godwin stood speechless as Edward turned on his heel and walked away. The delight he had felt at his daughter's marriage had vanished, along with all the hopes he had invested in the union between his house and Edward's. A joyful celebration had become a bitter, meaningless, empty occasion.

Oh my little girl, my poor, poor girl, Godwin thought. And then: I will make you pay for this, Edward, you cold, loveless, impotent bastard. I will make you pay if it's the very last thing I do.

In a stone-walled farmhouse whose roof of terracotta tiles was supported by sturdy oak beams, a woman was stirring a pot over an open fire. Within it was a mixture of garlic, onions, tomatoes and olives, which she planned to serve to her husband for his dinner, along with two grilled sardines bought fresh from the market in Narbonne that very day. She was smiling to herself as she cooked, partly because the act of preparing food for the man she loved was one that gave her great pleasure, and also because she had, quite by chance, entered into conversation with an elderly man who was waiting beside her at the fishmonger's stall.

His name was Solomon ben Yahuda, and he was a member of the Jewish community that had flourished in Narbonne for many hundreds of years. When he discovered that she had grown up in Damascus – the discovery came as a surprise to him, for as he said, 'I never met a golden-haired Syrian before!' – he had been delighted, for he had family in the city and had travelled there himself as a boy. Because she had warmed to him and instinctively trusted him, she had told him that she had been apprenticed to Zaid al-Zuhairi, one of the greatest of all Damascene apothecaries (she did not, however, go so far as to confess that he had been the first man she had ever killed). Solomon's interest had deepened still further, for he was, he said, a great student of the medicinal purposes to which herbs and flowers could be put. 'It would be my great pleasure and honour to discuss the subject with you, if you were agreeable,' he said.

'I would be agreeable . . . with my husband's permission,' she replied.

'Of course, of course, I quite understand. Please assure your husband that my intentions are entirely honourable. My only interest is scholarship. If I were thirty years younger, maybe not so much. But today . . .'

She laughed at the memory of the old man's face as he had said that, for he had put on such a comic expression of regret for his lost youth that it had been impossible to take offence. Then she brought her mind back to the food. The vegetables were almost done. It was time to place the fish on the grill.

Before she could do that, however, there was a rapping on the heavy wooden door of the farmhouse. When she went to open it, she saw before her a young woman whose dewy, unlined skin suggested she was barely more than a girl, though she had an air about her that told of a maturity beyond her years. She was lean and sunburned, with fair hair that was almost white from exposure to the sun. She was wearing a gown that had once been very expensive but was now faded and criss-crossed with patches and darning, and her feet were dirty and rough-skinned from countless leagues of walking.

'I have come here to find Jarl,' the young woman said.

The woman who had once called herself Jarl for professional purposes, but who had for many years been known only as Jamila, said nothing. Her immediate instinct had been to say, 'There is no Jarl here,' and slam the door, but then she had been struck by the young woman's eyes. They were very beautiful, with soft grey irises, and there was something feline about both their shape and the way they looked at her. They were simultaneously knowing and yet mysterious, as if they saw everything but revealed nothing.

'Who is asking?'

'My name is Mabel of Bellême.'

'And why do you seek Jarl?'

'Because I wish to learn from her.'

As she spoke, Mabel looked at Jamila with a cool insolence that seemed to say, 'I know your secret. Why are we even pretending that you are not her?'

But Jamila was not yet ready to reveal her true self. Her reply was noncommittal. 'Jarl? That is a strange name for a woman. Do you know what trade she practises?'

'Yes.'

Mabel said that one word with absolute conviction. Clearly she knew precisely what Jarl did and was determined to do the same. Her eyes were the proof that she would be a worthy apprentice. Jamila looked again at the slender limbs, the dusty skin and the sun-bleached hair and saw herself, many years ago, on the road that had taken her from Damascus to the sea.

'You have found the one you seek,' she said. 'You may come in. But I am afraid that I only have room for one guest.'

Behind Mabel there stood a scrawny, exhausted-looking donkey and beside it an old man with unkempt hair, matted with dirt and grease, who gazed around him with a simpleton's vacant, gap-toothed grin. Jamila could see that he was scrawny to the point of emaciation, for he was dressed in nothing more than a short kilt made of rags, and she wondered what kind of ill-treatment and deprivation he must have endured to be reduced to such a state. When she looked at him, he gave her a servile nod of the head.

'Do you have a barn, or a stable?' Mabel asked.

'Yes.'

'Then the donkey can spend the night there.'

'And your slave?' Jamila used the word for she knew that no paid servant would ever descend to such a state of wretchedness.

'Oh, the stable will do for him too. Where is it?'

'Behind the house,' Jamila said. 'Follow the path and it goes straight there.'

Mabel turned to address the man. 'You heard her. Don't just stand there like a gibbering idiot. Move!'

'Yes, ma'am, God bless you, ma'am,' the poor creature said, and as he scurried off, dragging the donkey behind him, Jamila realised that he was absolutely petrified of his mistress. He had good reason to be too, for a moment later, Mabel reached down, picked up a pebble and threw it at him, as hard and as accurately as any man. The hapless slave didn't see the stone coming, so the howl he gave as it hit him on the shoulder was as much one of surprise as pain.

Mabel laughed. Then she said to Jamila, 'He needs to be kept in his place, that one. Can you believe it, he thinks he's the Count of Bellême.'

Jamila understood then that there was a flinty cruelty in this young woman that she had never herself possessed, and for a moment she considered changing her mind and refusing Mabel entry. But then she thought of all the things she had done and the people she had killed, and realising that she was in no position to judge anyone, she said instead, 'Won't you come in?'

Book Four:

The Hungry and the Hunted

Autumn 1046–Spring 1048

1

The castle of Saint-Saveur-le-Vicomte, on the Cotentin peninsula of Normandy

Goles was a fool, an itinerant halfwit jester with sheep-shit for brains: a goggle-eyed, beak-nosed, big-eared buffoon whose presence was of no more consequence to the half-dozen men in the great hall than the dog greedily licking its balls before the blazing fire. Like a dog, Goles grovelled on the floor beneath the table, scavenging for discarded scraps and smacking his lips with exaggerated relish as he set about the shreds of flesh still clinging to chicken bones and sucked out the last soft morsels of marrow from the vertebrae of oxen.

Had not his hands both been gripped around the leg of lamb that was his latest trophy, Goles could have reached out and touched the boots of soft Spanish leather that clad the feet of Guy of Burgundy. His head was so close to the young aristocrat's cloak that every time Guy moved, the breeze from it wafted against his face.

'So we're agreed,' Guy said. 'The Bastard dies tonight.'

'You're sure we have to do it now?' asked another voice, which Goles recognised as Nigel Falconhead, Viscount of the Cotentin, whose castle this was.

'Yes, we may never again have an opportunity like this. He's just a few leagues away. The lodge has no walls or even a stockade, and William has no more than half a dozen men to guard him. It must be tonight.'

'Yes, tonight! Tonight!' Goles piped up. 'Go to Duke William and pledge your love for him tonight!'

There were a few desultory chuckles around the table, but all Goles received from Guy of Burgundy was a sharp kick, to which he reacted by flinging himself backwards and somersaulting twice, in a comic flurry of wildly waving arms and legs, before landing in a heap of rushes and food scraps swept up by the servants before they had been dismissed to leave the men in peace. A broomstick was propped up against the wall, next to Goles's scrawny sprawled body. He reached for his hat and stuck it back on his head before crawling back towards the table, murmuring, 'Poor Goles, poor, poor Goles. Be a good boy, Goles, and maybe the master will give you a penny instead of a kick.'

Guy of Burgundy paid him not the slightest attention. 'I must know that you are all with me. You must swear on your honour and your lives that you will not falter, or back down – that you will see this thing through until the duke is dead. Nigel?'

Silence fell around the hall. Goles muttered, 'I'll swear. The fool will swear.' Then Count Nigel steeled himself and said, 'I swear. The duke dies, or I do.'

'Good man. How about you, Grimauld?'

Goles was kneeling, but he sat back on his haunches and straightened his back enough to be able to see across the table. Like the duke they were plotting against, these were all young men, none of them more than twenty-five and one or two – including Guy himself – barely twenty. Grimauld de Plessis' face still bore a few white-tipped red spots, and the scars of many more. But despite – or perhaps because of – his immaturity, he did not hesitate before answering, 'I swear it. If I get the chance, I'll stick the Bastard like a fat pig on a roasting spit.'

They all knew that Grimauld's boasts were empty. William

of Normandy was younger than any of them, but his reputation as a strong, fearless, brutally effective fighting man was growing stronger with every year. However much they wanted rid of him, none of them doubted that he was a fearsome opponent.

Goles let out a series of loud porcine grunts and called out, 'I'm Duke Piggy! I'm the son of a swine and an unmarried slut! Roast me, Grimauld, roast me!'

This time even Guy of Burgundy joined in the laughter. But then his face grew serious again. He reached into the purse that hung from his belt, fished out half a penny piece and said, 'Enough, Fool. Let me buy your silence.' He flicked the coin across the room, Goles chasing after it on all fours.

Guy drew oaths from three more men. The first was Ralph 'the Badger' Taisson, Lord of Thury, so called because his lands were said to be so extensive that he could, like a badger, go to earth anywhere he chose. After him came Rannulf, Viscount of the Bessin, and Haimo de Crèvecoeur, Lord of Torigni, Évrecy and Creully, who was nicknamed 'Dentatus', or 'Longtooth Haimo', in honour of the unusually large front teeth that were revealed whenever he opened his mouth. As they looked around the table, crashing their goblets together in one toast after another, each proclaiming death to William and success for their rebellion, yet surreptitiously wondering who among them would be the first one to repudiate his oath, not a man noticed that the hall was just a little less full than it had been a few minutes ago. The plotters were still at the table. The dog, now asleep, still lay snoring by the fire.

But both Goles and the broomstick had vanished.

Goles was nobody's fool. Any idiot could stand beside a table, swear wine-soaked oaths and crow undeserving boasts about their prowess, but it took sharp wits to make quick jokes, and a lithe, nimble body to tumble across hard floorboards and come away unbruised. And Goles possessed a finer character than his social superiors. His loyalty was won not by the promise of personal gain, but by acts of kindness and fair treatment. He had performed many times for Duke William's mother Herleva, and she had borne no resemblance to an unmarried slut. On the contrary, in her beauty, her dignity and her generosity she had seemed to Goles like the finest of ladies. Her son he knew less well, but the very least that could be said was that he had never done Goles any wrong. And so the fool wanted the duke to survive, for his mother's sake if nothing else.

He scurried from the hall, broom in hand, let himself out of the keep and trotted down the steep slope of the mound on which the heart of the castle stood. An expanse of open land dotted with thatched wooden buildings lay between it and the castle walls. The sky was clear and the full moon cast black shadows across the blue-grey ground, making it easy for Goles to find his way to the gatehouse. He passed the stables on his way. At this time of night they would normally be dark and silent, but he could see the light of torches coming from them, and the flickering shadows of people and animals moving about inside. He could hear the horses whinnying and their grooms trying to quiet them. They were getting ready for the attack.

The castle's great oak gates had been closed since sunset and would not open without Count Nigel's express command. But there was a sally port cut into one of them, just big enough to let one man squeeze through, its specific purpose to allow movement in and out after lock-up. A nightwatchman stood beside it, clad in a hooded hauberk of chain mail with an arming sword at his waist. He towered over Goles like a great boulder of muscle and bone, exuding a dull-eyed miasma of truculent, obstructive stupidity.

'Where are you going, Fool?' he barked.

Goles looked up at the sky. 'Isn't it a lovely day?' he said breezily. He lowered the broom and mounted it so that it was grasped between his legs. 'I thought I'd go for a ride.' He slapped his own backside hard and cried, 'Giddy-up, Golesy! Giddy-up!' all the while skipping up and down in a stationary trot.

'You want to go out?' the nightwatchman asked.

'Of course! I'm going for a ride, aren't I?'

The nightwatchman thought for a moment. 'No.'

'No?'

'No.'

Goles felt a sickening lurch in his stomach. If he didn't get out of the castle, the duke would die. He had to find a way to change the man's mind. He put on his most gormless expression and scratched his head, 'Can you help me solve a puzzle?' he asked.

'Dunno.'

'Well then,' Goles continued, 'here's what I don't understand. You're on the inside of the wall, am I right?'

An impatient sigh. 'Yes.'

'And your job is to stop people on the outside of the wall getting to the inside where you are.'

'Suppose so.'

'And I'm on the inside, which is where you don't want people to be, and I want to get to the outside, where you want people to stay. So since I'm here when I should be there, and there's nobody there who shouldn't be here, isn't it your job, since you don't have anyone who's out there to stop coming in here, to kick me out of being in so that I can't come in again from being out?'

The nightwatchman made a brief, frowning attempt to make sense of Goles's words, then gave up the struggle and snarled, 'Shut it, Fool. I don't have to listen to this nonsense.'

'Oh, but you do. I'm a Fool and it's my job to talk nonsense, just like it's your job to stop people out there from coming in here and to get rid of people like me who are here but ought to be out there.'

The nightwatchman's right hand curled into a mailed fist. 'I told you, Fool, I won't listen to no more of this nonsense.'

'You don't have to. Just open the door and let me take my horsey for a nice ride and you won't hear another word from me ever again.'

Silence fell.

'Or I'll stay here and keep on talking, and if you want to hit me . . .' Goles started hopping from toe to toe and weaving his head, 'you'll have to catch me first.'

The nightwatchman's hand moved faster than Goles had expected. But the punches never came. Instead, he found himself grabbed by the scruff of the neck and dragged towards the door. As he struggled and gibbered, living up to his feather-brained reputation, the nightwatchman turned the heavy iron key in the sally-port lock and drew back a pair of massive bolts, top and bottom. Then he opened the door a little and gave the writhing fool a kick in the backside that would have done a bucking stallion proud.

Goles flew forward, genuinely out of control this time, and smashed against the studded oak door, which swung open, crashing back against the main body of the gate. He ended up lying face down on the rutted, hoof-marked dirt outside the castle wall. His arse and lower back were in agony from the kick. His arm, shoulder and skull all hurt where he had hit the sally port. He was winded, and as if that were not enough, the nightwatchman threw the broomstick at him like a spear and hit him on the head once again, leaving him dizzy and dazed.

Goles could not remember a time when so many different parts of his body were screaming with so much pain. But as he got to his feet, dusting himself down and leaving both the broomstick and his hat on the ground behind him, he did not care. He was out of the castle, and that was all that mattered.

Goles had spent his entire adult life walking through Normandy looking for someone, somewhere to give him food, shelter and maybe a penny or two in exchange for entertainment. He knew every road, lane, bridleway and path in the duchy, and on a night like this he'd have no trouble finding his way from Saint-Saveur-le-Vicomte to the hunting lodge near Valognes where the duke and his party were staying. But he had one fearsome enemy: time.

Valognes was about three, maybe four leagues away. Goles knew that a league was measured as the distance a man could walk in an hour. A fit young man could probably run almost three leagues in that time on a good path over flat country. But how fast could a horse go, carrying a large, fully armoured man? Goles had no idea. He'd never ridden a horse in his life, and the only thing he knew about them for sure was that a poor man going by foot did everything he could to stay out of their way.

As he imagined the sound of thundering hooves on the earth behind him and the sight of sword blades glinting in the moonlight, Goles broke into a frantic, full-pelt sprint. It was only when he started to breathe heavily that he realised that he had to pace himself. He settled into a steady, loping run, and as he ran, he tried to work out how far behind him the plotters would be when they too left the castle. Guy must have got them all to swear their loyalty to him by now. But they had to have a plan for what to do next. If Guy had already conceived one and it sounded good, he might be able to persuade the others to agree to it in no time at all. But if he was uncertain, or unconvincing, and they started arguing, well, they could still be there in the morning. And even once they were all agreed, they had to get themselves and their men on the move. The grooms were already at work in the stables, but how far had they got? And what about the soldiers: were they ready and waiting to go, or still fast asleep in the barrack house?

Goles's poor dazed, overworked brain tried to work out all the possible permutations, until his head was spinning with calculations he couldn't solve. But no matter how hard he thought about it, one fearful conviction became ever more deeply lodged in his mind: he wasn't going to make it in time.

2

Saint-Saveur-le-Vicomte and Valognes

Guy had hunted with Duke William many times, even staying once or twice in the lodge where he now lay sleeping. He knew exactly what had to be done to ensure that the building was surrounded, William's escape routes were cut off and the kill could be accomplished as cleanly as possible. He had even thought about ways to delay the final blow. He wanted William to keep fighting long enough to take some of the conspirators with him. It would suit Guy very well to have fewer men wanting to be rewarded and ready to start new rebellions of their own if they felt he had been insufficiently generous. Let them all fall, just as long as he himself was still standing.

This was not, of course, a point that he raised during the swift, decisive explanation of his plan that he delivered once he had secured the others' commitment to the plot. He spoke with a confidence and certainty that brooked no contradiction, knowing that if a leader did not demand obedience, but simply acted as if no other view than his own was even conceivable, people would almost always go along with what he said.

Longtooth Haimo and Ralph Taisson both had questions about their respective roles in the action, but they were simply seeking clarification rather than challenging his ideas. All in all, Guy was pleasantly surprised by the ease and speed with which the other lords had acquiesced to his commands. When they all left the keep, filled with good cheer about what the night had in store for them, they found their horses fed, watered and about to be saddled. The dozen knights Guy had picked for the task were adjusting their gear, checking their swords and bows and swapping foul-mouthed soldierly banter. There was no note of apprehension in any of their voices, no sense that they were trying to persuade themselves, against the evidence, that all would be well. These men were highly trained, experienced warriors, many from landowning families and even minor nobility. They were upbeat and confident, genuinely looking forward to a fight they would win.

Things were going so well, in fact, that they were ready even sooner than Guy's most optimistic expectation.

'Let's go!' urged Grimauld de Plessis, as desperate as ever to prove his eagerness for battle.

Guy wanted to strike in the early hours of the morning, when William and his men would be sleeping most deeply and slowest to react. But when he looked up at the moon, it was still less than halfway through its journey across the night sky. If they left right away, they would be too early. Then again, he thought, there was no purpose in keeping the men waiting too long, or their enthusiasm and energy might peter out and be wasted.

'Soon,' he told Grimauld. 'We'll be setting off soon.'

Goles was deep in the forest of Valognes, the only thing keeping him running his terror of what might happen if he tarried for a single instant. Here there were only occasional shafts of moonlight to break the deep darkness of the looming trees, and in that darkness lurked all manner of dangers he could hardly bear to even contemplate: wild animals like wolves and bears, and even wilder men, be they outlaws and brigands, or foresters out looking for poachers. And then, of course, there was Guy of Burgundy and his men. If they should encounter him along the way, they would realise at once what he was doing and waste no time in silencing him for good.

So Goles did not dare stop. But neither could he keep running much longer, not when the burning pain in his legs was so intense that they felt as though they were on fire and might at any minute give way completely, like the timbers of a flaming building. Not when he was breathing with the desperation of a drowning man coming up for air, when it did not matter how many rasping, heaving gulps he took, there never seemed enough to ease the agony in his lungs or slow the frenzied drumming of his heart.

His pace slowed until he was barely running at all, then just walking, then standing still, with his hands on his knees and his head bent over and retching. But then he heard, or thought he heard, a movement in the undergrowth, and the slow, steady breathing of a predator, and suddenly all his discomforts were forgotten and he was off and running once again.

Guy of Burgundy feared nothing as he cantered down the same forest track. There was no man or animal for miles around who would dare confront a company of knights as powerful as the one he now led. They had passed through a scattering of hamlets along the way, and he relished the knowledge that in every one of them the peasants would have been quaking in fear, dreading that they might be the target of the horsemen's wrath, knowing that if the knights were minded to do them harm, they could kill every man and rape every woman and there was nothing whatsoever to stop them. But filthy, lice-ridden peasants and their gap-toothed, saggy-breasted wives were not the sport that Guy and his men were after this night. They had a far mightier trophy in mind. And they were closing in upon it now. There was not much further to go. It was time to slow their advance and proceed with slow stealth and caution. Hardly conscious of what he was doing, Guy flexed his fingers. William of Normandy was so close that he could almost touch him.

3

When Goles arrived at the hunting lodge, he barely had the strength to beat his fist against the door, or the breath to call out for someone to let him in. It took several attempts before he could make enough of a sound, one way or the other, to wake anyone inside. The first response he received was the barely articulate protests of men who had been disturbed and wanted to be left alone. But after he had shouted, or at least gasped, 'The duke is in danger. For the love of God, open up or you will all be killed!' and managed to do so loudly and clearly enough for someone to make out what he was trying to say, the door did open a fraction and a bleary-eyed face peered out at him.

The eyes blinked. Their owner rubbed them and then scowled as he said, 'I know you. You're that fool, aren't you? What's your name?'

'Goles, my lord.'

'Well you can piss right off out of here, Goles, you son of a pox-ridden whore. What in the name of Satan do you think you're doing waking us all up? Do you think it's some kind of a joke? Get out!'

Goles fell to his knees and held up his hands in prayerful supplication. 'Gracious lord,' he said, though he knew full well there was not a drop of noble blood in the other man's body. 'I swear upon the blessed Virgin Mary that I am telling the truth. Guy of Burgundy is coming here, with five other great lords and their men, all mounted and well armed. They have sworn to kill Duke William tonight. They met at Saint-Saveur-le-Vicomte. I know. I was there. You have to believe me. I saw it all!'

The man at the door hesitated. He looked past Goles into the dark mass of the forest that rose up just a stone's throw from the lodge.

'I don't see Guy of Burgundy, nor any other lords or knights. Can't hear anything either. I think you're lying. I think you're spreading slanders about your betters. I think you need a good whipping, just to beat some damn sense into you.'

'No, sir, no, sir, please, I beg you, I'm telling the simple truth!'

Goles was desperate. He had been through so much to get here, and it was all going to be in vain. Guy's men would arrive at any moment. William and all his party were going to die. Goles was going to die.

'I must see the duke!' he begged. 'I must!'

The man at the door stepped on to the threshold, his fist cocked. 'I told you, get out, or—'

'What's going on out there?'

The question cut through the air, stopping the man dead in his tracks. He seemed to lose all interest in Goles, and spun round towards the inside of the lodge, saying, 'Your Grace . . .' And as those words were spoken, Goles's heart soared. For now he knew whose voice it was. And now, for the first time, there was hope.

William had spent most of his life as a pawn in other men's games, to be fought over, attacked or defended according to the strategies and interests of each particular player. His victory at Falaise had changed all that and made him, for the first time, an active player in the game rather than a passive piece on the board. Yet even if he was at last in charge of his own destiny, the threats that had long surrounded him still remained, and he knew it. Just two months past his nineteenth birthday, he was as hardened by bitter experience as a man twice his age. He could count the people he truly trusted on the fingers of one hand, and assumed that anyone he met was his enemy until they proved themselves his friend. The first question he asked himself whenever he was spoken to was 'Why is this man lying to me?' He always kept his sword in easy reach of his bed, and even as he slept, some part of his mind was alert to any sign of danger.

So when the sound of Goles's pleas, however faint, penetrated the upstairs room that William had taken for the night, he was out of bed in an instant. He came down the wooden staircase and into the lodge's great hall wearing nothing but a nightshirt over his breeches, but with his unsheathed sword in his right hand, ready for whatever threat might confront him.

'Bring him in,' he said, when he was told about the fool outside who was spouting an improbable tale of plots and imminent death. Goles was picked up off the threshold, manhandled into the hall and thrown to the floor in front of the duke. Half a dozen men emerged from the shadows and formed a ring around their leader and the sweat-soaked, panting figure sprawled before him.

When Goles looked upon William, he saw a man from whom all trace of boyhood had vanished. The duke was tall, but not exceptionally so, broad in the shoulders, with long, strongly muscled arms and legs. His red hair was cut short at the front and shaved up the back of his neck and the lower part of his skull: the style of a man with no personal vanity at all, who wanted to be as cool and comfortable as possible when his head was clad in a hood of leather or chain mail beneath a steel helmet. His facial features were strong enough to make him look older than his true age, though not particularly handsome. But good looks, like smartly barbered hair, were an irrelevance to William. For what struck Goles, as it did all who met the duke, was the overwhelming force of his will. You could see it in his eyes, the set of his jaw and the coiled tension of his body. It radiated from him like light and heat from the sun, an almost physical sense of power, determination, competitiveness and an absolute, uncompromising refusal to back down over anything, ever.

His voice was all of a piece with the man: gruff, steely, unbending. 'What do you want?'

I want to save your life, thought Goles. But how on earth was he to do that? How could he persuade the Duke of Normandy to listen to a man whose whole livelihood depended on talking nonsense? How could he convince him that he was speaking the truth and that his motives were pure?

Goles got unsteadily to his feet and stood before Duke William, wondering what to say next.

The duke looked down at him, waiting to hear the first lie.

In the forest just beyond the hunting lodge, Guy of Burgundy brought his horse to a halt and dismounted, taking care to slip to the ground as silently as possible. All around him his men did the same. He gestured to them to cluster round him, and then, keeping his voice at a whisper, he addressed them.

'Duke William lies sleeping just beyond those trees,' he said, pointing down the path. 'You all know what to do. If you follow your orders, neither he nor his men can escape. Are you with me?'

There were eager nods and whispers of assent.

'Good,' said Guy. 'Then follow me now, and by morning I will be your duke.'

With those words, he set off down the path towards the hunting lodge, on foot this time, his heart pounding with tension and pent-up aggression, steeling himself for the fight.

He felt no fear of what was to come. He had thought of

everything, he was sure of it. Close behind him, two men, picked for their size and strength, were carrying the battering ram with which he planned to smash his way into the lodge, breaking down the door before anyone inside had time to respond. He would catch William napping, and they would fight for real after all those years of practice. Then he would kill the usurping bastard and take the dukedom to which his own, unsullied bloodline entitled him.

Then, while he and his men were still hidden from the lodge by the trees all around them, Guy heard the barking of a hunting dog, and then another joining in, and then more still, until the whole pack was yapping and snarling and howling loud enough to wake the dead, let alone their masters asleep in the lodge. He muttered a bitter curse under his breath and picked up speed. They had lost the advantage of surprise, which would make matters harder, but still he had the edge in numbers, and no matter how much of a racket those blasted hounds made, there still wasn't time for William and his companions to get properly prepared for battle. Even if any of them had brought helmets, shields or chain-mail coats with them, which he very much doubted, they could not possibly get them on in time.

But why had the dogs barked? The thought struck him out of the blue, and nagged at him as he ran. He had made sure that he and his men were downwind of the lodge, so the animals could not have picked up their scent. And they had moved as silently as was humanly possible. No one had made any sudden noises – certainly nothing that would wake a sleeping dog. So why were they barking? And why was it getting louder?

He burst from the trees just thirty paces from the door of the lodge, which stood in a clearing, the main building forming one side of a U shape, with outbuildings and stables on the other two sides and an open yard between them. The moon was quite full, bathing the walls of the lodge in a pale blue-grey light and picking out Guy and his men as they ran, casting deep shadows on the ground beside them. There was enough light for a good archer to hit a target, even a moving one, and windows in the lodge walls for them to shoot from. Guy tensed himself for the first arrow, for he was in the lead and would be the natural target.

But no arrows came. He saw no figures at any of the windows and heard no bowstring twang, no fluttering of feathers in the air. And then he noticed something else. The door to the lodge was open.

They're coming out to meet us. Good! Far easier to cut them down out here than have to fight our way through a crowded building.

Yet no one emerged through the door. In fact, there were no signs of life anywhere in the building. Guy reached the open door and ran through into the hall. The remnants of the night's fire cast a dark amber light over the room. He stopped, tensed, looked around. This could be a trap! he realised. They could just be hiding, waiting to come out and catch us unawares.

He waited. Nothing happened. He shouted, 'Come out, William! Come out and fight! Or are you a coward as well as a bastard?'

Guy knew full well that of all the sins of which he could accuse his hated cousin, cowardice was the least plausible. No one in Normandy, no matter how much they despised their duke's illegitimacy, doubted his courage. He raised his voice even more and bellowed, 'William!'

There was no reply, no sound at all aside from the onrushing feet of Guy's own men and the distant barking of the dogs.

Guy strode deeper into the hall and found nothing except for the discarded bones around the dining table. He sent Longtooth Haimo with several of his men to search the outbuildings, while he led the rest through the few additional rooms that the lodge possessed, becoming more frantic with every one of them. They were all as empty as the Lord's tomb on Easter morning. Slowly it dawned on Guy. Those dogs had not been barking because strangers were approaching, but because their masters were leaving.

Haimo returned from his search and found Guy back in the hall. 'The dogs are in the kennels, going crazy. But apart from them, there's nothing. The horses have all gone. So have the servants and huntsmen. How the hell are we going to find them now? They'll have gone off through the woods. They could be leagues from here by morning.'

Guy let Haimo whine on. He was thinking. Then he said, 'I don't give a damn about servants or huntsmen, or anyone else. The only one I care about is William of Normandy. And I know exactly how to find him. Come with me.'

They ran through the building to the room William had been using as his bedchamber. It was strewn with his discarded clothes and possessions. Guy picked up a pair of his shoes and held one of them up to Haimo's face. 'Smell that,' he said.

'Mary Mother of God, that's disgusting!' Haimo exclaimed.

'Good. Because if you can smell the bastard's cheesy feet, then the hounds will feast on the odour. They're Alaunts. They chase scent. Let's set them to chase this.'

Goles had been too tired to run. It was all he could do to find an oak tree on the edge of the clearing in which the hunting lodge stood and climb up on to one of its lower branches. There he sat, with his back up against the trunk. There were no leaves to hide him, but as long as he remained quite still, he knew that no one would notice him. And so he saw Guy of Burgundy and his men dash across the open ground to the gaping door. He heard Guy's muffled shouts and the silence that greeted him, and sensed the confusion that must have gripped him when he realised that his quarry had fled.

The thought that he, a mere fool, had outwitted that arrogant, treacherous weasel had delighted Goles. But his pleasure was short-lived. For it was not long before Guy had reappeared in the yard between the lodge and the outbuildings, summoning his men and issuing a series of sharp, clear orders. One group ran to fetch horses, another to gather up the dogs, while Guy and his fellow nobles stood and debated William's likely escape route.

Valognes stood at the heart of the Cotentin peninsula, which jutted out of western Normandy. As long as the duke could be contained within the peninsula, he would be trapped, with the sea on three sides and only a relatively narrow neck of land opening out into the main body of the duchy. He would, of course, be well aware of that, so he would try to get off the peninsula as quickly as possible.

Guy drew a crude map in the dirt with his boot. 'This is where we are,' he said, digging his heel in. 'There are basically two ways he can go. South-east towards Bayeux and Caen. From there he could carry on towards Rouen, or go south towards Falaise.'

'He's got the militia to help him in Rouen,' Count Nigel pointed out.

'Yes, but he's got a castle and his peasant family in Falaise,' said Haimo.

Guy took control again. 'We mustn't get ahead of ourselves. He could be going due south towards Coutances and Avranches. If he does, he'll be making for Brittany, hoping to get shelter and support there. Ah . . . here are the dogs.'

Three of Guy's men had emerged from the kennels, each holding two dogs, their white coats gleaming silver in the moonlight. They were straining at their leashes, desperate to be off in search of their masters. Guy walked up to each dog and held the boot under its muzzle, letting it get a good long whiff of William's scent. The dogs started yelping with excitement, pulling even harder against their leads. They knew this scent. They couldn't wait to go and find its owner.

'Mount up!' said Guy, and all but the three men holding the dogs swung up into their saddles. He looked around and saw that his men were almost as eager for the chase as the hounds. Then he called out, 'Let loose the dogs!'

The Alaunts were released from their leashes and streaked away like spectral white demons of the night, with Guy and his men riding hard behind them. They all disappeared down a track, the same one Goles had watched William take not so very long before.

The duke was a fine rider, everyone knew that. Goles assumed that his horse must be the best in the duchy, for how could any lesser man dare to have one that was better? He had an advantage over his pursuers. But it was a very slender advantage, and he was just one man against a company of soldiers and a pack of hounds. If they should ever catch him, he would be as helpless as a lamb attacked by wolves.

Goles shivered, and not from the cold. He had done everything in his power to help William. He thought now of the duke's mother, Herleva. She would have no idea that her son was in mortal danger. He lifted his eyes to the heavens and prayed for her, hoping above all else that the next tidings she received about her son were not the news of his death.

4

The Cotentin peninsula and the Bay of Veys

William had listened hard to what Goles had to say. Fool or not, he had spoken with a conviction that overcame any scepticism. Besides, his story had been too detailed, with too many character touches that rang entirely true to William's ears, to be a matter of invention. So William had slipped on his signet ring, strapped on his belt and scabbard, wrapped a cloak around himself to keep the night's chill at bay and pulled on a pair of boots, for he could not ride far, or fast, barefooted. He told all his companions and servants to make their escape as fast as possible: 'But make sure to scatter in all directions so that it's harder for the traitors to track you.'

William's groom alone had stayed for long enough to race to the stables and throw a saddle on his stallion's back and a bridle over its head. He had barely buckled the girth before William had kicked the beast into action and set off at a gallop along one of the tracks that led away from the lodge into the surrounding forest, heedless of the danger that his horse might catch a hoof in a hole or a protruding tree root and send him flying as it fell, or that a stray branch growing out across the path might knock him clean out of the saddle. If he died making his escape, so be it. Such a fate was a risk. But to go carefully and slowly was to invite the absolute certainty that Guy of Burgundy would catch him and kill him. And that, so far as William was concerned, could never be allowed to happen.

William had acquired his horse a little over two years earlier, not long after his victory at Falaise, and named him Bloodfang, in honour of his father's favourite hunting dog. He was a towering stallion, chosen to make William stand out above the melee in the midst of battle, so that his men might see him and draw heart from his presence, and his enemies would know that he did not fear to show himself to them. The animal had a long stride, a deep chest and the heart of a true warrior. If he could have picked any horse in all Normandy to carry him to safety, William would always have chosen Bloodfang. Now he crouched in the saddle so that his head was almost lying on his horse's neck and spoke to him, encouraging him, praising him and telling him again, 'We can do it, Bloodfang. You and me together, we can do it.'

He had been riding for several minutes, ignoring the sting of leaves and twigs whipping against his face, twice having to use all his skill as a horseman to keep Bloodfang from falling and himself from leaving the saddle, when a thought struck him and chilled his blood, for all that he was sweating from the effort of riding so hard: *the dogs.* In the mad rush to flee the hunting lodge, no one had thought to take the Alaunts with them, or even just set them free to roam. William knew what Guy would do, for it was the same as he would do in that situation: he would use the dogs to hunt their master.

So now he would have to race even harder to stay alive. Before he had disappeared under the canopy of trees, William had taken a bearing from the Pole Star. He was heading south-east, making for the Bay of Veys, where four rivers flowed into the sea. The land thereabouts was marshy, treacherous and all but impassable for anyone who was not a native of the region. But right on the shoreline there were dunes and beaches. If he could just use one of the rivers to get to the sea, and ride along the water's edge, he would leave no trace for the dogs to follow. Maybe he could lose them that way.

The bay was around eight or nine leagues away across flat country. Under normal circumstances William would consider that a good, steady day's ride. But tonight he would have to ride flat out, for he had to be across the bay before the first light of dawn crossed the sky and made him visible to the eyes, somewhere behind him, that were even now gazing into the darkness, waiting for a glimpse of their prey.

On through the night he rode, thanking God for the light of the moon that made it possible for him to find his way, and marvelling at Bloodfang's ability to maintain a steady gallop for league after league, hour after hour, eating up the ground beneath his hooves, until finally William, pausing for a moment to catch his bearings, smelled the salt tang of the sea breeze blowing into his face and knew that he was near the Bay of Veys and must soon reach the western bank of the River Ouve, the first of the four waterways that emptied into it. The paths along which he rode were becoming sandier now, and he did his best to take those that seemed to be bearing towards the sea, often running along natural causeways, with reed beds on either side. Finally he caught sight of the river, which was quite broad, but with a slow-flowing stream that wound its lazy way to the sea. He followed the Ouve downstream as far as he could, until the path ran out and there was nothing for it but to walk Bloodfang into the river, his hooves slipping and sliding in the muddy water. The horse was so tall that they were almost in the middle of the stream before he was out of his depth. Then William turned him to face downstream and let him swim.

Bloodfang was as confident and powerful in water as he was on land, and William grinned as he thought of the pursuers and their dogs coming to that dead end and wondering where he had gone. He could hear the sea now, and then they were round one last bend and he could see the whites of the waves rolling in to the beach. Only now did it occur to him that he and his horse were in very real danger of being carried into those waves by the force of the river, and swept out to sea. With a sudden surge of alarm, he pulled hard on his right rein, trying to turn Bloodfang towards the bank. But there was no clearly defined separation of land and water, for the river seemed to be ending its life in a myriad of channels and rivulets that splintered off the main channel, so that even when he had guided Bloodfang away from the immediate danger, a new one arose. They were no longer going to be lost at sea, but they could yet be trapped in the mud and marsh, for there was nowhere for Bloodfang to get a solid footing as he scrabbled for purchase on the mud and sand beneath his feet.

The water was barely up to the horse's chest now, so William slipped off his back to lighten the load and dropped into the icy water, gasping at the shock of it against his body. He stumbled for a moment as he too struggled against the current and the treacherous riverbed, then grabbed the rein and led Bloodfang onwards. Up ahead he saw something glinting in the last of the moonlight, for dawn was not far away. He narrowed his eyes as he peered through the reeds and grasses and realised that the light was reflecting off sand. It was a dune: dry land. With renewed energy, he plunged through the marsh, which seemed still and almost completely silent as he and Bloodfang made their splashing, puffing way through it. And then, without warning, that silence was broken by a sudden deafening cacophony of honking, crying and frantic flapping as a flock of geese, disturbed by his presence, burst from the reed beds, crying out in alarm as they erupted into the sky and flew away towards the sea.

Damnation! William cursed beneath his breath. I might as well have shouted, 'Guy, I'm over here!' But there were any number of reasons why birds could be frightened into flight. Why should anyone assume that it was him that had spooked them? Calm down! he told himself sternly.

They had reached the dune now. William led Bloodfang up on to it and then down the other side on to the beach and the flat, hard sand by the water's edge. As he looked to the east, he saw the first hint of grey morning light on the horizon. The sun would be up soon and the same clear skies that had blessed him with moonlight would now expose him to the sun, and illuminate him for all the world to see, for there was no shelter here. Bloodfang was exhausted, but there was no time to rest. William stroked his muzzle and spoke to him again, then swung back up into the saddle and rode him hard along the beach, the horse's hooves splashing in the incoming waves. They covered almost a league, William guessed, swimming across the mouths of two more rivers, smaller ones this time, until they had gone most of the way across the bay. Then he saw a break in the dune, and below it a mass of footprints in the sand. This must be where the locals walked down to the sea, so there was probably a path beyond it, leading inland.

Sure enough, there it was, snaking away along a causeway. William followed it, and soon found himself alongside another river, which he realised must be the Vire, the largest of the Bay of Veys' four rivers. He had to cross it, but it was wide, and flowing much more quickly than the Ouve, and he hesitated to plunge Bloodfang into the water again. The horse was blowing hard, and even his indefatigable spirit might baulk at another such struggle. Then, up ahead in the dawn light, he spotted the sparkle of shallow water flowing quickly over rocks and stones.

A ford! William thanked God as he turned Bloodfang off the path and down into the shin-high current. He heard a bell ring somewhere close by, and as they came up the far bank, he saw a cluster of buildings around a church. It was a small monastery, and the bell was calling the monks to chapel for matins. For a moment, William was tempted to approach the monastery and ask for bread and water, and feed for his horse. The monks could hardly refuse a hungry, thirsty traveller, particularly if he was their duke. But that would be to expose them to danger, for Guy and his men might come this way, and he did not want to force some elderly abbot of a small and doubtless impoverished house to choose between betraying his duke and endangering his own life and those of his monks. Instead, William dismounted, bent a knee to pray and gave thanks to God for getting him this far, promising that if he were to survive his present danger, he would be sure to make a donation to the monastery. Then he led Bloodfang back to the river and let him drink. Every second they stayed in one place brought their pursuers closer, but the horse needed water and would not be able to keep going without it, so there was no choice but to tarry for a while.

The moment Bloodfang lifted his head and gave a snort of contentment, William was back up in the saddle and leading him onward, ever onward, once again.

'Damn and blast and fuck that bastard to hell!' Guy did not so much shout as scream in frustration as he and his men caught up with the hounds milling about in circles at the point where the path reached the Ouve river and stopped dead in its tracks. Behind him his men, too, were shouting and cursing as they crammed together in an ever tighter press of horses and riders and desperately tried to make room for themselves on the narrow causeway.

'If you ask me, he went in the water,' said Longtooth Haimo, trying to say something helpful to calm Guy down.

'No, you don't say? I'd never have thought of that,' Guy replied in a voice oozing sarcasm like pus from an infected wound.

'You don't have to be like that. I was only trying to help.'

'If you want to help, tell me where he went after he jumped into the river.'

'Downstream,' said Nigel of the Cotentin, who knew the Bay of Veys as he did the whole region, for it was his family's domain.

'Why?' Guy asked, seriously this time.

'Well for one thing, it's easier. His horse must have been shattered. Ours certainly are. Would you want to try to get them upstream against the current?'

'So then what? Did he just sail on out to sea? Where else is there to go from here?'

Nigel puffed out his cheeks. 'Well, you wouldn't want to go into those marshes. Not without a guide, that's for sure.'

'Not unless you were desperate and convinced you could survive anything, and William is both.'

'He wouldn't survive the marsh; there are quicksands all over them. Step in one of them and you don't step out again. And if you get caught when the tide comes in, that'll drown you.'

'Maybe he did go out to sea,' said Haimo. 'But not all the way out. Is there a beach?'

'Sure,' said Nigel. 'Stretches right across the bay.'

'So if he could reach that, he could ride along the sand . . . all the way across the bay.'

'If he could reach it, yes, but I wouldn't want to try it.'

'William would, though,' said Guy. 'Well done, Toothy. Maybe you don't have shit between your ears after all.'

'Thanks.' Haimo grinned, revealing the oversized incisors from which he took his name.

'You're not suggesting we go in there after him, are you?' Nigel asked.

'What, take that lot through a marsh?' Guy jerked his head towards his milling, swearing soldiers. 'No. But supposing William did go that way. He'd need to get off the beach somewhere and back on dry land. Where would he end up?'

Nigel thought for a moment. 'By the ford across the Vire. If he made it off the beach, that's where he'd go.'

'And if he didn't make it off the beach, or even on to the beach in the first place, we don't need to worry because he's dead anyway. So . . .' Guy looked at Nigel. 'Can you get us to that ford without getting us soaked in the process?'

'Of course.'

'Then what are we waiting for?'

5

The village of Ryes, Normandy

Hubert de Ryes was not one of the nobles who had become caught up in the fighting and banditry that raged elsewhere throughout the years of anarchy. He was a vavasour, which was to say a very minor baron, quite content to mind his own business on his estate, which lay to the north-east of Bayeux at the head of an inlet that ran down to the sea. His tenants were farmers and fishermen, so they and he all ate well enough, for even in the years when the harvests were poor, the sea still gave up its bounty. His health was good and he had the ruddy complexion and broad shoulders of a man whose life was spent outdoors and who was not too grand to lend a hand when work needed to be done. He had a wife he loved and three strong, dutiful sons, and if his castle was only constructed of wood, and protected by a wooden palisade rather than high stone walls, that was of no concern to Hubert. He had no enemies on land: the only reason he had any walls at all was to keep out pirates or raiders who might come in from the sea.

On this particular morning, Hubert was standing by the lowered drawbridge across the deep ditch that ran beneath his stockade, chatting to the local priest, whose church stood next to the castle at the heart of the little village of Ryes, when his eye was caught by the sight of a horseman coming up the dirt road towards him. Even at a distance, the man and his mount gave off an almost tangible air of extreme exhaustion. The horse was certainly a mighty specimen, yet it could barely put one hoof in front of another, and its rider was slumped in his high wooden saddle, his head hanging down, with a shock of bright ginger hair falling like a curtain over his eyes, so that Hubert suspected he might actually be asleep.

'Well there's a traveller who's been too long on the road,' said the priest.

'Hasn't he just,' Hubert agreed. 'I don't know who looks in more need, him or his horse.'

The man rode closer. 'Good day to you, sir!' Hubert called out. 'May I offer you some assistance?'

With a supreme effort, as if bearing a huge weight on his shoulders, the rider raised his head and looked towards Hubert and the priest. He said nothing. All he could manage was a feeble grunt before his head flopped forward again.

But that brief glimpse of his face had been enough. A year earlier, Hubert and the priest had both been at a mass at Bayeux Cathedral attended by Duke William and various members of his household. The priest, in fact, had taken part in the service, carrying the communion wine beside the Bishop of Bayeux, Hugo d'Ivry, as he went along the line of communicants. He had thus seen the duke at very close quarters. For his part, Hubert had been like every other member of the congregation, straining his neck to get a good look at his duke as he entered and left the cathedral and observing him as discreetly as he could during the service itself.

Now the priest looked at Hubert and said, 'It can't possibly be him, can it?'

'If not, he must have a twin.'

'What do you think we should do?'

'Help him, of course.' With that, Hubert stepped forward and took hold of the horse's bridle, stopping it in its tracks. The poor beast was lathered in sweat, and its bit was almost lost in the crusted white foam around its mouth. Hubert held a hand out towards William. 'Please, my lord, let me help you down from the saddle.'

The duke's eyes narrowed, and Hubert saw suspicion and also a trace of fear on his face as he asked, 'Who are you, sir?'

'Hubert de Ryes, my lord. But what brings you here like this, all alone?'

Again that look of anxiety crossed William's face, and Hubert's heart went out to him. He might be Duke of Normandy, and built like a full-grown man, but he was no older than his own eldest son, and Hubert knew how much uncertainty his boy concealed behind his bullish facade.

'Can I trust you, Hubert?' William asked.

'Of course, my lord. I'm yours to command.'

A bone-weary attempt at a smile pulled feebly at the corners of the duke's mouth. 'Thank you, Hubert,' he said. 'The truth is, I'm on the run. Some men tried to kill me last night. They've been chasing me ever since.'

'Then come with me, and I will make sure that they do not catch you.'

Hubert led the horse across the drawbridge and past his stockade with William still on it, for he looked too shattered to walk. They came to a halt in the yard before the castle keep, and he did not so much help William from the saddle as catch him when he fell into his outstretched arms.

The duke could barely stand. Hubert led him stumbling into his hall, sat him on a bench and asked the priest to look after him. Then he strode away, calling out to his wife. 'Where are you, dearest? Duke William is here! He needs our help! Where *are* you, woman? Come here!'

His wife appeared moments later, upbraiding him for shouting at her so, then fell silent as she saw the debilitated figure of her duke sitting bent over, with his elbows on his knees and his head in his hands. Rohaise was a practical woman, so she wasted no time on empty sympathy but began issuing orders at once. Servants were dispatched to fetch a large pitcher of water and wine, a loaf of bread and whatever cold meat was sitting in the pantry. The stable boy was sent for and told to water, feed and rub down the duke's horse.

Hubert, meanwhile, rounded up his three sons, who ranged in age from twenty-one to fifteen. 'Come with me,' he said, and led them back to the hall, where William, who had drunk the watered wine in a single draught, was demolishing a great hunk of bread in one hand and a chicken leg in the other. Hubert smiled as he saw the astonishing restorative effect the food and drink were having. The speed with which young men could restore their strength never ceased to amaze him. He sighed at the thought of the years that had passed since he too had possessed such vigour, then got down to the matter in hand.

'May I ask where you were planning to go next, fair lord?' he asked.

William had just washed down his food with a freshly brought pitcher. He wiped the back of his hand across his mouth and said, 'Falaise. If I can reach the castle there, I will be safe. I don't believe my enemies have the means to take me once I'm inside its walls.'

'Very well then, my sons will escort you. And I'll give you a fresh horse. Yours would collapse before you got a tenth of the way there. I take it you don't want to be seen if you can possibly help it, so this is what we'll do . . .'

Hubert gave his sons detailed instructions of the route they had to take to Falaise. 'The castle is at least fifteen leagues from here,' he told William when the boys had been briefed. 'That would normally be two days' ride.'

'I have already come a good fifteen leagues. If I have to ride another fifteen I will. But I'm not stopping until I'm safe in Falaise.'

'Then you'd better be off. I wish you God speed on your journey. Boys, you've got the future of our duchy in your hands. Take Duke William safely to Falaise, or don't show your faces in this house again.'

'What about you, Hubert?' William asked. 'The men who are after me will be here soon. They'll want to know where I've gone. I don't want you getting into trouble on my account.'

Hubert smiled. 'Don't worry, my lord. I can take care of them.'

'Then thank you.' William took Hubert's hand. 'You've been a good Samaritan when I needed one most. And I will never, ever forget it.'

Guy of Burgundy was shattered too. Not to mention frustrated, deflated and generally in a foul, cantankerous mood. For reasons he had still to work out, his apparently flawless plan had fallen apart. Somehow William had got wind that he was in mortal danger and, even more improbably, had managed not only to escape but also to stay ahead of the hounds, the horses and the men on his trail.

Not that there were many men or horses any more, nor any hounds at all. As the leagues had gone by, first the dogs had lost their enthusiasm for the chase, then one man after another had dropped out, pleading a lame horse or their own exhaustion as an excuse. Guy himself had only been able to keep going thanks to the spare horses he had brought with them. Nigel of the Cotentin and three of the men-at-arms had also taken advantage of the fresh mounts, and the five of them, Guy was sure, would be more than enough to kill William. First, though, they had to find him.

It had been some while since Guy had been able to move at speed, safe in the knowledge that the dogs were tracking William's scent. Instead he had been forced to ask peasants and shepherds in the fields, washerwomen doing their laundry, or the few travellers on the roads if they had seen a lone horseman passing by. For every ten he asked, only one came up with an answer, no matter how roughly he questioned them, or even on occasion whipped them. So it had been an increasingly slow, painstaking business to make his way along the coast, past Bayeux and towards a small village where he could see a man standing outside a pitifully meagre excuse for a castle – really not much more than a feebly fortified cottage, so far as Guy was concerned – talking to a shabbily dressed priest.

The moment Guy saw the man's clothes, which bore all the signs of a wife's repeated repairs, his sunburned skin and the amiable, almost half-witted expression on his face, he knew precisely what he was dealing with. He'd seen men like this up and down Normandy, petty barons in obscure rural backwaters who were barely more than peasants themselves. The man would know at once that Guy was far and away his social superior, and would act accordingly. That said, it never hurt to flatter the absurd pretensions of this kind of yokel.

'Excuse me, my good sir,' he called out. 'Have you by any chance seen a horseman riding by? He's a young man, bright red hair. Looking damn tired by now, I should think.'

The yokel grinned. 'You mean the Bastard?' he asked, and then chuckled at his own splendid wit.

Guy did his best to control the strange mixture of utter contempt for the man and huge excitement at his words that now swirled around inside his own, fatigue-fogged head. 'I do indeed mean William of Normandy,' he said. It pleased Guy to think that there were others, no matter how insignificant who might be ready to support his cause. 'I can see you don't think much of our Duke. I don't blame you. He's illegitimate, and his father killed his own brother to usurp his title.'

'You don't sound like much of a friend yourself, your

lordship!' the man said, grinning inanely. 'Would you like me to show you where he went?'

Guy looked down the road. There was a crossroads up ahead, with forks leading off in three or four different directions. 'That would be very kind. Perhaps you can point to the way he took.'

'I can do better than that, my lord. I can take you after him. He told me where he was going. Didn't mean to, but I got it out of him. Serves him right for taking me for a fool, eh?'

'Absolutely. No one could possibly think you were foolish, sir.'

'I should hope not. Well just you wait there a moment and I'll go and get my old nag and we can go riding after that bastard duke. Believe me, he'll get no mercy from me. It was a bad day for Normandy when he became duke, and if I've got anything to do with it, we'll have a new one by the time I get back here. Oh, when we find him, I'll strike the first blow all right, just see if I don't.'

Finally the man finished his blustering and wandered off towards his miserable abode. Guy called after him, 'Whom do I have the honour of addressing, good sir? You never told me your name.'

'Hubert's my name, Hubert de Ryes.'

'Well, Hubert, there'll be a shiny gold coin for you if we catch the duke.'

De Ryes disappeared behind his gates, only to re-emerge a short while later seated on a horse that Guy was convinced was at least a quarter donkey. 'Right, my lords, follow me,' he said, and cantered off to the crossroads and down one of the tracks leading from it.

Two hours later, having gone up and down hill, turning to left and right, across fields, through woods and over streams, and at least once – Guy was sure of it – returning to a point they had passed by some time before, it became clear that they were never going to find William.

'I don't know where that bastard's got to, I swear I don't,' de Ryes said, scratching his head. 'I know he came this way, for he told me he would, and I saw where he turned at the crossroads, too. He couldn't have lied to me, could he? I mean, a duke wouldn't lie, not even a bastard. I mean, he just wouldn't.'

You're the liar, Hubert de Ryes, Guy thought bitterly. You've tricked me, you filthy, pox-ridden peasant. I should whip the skin off your back, then run my sword through your guts and ...

But he was too tired even to think of what he would do to de Ryes, let alone actually carry it out. William had got away from him and there was no point whining about it, or fretting about the hows and whys.

Guy had lost the first skirmish, but this was going to be a war. And by God he would win that war and get his own back on William the Bastard, or die in the attempt.

6

The royal palace at Poissy, France

'Ah, Duke William, I was wondering how long it would be before you made your way here.'

King Henry of France, a tall, fair-haired, bearded man approaching his fortieth year, gave a little smile at the end of the sentence to indicate a degree of levity, and his courtiers all laughed at their master's wit, and at the sight that had inspired it.

William of Normandy had ridden from Falaise to Rouen and then on to the royal palace at Poissy, which stood on the left bank of the Seine at the edge of a forest famed for its hunting, about five leagues west of Paris. He was accompanied by his uncle Mauger, who might still be the same twitching bundle of nerves he had always been, but was nonetheless an archbishop and therefore added to the status of their embassy to the French court. Not that the courtiers had seen it that way.

'A bastard duke and a gibbering priest, marching in here without a by-your-leave,' one eminent French nobleman had sneered to his fellow peers. 'Really, these Normans are still just as savage as they were in Rollo's day.'

More than a century earlier, Rollo and his Vikings had rampaged through the towns and cities of northern France and pillaged half the country between Paris and the sea. In a desperate bid to prevent him wreaking any more havoc, King Charles the Simple had offered him Flanders as a place where he and his people could settle in peace. Rollo rejected the offer on the grounds that Flanders was too wet and muddy, and was equally dismissive of Charles's second offer of Brittany, as too rocky. He was, however, gracious enough to suggest that he would accept the old Roman province of Neustria, or Normandy as it soon became known, for it was large, fertile and could provide a man with a good living, without the need to fight for it.

Now, more than a century later, the tables had been turned, for here was Rollo's direct descendant – his great-great-great-grandson, to be precise – coming here to plead with the Frankish king rather than the other way around. To make the moment even more delicious, William had dropped to one knee before King Henry. That was particularly satisfying, for Rollo had flatly refused to bend his knee when Charles the Simple had demanded, or perhaps begged him to do so. Rollo was not minded to obey any man, and he made no exception for Charles. William could not afford to be so bold.

'We all heard about your flight from Valognes,' King Henry continued. 'Can it really be true that you rode from there to Falaise in the course of a single night and day?'

'Yes, sire, though it was well after dark by the time I arrived in Falaise.'

'And you were hotly pursued all the way?'

'Half the way, sire. I met a good man near Bayeux, Hubert de Ryes, who gave me a fresh horse and ordered his sons to escort me, then led Guy of Burgundy and his men off in the wrong direction while I got away.'

'This Hubert sounds like a good man. I trust you will reward him for his loyalty.'

'If I ever get the chance, yes, sire, of course.'

'And Guy of Burgundy . . . that's Reginald's son, isn't it?'

'Yes, sire.'

'Am I right in thinking he was brought up in Normandy?'

'Yes, sire, his mother was my aunt Alice, only she died when he was just a baby.'

'So your family took him in . . . huh! Doesn't sound very grateful of Guy to turn around and try to kill you.'

'He hates me, sire. He always has. He says that his claim to Normandy is stronger than mine because I'm . . .' William paused and looked around at the courtiers, knowing that they were aware of what was coming next and would look down on him for it. Then he pulled back his shoulders, held his head high and said, 'Because I'm illegitimate.'

'Your father wasn't, though, was he?'

'No, sire.'

'And he brought you to see me when you were just a boy. I remember it well. He declared you his heir, there was no doubt whatsoever about that, and you pledged your allegiance to me.'

'Yes, sire, that is why I'm here now.' William had been thinking for days about what he was going to say, and now that he had his chance, he wasn't going to let anyone, not even the king himself, stop him before he'd made his case.

'I remember that day too, Your Majesty. You told my father that he had given you shelter and help when you needed it, and that one day you would return the favour to me.'

'That's true, I said that,' the king agreed.

'Well, I need it now. Guy has got together with a group of barons to mount a rebellion against me. He's promised them all land if he becomes duke. They're already going on to my estates on the Cotentin, along the coast, down into the Hiémois, claiming them for themselves, taking property that doesn't belong to them, running my tenants off the land. I've lost half the duchy, and they'll take the rest unless you come to my aid.'

'Why, are you completely without friends?'

'No, I have men who are still loyal to me, and they have soldiers they can add to mine, but it's not enough. If I'm lucky,

I may be able to keep Guy and his followers at bay for a while. But in the end, they'll be too strong.'

'And why is this my problem?'

'Because you gave your word, sire. And no king can afford to break a pledge that he has freely made to one of his vassals. If men know that you had turned your back on me, having promised to come to my aid if I ever needed it, they might think, "I can't trust the king, so there's no point in following him or giving him help, because I might not get any back."'

There was a muted gasp from the onlookers. This young Norman was doubting the King of France's word.

'Be careful what you say, Duke William,' the king said, with the tone of a man whose patience was being stretched to the limit.

'Or you can keep your word,' William went on, 'and men will know that you are a man of honour who protects the vassals who look up to him for their care and safety. For if you and I fight together, Guy and his rebels cannot possibly defeat us, and when they are beaten, everyone will say, "Truly King Henry is a mighty ruler who stands by those who are loyal to him." And all your vassals here at court and out in your kingdom will know that you will come to their aid, and their enemies will know that too, and fear your wrath.'

The king chuckled indulgently at the passion with which William had made his case. 'So you're saying that I should help you for my good, not yours, are you?'

'Of course, for why would a man do anything if he did not think he would profit by it? I will also benefit, that's obvious. But you should help me because it is in your interests to do so.'

'What a persuasive young man you are, William of Normandy. You know, my sister Adela has a high opinion of you. She thinks you will go far. I'm beginning to understand why. So let us get down to practicalities. St Andrew's Day falls in two weeks' time, and the New Year a month after that. Do you think you can retain at least some of Normandy until next spring?'

William thought for a moment. Soon it would become impossible to keep soldiers in the field, for food would become scarce and the weather too cold to spend more than a few nights under canvas. Everyone would go back to their castles until the spring drew them out into the field again. 'Yes,' he replied. 'I will hold Rouen, Évreux and all the land east of the River Toques.'

'The eastern half of your duchy, in other words.'

'Yes, sire. I fear the rebels will have the rest until we are, together, strong enough to take it back.'

'Very well, then, I will keep my word.'

'Thank you, sire, thank you with all my heart.'

'No, you are right, it is my obligation to help you. You have my word that I will lead an army into Normandy next spring. Do I have your word that you will raise a goodly force of your own to greet it and share the burden of the fighting?'

'You do, sire, absolutely.'

'Then I will have our agreement written up and sealed. In the meantime, perhaps you would care to join me for dinner? Of all the obligations a king has to one of his dukes, the very least is surely the promise of a good meal, plenty of wine to drink and a bed for the night.'

'Thank you, Your Majesty,' said William. 'That would be almost as welcome as your army.'

7

Rouen and Val-ès-Dunes, just south of Caen, Normandy

The weather was especially harsh in the earliest months of the year, and King Henry was too pious to put his forces in the field during the season of Lent. But when the Easter celebrations were over, he kept his promise to William and entered Normandy at the head of an army several thousand strong. For his part, William had been hard at work throughout the winter, canvassing support among the soldiers of the Norman militia and urging the nobles still loyal to him to recruit every man they could find to the ducal cause.

He sent word to the citizens of Rouen and Évreux and the farmlands all around them; to those who lived in the Pays de Caux, which stretched north along the coast from the estuary of the Seine; to the people of Calvados, Lisieux and the Lieuvin region of central Normandy. Slowly at first, but then in greater numbers, the men of the duchy answered their master's call. And it was William who commanded their loyalty, for in the wake of his victory at Falaise, he had steadily come more and more into his own as duke. It had not been easy to wrest control from his elders on the council. Ralph de Gacé had posed a particular difficulty, for as long as he remained in control of the Norman militia, he would always have the power to impose his will on the duchy, and that power made him a very hard man to bring down.

And then William had a stroke of good fortune. Roger Montgomery, the son and namesake of the Roger Montgomery who had been exiled to Paris, and brother of the William Montgomery who had murdered Osbern Herfastsson, came to him hoping to rebuild the friendship that had once existed between his family and the House of Normandy. He brought with him a token of his good faith: to wit, a piece of information.

'Your Grace, my family's greatest disgrace is that my brother William murdered Osbern, your steward. I think I know who persuaded him to do it. Trust me, he didn't have the brains or the courage to plan and execute a crime like that by himself.'

'What will it help me to know that?' William asked. 'Osbern will still be dead.'

'You've been Duke of Normandy, in title, for ten years. But for all that, you haven't been the undisputed ruler of this duchy for a single day.'

William's face and body tensed. Those words were too close to the truth. 'Be very careful what you say, Montgomery,' he said. 'You wouldn't be wise to provoke me.'

'I came here to help you become that ruler, and to tell you that I will be your loyal vassal. That's why you should hear what I have to say.'

'Very well then, go ahead.'

'Shortly after my father's exile, Ralph de Gacé went to Jumièges to supervise the restoration of the land that my father had taken from the abbey. Do you remember that?'

'Yes. He went there under my authority.'

'Exactly. But did you also know that on his way, he stopped in Saint-Germain-de-Montgomery and went to our manor house?'

'Go on . . .'

'Only one of us was in: William. When the rest of us came back, he was looking pleased with himself, but also nervous. When we asked what had got into him, he wouldn't say. We pressed him, hard. Finally he admitted that Ralph de Gacé had come to see him. He wouldn't say why. A while later he left home, not telling anyone where he was going. That was when he killed Osbern. Days later, William himself was dead, killed by Osbern's estate manager Barnon of Glos. I had a word with Barnon soon afterwards. I said I'd spare his life if he'd tell me how he'd known where to find William. You know who told him? Donkey-Head, that's who.'

'Can you prove it?' William asked.

'Barnon's dead now, so no. But you must have heard the same stories I have about how it was one of de Gacé's men, Odo the Fat, who led the attack on Gilbert of Brionne. You know they say he did for Alan of Brittany and Thorold too. I'd believe it. I mean, one minute Ralph is the lowliest member of the council, only there because of his father's will, and the next everyone between him and you is dead and he's the most powerful man in the duchy. So what are we supposed to believe – that it's all just a matter of luck?'

William didn't believe in that kind of luck any more than Montgomery did. So he put the accusations to de Gacé, who of course denied them, claiming as William had anticipated that there was no proof.

'I don't need proof,' William replied. 'Montgomery's testimony is enough reason for me to throw you into a dungeon. And bad things can happen in dungeons. People get ill. They die. If I were to go down to your cell one night and kill you because I was convinced in my heart that you ordered the death of a man who was like a father to me, do you think anyone would care?'

'What's the alternative?' de Gacé asked.

'You retire from your post on the council, resign your command of the militia and go back to your estates to lead a quiet, peaceful, healthy life with your family.'

De Gacé was his father's son. He understood how the game

was played. He'd had a great run of luck and profited very handsomely from it. Now the dice that had long rolled in his favour had gone against him. The key thing was to stay in the game. That way, should the dice change once again, he would be there to profit. For now, though, there was nothing for it but to swallow his pride and do as William asked. It was, after all, better than the alternative.

Talou, however, was less easily placated. He was a decade older than William and the legitimate son of Duke Richard II. For all that Guy of Burgundy might tell his followers that he had a claim to the dukedom of Normandy, Talou's was very much stronger. It had eaten him up to see his half-brothers Richard and Robert become duke, and then, far worse, for his own claim to be ignored even when they both failed to produce a fully grown legitimate son to succeed them. For years he had played nursemaid to a bastard boy, and now that boy was becoming a man and showing him precious little respect. Talou saw no purpose in joining the present rebellion, for if it succeeded and Guy became duke, he would be no better off than he was now. Neither, however, was he prepared to give William any active aid. Instead he retreated to his vast estates, and sulked and plotted and waited for his moment to come.

William was all too aware of his uncle's burning resentment, but that was a problem for another time. For now he had the semblance of an army with which to fulfil his side of the agreement with Henry of France. And two days after Easter, he rode out of Rouen at its head, on his way to a rendezvous with the king.

Some men come by their nickname, be it Donkey-Head, Badger, Longtooth or Bastard, by means of cruel observation, wry humour or outright mockery. But none of those reasons explained why Nigel, Viscount of the Cotentin, was known as Falconhead. For this name was a badge of respect. His father, whose name he shared, had been a mighty warrior, famed for defeating an English invasion of Normandy in the time of King Ethelred, and later for defeating a Breton army who had attacked the town of Avranches. The present Nigel followed in the family tradition, and it was his prowess in battle that had earned him comparison with a falcon: his speed, his ferocity, his sharp eye and even sharper claws. Now he stood at the head of several thousand men from the Cotentin peninsula who had marched south and then east, past Bayeux towards Caen. He had led his men across one of the bridges over the River Orne and on to a plain known as Val-ès-Dunes that stretched for three or four leagues, uninterrupted by hills, woods or even the characteristic landscape of small fields separated by hedges, wooded copses and sunken lanes that the Normans called *bocage*. This was just open country over which men could march and ride without anything to get in their way.

'Hell of a place for a battle,' Nigel said to Guy of Burgundy. The two men had joined forces on the eastern bank of the Orne between the villages of Fontenay and Allemagne and were looking out across the plain, which was lit up by the afternoon sun. In the far distance, Nigel could just see the glint of sunlight on lances and helmets and the dots and dashes of colour that represented banners and shields. 'The king's men?' he asked.

'Henry's advance party,' Guy replied. 'His main force has set up camp between Mézidon and Argences.'

'How many men?'

'Some of my spies are saying he's brought ten thousand, but I seriously doubt it. You know how people exaggerate.'

'And the Bastard?'

'Not as many, I doubt he's got half the number of men with

him as Henry has. He's camped on the banks of the Muance, beyond the king's right flank.'

Nigel knew the land hereabouts well. The Orne flowed north through Caen towards the sea and marked the western boundary of the plain of Val-ès-Dunes. Its eastern boundary was set by three streams: the Laizon, on which the village of Mézidon stood; the Muance, beside which were Valmeray and Argences; and the Semillon. The three streams ran parallel to one another, all flowing to the north, before they joined, like the three spikes of a trident, to flow into the River Dives.

'How about us? Has everyone kept their word?'

'Longtooth Haimo's sent word that he's only a league away with a large force. Grimauld de Plessis has already arrived. He did well: more than a thousand men. Rannulf de Bessin's brought about as many as that too.'

'I wouldn't count on either of them,' said Falconhead, hawking up a thick gob of phlegm and spitting it contemptuously on to the ground. 'If Grimauld could fight as well as he brags, he'd be a much better warrior than he actually is. As for Rannulf, I don't trust him.'

Guy bridled. He took the comment as a personal insult. He had picked Rannulf as a co-conspirator. To belittle him was a slight on his judgement. 'You'd better have a damn good reason for insulting a man when he's not here to defend himself.'

Falconhead shrugged indifferently. 'If you're asking have I seen him break his word or run from a fight, no. But would I want him watching my back? Also no. Look, I hope I'm wrong. I'd love to be standing here tomorrow, with victory secured and everyone saying what a hero Rannulf was. But that's not what my gut tells me.'

Guy said nothing. A tense silence fell on two men whose unity was vital to their cause. At last Falconhead broke it. 'Ach! It's probably just nerves. I'm always edgy, the night before.

Don't listen to me . . . Anyway, where's the bloody Badger? Now he *can* fight. I'll be happy to have him on my side when we stick it to the French.'

'He's not here yet,' Guy said.

'Why not?' Falconhead asked, sensing the presence of words unsaid.

'I don't know. He was having a hard time with some of his senior men, I can tell you that much. They were getting the shits about betraying their vows of loyalty to the Bastard.'

'Bit late to get a sudden attack of conscience now.'

'That's what I told the Badger. I marched him into Bayeux Cathedral and made him swear on the holy relics that he wouldn't hold back from striking William whenever or wherever he might find him.'

'So if he happens to be in the battle and he sees William, he'll attack him?'

'Yes.'

'What if he's not in the battle?'

Guy was silent for a moment; then, trying to persuade himself as much as Falconhead, he said, 'But he will be. Christ, he's been with us from the very start. He's got a hundred and sixty fully armoured and mounted knights, and hundreds of foot soldiers and bowmen. He wouldn't bring them all the way here if he wasn't going to use them, would he?'

'No, he wouldn't. The Badger will use his men all right. But on whose side, eh? That's what I want to know.'

8

Bruges and Alençon

In the year that Matilda of Flanders was born, her grandfather Baldwin married for a second time, very late in life. His new wife was Eleanor, the daughter of Duke Richard II of Normandy, who two years later bore him a daughter, Judith. Thus it was that Matilda was two years older than her aunt, and so was less a niece to her than a surrogate big sister, even though, just to confuse matters still further, she was considerably smaller than Judith, whose Norman blood could be seen in her unusual height and auburn hair. Matilda, who was petite by any standards, was now sixteen and Judith fourteen. Their interests were entirely normal for girls of their age, which explained why they had sneaked out of their bedchamber and were now huddled behind the balustrade of the gallery that overlooked the great hall at the Count of Flanders' palace in Bruges, observing the festive dinner that was taking place there.

'I'm going to miss him so much,' Matilda sighed plaintively, gazing down at the high table.

Judith did not have to be told who Matilda was talking about. She had spent weeks listening to her niece going on and on and on about Brihtric Mau, the tall, fair-haired, broad-shouldered ambassador sent by King Edward of England to negotiate a trade deal that would encourage the sale of English wool to Flemish weavers.

'Oh, have you seen his wrists and forearms?' Matilda would swoon. 'They're so strong and muscly. I bet he has a really powerful grip. And his hair, the way it falls to his shoulders, it's like a lion's mane. And his eyes are so clear and blue, it's like looking into beautiful pools of icy water. But he's not cold like ice. He's lovely and funny and warm and kind.'

Judith only put up with Matilda's endless hours of wittering because she had a personal interest of her own in Mau and his visit to Bruges. The girls had befriended an English boy of their own age, Peter of Tewkesbury, who served as Brihtric's attendant. He had told them that Mau had a second, unofficial purpose, undertaken as a personal favour to Godwin, Earl of Wessex. This was to secure the betrothal of Lady Judith to Godwin's son Tostig, the Earl of Northumberland. Peter had kept the girls informed about the progress of the betrothal negotiations, which were, to Judith's relief, still very much at an early stage, and had done his best to satisfy Matilda's insatiable curiosity about his master.

'He's very rich,' he told them. 'He has estates right across the West Country, all the way from Gloucestershire to Cornwall, and his land covers almost four hundred hides.'

By asking a selection of monks, priests and members of the count's court who were known to have connections with England, the girls had established that the distance from Gloucestershire to the furthest tip of Cornwall was roughly the same as from Bruges to Paris: a very long way indeed, in other words. What was more, a hide was apparently a Saxon measure for the amount of land needed to support a family, so Brihtric had enough land for four hundred families, all of whom would have to pay him rent and tithes on their crops. He was, they concluded, a very rich man, and thus eligible. Unless, of course, he was already married.

'He can't be!' Matilda had wailed. 'I couldn't bear it!'

'No, Brihtric's not married,' Peter had smirked when they'd asked him, 'though there are plenty of mothers who've thrown their daughters at him. There's not a family in England that wouldn't want a marriage to my master and his money. He knows it, too, and between you and me, he doesn't mind taking advantage of it either. There are plenty of maidens, not nice ones like you two, obviously, who will give a man a taste of what they'd have to offer him if they were his wife, if you get my meaning.'

They didn't, not at first, but then Peter put it a bit more bluntly, explaining that there were women willing to give up their virginity ahead of marriage if it would help them win a man's hand.

'But why should he marry them if he's had that already?' Matilda asked.

'Good question, my lady, why indeed? But, see, not every young damsel's as clever as you. They don't understand that. They think that if they give themselves to my master, he'll like them so much he'll want to keep them.'

'I don't think he sounds very nice,' said Judith. 'I'm sorry, Matilda, but I don't.'

'I don't blame him,' said Matilda, defending her man to the bitter end. 'If they're stupid enough to throw themselves at him, what's he supposed to do?'

'I bet you wouldn't say that if you were already married to him.'

'Well no, of course not, but that would be different, wouldn't it? He'd have made a solemn vow to be faithful to me. If he broke that, I'd . . . I'd kill him, is what I would do.'

'I think you'd have a hard time killing Brihtric, Lady Matilda,' Peter had said. 'He's a mighty warrior.'

That had only added to Matilda's adoration of this English god. But for all her fevered fantasising, she had only been able to exchange a few words with him, spread over a handful of meetings. And now he was about to go back home. Her father had held a farewell banquet in his honour, but she had not been allowed to attend. Even her mother had stepped down from the high table when the night was still young so that the men could get on with their drinking and carousing.

'What are you going to do when he's gone?' Judith asked Matilda, as they both looked down at Brihtric.

'I don't know,' said Matilda. But then she clenched her jaw in an expression of absolute determination that Judith had known all her life, the one she called 'Matilda's getting-my-own-way look', and said, 'But I'm going to marry Brihtric Mau. I don't know how. But I absolutely will.'

Judith had no answer to that, except to say, 'Look, I hate to drag you away from Brihtric, but we should be getting back to our rooms. Your mother will be coming to say goodnight to you soon, and you'd better be in bed when she gets there.'

Matilda cast a last, lingering look at Brihtric, then scampered back to her room, just in time to be snuggled under the covers by the time her mother came in. Adela sat down on the edge of her bed. 'You like Brihtric, don't you?'

'No,' said Matilda indignantly. 'Why do you think that?'

Adela smiled. 'Because I know you, my darling, and even if I didn't, the way you look at him with big cow eyes and practically expire if he ever says a word in your direction makes it perfectly obvious.'

Matilda was horrified. 'Oh my God, does Papa know?'

'Of course not!' laughed Adela. 'Fathers are the last people ever to notice anything like that. And it's probably just as well, because heaven knows what he'd do to Brihtric.'

'But it's not his fault! He hasn't done anything!'

'Calm down, my darling, it's all right. Your father doesn't know. Brihtric doesn't know – at least I hope he doesn't.'

I bet he does, thought Matilda miserably. I bet Peter's told him everything!

'Anyway,' Adela went on, 'this just goes to show it's time we found you a husband, one your father does approve of. And I think I know just the one.'

In a tavern in Alençon, a man with a tankard in his hand was holding forth to a circle of listeners. 'So there's this nun, right, walking to market with this pig. And my lord Arnulf . . .' he looked around to check he was among friends and then spat, hard, on to the filthy wooden floor, 'he comes up to her with five or six of his bully boys and he says, "Give me that pig." So she says, "Please, I beg you, my lord. I can't give it to you, for me and my sisters have been fattening it up and it's all we've got to sell."'

There was a murmur from the gathering, whose numbers were growing as more of the tavern's drinkers were attracted by the prospect of a good story to be told and then to pass on in their turn. The man went on, 'Then Arnulf says, and I swear on my blessed mother's grave that I heard him with me own ears, "You and your sisters could always sell your bodies." And his men all start laughing and jeering at the poor sister, so Arnulf goes, "Though I don't think you'd get much of a price."'

'That bastard,' said one of the onlookers to many a nod and grunt of agreement. 'I thought his old man was a bad 'un, but he's no better. Come to think of it, he may be worse.'

'They've all got bad blood, the lot of 'em,' said a grizzled, wiry old man. 'I remember his grandad. Christ, he was a vicious, mean-spirited old sod.'

'As I was saying,' the storyteller called out, raising his voice to silence the interruptions. 'Arnulf tells her and her sisters that they should be whores, so she says . . .'

' . . . "Oh please, blessed lord, won't you give us a donation, for God will thank you for it?"' said Arnulf of Bellême, speaking in a ridiculous, high-pitched impersonation of the nun's voice as he helped himself to another great slab of the roast pork piled on to a platter on the high table at Alençon Castle. 'And I replied, quick as a flash, "No, I won't donate any money. But I'm happy to give you this." And I slapped her right across her face and knocked her clean off her feet!'

His hangers-on and toadies all roared with laughter, as did Arnulf himself, who was mightily proud of the wit with which he was recounting this hilarious tale. Soon he would come to the climax, where he and his men took the squealing pig from the weeping nun, but before he did, he needed something to wet his throat. 'Get me more wine! Now!' he shouted.

His sister Mabel, who was standing by the table with her eyes modestly downcast and a silver wine strainer hanging from a chain about her throat, scurried towards him carrying a pitcher of strong dark red wine. She had been back in Alençon for a few weeks now, and Arnulf had been pleased to discover that the hardships she had endured on her travels, particularly after their father had died, leaving her alone, had broken her haughty spirit and made her a far more obedient, submissive creature.

As she poured the wine into Arnulf's bejewelled goblet, he addressed the men around him. 'I'll show you how hard I hit that damn nun . . . this hard!' And he slapped his hand violently against Mabel's backside.

The blow caught her unawares. She almost lost her footing and she could not help but spill some of the wine over the table. But she did not cry out or protest. Instead she just murmured, 'Thank you, my lord,' and left the table.

Arnulf couldn't decide how he felt about that. On the one hand, he was pleased to find her so thoroughly broken. On the other, it frustrated him to put so much effort into striking someone and receive so little response in return. He was pondering this question as he got into bed later that evening and closed his eyes. But he never had the chance to reach a conclusion, one way or the other, for it was not very long before the slow-working poison that Mabel had slipped into his wine before she poured it killed Arnulf of Bellême stone dead.

For her part, though Mabel went to bed in the meagre cot in the servants' quarters that was all her brother had allowed her, she knew for certain that she would soon be living in far greater comfort. Arnulf was childless, and the only surviving male in the family was his and Mabel's uncle Ivo, Talvas's brother, who was Bishop of Sées. He would hold the title of Count of Bellême for as long as he lived, but since he was the one decent, honest member of the family and had kept his vows of celibacy, he had no children of his own.

Mabel, of course, could never hold the title herself. But soon after they had left Alençon, she had persuaded her father to take his revenge on Arnulf by drawing up a will, witnessed by an abbot and a bishop, no less, that left her all his land and chattels. As yet, she had kept the existence of the will secret, but when she revealed it, she would become a very wealthy woman. Since she was also, as she well knew, an exceedingly beautiful one, she would have her pick of prospective husbands. Their son would have an indisputable claim to the county of Bellême. And he would, for Mabel would make certain of this, love his mother very much indeed for giving it to him.

With this happy thought, she slipped into a deep sleep, filled with the most enchanting dreams.

9

The village of Valmery, Normandy

Father Louis, the priest of the church of Saint-Brise in Valmery, was a devout man. He conducted mass every day, even though he and his sacristan, Father Rodulph, a retired priest who now pottered about the church pretending to take care of its upkeep, were often the only communicants. Every day he would rise with the morning light, consume a modest breakfast of bread and watered ale, perform his ablutions and make his way to the church. He had passed a fitful night, what with the hubbub of men and horses, the hammering of the blacksmiths preparing horseshoes and repairing armour and weapons, and the visits from fearful villagers who knew that two great armies were massing at either end of the plain of Val-ès-Dunes, preparing for battle on the morrow, and dreaded what harm might befall any poor folk who happened to get in their way.

The King of France himself was said to be close by, and Duke William, with the rebel army led by Guy of Burgundy opposing them. Father Louis' particular concern was that Valmery lay smack in the middle of the line of march that the king and the duke would have to take in order to close on the rebels. So their army would pass through the village at least once, at the beginning of the day – in good order, it was to be hoped. And should God cast his lot for the rebels rather than the duke, then both armies would come through Valmery again at the day's close: the one in full retreat, the other in rampaging pursuit. And the Lord alone knew what would happen to the people, their possessions and their humble dwellings.

Father Louis was not in the best of spirits, then, when he went to the church on what he presumed would be the day of the battle. As he approached the church gate, however, Father Rodulph, who was not a small man, and less nimble than he might once have been, met him in a frantic flurry of movement, somewhere between a waddle and a skip, and blurted, 'You'll never believe who's in the church! It's the royal chaplain himself! And a choir! And other priest too, hordes of them!'

'What are you talking about?' Father Louis asked, unable to take in the magnitude of what the sacristan was saying, for though he could hear the words perfectly well, they seemed so far removed from anything that might happen in his small, somewhat ramshackle village church that he could not comprehend them.

And then, sure enough, as he came closer, there were horses, and grooms looking after them, and then the sound of singing – a glorious union of rich and tuneful voices – coming from inside the building. And as he walked in, a priest approached him and rather curtly asked, 'Who are you?'

'My name is Louis. I'm the parish priest.'

'Ah, excellent! Follow me, Father.'

Louis found himself being led in a daze past the normally empty choir stalls – filled now with monks practising a Magnificat and priests swinging silver censers that filled the church with the intense, heady aroma of incense – towards the altar. There stood a man in the richest vestments Louis had ever seen. His cope was covered in golden embroidery and studded with precious stones as crimson as blood and as blue as a summer sky.

The man who was leading Louis addressed this vision of magnificence. 'This is Father Louis, Your Excellency.'

'Good day to you, Father,' His Excellency said. 'I am Bishop

Bertrand. I have the inestimable honour to be His Majesty King Henry's personal chaplain. The king has requested a mass to be celebrated before he leads his army into battle. Yours is the nearest church to his encampment. I trust you will not object if the king worships here.'

'N-n-no, of course not. I would be honoured, greatly honoured,' Louis replied.

'Very well then, it is settled. The king is accustomed to hearing me conduct the mass, and will take communion from me too. But since this is your church and we are mere visitors to it, perhaps you would like to say the prayers thanking God for his mercy and bounty, pleading for the souls of the dead and, of course, asking Our Lord to watch over the king and Duke William and to reward the justice of their cause with victory today.'

'Yes, yes, absolutely. So you think it's acceptable for me, to, ah, take sides, as it were? I mean, there will be men with immortal souls in need of God's mercy fighting in the other army, too.'

'Then let their chaplains pray for them,' Bishop Bertrand said. 'For your part, let me put it this way. King Henry is your monarch on earth. Duke William is your master in this duchy. And Our Lord God Almighty rules over us in this world and the next. If you can make them all happy with but a single prayer, don't you think you should do that?'

Louis nodded dumbly, too overcome to say a word.

'You look alarmed, Father,' Bertrand said. 'Don't be. Just keep your prayer short, simple and heartfelt. And cheer yourself with this thought. Some of the mightiest men in all France will be under your roof this morning. They will soon be going out to fight, and some of them, sad to say, will die. Men facing the imminent possibility of death are, in my experience, keen to make their peace with God, and on the best possible terms. So rest assured you will probably make enough from this morning's collection to rebuild your entire church.' He cast a disparaging eye around the place before adding, 'It's about time you had a new one, wouldn't you say?'

Father Louis said the prayers with admirable aplomb, and the heartfelt sincerity with which he called upon God to look kindly upon the cause for which His Majesty the king and His Grace the duke were fighting, and to preserve them and all those who nobly and loyally fought alongside them, won him great praise and even greater charitable donations.

The two men themselves, however, took very different approaches to their private prayers. The king prayed for victory, yes, but above all else he prayed that he should be spared death, or, even worse, mutilation, and vowed to carry out a slew of charitable activities if he should avoid that fate. Duke William was every bit as heartfelt in his prayers, for he was a truly devout Christian, but he did not ask for anything from his Maker. Instead he simply gave thanks to God for cementing the alliance between Normandy and France, and for inspiring so many of the men of his duchy, from the highest to the most humble, to come and fight in his cause. He thanked Him for bringing his enemies to this place on this day so that they could learn the error of their ways. Above all, he gave thanks for the victory that was to come.

For it simply did not occur to him that he could possibly lose.

10

Val-ès-Dunes

'What's he doing?' Guy of Burgundy asked. He was standing with Nigel Falconhead on a low ridge, barely twice as high as a man, that rose just enough to afford a view over the heads of the massed ranks of mounted knights and foot soldiers, across the plain to King Henry and Duke William's forces in the distance. But neither man was currently looking at the enemy. Their eyes were focused on a point about halfway down the plain to their left, where a large body of men had taken up station between the two armies. Ralph Taisson of Thury, the Badger, had brought his men to the battle.

'He's like a fat man at a banquet, eyeing up a calf on one spit and a sucking pig on the other and trying to decide which to sample first,' Falconhead replied.

'He made his decision months ago. He swore to it again not two days ago. He had better damn well stick to his word. I'll make him pay for his treachery if he doesn't.'

On the far side of the field, King Henry was having a similar conversation with William. 'Who are those men?' he asked.

William informed him of the Badger's identity.

'Does he have any reason to bear you a grudge?'

'No, sire,' William replied. 'But nor do any of them. I've not given them cause to fight me. They just want what I've got.'

The king was about to reply, but then stopped himself and said, 'Now what?' half to himself as the Badger spurred his horse into a canter and rode away from his troops, accompanied by a knight bearing a white flag of truce. At first it was not clear where he was heading, but then he wheeled round in the direction of the French and Norman army and rode directly towards the point where Henry and William sat, side by side on their horses, with their standards fluttering around them.

The Badger rode right through the mass of French soldiers arrayed in front of their monarch, who parted to let him through. As he approached King Henry, he gave a short, curt nod of the head and said, 'Your Majesty . . .' then guided his horse right up to Bloodfang. He and William were now side by side, looking one another in the face, close enough to touch.

'Good day to you, Your Grace,' the Badger said.

'And to you, Taisson. What brings you here to see me?'

'I swore a solemn vow in the cathedral at Bayeux,' said the Badger, removing one of his heavy leather gauntlets. 'I swore to Guy of Burgundy that if ever I were to see you, I would strike you there and then. I don't wish to perjure myself by breaking that oath.'

With that he slapped William across the face with his gauntlet. All around the soldiers bristled, tensing themselves to pounce on the man who had dared hit the duke. But William raised his hand to still them. 'You kept your word. I can vouch for that,' he said, rubbing a hand over his smarting cheek. 'But you made another vow once, to me. You swore to be my loyal vassal, and your men with you. Will you be true to that oath too?'

The Badger said nothing, just gave a barely perceptible shrug of a shoulder, nodded again to the king, then wheeled round and rode away the way he had come.

'By God, I've seen some shameless individuals in my time, but that Taisson beats them all!' the king exclaimed, watching the Badger return to his troops. 'He as good as made it clear that he will come down on whichever side he thinks is going to win.'

'In that case, sire, we can be sure of his support,' William replied.

The king looked at him and saw that there was not the faintest trace of apprehension on the young duke's face. On the contrary, it bore a broad, almost exultant grin. It was the expression of a born warrior, for whom battle was not something to be feared, but to be relished. William exuded a confidence and certainty so absolute that anyone who saw him could not fail to have their spirits lifted and their courage stiffened.

'We should advance at once, sire,' he said. 'Let's go forward. We will not take a single backward step.'

He rode away, across the front of the army, until he came to his men massed on the right flank. There he stood up in the saddle, with Bloodfang pawing the earth beneath him, raised his sword in the air and shouted out the battle cry of Normandy: 'God help!'

Along the French lines, all the various battalions called out the mottos of their ruling families as the great mass of men began moving forward. They were led by the mounted knights, who lowered their lances to face the enemy as they urged their horses into a walk, then a trot, and then, gathering momentum, broke into a canter and finally picked up enough speed to gallop, until the whole army was thundering across the plain of Val-ès-Dunes towards the rebel horde.

'Here they come,' said Falconhead, and his eyes shone as brightly as William's, for he too was born to wage war. The cry of the Cotentin was 'Saint-Saveur!' and Falconhead gave it now and was answered by his men, then shouted the order they were longing to hear: 'Charge!'

'Holy Saviour! Holy Saviour!' cried Rannulf de Bessin,

hoping that if he could put enough volume and conviction into his voice, he could somehow persuade himself, as well as his men, that everything was going to be all right.

'Saint-Amand!' cheered Longtooth Haimo, urging his horse forward. Haimo lacked Falconhead's instinctive, unthinking conviction. What he possessed instead was a burning urge to prove himself. He was rich, his estates were substantial and he had raised as large a contingent as any of the other plotters. But he knew that they did not take him seriously, and so today it was his intention to show the world that there was more to him than anyone suspected. His only slight concern was that he did not know how exactly he was going to achieve this, other than generally making a show of taking the fight to the enemy.

Then directly ahead of him, and approaching him at high speed across the bare earth that now trembled beneath the terrible beating of the horses' hooves, Haimo saw the royal standard of France, and suddenly he knew exactly how he would make a name that would last for all time.

Longtooth Haimo was going to kill the King of France.

The two armies met in a juddering, percussive impact of flesh and bone and steel; of lances splintering on shields or piercing chain mail and plunging deep into the bodies beneath it; of rearing horses' hooves breaking bones and cracking open skulls; of swords against swords; of men shouting and screaming and gasping for breath. William exulted in the carnage and his power to inflict it. Few men on the field were taller or stronger than him, and none had a mightier horse beneath him.

One of Rannulf's men, a knight from Bayeux called Hardret, had sworn in public to kill William, just as Haimo had privately targeted King Henry. Now he rode to the head of the rebel army and aimed his horse at the duke, who was leading his men from the front, riding several lengths clear of them so that he could be seen by everyone on the battlefield. Hardret was not some vainglorious fantasist. He was a tough, experienced veteran who had, as he'd pointed out around the previous night's campfire, been colouring his sword with other men's blood when the Bastard was still in the cradle. He had every reason to believe that he was more than a match for a twenty-year-old duke in his first major battle.

But William put the sharp tip of his lance right through Hardret's throat, finding the one vulnerable spot between his hauberk, or coat of iron mail, and his helmet. The force of the impact lifted Hardret right out of his saddle, skewered like a roasting chicken, and dumped him on the earth behind his now riderless horse, stone dead, before he had been able to land a single blow on the duke. William threw away his lance, drew his sword and started laying about him, more than holding his own, until his own men caught up with him and he disappeared into the chaotic, swirling melee of the battle.

But as well as William was fighting on his side, Falconhead was matching him on the other. He drove his men between the French and Norman forces, trying to divide them so that each could be picked off separately, and as the corpses piled up in his wake, it seemed as though he might very well succeed.

For his part, Haimo was in something close to the furious fighting trance that his old grandfather, who was still at heart a Viking, had told him about back when he was a boy. 'Berserker', the old man had called it, describing a heady, almost drunken frenzy in which one fought without conscious thought, hardly knowing what was happening, yet somehow creating an uncontrollable force that no man could resist. Haimo had charged through the French army shouting 'Saint-Amand!' as he went, sometimes stabbing with the point of his lance, at other times swinging it like a staff at men's heads. Then, as if emerging from a thick forest into a sunlit clearing, he saw the king, perhaps twenty paces away, and there was nothing at all between them but bare earth.

Longtooth Haimo gave another war cry as he spurred his horse onwards, lowered his lance and aimed it straight at the king.

Henry heard the shout, and just had time to turn his body enough that Haimo's lance did not pierce his mail hauberk but instead was deflected to one side. Even so, the blow had the full force of a charging knight behind it, and the impact was enough to send him reeling in his saddle. His men raced to help him, and hands reached out to grab him so that he would not fall. But his horse panicked and reared, and the hands that had meant to help him back into his saddle actually pulled him out of it, so that he fell to the ground, right under the feet of all the men and animals around him.

The shock of the blow of his lance against the king's armour seemed to jolt Haimo from his trance. Suddenly he was very aware of where he was and how many French there were around him, with none of his own men in sight. He pulled his horse this way and that, trying to find a route back to the rest of his army, but there was no way out, just a ring of men around him, a ring that was closing ever tighter.

He drew his sword and tried to cut a path to safety. But there were too many enemies in his way, too many swords outnumbering his. He did his best to parry them with his shield, but then he felt his horse giving way beneath him as it was wounded, followed by the first excruciating pain of a blade entering his body, and another, and another . . . and then nothing at all.

The Badger was watching the battle like a gambler at a wrestling match, waiting to decide which man would get his bet. He saw the king go down, and was just about to order a charge against the exposed right flank of Duke William's force when there was a flurry of activity at the point where Henry had fallen. As his men lifted the monarch back up on to his horse, a great cheer went up from the French ranks.

That decided it. The Badger's knights were unscathed and their mounts were fresh. His foot soldiers had been standing still, waiting to be called into action, while their counterparts on either side had been fighting and dying. They had the power to turn the tide of the battle, and now he cut them loose and led them right at the heart of the rebel army.

Guy and Falconhead saw the Badger coming and knew that he had come down on William's side. Somehow they were able to turn their men to meet the new threat and with Falconhead seemingly tireless and invincible, it seemed that they might yet defy the odds and carry the day.

But then Rannulf of the Bessin, who had spent the whole battle desperately feigning activity while avoiding any serious action, finally lost his nerve completely. The threefold threat of William, Henry and now the turncoat Taisson was too much to bear. He called for his men to form around him and galloped from the field, racing towards the River Orne.

Still Falconhead fought on. But the sight of Rannulf's retreat did for Guy of Burgundy's courage too, and he turned and fled. With that the whole rebel army collapsed, and what had just a few minutes earlier been a disciplined force of brave fighting men became a disorganised, mindless rabble.

The rebels ran, and William and the king pursued them across the plain and all the way to the banks of the Orne, hacking down the stragglers as they went. There were bridges across the river, but the press of men was far too great and most of the rebels could get nowhere near them. Instead they were forced into the surging waters and even those few that could swim were weighed down by their armour. Into the river they went, by the tens, the hundreds, man after man, for even if they stopped and tried to surrender, the duke's men still pushed them into the cold, cruel water.

And so, as the sun set, the waterwheels of the mills up and down the river were jammed by corpses. And all the way across the plain of Val-ès-Dunes, the birds came to pick at the bodies of the dead and fight among themselves for the tastiest morsels of human flesh.

11

Conteville

Nigel Falconhead survived the rout at Val-ès-Dunes and escaped to Brittany, where he settled down to exile, secure in the knowledge that it was unlikely to be a long one. Sooner or later Duke William would forgive him his treachery and allow him back into Normandy. He was simply too good a soldier to waste, provided, of course, that he was willing to put his skills to work for the duke rather than against him. And if that was the deal that had to be done, Falconhead was happy to make it.

Guy of Burgundy, meanwhile, raced to his castle at Brionne, which stood right at the geographical heart of Normandy. The very last thing William wanted was to have an enemy in the depths of his duchy, but Guy had chosen a good bolthole in which to bury himself. The River Risle ran through the middle of Brionne, not as a single stream, but splitting into a number of rivulets. The castle was built on a small island, entirely surrounded by two of these rivulets, which both acted as a natural moat and guaranteed the castle a constant supply of fresh water. The island also provided land within the castle walls on which vegetables could be grown and a few pigs and chickens kept: not enough to keep its occupants well fed, but adequate to keep starvation at bay for quite a while.

William had no one inside the castle walls to help him as his grandparents had done at Falaise, and even he could not find a way past Brionne's defences of water and stone. So, unable to prise Guy out of Brionne, William made sure he was imprisoned within it. He built forts and siege towers on either side of the island so that the castle was completely blockaded, and then set off to deal with all the other castles that had been built without ducal permission during the years of lawlessness and anarchy. One by one the symbols of baronial power were demolished, and those that remained became symbols of William's power, for they only existed by his authority, and anyone who possessed a castle was thus, by definition, his man.

A year after the battle, with his position as secure as it was ever likely to be with Guy still holding out at Brionne, William received a message from Herluin, asking him to come to Conteville. His mother was not well and wanted very badly to see him.

Herleva was waiting to greet William outside the castle keep as she always did. But when he walked over to greet her, William was shocked by the dramatic change in her appearance. Her face, normally so full of life, was desperately pale, with gaunt shadows under her cheekbones. Her sky-blue eyes were clouded by pain and fatigue, with deep black rings beneath them, and when he reached out to hug her, the flesh seemed to have wasted away from her body, leaving just dry, brittle bones. Even worse, she winced and gave an involuntary little gasp as he held her, and he realised that whatever it was that ailed her was keeping her in constant pain.

Herleva saw the look of distress on William's face. 'Don't worry about me,' she said, forcing an unconvincing smile. 'I'm just having a hard time eating very much at the moment, and I don't seem to be able to get a good night's sleep. But I'm sure it's nothing and I'll soon be well again, God willing.'

Faced with a problem, William's instinct was to challenge it, solve it, or failing that, batter it into submission. 'Why did no one tell me you were ill before now? I would have come. I would have done something.'

'I didn't want you distracted. I knew you had other things to worry about. And there really isn't anything you could have done.'

'Nonsense! I'll find you the best doctors in Christendom,' William insisted, trying to convince himself as much as her. 'We'll summon apothecaries to give you medicines and priests to drive the evil spirits from your body. We'll—'

Herleva reached out a hand, its mottled grey skin so thin that the blood vessels beneath could clearly be seen, and laid it on William's arm to calm him. 'Hush,' she said. 'I don't need anything but good food, rest and prayers. If you want to help me, pray for me . . . and talk to me, my darling. Tell me how you are.'

And so, since she was the one person on earth who could command him, William sat with his mother and talked, basking in her absolute, unconditional love for him, knowing that with her he was always safe and always understood, and feeling deep within the cold tentacles of fear as he tried not to think about what life would be without her.

She knew, of course, what was going through his mind. 'You need someone else, you know, as well as me. Someone who'll love you and you can love in return. You need a wife.'

'I haven't got time to be thinking about things like that, Mother,' he said impatiently. 'I've got Guy to worry about. Geoffrey of Anjou is causing trouble along our southern borders. Then there's Henry . . . from what I hear, he's worried he helped me too well. And—'

'Enough!' Herleva snapped, and then had to take a couple breaths to regain what little energy she possessed. 'I know exactly how many troubles a Duke of Normandy has to deal with. But marriage isn't a distraction from your duties. It's a duty in itself. In fact, finding the right woman and having children with her is the most important thing you will ever do.

Without sons, you will have no heirs. Without heirs, the House of Normandy withers away. William, listen to me . . . I believe . . . no, I know, I've known since before you were born that you are going to be the greatest duke that Normandy has ever had. Your rule will spread far from here, across the seas. I saw it in a dream on the night I first lay with your father, a vision of a dynasty, growing from the seed we had planted.'

'Mother, please, you're exhausting yourself, you must rest . . .'

'No! I have all eternity in which to rest. So listen to me now. You know that I have been corresponding with Adela of Flanders. She and I are agreed that her daughter Matilda would be a perfect match for you.'

'Matilda? I've seen her. She's just a child!'

'That was years ago, you foolish boy,' Herleva said, and this time she smiled in a way that gave William a heartbreaking glimpse of the woman she had always been. 'Matilda's now in her seventeenth year, so quite old enough to be your wife. A match with Flanders would make political sense. And much more importantly from everything Adela tells me, the two of you would be the perfect match as man and wife. You need someone strong, William, to bear the load you will place on them. Matilda is petite. You will be far stronger than her in body. But she has strength of heart, of character and of will. Go to her, marry her, give her sons. That will make me feel better than any apothecary's potion ever could.'

12

Bruges

'Welcome to Flanders, Your Grace. I trust your journey was not too tiring.'

'Not at all, thank you, Count Baldwin, and you too, Lady Adela. May I say how grateful I am for your kind invitation.'

William gave a little nod of his head to the countess, in courteous recognition that she was by birth a princess of France and the sister of the man to whom he owed his present prestige. The victory at Val-ès-Dunes had not only made him undisputed master of Normandy – though he knew that it would not be long before someone, almost certainly his uncle Talou, would try to threaten that mastery – but it had also transformed his standing among the rulers of the lands that surrounded the duchy. The last time he had been in Bruges, he had been a young supplicant. Now he was a neighbour to be respected and even somewhat feared.

'May I introduce my brother, Odo of Conteville, and my cousin and steward William Fitzosbern?'

Adela greeted them both graciously before replying, 'And may I, in turn, present my daughter Matilda?'

So here was the reason for William's visit. He had only possessed the vaguest recollection of Matilda: a tiny figure dashing past him en route to her mother's throne, then pausing to watch as he left the room. Now, as he exchanged courtly greetings, he took a closer look.

'I just hope Matilda takes after her mother rather than her

grandmother Constance,' Herleva had said to William when he stopped off at Conteville en route from Rouen to Bruges. 'I only ever set eyes on Constance of France once, at Richard and Adela's wedding. She was one of the most beautiful women I've ever seen: dark eyes, as fierce and knowing as a cat's, olive skin, raven-black hair. My God, she was magnificent, but absolutely terrifying. She was King Robert's third wife. After she married him, she had his previous wife, Bertha, murdered because she feared they were still in love. ' Herleva had laughed at a memory that had suddenly come to mind. 'Fulbert, the Bishop of Chartres, once wrote that the only time he ever trusted a word Constance said was when she was threatening violence. When Henry became King of France, Fulbert refused to go to his coronation because he knew Constance would be there.'

Matilda did not look like a particularly frightening prospect to William at first glance, for she was still barely bigger than a child, and her skin was fair, rather than olive. But as he examined her more closely, he wondered whether she did take after Constance after all, for her hair was black and her eyes were dark and feline, and looked straight at him without the slightest pretence of feminine deference or modesty.

'Good day, Your Grace,' she said, and even curtseyed, which was more than he was strictly speaking due. Yet for all that, her tone and expression made it perfectly plain that she was not impressed by what she saw. William, who was always sensitive to the slightest hint that he was being belittled or insulted, felt his hackles rise at her impudence.

He took a small step towards her, the better to emphasise the difference between his height and physical presence and her diminutive stature. But Matilda did not quail or take a backward step. She merely tilted her head a little more, so that she could still hold his eyes with hers, and said nothing. She did not have to. Her silence was challenge enough.

William had no idea how to deal with this wordless defiance. A man would have backed down, for William's reputation was such that only the very bravest or most foolhardy would risk provoking him. But this was a girl, half his size. He could hardly just run her through with his sword.

Perhaps Adela sensed the duke's puzzlement, not to mention the sudden tension between her daughter and the man to whom she was about to be betrothed. For now she said, 'I'm sure you gentlemen will want to be getting on with your discussions. Come along, Matilda, it's time we rejoined the ladies.'

William watched the two of them walk away. He and his companions were about to negotiate the terms of a marriage contract that would bind him to Matilda for life. Well, Count Baldwin wasn't going to get his seal on the agreement without an exceptionally generous dowry. Any man who ties himself to that little terror, he thought, had better be damn well paid, because by God, he'll earn it.

'You might as well know now that I'm never going to marry that illegitimate oaf,' Matilda told her mother as the door to the council chamber closed behind them.

'You'll marry whomsoever your father tells you to marry,' her mother replied. She gave a short, sharp sigh of irritation as she considered her daughter's wilful fondness for unsuitable men. 'You're not still swooning over that Englishman, are you, Matilda? I thought we'd put paid to that one long ago.'

'You said you didn't want me having anything to do with him. I didn't say I agreed. Anyway, Brihtric's not just "that Englishman". He was King Edward's ambassador to Flanders. And even if he doesn't have a fancy title, he's got estates all over England, from Gloucestershire to Cornwall.'

'Do you even know where those places are?'

'No, but I know that it's like saying from here to Paris. And his lands cover almost four hundred hides . . . And before you ask, yes, I do know what a hide is. I'd be a rich woman if I married him.'

'You'd be a commoner, and you and I both know that you couldn't care less about Brihtric Mau's estates or his rents. You just took one look at his broad shoulders and strong arms and sparkling blue eyes and fell for him like a cow in season looking at a prime bull.'

'Oh, but you can't blame me, can you, Mama?' said Matilda, switching in an instant from steely defiance to wide-eyed charm. 'I mean, you wouldn't describe him like that if you hadn't noticed it too. He's the most beautiful man in the world.'

'He is passably good-looking,' Adela conceded. 'But he's also almost twice your age.'

'So what? Grandpa Baldwin was thirty years older than Granny Eleanor when he married her.'

'Hasn't it occurred to you that he might already be married?'

'Yes, and I found out that he isn't.'

'Well, married or not, it makes no difference, because he's at home in England, a very long way away. So put him out of your mind and concentrate on the duke, who's right here in Flanders, who's only a few years older than you and also, to my certain knowledge, single . . .'

'Which doesn't surprise me; just look at the great oaf.'

'. . . and who is both a perfect match for you and a politically advantageous union for Flanders.'

Mother and daughter had by now reached the solar, the chamber where the women of the count's household spent their days. They sat on a long wooden settle, softened by a richly embroidered cushion, and Adela took Matilda's hand. 'You know how things are, my darling. Young men serve their families by fighting for them. We women serve them by marrying well and providing our husbands with sons. That's how bonds are made between royal and lordly houses. That's how we help to keep the peace.'

'Well that doesn't seem to work, does it?' Matilda protested.

'Not all the time, no. But think how much worse it would be if men had nothing to restrain them. Your father and I both think that William of Normandy is an ideal match for you, and for Flanders. And it's not as if he's a bad-looking boy. He's at least as tall as Brihtric, and even more strongly built. He's got quite a handsome face, actually.'

'I don't think so. He always looks so cross about everything.'

'Then it's your job as a wife to make him happier.'

'And his clothes are awful.'

'Then get him better ones. It's not as if the Normans can't afford to dress well. Any wife worth her salt can change her man without him even knowing that she's doing it, if she goes about things the right way. As mistress of Normandy, you will be one of the grandest women in Christendom. You'll be able to commission beautiful things for your homes and give endowments to churches and convents. And I'll tell you this: being William's wife will never be boring. When he first came here, I told your father that I thought that boy was destined for greatness, and I still think that. Imagine being beside him – his consort, adviser, best friend, the mother to his children. What woman could hope for more than that?'

Adela let go of Matilda's hand and sat back, satisfied that she had made her case. But her satisfaction disappeared in an instant as Matilda said, 'Me. I could hope for more. In fact, I hope – no, I expect – to be the wife of Brihtric Mau. So William of Normandy can look for another consort to be his brood mare.'

'What?' gasped Adela, glaring at Matilda with a fury that suggested that Constance's character traits had not entirely passed her by. 'Are you seriously intending to defy your parents' wishes? How dare you? And what in God's name makes you think you have the slightest chance with that damn Englishman?'

'Because I've sent a messenger to England asking him to marry me. I'm expecting a reply within the next month.'

Adela was aghast. If anyone discovered that her daughter had been offering herself up in marriage to visitors to Count Baldwin's court, the House of Flanders would be the laughing stock of Christendom. 'But you haven't asked your father's permission!' she protested.

'No,' replied Matilda flatly. 'And I don't expect Brihtric will ask his permission either. We'll just get married because we love each other, and there'll be nothing anyone can do about it.'

Matilda looked at her mother, saying nothing, daring her to object. And for once in her life, Adela found herself completely at a loss for words.

That night, when he retired to bed with his wife, Count Baldwin discovered what his daughter had done. Having promised Adela that 'I'll tan that little minx's backside for her impudence!' he took a deep breath and did his best to take a calm and rational view of the whole situation.

'I have to say that Brihtric Mau did not strike me as the kind of man who would try to steal his host's daughter and take her away as his bride. He seemed like a perfectly respectable, honest type, as boring as the rest of his race. To be honest, I can't imagine what Matilda saw in him.'

Adela stopped herself from saying, 'I can.' Instead she said, 'He's a man. And no man cares about being respectable if a pretty young woman is throwing herself at him.'

'Well I'm not sure that's quite true, my dear, but even if it were, what exactly are these two lovebirds going to do about it? She still has to get from here to England. How is she going to do that?'

'On a ship. You may have heard of them, my lord. They sail across water.'

Baldwin looked to the heavens for strength. He loved his wife dearly, but she certainly knew how to infuriate him sometimes. 'Yes . . . my lady. But she has to get on that ship, and I can have every vessel bound for England watched and if needs be searched. If Matilda tries to escape, she'll be spotted and caught, you have my word on it. And if by some miracle she does get to England, I'll write to King Edward . . . no, I'll write to Earl Godwin and tell him that if he wants his son to marry Judith, he'd better find a way to stop Master Mau from marrying Matilda. I will also make it worth his while to be discreet.'

'Well I hope your confidence is justified. I wouldn't put anything past that girl. I love her with all my heart, but by God she tries my patience.'

'Don't worry, Adela my darling,' Baldwin said, taking her in his arms and feeling an agreeable hardening as he did so. 'I won't breathe a word of this to young William. Within the next few days we will conclude our negotiations, a dowry will be agreed, and then our beloved Matilda can be packed off to Rouen to try his patience instead.'

13

The days went by in a drudgery of negotiation and joyless feasting. Baldwin had to admit that Duke William did not seem remotely enthused by the prospect of marrying his infuriating but beloved daughter. Here was a young man who might have a fine title, but whose eligibility among families for whom bloodline was everything was seriously marred by his illegitimacy. Yet he was being offered the daughter of the Count of Flanders, ruler of some of the wealthiest cities north of the Alps, with a magnificent dowry to match. He should have been champing at the bit to get her on his arm and in his bed at the first possible opportunity, particularly since Matilda was a stunning little creature whose shameless pursuit of that great oaf Brihtric Mau suggested she would take very happily to conjugal relations. Her mother had certainly done so, Baldwin reflected with the contented complacency of a happily married man.

William, however, seemed oddly passionless. He could barely bother to hide how tedious he found the entire business, and only showed the faintest trace of good humour and enjoyment when Baldwin, desperate for a break, suggested that a day's discussion should be replaced by a hunting expedition. Then, one morning, the entire question became moot as Adela burst into the council chamber, clearly in a furious temper, and virtually dragged Baldwin out into the hallway, while the Normans looked on in amazement at the sudden intrusion of raging disorder into the well-ordered tedium of life in the Flemish court.

'That beef-eating piece of Anglo-Saxon *merde*!' Adela shouted, loud enough for William to hear, even though she had slammed the door to the chamber shut behind her.

'I'm sorry . . . who?' Baldwin replied, still too amazed by the fury of his normally placid wife to be able to think straight.

'Who do you think, idiot? That no-good, useless, unwashed English oaf Brihtric Mau, of course!'

'Why, what's he done?' A look of horrified comprehension passed across Baldwin's face. 'My God! He's not gone and stolen Matilda away, has he?' he gasped.

'No, no, of course not. He does not have the balls for that. No, he's written to her to say that he cannot marry her!'

'Oh, thank God for that . . . I mean, that's good news, isn't it? After all, now she's free to marry William.'

'No, it's not good news, you fool! It's terrible news. Matilda is desolate. She has locked herself in her chamber and refuses to come out. She says she'll never marry anyone. She wants to be a nun.'

'Oh come now,' said Baldwin, deciding that this was the sort of time when a man's duty was to calm the nerves of his overexcitable womenfolk and try to restore them to some kind of good sense. 'She doesn't mean that. She's just got herself all worked up about an unsuitable man. She may be throwing a tantrum now, but she'll get over it soon enough. I'm sure if you sit her down and talk to her about marrying William, tell her how pretty she'll look, promise her a beautiful wedding gown, that sort of thing, she'll soon cheer up.'

To Baldwin's horror, far from making Adela see sense, these words changed her mood from raging fury to the icy calm that he knew from experience was actually a far more dangerous sign. 'No, Baldwin, that is not what will happen. Matilda's mind is made up, and if you think that a young woman with my mother's blood in her veins is going to be persuaded to come round to your way of thinking by the promise of a pretty dress, then you are out of your simple Flemish mind. Tell William to go home. He is wasting his time here.'

'That's quite enough!' Baldwin said. He was fed up of being patronised by his wife, and he wasn't about to be defied by his daughter. He was the Count of Flanders, by God, and these women had better remember it.

He stalked to Matilda's chamber and hammered on the door. 'Matilda, open up!' he commanded her. 'This is your father. I demand to come in.'

'Go away!' her furious voice shouted through the door.

'Open up, young lady, or I'll have the door smashed down.'

'Go ahead, but I'll be dead when you come in. I have a very sharp knife.'

'Don't say that, my little darling,' Baldwin cooed, trying a more gentle approach. 'Look, I know you feel sad now, I understand. Everyone has their heart broken when they're young, it's normal. But William is here. He's bursting with love for you. He'll be devastated to hear that you are unhappy.'

These were blatant lies, but desperate times called for desperate measures.

They did not work.

'I don't care about William. I think he's ugly and stupid and boring,' Matilda said, causing her father to admit that she was right about one of those, at least. 'I am going to give my love to God. I know He won't let me down the way men do. Either let me enrol in a monastery, or let me die. It's your choice.'

Baldwin was appalled, but also oddly impressed by Matilda's patent sincerity, for he had no doubt that she meant what she said. Adela had been right. This wasn't a spoiled princess's tantrum. It was a serious threat.

'Very well then,' he conceded, 'I will tell William that you have decided to take up holy orders and that therefore you will not be betrothed to him under any circumstances.'

'Good. What about the nunnery?'

'I shall consult with the senior clergy to find the best possible convent for you to enter. In the meantime, I suggest that you spend time in the chapel, praying to God for guidance. You must make sure that this really is the right thing for you.'

'Oh thank you, Papa. I knew you would understand.'

The door opened and Matilda's face peered round the corner. 'Are you going to tell William now?'

'Oh . . . yes . . . now . . . absolutely,' Baldwin muttered and scurried off back towards the council chamber, with Matilda's voice echoing in his ears: 'You're the kindest, sweetest, loveliest papa in all the world!'

Back in the chamber, Baldwin did his best to explain to William that they had all been wasting their time for the past several days. Matilda, he suggested, had been visited by the Holy Spirit and called to do God's work. He insisted that this was in no sense a reflection upon William. It was just one of those acts of God before which all mere mortals had to bow.

William listened without comment. His face showed no expression, either of anger at being humiliated or even of relief at avoiding an unwanted union. He simply heard Baldwin out, asked, 'Is that all?' and, on being told that it was, said, 'Very well, then, we'd better be on our way. Thank you, Count Baldwin for your most generous hospitality. Do pass on my best wishes to Countess Adela. Good day.'

'Are you leaving right away? Won't you stay for lunch?' said Baldwin, feeling somewhat ashamed now by the way the Duke of Normandy had been treated, and also distinctly worried by the thoughts that might be festering beneath that expressionless exterior. The duke had already shown that he was not a man to be trifled with, and Baldwin had no desire to make an enemy of him. 'It will take your servants some while to pack everything,' he went on. 'And you will need feeding before you travel.'

'Thank you, but no,' William said. 'The servants can remain here and follow later with the baggage, but I see no point in staying any longer. I have other things to do elsewhere. It's time I went and did them. Good day to you, Count Baldwin.'

And with that the Normans left, grim-faced, to begin their journey back to Rouen.

Oh well, thought Baldwin, watching them go, at least I saved myself a dowry.

William was not a man who ambled anywhere. He would always rather walk fast or gallop hard than go at a gentle pace. But the pace he set on the ride from Bruges was punishing even by his standards. Finally, when even he had to admit that the horses were at the end of their tether, he was obliged to slow down and stop by the banks of a small stream so that they could rest, graze and drink a little before resuming the journey. But even as the animals relaxed and the men stretched their legs, William's face was set in a brooding expression that warned of a fury building within him like gathering clouds before a great storm.

'Something's troubling you, brother,' said Odo a little nervously, because it was obvious that it wouldn't take much provocation to set William's temper off.

William said nothing.

'My lord . . .' Fitzosbern began, then paused, not knowing how to go any further, before adding, 'Can we help?'

'Nothing's the matter,' William replied.

The other two stayed silent. They had registered their concern; now it was up to William to decide whether he wanted to respond to it. As close as they all were, he was the duke, their liege lord, and it was not for them to press him as they might another man. Still, it was permissible to offer him a drink.

'Wine?' asked Odo, holding out a leather skin.

William took it and drank thirstily, then wiped his mouth and gave the skin back to Odo. 'That bloody girl,' he muttered.

The other two looked at one another and silently agreed: *Say nothing. Let him spit it out.*

'I mean, it's not as if I even wanted to marry her. I only went to Bruges to please Mother, you both know that.'

'Absolutely,' said Odo, and Fitz nodded his agreement.

'God knows I've got better things to worry about. Guy's still sitting behind his walls at Brionne, laughing at us. And don't think I'm not well aware that my uncles start plotting against me the moment I set foot out of Rouen, but . . . but . . . Damn it, I'm not having some spoiled little madam from Flanders making a fool out of me.'

'She didn't make a fool of you, lord,' said Fitz. 'Of her father, maybe. But not you.'

'Kind of you to say so, but that's rubbish. And it didn't have anything to do with Matilda suddenly getting a religious vocation, either. You only have to look at her to see that she's no nun. Everyone knows she was wet for that Englishman with the stupid name, Brit-something . . .'

'Brihtric Mau,' said Odo.

'Right, him. Anyway, she wanted him and she thought she was too good for me. I'll bet you anything you like that she's sitting there right now with my cousin Judith, having a good laugh about how she turned down William of Normandy. Here, pass me the wine again . . .'

Odo did as he was told, and William drank some more.

'I won't have it,' William said. 'I won't have people laughing at me, calling me the bastard, saying I'm not good enough for them.'

'Just forget it, she's not worth even thinking about,' said Odo. 'You said it yourself, you've got better things to worry about.'

'No, I won't stand for it,' William repeated. 'I'll teach Matilda a lesson she won't forget.'

He strode towards Bloodfang and swung up into the saddle, ignoring the other two as they tried to persuade him not to do anything foolish.

'Ride on without me,' he called down to them as he turned Bloodfang back along the road towards Bruges. 'I'm going to deal with Matilda.'

Matilda was feeling particularly pleased with herself. Brihtric had broken her heart and, which was much worse, humiliated her. But the fact that she'd been able to do precisely the same to William, and within the same day too, had cheered her up no end. Of course, there was the minor problem of her upcoming life as a nun to think about. But she was absolutely certain that if she just spent a little more time dressing in her dullest gowns, moping about in the chapel and generally acting like a pious misery-guts, Papa would be only too happy when she changed her mind and wanted to go back to being her usual self. She was his favourite child, and wrapping him around her little finger had long been one of her favourite pastimes.

She got up from the ornately carved family pew where she had been contemplating her next moves, and walked down the aisle of the chapel thinking of the ride she was about to take. Before setting off for her prayers, she had ordered her horse to be brushed and saddled. A brisk ride would work up a nice appetite for supper, although, it now struck her, this new passion for monastic simplicity might mean she'd have to stick to bread and water. No, on second thoughts, there were lots of very well-fed priests, monks and nuns about the place. Even if they denied themselves love, they didn't seem to stint on food.

As she walked towards the stables, she was dimly aware of a commotion in the distance: a lot of shouting and clattering of hooves. And she thought she heard a voice she recognised, but no, that couldn't be possible.

When she reached the stable yard, the head groom was waiting for her. 'Is she ready?' she asked.

'Yes, my lady, exactly as you ordered. I will have her brought out immediately.'

A moment later, a stable boy appeared leading a very beautiful, fine-boned palfrey: a horse fit for a princess. 'Oh, my pretty White Dove,' Matilda cooed, running to greet her beloved grey mare. She stroked her muzzle. 'How are you, sweet one? Have all those horrible stallions been beastly to you, hmmm?'

She was helped up into the saddle, where she sat with the relaxed confidence of a woman who'd been riding all her life. Matilda had two brothers, and what she lacked in size and brute strength, she more than made up for in lightness and courage. She would gallop just as fast as them and jump just as high or wide, and she was in the process of planning where she would take White Dove now, for she needed a really good, hard, thrilling ride that would set her heart pumping, when— Mary Mother of God, what was *he* doing here?

William of Normandy was marching into the stable yard like a man going to war. The head groom went to speak to him and William just shoved him out of the way without even looking at him. His eyes, which were the most piercing shade of lapis lazuli – how had she never noticed that before? – were fixed on Matilda. She felt as if they were burning into her, right down to her very soul, and they seemed to have some kind of sorcery about them, because she simply could not turn her head away and escape his fearsome gaze.

Now he had come up to White Dove and was standing right by Matilda, still looking up at her, not saying anything, and she suddenly understood what it must be like for a man to confront him in battle and have to face this extraordinary physical presence, this sense that he would not be beaten or denied.

Then he reached his arms up and grabbed her, and though she screamed and kicked and punched the air in protest, he lifted her up, right out of the saddle, as easily as if she weighed nothing at all. She found herself standing on the ground, still completely caught in his grasp, and she realised he was getting down and kneeling before her. For a second she thought he was going to vow eternal love, but then he was lifting her again and spinning her, and she realised: no! He can't be! He's putting me over his knee!

And then he was spanking her, hard enough to hurt, and she was yelling, more in fury than in pain, and finally William spoke, timing his words to his blows as he snarled, 'Don't . . . you . . . ever . . . dare . . . make . . . a fool . . . of me . . . again.'

When he was done, he put her back on her feet, and without a word or a backward glance strode out of the stable yard. Matilda stood in stunned silence for a moment, and then ran after him, screaming, 'I hate you! I hate you! My father will kill you for this! He'll go to war! You'll be nothing, William of Normandy . . . nothing!'

But he continued to walk away as if she did not even exist, and as he remounted his horse and rode back out of the palace gates, Matilda stormed up to her room and threw herself sobbing on to the bed.

When Count Baldwin found out what had happened, he was just as angry as Matilda had promised. He stormed around the palace shouting orders for his barons to be summoned for a special council of war. 'After all the kindness, all the hospitality

I've shown to that barbarian, how dare he assault my daughter!' he raged at Adela. 'He insulted her, he insulted me, he insulted our family and he insulted Flanders itself! This infamy cannot be allowed to go unpunished!'

To Baldwin's surprise, Adela did not seem nearly as shocked as he was. She said nothing, and if Baldwin hadn't known better, he might almost have thought she was amused by the whole affair.

The count spent the remainder of the afternoon drafting an official letter to be sent to the Duke of Normandy demanding a formal apology for his conduct, accompanied by significant restitution for the slanderous damage he had done to Lady Matilda's good name and the reputation of the House of Flanders.

He was just pressing his official seal into the wax at the bottom of the letter when Adela appeared, accompanied by their daughter, and informed him, 'Matilda has something she wishes to say to you.'

'Of course, my dearest. You poor child, what can I do for you?'

'Father,' said Matilda, 'I've come to a decision.'

'Yes, yes, just name what you desire and it will be done.'

'I want to marry William of Normandy.'

And so an official letter was indeed sent from Bruges to Rouen, addressed to the Duke of Normandy. But it made no demands and its tone was conciliatory in the extreme as it offered him the hand of Matilda of Flanders in marriage.

This was not, of course, the first time that a man had been given the chance to take Matilda as his bride.

But this time the answer was yes.

14

Conteville

Herleva was delighted by the news from Bruges, and even happier when William came to tell her in person about what had happened. She had retired to bed now, and the hair that fanned out around her head as it lay against her pillows had lost the glorious copper glow it had once possessed and become as flimsy and colourless as the rest of her. But she still had her smile, and her laughter had returned, for a peace had come over her, an acceptance of God's will and a faith that a better life awaited her when her time on earth was done.

His mother's serenity made it easier for William to relax and tell his story. 'Anyway, I got to Bruges and rode right into the palace, and to tell you truth I had no idea what I was going to do or say. I just wanted to give Matilda a piece of my mind. So I asked where she was and one of the servants said she was about to go out for a ride and I should try the stables. Well, I rode into the yard and jumped down off Bloodfang's back, and there she was, sitting on this grey mare, a real girl's horse, but a pretty little thing, and she looked . . . Christ, she just looked so incredibly beautiful.' William stopped for a second with a look of surprise on his face. 'You know, it's funny, I've not said that before. In fact, I haven't even thought it, really, but it's true. She looked so gorgeous and pleased with herself that this feeling – I can't explain it – came over me and I just had to do something, anything, you know, to her. So I grabbed her and pulled her off her horse and . . .' He burst out laughing. 'I'm sorry, it was wrong, I know. I mean, you can't treat the daughter of a count that way, but I put her over my knee and spanked her.'

'William!' exclaimed Herleva, trying to sound cross but failing hopelessly.

'I'm sorry, Mama, but I didn't know what else to do. And Matilda was kicking and punching and screaming blue murder and I was saying I wouldn't let her make a fool of me ever again, and then I finished and didn't know what to do next so I just got back on Bloodfang and rode off. You were right about her having spirit. She didn't just lie there like most girls would, weeping and feeling sorry for herself. She came running after me, waving her fist, cursing me and threatening me with war.' He burst out laughing. 'The crazy little minx actually declared war on me!' He stopped and looked at Herleva, who was lying very quietly with an expression he could not quite read. 'What is it?' he asked. 'Did I say something wrong?'

'No, William, you absolutely did not. I was just thinking how wonderful and mysterious love is. Just look at the two of you, neither one the slightest bit interested in the other. Then she rejects you, and you can't bear it. And you treat her quite abominably—'

'I know! That's what I don't understand. Why did she suddenly decide she wanted me after I'd done that?'

'Because she saw how much you wanted her. She knew that she'd awoken feelings in you that no other woman had. Is it good for a man to hit a woman? No, absolutely not, and don't you ever dare do it again.'

'No, Mama, I won't,' William promised, as if he were still her little boy.

'But is it thrilling for a woman to know that she has driven a man so wild that he simply can't control himself? Yes . . . oh yes, it is. I remember the first time I saw your father, looking so handsome, so impossibly far removed from a girl like me . . . and I made him, the son of a duke, turn his horse and gallop back towards me. And he didn't know what to say, or what to do, either . . . It was the most exciting thing that had ever happened in my life.'

'But he didn't spank you.'

'No, he did not! But he did more or less order me to present myself that evening, and we both understood why.'

'And you went.'

'Yes, and for the same reason that Matilda said she would marry you. I knew I had met my man.'

Herleva was exhausted by their conversation. But the next day, when she and William were talking again, she said, 'I'm sorry that I won't be here to see you and Matilda together, to hold my grandchildren and watch them grow.'

William did not protest that of course she would. He too had come to accept that his mother would soon be gone. 'I'll tell them all about you,' he said. 'How wonderful you were and what an extraordinary life you led.'

'Thank you, my darling. But please don't be sad. My spirit will always be with you, watching over you, and your family. Mine and your father's. We'll be together again, I know we will.'

'Have you loved him all this time?' William asked.

'Every hour of every day.'

'But what about Herluin? You must have loved him a little, surely.'

'I loved him very much, but in a different way. He's a fine man and as good and kind a husband as any woman could have. He gave me my two lovely boys . . . promise you'll look after them.'

'Of course! Odo and Robert are my brothers. I'll look after

them, and Herluin too. He has never once let you or me or Papa down.'

'Could you get him for me now, please, and tell the boys to come too? And William, my darling, I think you should also fetch the priest.'

Postscript: A Visitor From England

Rouen, June 1051

Herleva was not the only person in Normandy to appreciate the dynastic significance of William finding a bride. For Mauger and Talou, the news was as bitter as it had been sweet for her. They knew at once that if William produced an heir, and lived long enough to see him reach maturity, their hopes of controlling Normandy and even seizing the dukedom itself were gone for good. Mauger therefore asked Pope Leo IX to forbid the marriage, claiming that William and Matilda were too closely related to wed, through her mother's marriage to William's uncle Richard, and her grandfather's marriage to William's aunt Eleanor.

William was painfully aware that a generation earlier, the previous Archbishop of Rouen, his great-uncle Robert, had forbidden his mother and father to wed, and had been powerful and ruthless enough to force the issue in his favour. In the process, he had condemned William to a lifetime of illegitimacy and an emotional scar, caused by the pain of his parents' break-up, that had never healed. But Archbishop Robert was a far tougher, wilier politician than Mauger, and William a far harder man than his father.

The duke refused to give way. He knew he had right on his side, for there was no blood link whatsoever between him and Matilda. When the Pope came to the Council of Rheims in 1049, William sent a strong contingent of loyal bishops, including his half-brother Odo, whom he'd named Bishop of Bayeux, to lobby against the ban. Then he married Matilda and dared the Church to do its worst.

In June 1051, when Matilda was pregnant with their first child, and William was just hearing the first stirrings of trouble on the border between Normandy and the county of Maine, an eminent visitor from England arrived in Rouen. Robert Champart, once the abbot of Jumièges and then – thanks to the patronage of his friend King Edward – Bishop of London, had now been promoted to the archbishopric of Canterbury. He was on his way to Rome to receive his pallium – the woollen band worn around the neck to denote rank – from Pope Leo. But first he requested a private audience with the Duke of Normandy.

William was now twenty-three years old, still very much a young man, yet blessed, or perhaps burdened, with the political and military experience of one a decade older, or more. He still, however, possessed the impatience of youth, so he wasted little time on pleasantries before launching into an impassioned defence of his right to be married to Matilda.

'So you see,' he concluded, 'there's no justification at all for saying that Matilda and I are too closely related. And our union must be acceptable in God's sight because He has ensured that we love one another with all our hearts, and He has blessed us with a child.'

'The baby is not yet born,' Champart murmured. 'One must not take Our Lord's will for granted in these matters.'

'Matilda will have a healthy baby and it will be a son, I know it,' William insisted, giving Champart his first sight of the force of the duke's convictions. 'In any event, Archbishop, it would mean a very great deal to me if you could feel able to express your approval of our union. Will you be attending evensong at the cathedral today?'

'Of course.'

'Then I will bring Matilda to the service, and you will see for yourself that she is as fine a wife as any man could hope for, and that the love between us is true.'

'I have no doubt of that,' said Champart. 'For myself, I am minded to agree with you that these attempts to prevent your marriage from happening and then to declare it invalid have little merit. And of course, your cousin King Edward has nothing but good wishes towards you and would naturally seek to increase your happiness.'

'I thank him for that. I hope he is well.'

'Oh yes, very well, though I know he will be grateful for your good wishes. But to return to the question of your marriage, I can foresee one minor problem.'

'How so?' asked William, with a slightly nervous edge to his voice, since he had thought that Champart's position was settled in his favour.

'As you are doubtless aware, your father-in-law Count Baldwin has agreed to the betrothal of his half-sister, Judith, to Tostig, son of Earl Godwin.'

'Yes, I know about that,' said William. 'But why should that be a concern? Surely Godwin is the king's most senior and loyal retainer. He is the king's father-in-law, after all.'

Champart cast a shrewd look at William, as if trying to decide whether the duke was really as naive as he sounded, or simply pretending to be so for his own purposes. He decided on balance to treat the remark as an innocent one and answer accordingly.

'As you say, Duke William, the earl and the king are bound by many ties, and of course Her Majesty the Queen, being blessed with the naturally gentle and peace-loving qualities of her sex, and being both a dutiful wife and an equally loyal daughter, does all she can to encourage the best possible relations between the two. Sadly, however,' and here the archbishop gave a heartfelt sigh, 'the earl acts in ways that make His Majesty the king uneasy about his subject's true intentions. You see, Godwin and his sons control the land from the very west of England right along the south coast to Kent and then around into Essex and East Anglia. The king would only be human to find this encirclement somewhat suffocating.'

'His other earls can't be happy about it either. No one likes to see one family becoming much more powerful than all the others.'

'How very true. Your Grace has hit upon the precise balance that exists at the moment. His Majesty is not, as yet, in a position to rid himself of the Godwins,' Champart gave a wry half-smile, 'though who knows how events may unfold.'

'I only ever know by making them unfold in the way I wish,' William said.

'And do they always do so?'

William laughed. 'No, they don't, damn them.' He held up a hand of apology. 'Excuse me, Archbishop, I should not blaspheme in your presence.'

'Forgiven, my son. But there is a matter arising out of King Edward's present situation that I wish to raise with you. Sadly, though Queen Edith is an ideal of womanly virtue in many respects, she has not been able to furnish King Edward with an heir.'

'Then he'd better find another wife who can.'

Champart frowned thoughtfully. 'Yes, I can see that might be a possibility for another monarch, one who puts his dynastic responsibilities ahead of his duty to God. But King Edward is a very holy, one might almost say saintly, man. I cannot imagine him divorcing the wife to whom he has pledged himself for life. Nor, were he to be widowed, which God forbid, would he ever take another bride. His grief, and the depth of his mourning, would simply be too great.'

William thought about his cousin Edward. It had been several years since he had last set eyes on him, but the thought of him being plunged into grief on anyone else's account seemed improbable. He had not mourned his brother Alfred's death. Why would he mourn a barren wife?

These were, of course, thoughts best kept to himself. So he just said, 'Of course, I quite understand. I could not imagine life without Matilda.' (There, that's reminded him, he thought.)

'That means, therefore, that King Edward is highly unlikely to have a son of his own to be his heir,' Champart continued. 'Might I ask, are you aware of the rather unusual way in which the English choose their kings?'

'Isn't it done by the nobles? They all get together and decide which possible heir has the best claim and would make the best king, something like that?'

'Precisely. Of course, you or I may find this an absurd way to determine kingship, and the truth is that when there is an undisputed male heir presumptive, he can count on the nobility's support. It is only when there is some dispute over the succession that difficulty arises.'

'I imagine so,' said William, 'but I don't quite understand what the ins and outs of English custom have to do with me. Excuse me if I sound discourteous, but my time is precious, and—'

Champart held up his hands. 'Of course, of course, I am detaining you too long. Let me get to the point. His Majesty met recently with his most powerful earls, including Godwin, I might add, along with a number of senior churchmen, one of whom I was privileged to be. He named his chosen successor as King of England, and required every man there present to swear a solemn oath that he would do nothing to oppose this successor's right to the throne, or to challenge him once he was king.'

'Huh, that's certainly a bold move.' William paused and frowned as he tried to muster the names of all the English and Scandinavian nobles and monarchs who had expressed, often violently, an interest in ruling England. 'Who was King Edward's choice?'

Champart smiled. He let a few seconds elapse, just to draw the moment out, and then he looked at William the Bastard, Duke of Normandy, this powerful young bullock of a man, with his fiery red hair and his chilly blue eyes, filled to bursting with energy, pride, and ill-concealed resentment for all the indignities he had endured. 'You, my lord duke,' he said. 'You are King Edward's chosen heir. And thus you, William of Normandy, will be the next King of England.'

opportunity arises: thus it was my choice, for example, to follow a source that claimed Ralph de Gacé was born out of wedlock, rather than those that declared him a legitimate son of Archbishop Robert. But I very much hope that I have not distorted the events I describe to the point where they just don't match what is known to have actually happened. Thus, irrespective of his parentage, de Gacé certainly does seem to have ordered at least one of the assassinations I ascribe to him.

Much of the time, I am using fiction to fill in very glaring gaps in history. For example, every death of every named historical character is based on fact: the person in question really did die in a manner consistent with my description. But early medieval people could frequently not explain why a person had dropped down dead. They simply lacked the scientific knowledge to determine whether they were ill, let alone what the disease might be, or were the victims of homicide.

Norman chroniclers in particular often suspected murder (for some reason Anglo-Saxons were more trusting and tended to think that sudden deaths were acts of God rather than man) but they often had no idea who had murdered a given victim, or why. So in some cases I have provided my own accounts and explanations. But that still leaves plenty of killings – those of Gilbert of Brionne and Osbern Herfastsson, for example – whose descriptions are taken directly from specific accounts written not long after the events in question.

This is fundamentally a story about conflicts between and within great families, whose influence stretched across the whole of northwest Europe and whose fortunes were interlinked by events, marriage and blood. Just to illustrate the point, Harold Godwinson, future adversary of William of Normandy, was the son of Godwin, Earl of Wessex. Godwin's wife was Gytha, the sister of a Danish noble, Ulf Jarl, whose wife was Estrith, daughter of King Sweyn of Denmark and sister of King Canute of Denmark and England. Canute's wife was Emma of Normandy who was not only the mother of his son and potential heir Harthacnut, but also the widow of King Ethelred and mother of his son and potential heir Edward, and was also the sister of Duke Richard II of Normandy. His son Duke Robert I was, of course, father of Duke William of Normandy and also the younger brother of Duke Richard III, whose widow Adela was wife of Count Baldwin IV of Flanders and mother of their daughter Matilda, who became the wife of, yes, William of Normandy.

This is a deliciously complicated web of relationships – hence the need for a family tree. But the situation is made harder, from a writer's point of view, by the problem of names. Early medieval folk had a very limited number of names for their children, and boys in particular. If a Norman baron had five sons – and plenty of them did – they were almost certain to include a Richard, Robert, William and Ralph, with either an Odo, a Geoffrey, a Fulk or a Hugh to make up the numbers. Scandinavians liked nothing better than a Sven/Sweyn/Swegen or a Harald. Women were marginally more varied in their names, though both Emma of Normandy and Elgiva of Northampton (as I have called them) were known to their Anglo-Saxon contemporaries as Aelfgifu, and the number of Ediths surrounding the English court in the later years of Edward the Confessor and the brief reign of Harold II will, I am sure, prove very troublesome in the next volume of my story.

The problem is made worse by the fact that surnames as we know them were really not a part of early medieval life. In Scandinavia, as in Russia, people were distinguished by patronyms. So Gytha, the Danish-born wife of Earl Godwin of Wessex, was known as Gytha Thorkelsdóttir (Thorkel's daughter) and their son Harold was Harold Godwinson. The

Norman equivalent was the prefix 'Fitz', which was a corruption of the French word 'fils', meaning son. Thus Osbern the Steward was known as Osbern Herfastsson because his father (brother to Duchess Gunnor, wife of Duke Richard I of Normandy) was a Dane called Herfast. His son William was William Fitzosbern because the family now used a Norman equivalent to their old Viking style.

Another way people got around this problem was by telling, say, one John from another by their profession, as in 'John Baker'; or origins, such as 'John of Rouen'; or by a nickname like 'John the Bold'.

I have tried a number of similar stratagems. So, for example, the only William in this book who is regularly referred to by that name alone is our hero, Duke William, known at this point as William the Bastard, though remembered by posterity as William the Conqueror.

There are, however, many other characters who were christened William. The Duke had an uncle William, the Count of Arques and Talou. I decided to call him 'Talou' because that is easier for a non-French speaker to read and pronounce than Arques. Of course it does look a bit like 'Talvas', which was the nickname (meaning 'hammer') that contemporaries gave to William Count of Bellême and which I used to identify him. But since Talvas and Talou are never in the same scene, I chose to ignore that problem. Finally William Fitzosbern becomes 'Fitz', because he is one of William's closest friends and that sounds like a name one friend might use to address another.

A few years ago, writing a novel about a very different period of history, I received a great deal of help from an academic expert in the field. I sent him a copy of my first draft, to check that I had understood everything correctly and not made too many glaring mistakes. He called me up, having read the manuscript and said, 'The history's fine. But this is meant to be a novel. So stop trying to be a historian and go back and write like a novelist.'

That proved to be wonderful advice. And that is the basis on which I have written this novel too.

David Churchill
West Sussex, 2016

THE LEOPARDS OF NORMANDY

Timeline

Many of the dates below are not known to historians, open to debate, or relate to fictional occurrences. Count Alan of Brittany, for example, is frequently said to have died in 1040, rather than 1039 and the entire sequence of events leading to William's marriage to Matilda, including the date of the wedding itself is a matter of legend and conjecture. So while the dates below relate as closely as possible to known historical facts, where those are available, this timeline is primarily intended as a guide to events that occur in *Duke*, giving readers a general sense of what is happening when. Anyone revising for an exam in Early Medieval History, however, is advised very strongly not to rely upon it!

1035

- Harold Harefoot becomes King of England

1037

- Death of Archbishop Robert in Normandy
- Alan of Brittany, Osbern Herfastsson and Gilbert of Brionne take on guardianship of William the Bastard, seventh Duke of Normandy
- Mauger becomes Archbishop of Rouen

1039

- Sudden death of Alan of Brittany while besieging the town of Vimoutiers
- Ralph de Gacé becomes one of William's guardians and a key member of his inner circle
- Harthacnut signs a treaty with King Magnus of Norway by which if either dies without an heir, his kingdom would go to the other

1040

- Death of Harold Harefoot in England
- Gilbert of Brionne is murdered while out riding near the village of Bec Hellouin
- Harthacnut takes the English throne

- Posthumous execution of Harold Harefoot
- Osbern the Steward is murdered at Vaudreuil while protecting the young Duke William

1041

- Harthacnut orders the harrying of Worcester
- Edward returns to England

1042

- Queen Emma of England is arrested by Edward and survives trial by fire (legend)
- Death of Harthacnt in Lambeth, England

1043–1044

- Edward the Confessor succeeds Harthacnut and is crowned King of England
- William goes to the court in Bruges to seek the assistance of Count Baldwin
- William takes the castle at Falaise

1045

- Edward married Edith, daughter of Godwin of Wessex

1046

- Guy of Burgundy mounts a rebellion against William
- William entreats King Henry of France for help in resisting Guy

1047

- King Henry's army enters Normandy to aid William's cause
- William's army defeat the rebel army led by Guy of Burgundy at Val-ès-Dunes
- Guy retreats to his castle at Brionne. William blockades the castle and becomes the undisputed power in Normandy

1048

- William and Matilda of Flanders meet as adults at the court in Bruges
- William proposes marriage to Matilda. Initially she resists him

1050

- Marriage of William of Normandy and Matilda of Flanders

1051

- Duke William is named as Edward the Confessor's heir to the English throne

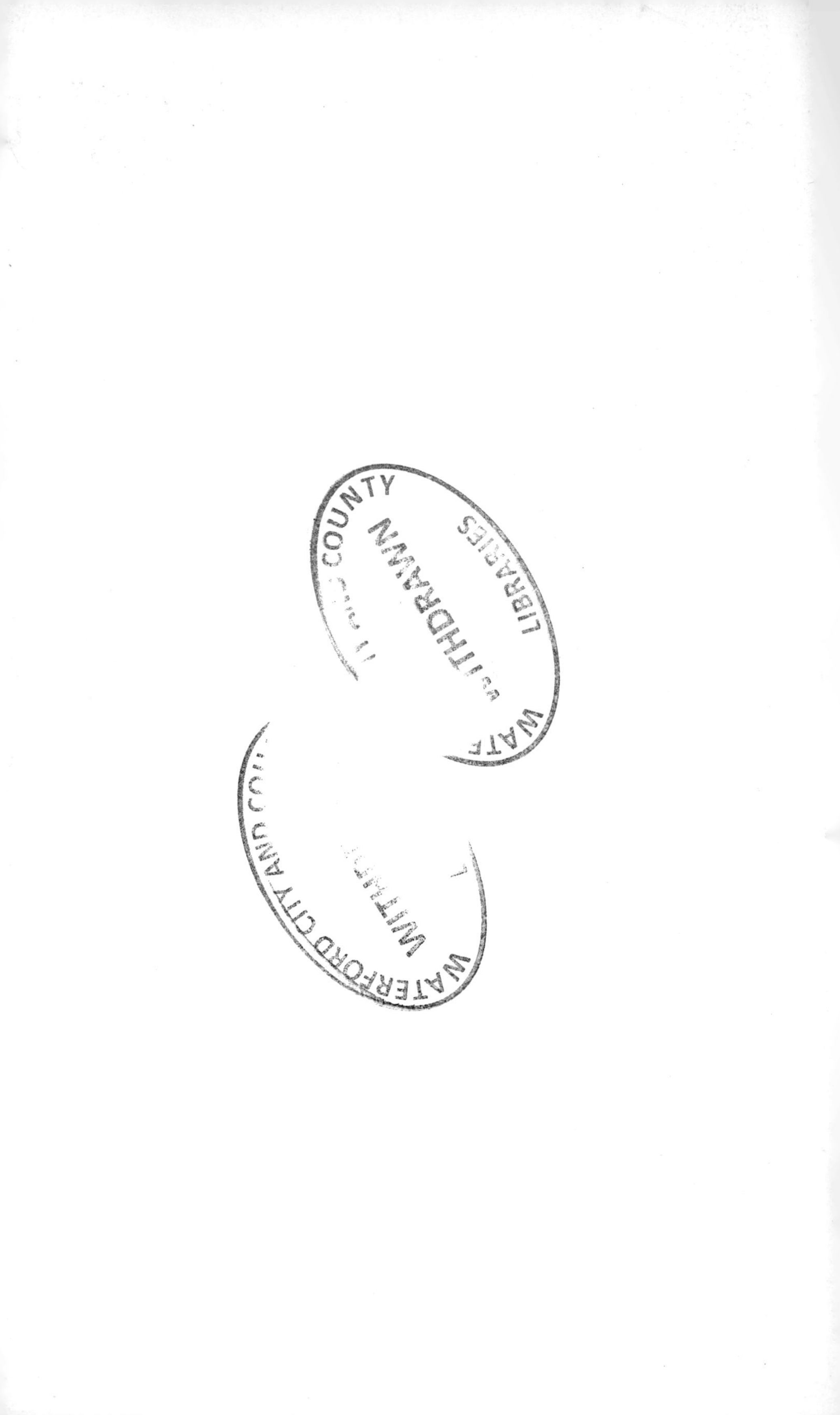